GW00471430

Jasmine's War

Daniel Hyland

Jasmine's War

GREEN PRINT

First published in 2014 by Green Print
An imprint of
The Merlin Press
99B Wallis Road
London
E9 5LN

www.merlinpress.co.uk

© Daniel Hyland, 2014

ISBN 978-1-85425-107-7

The right of Daniel Hyland to be identified as author of this work has been asserted in accordance with the Copyright, Designs and Patents Act 1988

All rights reserved. No part of this publication may be reproduced, stored in a retrieval system, or transmitted, in any form or by any means, electronic, mechanical, photocopying, recording or otherwise, without the prior permission of the publisher.

Printed in the UK by Imprint Digital, Exeter

Daniel Hyland served for eight years as a police officer with the West Midlands police. He later emigrated to Central America, eventually settling in El Salvador where he worked for TACA Airlines and published poetry. After twelve years there he returned to the UK and currently resides in Birmingham.

Acknowledgements

I would like to pay tribute to my wife Carolina and our family who have supported and encouraged me in writing this book despite the time it has taken me away from them.

I would also like to thank all those who agreed to be interviewed, offered advice and shared their experiences; and those who took me to places mentioned in the book, acted as guides and on whose input I drew as I wrote.

To the editor Chris Edmondson, whose patience I tested and whom I found to be tireless, and whose editing skills made all the difference; to Adrian Howe of The Merlin Press for his sound guidance and advice and steadfastness in the production of the book; and to Tony Zurbrugg for signing me up in the first place, I offer my profound gratitude.

Daniel Hyland

Acronyms and Spanish Words

Alcalde – Mayor

Alumna – pupil, student

ARENA – Alianza Republicana Nacionalista – Nationalist Republican Alliance

Caballero(s) – Gentleman (men)

Cafecito negro, por fa' – black coffee, please

Campesino – peasant

Camposanto – graveyard

Cantón – Small village

Catracho – Honduran (colloquial expression)

Champas – Shanty towns

Colectivo – bus

Comandante en Jefe – Commander in Chief

Compa – guerrilla

Compañera – companion / comrade

Damas y Caballeros – Ladies and gentlemen

Despulpadora – Coffee pulping machine

Encanta'o – enchanted

Escuadrón de la muerte – Death Squad

Guarro – alcohol / cheap alcohol

Hasta la Victoria y Siempre! – Until the Victory and Always!

Hija de la Luna – Daughter of the Moon

Linda – pretty

Matanza – killing, massacre

Mi Pais – My Country

Muchachos – boys, guerrillas

Patrón – boss

Poochica! – Shucks!

Propina – tip, backhander.

Punto! – And that's that!

Pupusas – corn pasties filled with melted cheese, pork, and refried beans

Que bonito! – How pretty!

SAF – Salvadoran Air Force

Soy – I am

Teniente – lieutenant

Terratenientes – Land owners

Tiro de gracia – Coup de grace

Tonto – silly

Vaya con Dios – God be with you

Wacala – Yuck / disgusting

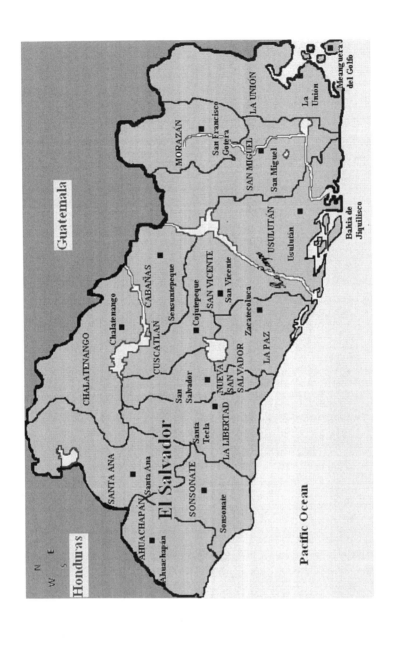

Chapter 1

March 1984

FROM THE SHADOWS BETWEEN COLOSSAL TREES the dawn mist drifted across the trail. A girl was running hard, a basket of washed laundry on her head, hands struggling to keep it there. She'd have to ditch the basket if she was serious about putting distance between her and her pursuers, but she pictured her mother, hands on hips, enquiring after the whereabouts of what was almost their entire wardrobe.

Breathless, she looked behind. She could see nothing and now the path, too, faded beneath the mist. She ran on, instinctively picking out the way ahead.

A male voice barked somewhere behind her and seconds later, three short bursts of automatic rifle fire thudded in quick succession. The soldiers must have seen or heard her and followed her back into the forest.

Jasmine Gavidia had been the last of four laundry-bearing girls to file on to the black road that led to El Zacate. She had joined in the baiting of Elena the Dreamer with a couple of playful taunts of her own, which earned her a peal of laughter from all except Elena. Elena, given to dreaming of storybook romance, held her head high and, picking notes at random from a Nahuatle love song to show she could not be baited, sauntered straight into the middle of the road. Automatic gunfire blasted over her song, battering the dawn with such startling violence that for an instant Jasmine froze to the spot. Elena's arms shot up, fingers splayed, basket in the air, dyed

9

tiers of cloth winging after it. Her scream rose above the gunfire and then broke off with tragic abruptness. Her arms craned down to horizontal, moon-white palms now upheld towards her attackers, head turned aside. She fell to her knees where bullets, shaking her body, shoved her over backwards until her bended legs sprang from beneath her and she landed on her back. The basket rolled into the ditch. The guns went silent.

Jasmine rediscovered her limbs and recoiled in horror, backing away deeper into the shadow and scanning to her left. Two figures in rounded helmets with rifles across their midriffs were striding through the mist towards her. She turned and fled back into the forest. At first she heard the desperate footfalls and terrified squeals of her companions behind her, but they faded as she ran and now, looking back over her shoulder once again, she saw no sign of either girl, nor did she hear their screams.

But she heard more gunfire, spurts of it filtering up from El Zacate.

'*Madre.*' She came to a shambling halt, swivelled round, and hesitated. Her mother had been lighting the clay oven in the courtyard when Jasmine had left home a little over an hour ago. Other shooting, this time from the road, decided the matter. The basket had to go. She tucked it behind a bunch of ferns sprouting between the roots of a ceiba sapling, hidden from casual observation. Now unencumbered, she sprinted over the uneven path in the direction of the river, the thin mauve dress fluttering about her body and her hair spiralling out behind her. She could smell the river, the musty sweetness of wet rock, moss and damp sands. She would follow its near bank and cross at a point she knew well, a ten-minute jog upriver where a balsam poplar had fallen and where the water was only shoulder-deep. From the other side she would take the farmers' path that climbed to La Molienda, where once the co-operative had run its processing plant. And from there she would have a clear view over El Zacate.

She was hoping that she'd gained a decent lead on her pursuers when a sharp exchange of what sounded like hastily issued instructions brought her skidding to a halt. More soldiers, she guessed, scanning the fog for them. They must have crossed the bridge at the edge of the village and come up the riverbank to cut off the runaways. She looked desperately around. Must get off the path. She slipped into the undergrowth and moved forward, pushing past branches that yielded against her body, easing them back into place to avoid whipping up giveaway noise. She was patting her way past another giant tree trunk when she heard breathless voices behind her – two of them:

'You seen any more?'

'Finished off two back there but another gave me the slip. Couldn't have been more than eleven but runs like a deer. Didn't come your way, did she?' A pause, perhaps allowing the question to be answered with a nod or shake of the head, before the second voice resumed. 'This Salvadoran army gear is useless, you can't run in it. No way could I catch her.'

The men were now on the path behind her. With aching caution she lowered herself and settled on her haunches between two roots, breathing through nose and mouth together, the pulse in her ears like the beating of a bird's wings on the air, all senses fully alert.

'She'll be in the undergrowth, then,' the first voice decided, and Jasmine bit into her knuckle. But she dared not move. Inches beyond her toes the flowers of a yellow sage weed stood as motionless as a still-life painting. A minute black ant, waving a jagged shred of orange amaryllis petal that outsized it a hundred times, hiked erratically towards a curled leaf edge.

Then there was an eruption of gunfire. Automatic rounds tore through the forest with appalling ferocity.

Jasmine screamed, wished she hadn't and fell back into a sitting position, arms crossed over her head. With an effort she stifled a second scream, and peered out. The sage flower heads were chopped to smithereens. The black turf was churning and spitting into the air. Whole branches came crashing down around her. Airborne leaves, bits of twig, fern and bark whirled, danced and collided in a deafening frenzy of bullets that smacked into the trees. She screwed up her eyes and flattened her palms over her ears. Drawing her knees up to her chest she shrank deeper into the silk cotton's roots. She could smell the saps of the forest as they were released into the mist, and taste the metallic tang of blood.

An interval while they reloaded, and the mayhem resumed, yet she sensed the gunfire was indiscriminately placed. Uncertain of her precise position the pursuers were laying down blanket fire hoping for a chance hit, the assault gradually moving along the path. Encouraged by this, Jasmine relaxed a little and, quite abruptly, the shooting cut out altogether.

The pitter-patter of debris falling on ferns. Somewhere a partially severed branch was creaking as it was wrenched away by its own weight and crash landed among the stirring of an unsettled forest.

Perhaps the greens were reloading. Perhaps they were listening out for her. She kept her eyes tightly shut.

'Come on, Ángelo. She never survived that. We practically shaved the undergrowth.'

When finally the other answered it was to suggest they head back to the village and rejoin the battalion. Jasmine stayed put, listening to the casual banter as it dwindled with distance.

'No matter how carefully you plan an operation you always overlook some small detail. No-one considered the girls… leaving at dawn to do laundry by the river.'

A while passed, she wasn't sure how long, before she heard more gunfire. But it was much further away this time. She drew in a long breath and exhaled slowly. Had it not been for the shield of the silk cotton tree she would surely have been cut down.

Her hair felt laden. Shaking her head she hand-brushed twigs, leaves and soil from her curls. She paused to stare incredulously at the ant as it scaled a crooked twig, still waving its merry sail despite the gale it had weathered. She tugged a couple more twigs from her hair and then, clutching her knees to her chest, she began to tremble.

Do the soldiers really think they got me? Or are they just pretending to walk away, to give me a false sense of security and lure me out on to the path? She waited, occasionally rubbing her arms, wondering how many other soldiers might be about, and assessing her chances of giving an unknown number of them the slip. She knew these forests intimately, having undertaken long expeditions on her own, following the river north. Flouting her mother's severe instruction to steer clear of the red zones, she had on more than one occasion ventured into Chalatenango Province to quench her thirst in natural springs and even bathe in their icy waters. But this was also home to the guerrillas, their camping and training grounds. Although, despite their stealth, she could pick out their scent even at a safe distance, the same bitter smell that tramps give off, but as guerrillas regularly moved in columns, that smell was multiplied. And she had seen them – men and women of all ages in a motley combination of peasant clothing and camouflage gear – sneaking their way through the undergrowth. She had heard the unconvincing bird-cooing of flanking scouts, and stumbled on their abandoned camps. On two occasions she had spotted boys, eight or nine years old, darting with such speed that she had merely glimpsed them before they were gone.

Feeling equally at home in forest and village had given her an edge over her friends when it came to giving their pursuers the slip, if only temporarily. Now there were too many sounds for Jasmine to feel at all confident of detecting an approaching adversary before they found her. She felt as if she was waiting to be discovered rather than waiting it out. Besides, she must get to La Molienda.

13

So she came to her feet. Stooping, she picked her way back to the path where she paused to check out both directions.

Morning had broken and the forest canopy was shot through with the first pale rays of sunlight. She turned to her right and trotted along the path, hopping over roots and ducking beneath branches. A muddy clamber led her up a cone-shaped mound and down its other side. Soon she was on the sandy riverbank where clear ripples negotiated black boulders, the far bank an abstract of woodland greens. She set off along the soft sand, leaving a trail of small footprints.

In places the bank narrowed and she splashed through the shallows; in others she had to clamber over rocks that were slippery with running water or moist green moss. Her heart stopped at the popping of renewed echoing gunfire, her mother the foremost of her anxieties. But to go back to the road would be fatal. No, her best chance was to make for La Molienda and get a clear view of El Zacate from above.

She had followed the bank for almost a mile before the mist had lifted sufficiently to see across the river. Not long after, she spotted the fallen balsam poplar, half its branches submerged in the water. Wider here than at any other point that Jasmine knew, the river was also shallower, and ever since she had discovered the overgrown trail on the other side almost five years ago, she had made this her regular crossing point.

She waded into the chilly water, sand and pebbles riding in her sandals. Her dress clung to her, cold against her skin. She pushed forward, deeper, with the current tugging. Minutes later she reached the fallen tree and after clambering through its tangle of branches she plodded ashore. She took a scouting glance round while wringing the hem of her dress before setting off. She launched herself up a shoulder-high bank and with the sand subsiding beneath her feet, grabbed the stringy roots of a thorn bush and hauled herself on to the track, earning a brace of inch-long welts across her brown upper arm.

She hurried up the trail, which local plantation owners once used to ferry harvests to La Molienda; that was before

14

an earthquake had brought down most of its walls. The co-operative, renamed "El Beneficio", had since relocated to the neighbouring village of Nejapa. The new building was modern, smart-looking and incorporated the latest anti-seismic components within its walls. There had been more than a little resentment in El Zacate, resentment that their larger neighbour should be the beneficiary of this new coffee processing plant when previously it had been housed, if not within El Zacate, at least close enough to elevate the prestige of the tiny hamlet.

With the intermittent crackling of distant gunfire urging her on, she hurried up the steep hillside. On any other day Jasmine would have paused to catch her breath. But with her mother on her mind she put in a remorseless effort and eventually came out at the top of the rise. Breathing heavily now and not too steady on her feet she followed a narrow ridge high above the forest and coffee orchards until, within catapulting range below, there was La Molienda – broken walls upon a ragged cement terrace wedged into a sloping hillside. She pelted down the hillside through an avenue in the orchard. This was where she and her schoolmates played tag and hide-and-seek amid the few upstanding adobe walls whose irregular maps of whitewash they had daubed with graffiti: *"Corazón, corazón, dame tu amor." "El Águila, ganador de la Copa de América." "Juan e Isabela."*

Sprouting stringy weeds from its cracks the cement flooring covered an area equal to the combined footprints of five regular houses. All useable roof tiles had been barrowed away by villagers, and now the timber rafters lay in splintered segments, scattered like the dead leaves and the unsalvageable tiles.

With her heart in her throat she walked across the derelict processing plant, faltering as she approached the edge, scared about the view it would afford her. To avoid being silhouetted on the skyline she got down on hands and knees, crawled to the rim, and peered over.

Jasmine could see the layout of El Zacate well from this height and angle. A standard colonial grid plan of the type employed by the Spaniards in the Americas from the earliest years of the conquest, with single storeys of whitewashed walls and wood-shuttered windows, pitched terracotta roofs, and waves of bougainvillea washing into courtyards. A cobbled thoroughfare ran down the middle of the village. The domed church of Santa Teresa and the town's colonnaded committee offices faced each other across the plaza. And from the plaza a quaint arched bridge of volcanic rocks joined the black road where it entered the forest. Faded Partido Demócrata Cristiano campaign posters of the President of the Republic, Martin Aragón, gazing benignly upon his loyal partisans, were plastered on walls and doors.

And behind it all a football pitch was scratched into the light brown earth, where Jasmine, having risen to the coveted rank of centre-forward for Los Halcones, gave as good as she got in the male-dominated sport.

And here the normality ended.

About El Zacate today was an abnormality that squeezed the air from Jasmine's lungs. Across the plaza and along the road as far as the alley that cut through to the school, a thousand people – the entire population of El Zacate – were lying belly down, side by side, in straight rows. Folded arms cushioning a cheek or forehead. Heels knocking together, toes kicking down, ankles crossing and uncrossing. Others lay perfectly still. Dresses were vivid splashes of colour, a single or double braid of hair weaving down the backs of the women. Men in reed hats and Wellingtons. Others barefoot, the skin of their soles startlingly pale. The shorter stature of the kids cut them out beside their parents, the infants just bundles in their mothers' arms.

A swarm of soldiers were striding about the recumbent villagers, most of them in belted olive-drab rolled up at the sleeves, helmets, sagging field packs strapped to their backs;

but others had saucepan caps crammed down to their sunglasses, and well-stocked equipment belts pinching puffed camouflage fatigues. All of them hefting M16 assault rifles and doing a lot of shouting. Jasmine couldn't be certain how many greens were down there because they were constantly shifting, disappearing beneath the eaves while others emerged from alleyways or open doors, driving stray villagers forward at the end of prodding bayonets, kicking spaces into the already compact rows and slotting in their hesitant prisoners.

La Guardia Nacional, Jasmine recognised without difficulty. Why are they here?

She gazed across the freakish scene, scanning for her mother. With only the back and sides of the villagers' heads and their miscellaneous clothing to go by, telling who was who down there was tricky. She picked out her home – second to last on the right before the plaza – the one with the colourful hammock dipping between the lemon tree and the vine-plastered courtyard wall. No signs of her mother there. She scanned away. Her eyes settled on three guardsmen who were using their bayonets to tap some backs. Thus selected, ten men obediently pushed themselves to their feet and then looked around as if awaiting further instruction. In their ill-fitting trousers, grubby singlets and *campesino* sombreros they looked pitifully ragtag amid the uniforms of their unwelcome guests.

Jasmine tilted her head to listen, but stunted syllables and half words were all that carried to where she lay. Still, it was apparent that the chosen ten had understood their orders well enough, because now they shuffled about and managed to assemble themselves into a single file along the middle of the road. They understood their next orders also, turned to face the plaza and then they were on the move, the individual parts of the column compressing and expanding like an accordion, stepping gingerly between the heads and feet that bordered the aisle. A uniform moved in to flank them. Confident shoulder movements, confident strides, he swung his bayonet-fitted rifle like a battering ram – a gesture not wasted on his nervous captives. They shied away from the steel whenever it swung near. Another green eager to lend a hand marched to the head of the column, turned and facing the captives, reversed up the road, waving his rifle to beckon the lead man forward. A third fell in behind the last man. It didn't take long for the column to make the top of the street, where it folded left and squeezed and stretched across the plaza towards the church. Behind it another uniformed trio moved in and prodded ten more reluctant volunteers to their feet. Bellowed at and manhandled they too shuffled and organised themselves into a queue, and were then shepherded towards the church.

Minutes later a third group followed. And then a fourth. And a fifth. A precise military operation was underway.

Jasmine turned her attention to the church. Above the gable twin bell-towers reached into the glossy foliage of a catalpa tree. On the flat chancel roof roosted a grubby rotund dome, liberally mottled with light and shadow. Heavy wooden doors, studded with iron, stood marginally ajar in the portal which, like the bell towers, was round-arched. The leading column was now at the foot of the steps.

Guardsmen, stepping over huddled villagers who shielded their heads with clasped hands, took up new positions, forming a rough semi-circle behind the now disintegrating queue and began herding the men towards the portal. Backing away from the bayonets, the peasants stumbled up the stairs, arms extended in gestures of pleading, others in outrage. One plucky lad stepped forward and waved a threatening fist. Juan Antonio in his precious Barcelona football shirt. Jasmine knew the squat coffee-picker from the orchards they had worked together.

A camouflaged green volunteered an underarm swing, bayoneting Juan Antonio a stabbing stroke to his flank, before slipping tidily back into formation. Jasmine gasped aloud. Despite the menace with which the soldiers were carrying themselves, this act of brutality took her by surprise. Soundlessly, the coffee-picker doubled over and clutched his side and dropped on his knees. He plucked his hand away from his blood-soaked shirt, glanced at it and then up at his attacker. Jasmine held her breath as the guardsman volunteered again, brandishing his rifle for a second dose which Juan Antonio narrowly evaded by rising unsteadily to his feet. Applying both hands to his wound he stumbled back to join the others who were packed together, horror showing on their faces with a clarity that brought the first sting of tears to Jasmine's eyes.

But a couple of petulant-faced youths, perilously incensed at the treatment meted out to Juan Antonio, were gesticulating, leaning forward, and gabbling back at their forbidding tormentors. This led only to further aggression, and Jasmine saw one of them drop although she didn't see the strike; but now he was wriggling on his side on the top step. A uniform lunged forward and ploughed a bayonet into the boy's upturned hip. He flipped like a fish in a pan of hot oil, and it took a second for his squeal of pain to resonate up to Jasmine. The blade hovered above his cheek which was flushing a deep maroon colour. Jasmine held her breath again. She wanted to look away, yet she had to watch. Please don't. Please don't. She sobbed with relief when the boy lurched to his feet before hobbling up the last step and disappearing into the church. The second file of ten had reached the steps. They received similar treatment to the first, before they too were bundled through the door. Again two of them decided they weren't going quietly, and were throwing up their arms as if shooing away an approaching herd of cattle. Suddenly both broke into a mad dash across the plaza. They promptly parted company and, leaping from aisle to aisle, took separate routes towards the main street. Heads raised themselves from the ground and shouted after them. From every quarter ill-tempered greens flooded across the street. Surrounded on all sides the would-be escapers came to a stuttering halt, their heads swivelling, looking desperately about them. With the circle of soldiers closing in swiftly there was no escape. The two dissenters, twisting and arching away from the lashing blades while their clothes turned to bloody rags, were marched back to the church. Jasmine bowed her head and screwed up her eyes in disappointment.

* * *

The sun was baking the concrete floor on which Jasmine lay, drying her hair and dress. There was still no sight of her mother, despite the repetitive cycle of single files being stewarded into the Church of Santa Teresa. And Jasmine harboured a fool's hope that her mother had taken to the woods.

When the last of El Zacate's young men had been herded into the church, three grim figures stood at the open door, rifles levelled to deter further insubordination, and waited. By now the rush of adrenalin was wearing off, and Jasmine felt strangely weary, even numb. She yawned into the back of her hand. In the bowing grass just below the ledge where she lay, swallow-tailed butterflies fluttered, settled, and fanned wings of orange and black. An army of tiny black ants trickled through a crack beside her right hand. Seeing the colour drained from around her fingernails, she relaxed her grip on the cement. Jasmine felt thirsty.

The hush was brought to an end by a fresh round of shouting. Again bayonets sought out dissenters. Now the women, children and the elderly got uncertainly and stiffly to their feet. Kids clung to their mums while others, perhaps the brave and foolish, stood aloof, almost insolently so. Yet more rifle-brandishing greens appeared and one by one they drew up new positions and halted, feet wide apart, heads swivelling. Orders were barked but the barker didn't show himself. And the remainder of the villagers were forcibly ushered into nine consecutive columns that, end to end, extended almost the entire length of the main road. But these latest queues were not destined for the church where the men folk called out what sounded like names, probably those of their wives and kids. Instead, they faced south. Still no sign of her mother, and Jasmine's hopes for her safety dared to grow some more.

One of the guardsmen slung his rifle across his back and

began drawing away girls and even some children by plucking at their sleeves and pointing towards the raised pavement at the far side of the street. With their faces clearly visible now, Jasmine recognised all who gathered there, schoolmates, friends, and neighbours. A lone school-age soldier was dispatched to guard them. It was left to the old folk and the very smallest of the infants to fill the columns.

Another bellowed command, delivered by someone Jasmine still could not see, prompted the columns into sluggish motion. A faltering procession shuffled down the street. Jasmine's heart took a sickening plummet when the lean figure of her mother, still in her green nightdress, shuffled into view from beneath eaves that shared a corner with the plaza.

'*Madre! Madre!*' Jasmine cried out wildly. While her mother gathered up her hair and clamped it into a toothed clasp, she wandered fractionally from the line. A soldier who cared too much for discipline stepped in with his poised bayonet. 'No,' Jasmine yelled directly at him, unable to contain herself. Her mother, feisty as ever, sprung a strict finger at the soldier in an attitude of sharp admonishment. Jasmine knew the menace that finger could carry, and wasn't surprised when the soldier backed off.

On another command from the conspicuously invisible man the wretched line managed a ragged halt. A rowdy interval followed during which some tidying up was undertaken and while this was going on the incessant wail of an infant carried shrilly on the warm air, and Jasmine noticed a soldier making a beeline for a bafflingly placid-looking woman who was clutching a tiny newborn to her breast. Tugging at her arm he drew her from the queue, and with his hand to the small of her back in a sort of semi-embrace, guided her to the side of the road where he left her unattended.

From Jasmine's elevated position it was easy to pick out the escape route; and she willed the young mother to make for it. Look right. The corner house, ten paces if that. Even with a baby in arms you could make a dash for the alley.

With everything else going on right now, you might even go unnoticed, and once in the warren of shaded lanes, head for the football pitch and disappear into the plantation. And call for help. Run woman, run!

But instead of running, she unfastened the buttons of her spotlessly white blouse, pulled up her brassiere and pressed the child's face to her swollen breast. With elaborate care she began to arrange her headscarf to shield the child's head from the sun's glare. But the baby, having none of it, turned a pinched reddened face towards Jasmine and screeched at the top of his small voice. The scarf drifted away to the ground.

Another tirade of orders from the hidden officer startled Jasmine. Nine columns on the move. Synchronised, they turned inwards, approached nine neighbouring houses and began filing in beneath the eaves. Sucking at the back of her hand Jasmine kept her eyes fixed on her mother, watching her edge towards the bend in the column, edge round it, heading now for the eaves. Finally, like the others, she slipped from view.

'*Madre!*' she whispered as her hopes fell. She shut her eyes tightly and prayed: Please, help her, and help me know what to do.

Aside from the woman cradling her infant and the forlorn group of schoolgirls, the streets of El Zacate were now empty of civilians yet filled with soldiers.

A flurry of military activity. Nine squads of three aligned themselves along the fronts of the houses into which the columns had marched, and another outside the church. From beneath an overhanging roof far below, a uniform strolled into the middle of the street. Tall, elegant, with a posture that shouted self-belief; face cast in the shadow beneath the sharply pitched cap. In his left hand a radio into which he was speaking. A colonel, perhaps, Jasmine thought grimly. Now the sound of an entire village screaming filled the valley. Harrowing overlapping wails, pleadings, and enraged male voices that Jasmine would never forget.

The colonel punched his right fist vertically into the air and held it there, a high salute that prompted the men positioned in front of the church and houses to shoulder their M16s and direct their aim through the open doors. The screaming rocketed to new heights. The colonel plunged his fist to shoulder-level and hollered, '*Fuego!*'

Caught in a silent time warp Jasmine watched, amazed that such cruelty even existed. Hundreds of muzzle flashes like sparklers. Guardsmen hunched over their rifles. Then reality kicked in, slamming her chest and unblocking her ears to an appalling drumming, and the muzzle flashes began to dissolve into drizzly blurs behind her tears. And even above the sustained ear-battering cacophony of the guns soared the shrill entreaties of the dying.

'Santa Maria, mother of God!' she managed on a whisper, and then louder and louder – 'No! No! No! No!' – trying to undo the scene with one word. '*Mi Madre! Mi madre! Mi madre!*'

The colonel had moved; there he was, closing in on the mother and child.

'*Mi madre. Mi madre!*' Jasmine watched through tear-blurred eyes as the colonel rushed the blade into the woman's abdomen and plucked it out in a single stroke, then ripped it free of the clinging dress.

'*Por que?*' Jasmine shrieked at him, pleading for the consolation of some sense to all this. '*Por que?*'

Still clutching her son the woman staggered sideways before her legs failed and she began to sink. The colonel leaned in, seized the child's neck in one hand, and with a hefty boot stamped on the woman's forehead. As she flopped away he snatched the baby from her desperate fingers, tossed him high, hoisted his rifle and waited with nonchalant patience. Face-up and kicking, the infant landed plum on the poised bayonet. The blade slid in cleanly and sprung out of his stomach. His kicks subsided. The colonel lowered and shook his weapon until the tiny body became unstuck and slid from the bayonet on to the road. The child was still moving. He rolled on to his side, drew his knees to his elbows, put his head forward, and then appeared to sleep while blood seeped into the grooves between the cobbles. Wiping away her tears with the back of her hand Jasmine swerved her eyes to look blankly back at the empty space where her mother had been. This cannot be happening.

Now the screams were ebbing away against the thudding artillery. She did not see where he came from, but a young hopeful was sprinting away behind the shooters. He must have escaped from the church. As if running a slalom course he dodged past one guardsman and then another, both of whom were engrossed in watching the macabre work of their colleagues. By some miracle he had not been brought down, and Jasmine willed him to escape. A last semblance of hope in a hopeless place.

'Run, Don Pedro. Run!' She squeezed the tears from her eyes with her palms. He's making for the gap at the end of the block. 'Yes, Don Pedro, it's clear, to your right.'

Pedro sped behind another soldier. Jasmine gripped the edge of the floor, her knuckles paling. Pedro would escape. He was less than five paces from the alley when for no apparent reason he threw up his arms and went down on folded knees.

'What happened?' Jasmine hammered a bunched fist on the concrete.

Pedro tipped forward on to his stomach and lay flat, sluggishly moving his limbs.

With his languid gait the colonel moved in to kneel on Pedro's upper back. He plucked a long blade from his belt, grabbed a clump of Pedro's thick black hair and yanked back his head, and with an efficient series of sawing movements to the side of his neck, decapitated him.

Jasmine retched. '*Madre de Dios Santo!*'

The colonel paraded the severed head before the youngsters on the pavement. They hopped about, clawing at their own cheeks and dragging down the skin until their eyes were as oval-shaped as their mouths. Some turned their backs on the gruesome scene and clawed the wall with their fingernails, and others drew the youngest protectively behind them while they gaped on, the fingers of one hand curled into their mouths.

Jasmine rolled on to her back and cupped her hands over her face, choking on her pain, kicking out with both legs.

By now the terrible screams from the houses and the church had stopped, and the guardsmen, many of whom had disappeared through the doors, were firing only intermittent bursts and single shots, snuffing out the odd wail here or frantic jabbering for clemency there.

Jasmine heard another sound. It grew and seemed to come from all around. She took her hands from her eyes and craned her head back on the concrete, searching the sky. Silhouetted black against the blue of the sky, it drew closer at speed, the sandy brown and jungle greens of its fuselage materialising. UH-1M Hughes gunships formed the backbone of the Salvadoran Air Force's *Escuadrón de Helicópteros,* and she had seen them on countless occasions before today. She rolled back on to her stomach and glared down at the village where the greens, ignoring the approach from the sky, continued about the business of finishing off the last of the living. Only the tall colonel paid any attention to the gunship; arching his back, radio to chin, he was tracking its flight.

Jasmine sprang to her feet, ran back across the terrace and squatted in the cover of a coffee bush. As the helicopter thudded overhead she looked up at its wide underbelly before it swept away towards the east then banked steeply and descended towards El Zacate, evidently aiming to land on the football pitch. She made off, sprinting hard up the avenue of coffee bushes until, at the crest, she plunged into the forest.

Coughing up her sobs, she ran aimlessly until, abruptly and for no other reason that she couldn't run forever, she stopped. She sank to her knees and, burying her face in cupped hands, screamed at the top of her voice, 'Mother. Please, God, no!' She rocked forward and fell on her elbows, forehead to the ground, arms flung out ahead. While her hands grappled with fistfuls of soil and fallen leaves, she forced her thoughts into some semblance of order. She would run to Nejapa and seek help. Pushing excruciating scenes from her mind she came to her feet, brushed away the dirt from her knees and elbows and made off at a jog.

CHAPTER TWO

FERNANDO MENESSES HAD SHUFFLED a bunch of invoices into a wad and was now straightening the edge on his cluttered desktop, and before he could shout *come* at the brisk tap on his office door Liana had entered and was nudging the door shut by backing into it.

'Nancy Portillo has been waiting in reception for half an hour already,' she reminded him.

'Did you tell her I'm in a meeting?' he enquired.

'I did, and that it may go on a while, but she insists she has a matter of some considerable importance to discuss with you personally.'

'It's always important with her,' he muttered, as he shelved the invoices in the dealt-with tray. He was sobering at the prospect of Nancy's visit. Nancy Portillo, part-time wife to an ancient entrepreneur whose lucrative shoe factory sustained her wastrel ways. Town gossiper and scandal-raiser with nothing on her overactive mind except pursuing her leisure in earnest.

'All right, show her in,' he agreed. From the bottom of Nancy's gossip bin the odd morsel of use could sometimes be scraped up.

Nancy Portillo entered. In vogue, but by no means sophisticated, in fine shape for a mother of three pushing fifty, though overdoing the eyeliner, perfumed but nothing subtle.

Fernando rose from his chair. 'Señora Portillo, good to see

you in such fine health in times like these,' he said, if a touch ironically.

But his satire went over Nancy's flared straw hat as she approached his desk in a yellow dress, pulled off a whopping pair of sunglasses and looked up with an expression that was both demure and coquettish. She was followed by a slender, fine-boned girl who moved with a lithe grace that made Nancy appear awkward by comparison. The girl's head was down, tumbling curls covering her shoulders. A knee-length dress of home-grown cotton and indigo, simply embroidered in turquoise around the neck.

Fernando nudged his spectacles up the bridge of his nose to better inspect this stranger. A cherubic face with small tapered chin, full Mayan lips, and a button of an up-tipped nose. Wide eyes so darkly lashed as to cast a shadow over huge irises which, swimming in un-spilt tears, were of such high brown as to be almost yellow. A regular *mestiza* peasant, Fernando concluded. Regular, in a predominantly mestizo nation.

'Don Fernando, forgive me for interrupting,' Nancy opened with her usual entreaty, squeezing down with both hands on yet another new handbag, 'but I found this child wandering the outskirts. Says something very bad has happened in El Zacate. She may be lost or something. So where else could I bring her, but to the mayor, right?' Nejapa, boasting a population of over twenty-five thousand souls, was a town in every sense of the word, with a mayor instead of a community leader, and a mayor-sized house to go with him.

'Right.' Fernando agreed she had taken the appropriate course of action under the circumstances, and indicated a pair of chairs in front of his desk. When they were all seated he reached for a pencil and poised it over his note pad. All visitors' details to be recorded. His rule.

'Now daughter, name and where you're from, please.'

'Jasmine Maria Gavidia. Soy del cantón de El Zacate.'

The clear lilting accent common to Cuscatlán Province.

'Age?'

'Fourteen, *Señor Alcalde.*'

School age and judging by the abundance of copper-blonde locks spiralling amid the black, she was accustomed to direct sunlight. At play perhaps? Though in these parts kids regularly worked the plantations too.

'Occupation?'

'*Soy alumna del Colegio Santa Teresa, Señor Alcalde.*'

'So, daughter,' he continued, tendering for her use a box of paper tissues that he, in his other capacity as marriage counsellor, kept on standby for the domestic squabbles he was regularly called upon to arbitrate. 'What do you have to say for yourself?'

As soon as he realised where her narrative was leading, he interrupted to dismiss Nancy with as much consideration as he could muster: 'Doña Nancy, I needn't keep you any longer. Thank you for bringing this matter to my attention.'

Nancy's face dropped as if she'd been handed an eviction notice, but she swallowed any pride and kissed Fernando in a chaste cheek-to-cheek effort, replaced her huge sunglasses, and after stalling to assure Jasmine that she was in very good hands, finally took her leave.

Fernando bade Jasmine resume. 'Starting from the point you reached La Molienda, if you please.' And he gave her his full attention while he pondered the reliability of this young witness. But he judged himself a keen reader of personalities – a mayor had to be in this town – and so once he had satisfied himself as to her reliability he pondered whether the Guard might pick out Nejapa for a similar dose of commie purging. In a contested zone like Cuscatlán, boys of twelve and over were routinely shanghaied into the army, so the fact that Fernando's son was an officer in the Guard was not necessarily a ticket to favourable treatment. A sense of foreboding welled up inside him.

At the end of what was by any standards a harrowing tale the mayor placed half a dozen telephone calls to acquaintances in El Zacate, and the foreboding grew as each call remained unanswered.

He pressed a buzzer on his desktop which summoned Liana with notebook and pen in hand, like a waitress ready to take his order.

'Call absolutely everyone you know in El Zacate and let me know the instant you get through to someone. Don't ask why, just do it.'

And as Liana left to perform his bidding, Fernando pointed his pencil directly at Jasmine. 'Listen to me, daughter,' he said, hearing an unintended frostiness hijack his voice. 'The war is in its fourth year and these are very delicate times. Watch what you say, and to whom. Understand?'

Local protocol prevailing, peasant girls would rarely meet eyes with a man of Fernando's important position, but she held his stare with no flinch at all. 'I am not lying, Señor Mayor.'

He sighed at her apparent gullibility. 'How many people have you told about this?' Meaning – how much have you told Nancy? But Liana was back before Jasmine could answer.

'Don Fernando, you should come and see this.' And her expression told him that indeed he should, so he bid Jasmine stay put. He'd be back in a minute.

Hands deep in pockets, feet wide apart, Fernando stood over the colonnaded veranda and glared across the plaza where townsfolk were gathering in their dozens, their conversation overlapping, in a low constant hum. He watched a woman draw a neatly folded handkerchief from her bodice and press it to her nose. Arms started pointing across the rooftops due south, and the hum grew louder.

He followed their gaze and saw a smoke cloud soaring against the first vivid hues of dusk. In the midst of the cloud reds and greens and purples were folding into its otherwise sooty character, and Fernando's puzzled mind likened its outline to a giant cauliflower, except for where its upper heights were bending into a wind current. Had the cloud been a simple shade of black or dark grey it might have signalled a plantation fire. But multi-coloured? He hadn't seen smoke quite like it before.

'People are saying it comes from El Zacate.' Liana was standing beside him now. Despite her liberal application of perfume Fernando wrinkled his nose at another odour that carried on the warm evening air. It was the scent of a barbecue, of tons of burning meat.

* * *

By evening rumours of a massacre in El Zacate were widespread throughout Nejapa.

'Her story makes little sense,' Fernando confided in his wife Elsa that night as they lay, elbows touching, on their king-size divan, he cradling the remote control, she reading a fairly recent issue of *Hola*, both waiting for the National Television's news reader to get through the State's catalogue of isolated killings and accompanying accusations and say something – anything – about the massacre.

'Seems like a nice girl,' Elsa conferred her first impression of Jasmine. 'It was thoughtful of you to take her on as our maid.'

'What else could I do? Poor elf's got no family, the orphanages are overflowing.'

'Well, since Maria left I haven't had a chance to do much housework or laundry, so there's work for her.'

'Now why do you suppose Maria left like that? Not even a goodbye,' Fernando chanced during yet another obscure polaroid of partially burnt wayside corpses in ill-fitting Guard uniforms.

Elsa shrugged in a non-committal way, leaving Fernando with a compelling suspicion that she knew more than she was telling. But mother-son relationships shared their secrets with no one.

'I put Jasmine in the maid's quarters,' she informed him. 'And bought her a couple of nice outfits from the market.'

But his remote control was scanning the channels for more news. 'There's still nothing on the TV about it. Can you believe it?'

'Actually, Radio Venceremos is airing the news every half

hour, accusing the military of a great *matanza*.'

'What do you expect from the rebels' station? But please, Elsita …'

'It's banned, yes I know. I'm a discreet listener.'

'Her story makes no sense,' he repeated distantly. 'Only last month …'

'June.'

He thrust out splayed hands and put the tips of his forefingers together. 'After decades of military dictatorships,' he grabbed a middle finger and bent it back, 'fraudulent elections,' index finger back now, 'mass riots,' he clinched the little finger too, 'a coup d'état in 1979,' he throttled a thumb, 'one provisional junta,' the hands swapped roles to continue the count, 'and four years of civil war, finally the fairest general election in the country's history ousts the right-wing ARENA party and sees into government the Partido Demócrata Cristiano. Granted, while the Frente Farabundo Martí para la Liberación Nacional …'

'The guerrillas…'

'They're not all guerrillas …'

'Most are …'

'The point is, even though the FMLN was not granted political legitimacy to compete for the presidency, we do now have a new president whose ambitions to engage with the guerrillas instead of shun them show a commitment, however flawed some might see it, to securing an end to the conflict. So tell me, Elsita-*linda*, why would President Martin Aragón, a man generally considered to be liberal-minded, send troops to massacre a village that voted for him?'

Elsa delayed her answer, supposedly to give his question the consideration it deserved. 'Perhaps they weren't soldiers. Perhaps they were guerrillas,' she suggested gamely.

'Nah! For kit, the guerrillas are cobbling together homemade rifles. And the girl mentioned seeing a helicopter. That's one piece of kit the *muchachos* don't have. There's still nothing on the news. Look at that. They must have heard reports of a massacre. Even foreign embassies listen to Radio Venceremos, if only to stay abreast of what the rebels say about them.'

'We'll ask Anastasio when he gets home. He'll fill us in on what really happened in El Zacate,' Elsa proposed on a note of finality, and shook her magazine in readiness for an earnest read.

Fernando sighed. His son may have answers to this and other *matanzas*. But would he divulge them, even to his mother? Unlike the countless conscripts wrenched from their classrooms, Anastasio was a career soldier, married to the army for better or worse. He was unlikely to betray his true love. 'Whoever's behind this will kill the girl when they discover she witnessed the massacre.'

Elsa slapped the magazine down on the duvet and stared aghast at her husband. 'Then nobody must find out,' she instructed him.

But who can halt the advance of gossip?

'Too late. We're all familiar with the idler's talents of Nancy Portillo. The list of people who shouldn't have found out will soon be endless.' But in his heart he wanted to add his own son to that list.

* * *

Below the crumbling edge of the concrete floor on which Jasmine lay, gorgeous butterflies settled in the long grass and fanned their wings leisurely.

Echoes of screams began to fill the hills.

She frowned, and looked beyond the butterflies, over the orchard canopy and down upon a nest of pink roofs surrounded by sloping cloud forests and perfectly still coffee orchards. A warping queue of villagers was processing down the main street, and from it she picked out her mother wearing green and feeding long hair through a black clasp. Guardsmen flanked and a guardsman led and another followed. Yapping away and brandishing bayoneted rifles.

'Run. Run, *Madre*, run.'

Her mother angled her head and stared directly up into

Jasmine's eyes. A what-are-you-doing-up-there expression showed no inkling of the fate towards which she was being ushered. Moving her lips now, uttering something incoherent.

Jasmine wriggled forward, taking herself way over the edge, pushing her tipping point to its absolute threshold. She cupped a hand behind one ear. 'What? I can't hear you.' But the all too brief exchange was lost somewhere in the distance between them, and her mother, borne forward by the queue, disappeared beneath the eaves.

On a troubled ascent towards consciousness yesterday's horrors hastened to greet Jasmine, crowding her mind with images, most of them abominable. And her mother wandered like a lost soul through the storm of them. An upsurge of something that felt like guilt erupted in a whimper. She opened her eyes to blackness and reached blindly for her mother. Not finding the anticipated warmth, she swung her legs out of bed – a bed whose coiled spring mattress chirped unfamiliarly. She padded over to the wall and groped along it until she felt the light switch. The forty-watt bulb illuminated the room with a parsimonious glow. She saw immediately that this was not the bedroom she shared with her mother, but the servant's quarters of a strange house. The loneliness that flooded in threatened to plunge her spirits into an abyss of grief. A sob spluttered from her lips, but she lifted her chin and sniffed back the next.

She climbed on to the bed and lay on her back, staring through tear-blurred eyes at the kamikaze ant flies colliding with the light bulb, shedding their slim transparent wings in the process. An image surfaced of her mother, terribly wounded but alive amid the remains of all the people she knew in El Zacate. Could she have returned to guide her mother out alive? Perhaps not. But she'd have to return to retrieve her body, and give her a decent burial. How was beyond her right now.

She went to the window, opened the shutters, and shivered, exhaling vapour wisps into the chilly air, air that smelt of damp cement and ulmo blossom. The night was dotted with stars, and she caught glimpses of an almost full moon through silhouetted branches. She watched a black and white cat run on silent paws along the pitched roof of the main house directly across the walled courtyard. The cat paused and stared at her, eyes startlingly luminescent.

Jasmine closed the shutters and switched off the light. She rolled on to the bed and lay on her side, using her palms flattened together as a pillow. Afraid of her dreams she stayed awake, yet tortured images insisted on rolling over in her mind. The night dragged on in a succession of black and endless hours.

* * *

A cockerel close by let rip a vociferous dawn crowing. Not to be outdone, another more distant bird blurted his wake-up call at the town.

Jasmine showered and it didn't matter that the water was icy-cold because she felt as if nothing could have warmed her, and she pulled on a pleated white skirt and a pink sweatshirt with a printed pattern on the front that she didn't bother identifying.

With yesterday's clothes tucked under one arm she stepped barefoot into the courtyard. The familiar aroma of boiling maize lent sweetness to the chill. She stumbled against something and, with an outstretched hand, steadied herself on the wall. A plastic basket of imitation wicker piled high with dirty laundry had been left right outside her door. She added hers to the pile. Teeth chattering, she rubbed her hands over her arms and looked around. At the foot of the garden wall that ran between the main house and the maid's quarters lay a flowerbed, its soil in hard dry clumps. Above it a wooden trellis was mounted on the courtyard wall. Jasmine went over and squatted beside the flowerbed and put aside the laundry basket and peered at the crumbling clusters of dark soil.

'Mountain rose,' she told herself, and gathered the limp stems in her hands. She got up and scooped a bowlful of water from the deep concrete basin known as a *pila* annexed to the main house and slopped it generously over and around the roots.

Sleeves rolled up to above her elbows she set about scrubbing the clothes in the *pila*. And by the time Elsa bustled from the kitchen into the courtyard, the laundry was almost done.

The morning greetings taken care of, Elsa said she would take over the washing because she wanted Jasmine to pop to Carmencita's store at the top of the street, on your right, you can't miss it, and here's a list of groceries I need for tonight's supper because my son's coming home and I want to prepare his favourite cheese *pupusas*.

With a huge wicker basket in one hand and a leather coin pouch in the other, Jasmine stepped on to Nejapa's main street and felt the sun's agreeable warmth upon her face.

On the way to the plaza she passed a barber's shop and heard the snip-snip of busy scissors. In the pharmacy a length of polished cedar wood served as a counter. A couple of dishevelled men in rags loitered impatiently for the liquor store to open its shutters. A knot of teenage girls in colourful frocks paused to engage in outburst of giggles with a boy in a Stetson and jeans leaning at the door to a billiard hall. From the pavement a street seller in a frilly white apron offered Jasmine a calabash of steaming maize gruel. '*Un poquito de atol, mi amor.*'

Jasmine declined with a pursed-lipped smile.

Twenty minutes, by her estimation, to walk the easy gradient from one end of the street to the other. Quicker if you're not a tourist. Bang in the centre of the plaza stood a cotton tree, its slender trunk spreading reddish branches into a flat crown festooned with clusters of yellow flowers. In its ample shade, concrete benches were situated at regular intervals along paved walkways.

Jasmine continued past the plaza, past one elderly man in a wide-brimmed reed hat who was puffing at a rough-looking cigar, and past another two who were vigorously slapping dominoes on a concrete table.

In stark contrast to the vibrant, sparkling morning outside, the interior of the store had a muted church-like dimness. And while Jasmine waited to be served, conscious of the inquisitive stares of several other clients upon her, she could smell nutmeg, cinnamon and ground coffee.

A short while later she left Carmencita's Store, her basket laden with purple onions and fresh tomatoes and hard *queso-duro-blando* cheese.

'*Hola*, Señorita Jasmine,' a stranger – male, adult – addressed her out of the blue. 'My name is Chachi. Can I walk with you?'

She looked up, somewhat startled. A lean-bodied man in a stripy red shirt and glossy shorts lumbering at her side was pushing a lock of black hair off his sweaty forehead. And he had the dried sweat pong common to her football pals back home.

'Sorry I frightened you,' he said, sounding anything but apologetic.

'You didn't frighten me,' she denied on impulse, and glowered straight ahead to show how much she was ignoring him, but then thought to enquire as to how he knew her name.

'A new face in a small town is news.'

That's how it was in El Zacate, she reflected.

'My brother sent me,' Chachi blurted rather forcefully and added a conspiratorial 'shush' as if she'd been the loudmouth. 'He would very much like to meet you, to discuss what happened in El Zacate.'

'Your brother?' she retorted.

'Leonel Flint.'

The penny dropped. Leonel Flint: guerrilla *comandante* with the *Partido Comunista Salvadoreño* – otherwise the PCS – in coalition under the FMLN's inclusive umbrella. Obscure photographs of Flint taken at distance by a telescopic lens were habitually plastered on the pages of the national tabloids and graced the army's monthly Most Wanted lists with the accompanying warning: A most sadistic murderer of innocent civilians.

'He's a *compa*, isn't he?' she accused.

'Señorita, we can't speak here. He and I will wait for you at La Molienda, in one hour exactly.'

She flicked her head away and gave him a dismissive laugh. 'I can't possibly meet you anywhere,' she said, and picked up her pace.

'Listen to me, señorita.' He seized her arm and gave it a tug, swinging her right round to face him.

'Let go,' she snapped, trying to recover her arm by twisting it.

'Listen,' he snapped back, clamping her arm even tighter until her skin smarted. 'Major Anastasio Menesses will return from San Salvador *this evening*.'

'I'll scream,' she cried out, drawing in the prying eyes of a couple of passing nuns in white habits. But Chachi carried on regardless: 'His return is no coincidence. You are the only known witness to an illegal operation ordered by Colonel Santamaria and carried out by his battalion.'

Jasmine stopped wrestling. 'Colonel Rubén Santamaria? *Batallón Liberación?*' Other names that sent shivers up the spine of even the hardiest *campesino*, and to which, if her mother was to be believed – and Jasmine believed everything her mother said and more so now that she was gone, the label "sadistic murderer of innocent civilians" could equally be applied.

'You've heard the name before,' Chachi suggested.

She nodded slowly and he relinquished her arm.

'Then you know the colonel's reputation. The El Zacate *matanza* isn't his first. He's bloodied his hands in many towns and villages in the department of Morazán and in Chalatenango. The mayor's son Anastasio is attached to *Batallón Liberación*. He reports directly to Santamaria.'

She felt her mouth go dry. Up ahead waited the sun-dappled façade of Casa Menesses. With a long sigh she looked searchingly into Chachi's face. Beneath heavy eyebrows, brown eyes too close together held her stare. The faint lower-jaw beard and outer-edged moustache of a man who scarcely needs to shave. She put his age at mid-thirties, though he stood before her shuffling his feet like an adolescent desperate for the urinal, which, together with his footballer's outfit, she found rather disarming. He shared her absolute passion – the *beautiful game*. With a fractional nod she cued him to resume.

'The gringos are asking hard questions of the PDC about El Zacate. It's rapidly becoming an international concern, thanks to Radio Venceremos.' Chachi put his hands on her shoulders and stared into her eyes. 'Anastasio will definitely cover for Santamaria, of that you can be sure. They won't let you live.'

* * *

La Molienda was bathed in sunlight yet a chill mountain wind tossed Jasmine's hair while she stood at the edge of the fractured floor and raised a hand to her lips. Is that El Zacate?

Not so far below her lay a ghost town, skeletal rafters where rooves had caved in, sooty smudges lapping at rows of gaunt windows. The school and the football pitch remained untouched, but beneath the withered branches of the once majestic catalpa, the little church was a roofless husk of blackened walls. And half a dozen people moved silently amid the clutter, a small coffin on the shoulder of one old man in baggy trousers, a mule cart parked at the wayside, more coffins aboard.

And somewhere down there lay her mother.

Behind her someone had called her name, and she turned her back on El Zacate to face her caller. Shoulder to shoulder two men approached across the flooring. Chachi was still in his football gear, and still mangy-looking. The other was the taller by a head. Clad in a military-green jungle suit, he had the gait of a man much lighter on his feet than his stature would suggest. Through his dark beard, Jasmine made out a firm jaw squaring into a neat chin. And in his lean and suntanned face he had a narrow but flattish nose with flared nostrils, and alert brown eyes that had already settled on her. Of course she recognised him, not only from his Most Wanted pictures but also from her covert observations in the forest.

With a wave of his bony hand Chachi made introductions. 'Jasmine, Leonel. Leonel, Jasmine.'

Leonel thanked her for coming at such short notice. She heard herself state firmly that she hadn't much time because Doña Elsa would be wondering where she was. 'I understand,' Leonel assured her.

'Have you been down to El Zacate?' she got in the first question.

'At dawn, today.'

'Did you find any survivors?'

'We searched the village, and right now my column is combing the surrounding hills. Other than you, we have found no survivors.'

Although she had suspected as much, the news came as a sickening blow. She hung her head and nodded in bleak acceptance.

Leonel offered condolences.

'What about my friends?' She looked up on a fragile upsurge of hope. 'I saw them being pulled aside to be spared. I *saw* them.'

'Don't know about your friends. But the plantations are littered with small cadavers. Our medic Adrian examined many of them, reckons they were killed while being raped.' If Leonel was trying to shock her, he was succeeding. He tugged the tip of his nose and cleared his throat. 'As we speak, relatives from Guacamaya are recovering the bodies and transferring them to the *camposanto*. The adults were shot in the village. Those in the church were doused with petrol and set alight.' He paused, and then repeated that he was sorry. A tear spilled from one of Jasmine's eyes, and she dashed it away.

'How could anyone have done that?' she stammered, bottom lip quivering.

'War brings out the worst in people,' Leonel suggested, 'and a cocktail of drugs smothers misgivings. The guardsmen will have been well doped up to carry out those orders.'

She shook her head in bewilderment before asking why he had invited her here.

'To apologise. To explain. To offer any help we can.'

She shrugged uncertainly, appealing for clarification. 'Apologise? What for? I thought it was the greens who did…' – a cogent description of what the National Guard had done escaped her – 'did what they did.'

'There was some doubt as to which side of the political fence El Zacate fell. No National Guardsmen deployed to patrol the streets. The mayor a Democrat, wanting nothing to do with us or the right-wing ARENA.' He scratched his jaw in thought. 'Possibly he tried to strike a balance between the soldiers and the guerrillas, believing that if he offended neither side he and his people would be safe.'

'He offended someone,' Chachi chipped in scathingly.

Leonel agreed. 'Had the community leader sought our protection I would have dispatched a defence squad to take up positions in El Zacate. That's part of what we do. But being a PDC supporter, he probably felt he had no reason to ask for *compa* support, because his party is in government. Still, knowing the haphazard way the military does its profiling, I'm not that surprised they went in. I don't like sending squads into a town against the wishes of its mayor or administrative committee, but in this case I could have made an exception.'

'You'd better hurry up,' she urged. National politics and The Conflict had been weighed on every *campesino* tongue for the last four years, so she followed his rhetoric readily. 'What exactly do you want from me?'

'The media reports of the massacre are ambiguous or biased,' he picked up the pace now. 'At noon today Radio Nacional responded to Radio Venceremos' allegations by transmitting live interviews with military personnel who claimed to have visited El Zacate, apparently to investigate a *matanza*. Those investigators reported the massacre to be the work of the Frente Farabundo Martí para la Liberación Nacional. Aside from being highly detrimental to our cause, this is quite untrue. Radio Venceremos, on the other hand, accuses the military of this act of aggression against an unarmed civilian people. *Your* people. Neither side has an eye-witness to support its accusation of the other.'

'You want to interview me on Radio Venceremos?' she guessed.

'Señorita Jasmine, clearly you understand our predicament.'

The mere notion of trawling through every detail of *la matanza* was enough to make her quail. Without giving the matter a second thought, she refused flatly.

Leonel paused, presumably to rally an apt response. 'Before El Zacate there were others. Morazán, Chalatenango, they share your loss…'

'Yes, yes, I know,' Jasmine cut in irritably. 'Chachi gave me that lecture. Please, hurry. Or have you finished already?'

'The difference, Señorita Jasmine, being that the entire Morazán Province has always supported the FMLN, whereas El Zacate, in a divided Cuscatlán Province, has not. Further military incursions are likely in the coming weeks, and your assistance may help prevent these from happening.'

It seems like a perfectly reasonable request, she thought. But the prospect of being escorted by a bunch of guerrillas to a dark and secret place deep in the woods was daunting. And to publicly declare her true name and relay to a radio-phonic world memories she would rather never again contemplate went far beyond daunting. Yet she would consider his request on the back of one equally reasonable request of her own.

'Señor Leonel Flint, it's only because none of the soldiers ran away when the helicopter arrived that I realised the army and not the FMLN had destroyed El Zacate. But I didn't start this war, you did, you and your Partido Comunista Salvadoreño.' She purposely enunciated the appellation with a high degree of contempt, and added with a tilt of her head, 'All I can think about now is my mother, down there.'

'We understand your concerns, señorita. But you must think about yourself now. And perhaps spare a thought for the other villages that might be in the firing line. Meanwhile, we can offer you some reasonable protection.'

'Reasonable protection!' she blurted, and gave a scornful laugh. 'How? By my coming to live with the *compa's* in the mountains?' And wagged a forefinger at him. 'No thanks! My best option is to stay in the mayor's house, under his protection. Right now that's the safest place for me.'

'You will at least think about giving Radio Venceremos an interview?' he urged.

'Perhaps,' she gave an inch and added, 'but I have a condition.' She spotted his slight nod. 'You help me bury my mother.'

A sharp intake of breath. 'Don't go down there, Señorita Jasmine. It's not a pretty sight.'

'Mother will have a proper burial, *with* or *without* your help.'

'Go on,' Chachi coaxed. 'Help her out. Then maybe she'll help you.' He hunched his shoulders and thrust forward upheld hand. 'What've you got to lose?'

Leonel transferred his steady gaze to his younger brother. 'You're right, Chachi. But you're coming too. And you arrange the transport, because the pickup's being used by my courier.'

'I have a second condition,' Jasmine blurted.

'You drive a hard bargain,' Leonel said with the first smile of the day. It was an engaging smile to which Jasmine felt compelled to respond in kind, but her face muscles refused to budge.

'I want to play football, in a proper team.' She was plainly aware of the incongruous nature of her second condition, but the way she saw it, the thrill of a good soccer match might return a sense of normality to lift her spirits.

'I'm not sure the other players will agree,' Chachi began, but under a crushing glare from Leonel he continued smoothly – 'but I'm sure I can persuade them.'

'A word of warning,' Leonel said as she was about to take her leave. 'I understand you're staying at Casa Menesses, yes?'

'Yes.'

'Anastasio will want to speak to you. For your sake, not for mine, I suggest you neglect to mention our little conference here. Watch what you tell him, and under no circumstances allow him to take you away from the house.'

'*Adiós, Señores* Flint.' She was already backing away from the brothers. She had heard quite enough.

* * *

Jasmine's return to Casa Menesses was met by a flurry of questions from a flustered Elsa in a pink flour-powdered apron. Where've you been, child? You all right? Did you get the groceries?

And when Jasmine confessed that she'd sidetracked to La Molienda, Elsa bestowed on her a sympathetic expression before relieving her of the hamper and scuttling off to a kitchen that was sharing its garlic-laden aromas with the connecting room.

Fernando hadn't returned from work yet. No sign of Anastasio either, though he could be in his bedroom.

'Shall I help prepare the supper?' Jasmine asked, somewhat at a loss for tasks to perform.

'Tidy up the lounge and lay the table for me, will you?' Elsa bid without looking up from the chopping board.

Thus Jasmine was engaged when a sweating Fernando turned up and paused with briefcase in hand to enquire after her wellbeing before subsiding into a sofa, bellowing, 'Elsa, I'm back,' and clicking on the TV by way of remote. And thus too Jasmine was engaged when against the blare of the canned hilarity of *La Risa en Vacaciones VI*, she heard the front door being opened. So for that matter did Elsa from the kitchen, because she darted behind Fernando who continued heaving with amusement at the antics mustered by his favourite comedy show. Elsa stopped short of the door and flung out plump arms in readiness to embrace her son with enough motherly affection to make up for the fatherly deficit in this regard.

Green cap in hand and in full camouflage Anastasio crouched stooping and Elsa hitched herself up on tiptoe and thus they could more or less engage in the hearty embrace they had prepared for each other. Jasmine prudently averted her gaze, and continued to lay the dinner table. Fernando batted not an eyelid in his homecoming son's direction.

The dinner table was laid and Jasmine proceeded to the kitchen to await orders from her *patrones*. Once they had eaten she would take her meal in the servant's quarters. She settled herself on a stool hedged between the refrigerator and a kitchen cupboard, and waited, a tea towel draped across her knees.

'Señorita.' Shirted now in glossy black satin, fingers tucked into the pockets of faded jeans, flat-top hairdo bristling and smelling of refined citrus, Anastasio Menesses towered from the doorway. In a strikingly symmetrical face his smile was easy and white while the outer corners of friendly eyes crinkled. 'I'd like to ask you a few questions, if you don't mind, so Ma says why don't you join us for dinner tonight?' Suggested in a grating voice that detracted from his handsomeness, of which Jasmine was very aware.

Don Leonel was right, she mused. Here come the questions. But it was far from Jasmine's sense of duty to her kindly patrons to decline, even politely, an invitation to dinner on the grounds that a most wanted guerrilla leader had forbidden it. So it was with stifled reluctance that Jasmine followed Anastasio through to the lounge where her patrons were waiting seated at the dinner table.

'Opposite me,' Anastasio invited.

And so she did, noticing that someone – who else but Doña Elsa? – had made up an extra place of plate and cutlery and plastic beaker.

Elsa smiled her approval. 'Do please relax, child.'

Jasmine dropped her shoulders in a studied act of relaxing and then shut her eyes while Elsa improvised on an already elaborate version of *For what we are about to receive* to include a touching supplication for Jasmine's safety, and recovery, and wellbeing. Amen.

Elsa managed to dish out piping hot pupusas and launch into a merry monologue designed to bring her darling son up to date on local gossip – help yourselves to salad and salsa – and Carmencita of the veggie shop was quoted verbatim as the reliable source because she's got her ear to the ground, hasn't she, darling?

Which went over Fernando's head.

'Any news on your promotion, dear?' Elsa swerved off topic and fluttered her hand on to her son's wrist.

With a well-ironed napkin he delicately dabbed the corners of his mouth before answering. 'Promotion purely on merit is unlikely, Ma. Depends on *el tandón* – not what you know, but who you know, and more to the point, who you impress.'

'Your key is the colonel,' Fernando piped up. 'Get him to notice you, and you've cracked it.'

'Not that easy, actually, not these days, not since Santamaria's mind went one-track.' He broke off for a sip of freshly squeezed orange. 'I kid you not, *El Indio* is obsessed with Serafin Romero and his pirate radio station; he's convinced General Levi to divert resources badly needed elsewhere to scour the countryside for the transmitter. Needle in haystack stuff.'

'Find that transmitter and even General Simón Levi will notice you,' Fernando, eyes on his plate, stated the bleakly obvious.

Another familiar name to Jasmine. General Levi – the army's highest ranking commander, with the exception of the President of the Republic, of course, whose inherited title of Commander in Chief held little in the way of tangible authority. So Mother had claimed.

'What does he want with a transmitter anyway?' Elsa pulled a face to show how ridiculous transmitters were.

In reply Anastasio flogged her a stock media quote: 'Venceremos spreads its lies and propaganda through it.'

'When fifty-five thousand soldiers and masses of technology can't track down a paltry radio station in a country as small as ours…well…' Fernando muttered with heaps of amusement, and earned himself a reproachful stare from his wife.

The trace of a smirk implied that Anastasio was also amused. 'Not as easy as it sounds, Pa. Even within the guerrilla ranks only a select few know its whereabouts. Besides, we don't have the whole army looking for it, just the security forces.'

'Security forces, you mean the National Guard, and they number – what? – eleven thousand by the last count? Still a hell of a lot of manpower for a single purpose. And what about the Hacienda and the National Police?'

'Surely not the Police,' blurted Elsa, her tone laced with scepticism.

'Unlike police in other countries,' Fernando would have her know, 'besides carrying out routine duties like chasing bad guys and extracting the odd backhander from motorists, our police function as combat and intelligence units alongside the army. And the Guard and the army are like that…' Upheld fingers crossed. 'Tight.'

'Unlike the Guard, Pa, the police are assigned to the cities, whereas our search focuses on rural territories.'

Not so ridiculous now, Elsa was saying – if only through a smug little smile to hubby.

'So I suppose what they're saying about El Zacate is propaganda too,' Fernando tested.

Anastasio wiped his hands on his napkin, plonked his elbows on the table and turned with composure to his munching father. 'Radio Venceremos is right, for once.'

Fernando's jowls stuck fast in mid munch. He lowered a salad-laden fork and stared back in evident astonishment. 'You admit it, then?'

'Admit what, exactly?'

'The army's responsible for the *matanza*?'

Anastasio made a disparaging gesture with his right hand and leaned back in his chair. 'I'm compelled to admit it. After all, the evidence is overwhelming.'

This was not what Jasmine had expected at all. The army kept its mouth zipped up. The army brushed under the carpet. Others were involved in such contentious exploits as *matanzas*. The army was blameless, or so it would have you believe.

'Are you sure, son?' Elsa looked concerned.

'Fairly sure. A rogue unit perhaps, acting independently. Such an operation wouldn't have been sanctioned by any reasonable commander.'

Elsa narrowed her eyes in awe and declared, '*Un escuadrón de la muerte.*'

'Unlikely,' Fernando stated with all the certainty in the world and then crammed the fork-load of salad between his moist lips.

'Why not death squads?' Elsa asked. Fernando swallowed hard before tackling the plate again. 'Military officers, paid civilian mercenaries, opposed to the PDC or the FMLN, pushing Mary Jane and crack-cocaine on my humble streets. But I tell you this,' he sucked his forefinger and aimed it directly at Anastasio, 'they couldn't have mustered enough troops to round up a thousand villagers. A thousand mind. And that's why it wasn't a death squad.'

Anastasio conceded that the El Zacate operation must have been the work of a military battalion, but insisted, one that acted independently. 'You and I both know there are rogue elements in the military. It's no secret.' And turning a gathering frown on Jasmine he asked, 'You wouldn't by any chance recognise the ground commander, anyone who was giving orders, would you?'

A shake of her head might have sufficed, but she managed to add, 'From up at La Molienda looking down on the scene, I could see only the top of his cap, and with his visor pulled down hard, I couldn't see his face at all.'

'That's a real pity.'

A pity for whom? Jasmine speculated, yet to come to terms with a soldier pointing the finger of accusation at his own kind.

'What evidence?' Elsa again. 'You said there was evidence.'

'I did, Ma. Evidence in the form of army-issue cartridges and bullets recovered from the crime scene by investigators. That's your evidence.'

Means SFA reckoned Fernando, apparently playing devil's advocate. 'Soldiers sell rifles to anyone with the right notes to buy them. The *muchachos* have their fair share of army-issued weapons too.'

That was also true in Anastasio's soldierly opinion. 'The FMLN is increasingly equipped with M16s. But they lack sufficient supplies to go round their nine thousand combatants. Most are armed with Soviet AK47s, and there's a bunch of Chinese and Yugoslav replicas knocking about besides, and some make do with home-made examples. Now, AKs chamber 7.62 x 39 mm rifle cartridges, a few will take 5.45 x 39 mm ammo.'

'All these chambers and millimetres, means what?' Elsa asked, with a bewildered shake of her artificially blonde head. 'Is that the evidence?'

'It means El Zacate is full of NATO rounds,' Fernando translated.

But Anastasio had more of the same to get her head round: 'M16s chamber standard NATO 5.56 mm cartridges, of which there are literally thousands scattered on El Zacate's street. In fact, Ma, all without exception of the spent shells and bullets recovered from the scene come from M16s, which are standard military-issue rifles. If the *muchachos* had massacred El Zacate, I'd expect to find at least some spent AK ammo in the mix.'

Fernando pressed a forefinger vertically to the tabletop, bending the tip so far back that only a double joint could have allowed it. 'Do we know who led this rogue unit?'

'Not yet, Pa.' Even white smile spreading as he turned to Jasmine. 'But I'm assigned to the investigating unit, and I'm to submit a findings report before the National Congress and the American Ambassador next Friday morning. And with your help, I will expose the murderers responsible for this unspeakable crime against your town.'

So both Don Leonel and Don Anastasio sought her help to expose those responsible for the El Zacate *matanza*. What Don Leonel could never have expected, in Jasmine's considered opinion, is that Don Anastasio would break with the official version of events by implicating the army instead of the guerrillas. And this highly unexpected factor tipped the oppressive balance of trust under duress, if ever so slightly, in Anastasio's favour.

'*Gracias*,' was all she could muster by way of reply. But as she would later discover, *gracias*, to Anastasio's way of thinking, meant *yes*.

CHAPTER THREE

A PAIR OF mules in leather collars and chain traces pulled a four-wheeled dray – pride and property of farmer Ignacio Molina – down the road. Jasmine was perched beside Leonel on the plank of a headboard, Chachi lounging behind with a rolled up canvass stretcher at his flip-flop clad feet. Leonel lashed the mules' backs and they acknowledged with an irritable flick of ears, and Jasmine's appeal for less of the whip was lost in a fraternal debate on how to drive Don Ignacio's cart.

'So quiet,' she murmured, sizing up the soaring pines that walled them in on either side. The nearside mule gave a huff and swung his log-like head from side to side. Leonel lashed him again and the animal snorted bitterly, so Jasmine leaned across to try and wrest the whip from Leonel but he winged it far out of reach with a long straight arm.

They turned with a slow bend and through the trees Jasmine could see sun-splattered rooftops so ordinary-looking that for a fleeting moment she made herself believe she would find everything as it should be; and her mother in the courtyard with a caldron of frijoles on the go.

'What a stench!' Chachi gasped. And he abandoned his latest debating point to clasp a hand over his nose and mouth like a man trying to rip off his own face.

They trundled into El Zacate and Leonel pulled the cart to a halt, and offered Jasmine a handkerchief to filter out a vile vinegary smokiness that came in wafts, but she declined and stared directly ahead.

'I hardly recognise the place,' she told him.

Dozens of black vultures picked their way over crumbled masonry, smashed roof tiles, and dry stalks. They assembled around fallen statues and severed branches that with a second look became carbonised human contours drowning in waves of debris, and with a third blink became human skin, blackened by fire, curling from naked limbs. And from these eye-watering wounds oozed butter, but of course, reasoned Jasmine, it couldn't be butter. A town elder lay on his back not ten feet away. His head angled back, teeth exposed, skin sunken into his ribcage. And beyond his bare feet a boy lay on his stomach, face into the rubble, the back of his head missing, his skull open like a calabash bowl. Jasmine's eyes began picking out still more twisted, crumpled mounds among the debris.

Humming clouds of flies eddied above the featherless heads of the feasting birds, and poured through bullet-pocked doorways and soot-smeared windows and round a ballooned mother pig, a bald mongrel, and a collapsed black horse with a party of two vultures on its bloated belly.

'People,' Jasmine said, feeling numb.

'We could leave, leave things as they are,' Leonel suggested in a subdued murmur.

But his suggestion was rejected. 'I must bury Mother.' Jasmine leaned forward and identified the house into which she'd seen her mother being driven.

Leonel flicked the reins and the mules lurched forward, the iron-shod wheels crunching the brittle tile fragments. He parked and driver and passengers dismounted and snapped on rubber gloves, thoughtfully provided by the driver.

'The ninth house down from the plaza,' Jasmine confirmed, glancing back at Chachi whose face had acquired a pasty hue. His cheeks began pumping as if he was about to vomit.

As they stood on the threshold of the marked house, Leonel squeezed his handkerchief over his nose and mouth. Creases gathered on his forehead and his eyes narrowed to slits. 'You shouldn't go in there, Jasmine. Chachi and I will take care of this.'

'Chachi's about to throw up. Besides, only I can recognise my mother.'

'She may be unrecognisable. As you can see,' a single nod towards the street, 'many of the bodies are burnt beyond recognition.'

She met his eyes, shook her head and stepped through the open door.

Two huge vultures shuffled out of her way. As her eyes adjusted to the dimness she saw more of the scavengers inside. Within the fly-clouds they stalked indelicately upon a mass of bloody human wreckage; over corpses – some resting slackly while others, still racked by rigor mortis, were frozen in stiffly warped poses – and over plastic lawn chairs that must have made a set with the upended table. They had picked at the destroyed faces, at bowels torn open by bullets, and at fly-infested ears. The open mouths of adults held their final screams, and on the faces of the children the terror of their last moments was cast with heartbreaking clarity.

Bullet craters patterned the walls on which bloody handprints scored downward channels faithfully describing fall after fall. And in the dark gelatinised mess on the floor, blackened bullets were set alongside severed fingers and random shoes and chips of porcelain except that they weren't porcelain but teeth. If there was one saving grace, it was that this house had thankfully escaped most of the flames. Aside from singed holes to clothing the edges of which were glued to festering burns, the cadavers gave the impression of having had their flames considerably doused with blood before further fire damage was done.

Speechless Jasmine advanced, plucking each breath in short sharp intakes, and swallowed back the bile that crept up to her larynx. She put the back of her wrist to her nose and reached out her spare hand as if seeking reassurance; and Leonel clutched her fingertips, but she felt numb and the gesture gave her neither comfort nor reassurance so she wriggled her fingers free.

At the sound of Chachi retching outside followed by the heavy splatter of vomit, the search began. Jasmine and Leonel studied corpses through whining fly-clouds, shoved aside cold punctured arms that bent unnaturally where the bones had broken and saw body parts that Jasmine struggled to recognise. They pulled one body off another and for a while recognition failed. The woman lying on her side had black hair flooding across her cheek. Her semi-fisted hand was touching the tip of her nose as if she was about to suck her thumb. For Jasmine this brought full acceptance that her mother had indeed died.

'Yes, that's her,' she said, although her voice was no more than a whisper.

She knelt on the floor, gathered up her mother's head and drew aside several wisps of silver-streaked hair. The normally plump folds of skin had sagged and her prominent cheekbones looked as if they would tear through the taut brown skin. There was a peculiar colouring to her lips: maroon overlaid with transparent grey. Her eyelids, finely crinkled like moths' wings, had sent out trickles of black mascara. Jasmine bent over and kissed her lips and then set about tenderly caressing the cool and flaccid face. No rush, she thought. Although this was hell on earth, here is where she wanted to stay for a while.

Leonel squatted beside her. 'May I know her name?' he mumbled, close-lipped like a ventriloquist, blocking his mouth to random flies.

'She is Señora Inocenta Maria Gavidia, my beautiful mother,' Jasmine announced as if electing her Queen of the Coffee Festival. And to that queen she murmured, 'This is Don Leonel Flint.'

Under Jasmine's exacting supervision the brothers lifted the mortal remains of Inocenta Gavidia on to the stretcher and carefully carried her from the house. At the cart, Jasmine lowered the tailboard and Leonel slid the stretcher on to the deck and she watched silently while he drew the white linen over her mother.

He snapped off his gloves and laid a consoling hand on Jasmine's shoulder. 'Chachi reserved a good place for her in Nejapa's *camposanto*.'

She could only turn away. Leonel squeezed her shoulder gently but that made it all the more likely that she would weep, so she shrugged off his hand. She climbed aboard and lay cuddled up to her mother as she used to do, and whispered comforting words as her mother used to to her.

No doubt very relieved to be leaving, Chachi sprang on to the headboard beside his elder brother.

'Hup.' Leonel flicked the reins and the cart rocked away with a well-executed U-turn.

In the evening of that same Saturday, during a private ceremony held at the *camposanto* overlooking Nejapa, Padre José Maria Melgar buried Inocenta Gavidia, while her daughter Jasmine Maria, who stood between the Flint brothers, bowed her head and wept.

CHAPTER FOUR

IT WAS LIKE A date, but not a date. Like one because he properly fancied this latest house-*muchacha* who he, with Ma vouchsafing his good character and usefulness as a protective benefactor, had persuaded to accept a friendly restaurant dinner on the strength it would do her the power of good. Not like one because unlike Ma's previous maids this one showed not the least bit of romantic inclination towards him. Fancied? Okay, that was an understatement, he conceded. Though those pills were working their evil – the irritability, the abrupt mood-swings, the explosive losses of temper. But Santamaria's plan for El Zacate was gruesome in its conception, and nothing short of hellish in its realisation. To get through it he and his men had hit the go-pills and cocaine and smoked spliffs laced with gunpowder. Short of overdosing on these, most of the boys, including Anastasio, would have lost their bottle either before or during Hammer and Nail, and the whole thing would have gone belly-up.

He'd never had one of his victims stay in his house. That was likely to work your conscience like nothing else. And since Jasmine had come to stay with Ma and Pa, the depressive withdrawal effects of the pills were enhancing his natural revulsion at what he and the rest of *Batallón Liberación* had done. Having sight of this innocent victim, seeing the tragedy in those same eyes that had learned to trust him, was enough to bring him close to a place he hadn't known since before he'd sussed The Game and that place was repentance.

So then, to San Salvador in Pa's air-conditioned SUV. Choice of restaurant: La Pampa Salvadoreña in Colonia San Benito. A polished timber dance floor surrounded by rustic tables clad in red linen and inward facing fake outer walls topped with fake tiled eaves and punctuated by equally fake shuttered windows, all failing to reflect Salvadoran vernacular architecture because Swiss Cabin was how Jasmine described it, and Anastasio searched his memory for anything on architecture and, coming up with nothing other than Gothic – which he wouldn't have recognised if he bumped his head on a pointed arch, and colonial – which was probably like Pa's house, he conceded a thoughtful yes, definitely Swiss, where did you pick up such extraordinary architectural knowledge?

'Heidi, Girl of the Alps.'

Which left Anastasio with his first stalling of the night.

The second came when the sullen-faced waitress, having taken his order for a glass of Lambrusco, medium or large? Large – thank you – asked, 'And for your daughter, sir?'

While Jasmine was looking over the menu, he consoled his dented feelings by reminding himself that girls as young as Jasmine often married men a lot older than him. Besides, at twenty-six, he was hardly on the shelf.

Skipping the starter she went for grilled corvina with king prawns and asparagus, which told Anastasio that despite her peasant upbringing she believed she had a right to the best. Others from her town would have meekly gone for the cheapest option on the menu, in keeping with their social class. Jasmine was no cheap date. Just as well he'd brought along enough cash. After all, his intention was to impress, gain her confidence, and then, unless he could come up with a clever way out, he'd have to carry out Santamaria's intention: eliminate every last witness. And the shithead was likely to be on his back about her very soon.

She was easy company, so chatty in fact that he needn't have feared embarrassing pauses. Oscillating between child and woman she disarmed him and surprised him with snippets of insight far beyond her years. Her chatter journeyed from the European football leagues to the construction of sonnets, the latter sailing a bit close to the wind when she heaped praise on the late Roque Dalton; so Anastasio put a discreet finger to his lips because Dalton had been as red as they come.

'I like him anyway,' she retorted.

'Him or his works?' Anastasio retorted back, irritated to be quelling a drop of jealousy.

'Him and his works.'

Besides being as red as they come, Dalton had been handsome. And even though Anastasio gave himself a ten for good looks, he resented having to compete in that department with a dead poet. Suddenly he hated the girl sitting on the opposite side of the table, eating fine food at his expense. Then he forgave her, but when she confessed an appreciation for Adonai Limeño's prose, he went back to hating her.

'His works are banned,' he snapped.

'Why?' Challenging him to explain.

'Insurrectional. Why else?'

'He writes lots of tender stuff too, why ban those? And the other stuff, well, the sort you hear all over the place.'

'Hear? Like we should arm the peasantry and bring down an elected government?' – guessing now, because he'd never actually read the work, just believed the party line against him.

After a pause for thought – 'Like the gringos imposing their vampiric will on us.' Quoted far too loudly for his comfort, so with finger to his lips again he pleaded, for pity's sake, keep your voice down. Where the *gran puta* did she hear that?

He looked round and spotting no potential hazards within earshot, he leaned across the table. 'Allow me to impart for your wellbeing a spot of free advice,' he said, forgiving her all over again and wanting desperately to be her protective benefactor. 'It may surprise you that I despise the gringos' meddling hand in our country, but since they've succeeded in turning our survival into a question of choosing sides, I buy into it. And don't think I've got the time of day for those pretend-gringos who own most of our country, because they're the savages who pit us against each other and opened the doors to your so-called vampiric meddling in the first place. Politicians are here to stuff up Average José's life, pocket the national bounty and get paid big bucks for doing so. Only one problem: that approach can sink a country. So our job, and by ours I mean any Average José with more than half a brain, is to head for the highest ground we can reach, and be sharpish about it lest we get dragged under.'

'Come again?'

'Deprivation.' He was on a roll. He was not your regular Party-bought soldier blindly following orders on the simplistic doctrine of blue was good and red was evil. Unlike his peers he could even confess to a certain sympathy towards the Reds, but not here, it was too risky. But he had The Game sussed, knew where he stood in society, and was placing his cards where they were most likely to come up trumps.

'Did you know that the world's richest country…?' he started, but was rudely interrupted.

'*La USA.*'

'Indeed. That *la USA* will continue to pump massive resources into our modest pockets – a whole lot of it destined for the military?'

'Yes, but continue pumping for how long?' – taking it to another level, and surprising him again.

'Ad infinitum, or at least until our president says thanks very much but we want no more of your military aid or your awards and contributions and spare parts and any of the other tricky tickets by which aid is converted into hard currency. Which, take it from me, our good president will not say.'

'But the *muchachos…*'

'A flock of sorry-arses living hand-to-mouth in the jungle,' he said dismissively. 'However much sympathy money they eek out of poverty-ridden peasants or French *sandalistas* and Canadian hippies, they're not going to head off the endless

59

resources the US government is hell-bent on committing here to wipe out the Red Dread. You don't need a degree in rocket science to put your money on the military winning sooner or later. Only two questions you need ask yourself, Jasmine: which gang do you choose? And what are you prepared to do to remain a member?'

* * *

'I want you to describe the El Zacate operation from where you saw it. Battalions have preferred tactics which from an investigator's point of view we sometimes call Modus Operandi. With a clear visual understanding of how the operation proceeded, I should be able to tell who was in command.'

That was how Anastasio had enlisted Jasmine's 'vital help if we are to root out the offending battalion.' And that was why, for a second time in as many weeks, she found herself out with Anastasio. No SUV today, but the back of an open-top jeep that had the suspension of an unbroken colt. Okay, so Don Leonel had cautioned her against going off with Anastasio. But wasn't he out to enlist her for his own aims too? Who was he to declare himself the safest murderer in town to hang out with? Hadn't he put away his fare share of innocents in his time? And if these inward debates didn't quite mollify Jasmine's underlying unease at conceding to this trip then it was none other than Doña Elsa, wholly trusting of her beloved son, who had again clinched it when in a merry voice she had reminded: "Everyone needs a protective benefactor these days. My son is ours, so I recommend you get on side.'

In the front passenger seat the protective benefactor, in full military fatigues, sat half-sideways, thus presenting for Jasmine's grudging acknowledgment the refined profile of his undeniably handsome face. Labouring at the wheel was a dumpling-cheeked captain who kept eyeing her through the rear-view mirror, and beside her a bespectacled corporal uniformed in swirling greens.

Jasmine recognised the route, having bussed this way

with her mother on the occasional daytrip to Nejapa. Several kilometres longer than the short cuts possible on foot through the woods, this was a narrow mortar-cratered trail winding between a soaring wooded escarpment to the right and a sinking valley to the left.

Away to the east veins of white light flickered against dark thunder clouds.

'It's going to rain,' Jasmine announced, hoping the trip would get rained off.

Anastasio gave a tight smile to simply agree with her weather forecast.

As their bumpy route took them higher so the great shelf of cloud hastened towards them, breaking over mountain peaks and skimming across valleys, and with a rushing onslaught of torrential rain and shrieking winds it smacked into the jeep from the left. In the sudden dusk-light Jasmine blinked the running water from her eyes. Within seconds her mauve cotton dress clung saturated to her skin. Giant curtains of driven rain swept across them, pelting the embankment and disintegrating into a series of mini cataracts that hauled sliding mud and rocks down on to the trail. 'We should turn back,' she yelled into Anastasio's ear. Anastasio shouted something that was lost in the wind, pointed to his ear and shook his head. Then he tapped the forward-leaning driver on the shoulder and by patting the air with a flat horizontal palm signalled him to decelerate.

Thankfully the driver responded by changing down to first but despite moderating his speed to a crawl, he completely missed the turnoff for El Zacate. So an utterly drenched Jasmine, more eager than ever to get this trip done and dusted, spoke to Anastasio again. 'This is not the way to El Zacate. We should have taken that turning.' She pointed back over her shoulder.

The captain piled on the brakes and cut the engine. The soldiers dismounted, and with a wave Anastasio beckoned for Jasmine to proceed likewise.

The unscheduled detour and now this stop in the middle of nowhere confirmed Jasmine's belated fears that Anastasio, by readily implicating the army in El Zacate's demise and taking her out to dinner, had gained sufficient of her trust to lure her into his snare. So she looked round, not in bewilderment, but hunting for escape. The forest to her right had thinned – trees and clumps of wild thorn scattered amid tall meadow grass. To her left the scrub sank away abruptly.

But strong hands had clamped over her arms. They yanked her out of the jeep and hurled her down, and with a splash she landed painfully on all-fours.

The half-submerged tread of Anastasio's boots appeared so close that she could smell the new rubber. His face was distant and shadowed beneath his cap visor, and beyond it glided the vast flickering storm.

'A little detour,' she heard him say.

She began to push herself up, but his boot whipped up and stomped between her shoulder blades, sending her splashing flat to the road. Her wrists were forced up her back and cold metal handcuffs locked them together.

Coarse hands hoisted her to her feet, frogmarched her off the road and into the forest. Dozens of paces later, she emerged into a glade of waist-high grass and slender eucalyptus saplings.

'Halt. Turn about.'

On obeying she discovered that her handler – a grim-faced Anastasio – was alone. The others must have remained with the jeep. Despite the poor light in the glade, he was wearing sunglasses. Even now she could smell the tang of citrus lotion. His uniform, wet through, had taken on a deeper shade of green. He drew up to her and laid a huge thumb on her temple and rammed it with such sudden force that her head snapped back, and she took several back-steps to recover her balance. When she looked up, he was drawing his pistol from its hip holster. He levelled it at her. She shut her eyes, and waited. Long seconds drew by during which the howling gale seemed to close in around her. She opened her eyes and saw a shift of Anastasio's head. She looked down at her own body. The wet fabric of her dress clung to her small breasts. Her nipples, hardened by the cold rain, pushed out the material. She raised her chin defiantly, glaring into the sunglasses as if to penetrate them with her accusation.

Anastasio leaped forward and thrust the pistol to the side of her head. With his free hand he wrenched at the embroidered neck of her dress, jerking her into his sodden shirtfront. But the embroidery held the fabric intact. His hand delved into her hair, found the zip at her back and slid it all the way down. The dress stuck to her wet skin, so he peeled it off her shoulders. With a second wrench the zip tore, and she felt the dress being tugged down until it gathered on her feet. Now he poked the gun muzzle between her breasts and, descending on bending knees, used his free hand to drag her panties down her legs. She gazed up at the treetops and prayed: '*Virgen Madre, protéjame…*'

Now he was backing up through the tall grass. She was shivering, and with her hands manacled at her back was unable to cover any part of her nakedness. He plucked off his sunglasses and made several poorly aimed stabs for his breast pocket before they slid in.

'Santa Maria, mother of God,' Anastasio exclaimed, as if in triumph, 'you are a creature of glory.'

'I'm cold,' she stammered, through chattering teeth.

With the pistol levelled at her forehead, he reached down with his spare hand and began kneading his groin. With a look of resignation he stopped, stuck his sunglasses back over his eyes and cupped both hands over the pistol grip.

'Just obeying orders, Jasmine. *Disappear* the witness,' he admitted with – dare she think it – a note of regret.

'What about the other evidence?' Jasmine blurted above the downpour, hoping to seize on any regret, if regret was indeed what she'd heard in his voice. 'The cartridges you found.'

'Santamaria went and scattered the place with AK cartridges. The investigators found a lot of Soviet-made ammo. You have the only evidence, which makes you the loose end. You leave me no option, Jasmine.'

First regret, then accusation. And now, sensing a hesitance, Jasmine played her trump card: 'I can show you where the transmitter is hidden.'

A prolonged pause until Anastasio removed his shades again and glared at her, his jaw muscles knotting.

'Don Leonel Flint asked me to do a radio interview. He'll take me to Radio Venceremos and when I return I'll tell you where they hide out.' There. Simple. She had said it and felt defiled by her own perfidy. Especially now that Anastasio had shown his true colours.

'You saw Leonel Flint in Nejapa? He came down from the mountain?' Anastasio asked, incredulous enough to dip his gun beneath the height of the grass.

'His brother took me to meet him.' She swallowed hard.

But her betrayal hadn't worked, because Anastasio raised his gun back to a level position. The crack was deafening. Even before Jasmine flinched the bullet had swept inches past her right ear and skittered into the undergrowth. But she didn't know that because she was trying to figure out which part of her body the bullet had hit and when she was likely to feel the pain and whether she should keel over now or wait for the injury to prompt her collapse. But she hadn't long to ponder because Anastasio's shirtfront was now pressing hard to her cheek, the wet fabric sucking at her skin and she realised that her wrists were free.

'Convince them not to blindfold you.'

'I will,' she promised, rallying her stunned senses.

'Look out for landmarks. Memorise the route. Tell me and *only* me where they take you.'

Rubbing her wrists she nodded her agreement.

'Run, girl, back to the house.' His voice oddly thick, as if his throat was closing up. 'I'll tell the others I killed you. I'll take care of you. No-one can harm you now.' Then, unaccountably, he planted his lips on hers, and she felt his hand spread on the small of her back, squeezing her up against him. Another blow to the senses, which made her open her eyes as wide as they would go; but then indignation kicked in, and she made to push him off, but her indignation became strangled mumbles against the hard press of his lips.

Abruptly he pulled away and took a drunkard's step backwards, a flicker of bewilderment in his eyes. With trembling hands Jasmine pulled up her panties before knotting the torn and muddy dress straps over her shoulders. Without looking back at Anastasio, she tore across the glade and into the woods.

* * *

Loyal spectators would have observed that today the regular players of Manchester United and Los Aztecas displayed their most exuberant footwork, which invariably led to blundering losses of possession followed by erratic spurts of speed across the threadbare field. Tempers flared. Messy scraps broke out. Sam the referee worked his whistle overtime, bluish veins standing out on his neck. But Jasmine, drowning in one of Chachi's spare football outfits, had seen it all before, and she assumed her assigned position as right-back for Los Aztecas unfazed by even the most extravagant play from her male peers. And if she pushed her luck by fouling The Mantis – as Jasmine had secretly branded Manchester's all legs and no style centre-forward – in the unmarked and arbitrarily decided upon penalty area, thereby conceding a penalty-taken goal, it's true to say she went a long way to redeeming herself when, breaking position, she dribbled the semi-deflated ball forward to set up the equalizer, which Juan the team captain scored with possibly the first true flare any regular spectator would have observed thus far during the match.

And after Los Aztecas had gone on to thrash Manchester in a five-one victory the exhausted players took to the short pebbled track back from the field to Nejapa.

'I heard…' Chachi began, but Jasmine was off into the huge shadow of a conacaste tree. Legs together, she leapt from one light spot to another in a private game of hopscotch, and only broke off to allow an oxen-drawn cart to pull past, its wrinkled old driver in a pointed reed hat with wide brim, wistfully puffing on a fat home-rolled cigar, pungent tobacco smoke trailing.

'Mother used to roll cigars,' Jasmine announced cheerfully, skipping over to join Chachi when the cart had clattered past. 'And when there was no pruning to do in the orchards, I'd sell them from home.'

The football match had indeed served as a tonic for her, thought Chachi as they happily speculated on the Manchester players' embarrassment at what was by any standards a stunning defeat. Chachi would have liked to talk further on the match because he was punctuating the banter with gags and one-liners that were witty enough to prompt from Jasmine peals of unaffected laughter and dimple-cheeked responses that he found truly endearing. And when his quips went borderline reddish, her infant-like frown – curious or disapproving, it was hard to tell which – triggered in his innards an upsurge of protective fondness towards her. But he must change the subject for her own good, because unkind rumours about her were afoot in Nejapa.

Striking what he hoped was a casual note he launched the change of topic into a natural pause: 'I heard you went for a little jaunt with Anastasio and three of his goons.'

'Yes, Chachi, I did,' she admitted readily enough, but offered nothing further on the matter.

'Well, what did they want?'

'Just to talk about...' she started, and after a suspiciously long intermission rushed in with, 'about El Zacate.'

He tried another approach. 'Is there something you want to tell me, Jasmine?'

'I'll do the interview,' she blurted, rather too abruptly to equate naturally to what he considered his sensitive line of questioning.

'Not on the cards any longer,' he said. 'Leonel reckons it would be unsafe for you to do so while you're with *Los*

Menesses.'

'Why? They're not going to *do* anything to me, are they?'

'Don Fernando won't, nor will Doña Elsa. But don't overestimate their power over their son. With a word from Anastasio, Nejapa could be reduced to ruins, just like El Zacate.'

'But Don Anastasio said he would protect me,' she retorted.

While they stopped to allow a couple of Aztecas team-mates to saunter past with a *Hi* and a *Bye, see you later*, it dawned on Chachi that she had let a rather large cat out of the bag.

'Oh really?' he said, when they were out of earshot. 'And why do you suppose he would undertake to protect you? Perhaps you have something he desperately wants?

She had already hung her head. And when he faced her and took hold of her shoulders she could only meet him with a fleeting upward glance before her gaze dipped again.

'Did he hurt you, Jasmine? Force you to agree to something in return for his protection?'

He had not, she sought to assure him.

But Jasmine was no liar. She couldn't even look him in the eyes, and it wasn't as if he were a *patrón* or something. He urged her to trust him. Reminded her that Nejapa's fragile security floated on Anastasio's homicidal whims, which left the mayor – a Partido Demócrata Cristiano supporter – in the precariously awkward position of relying on his high-ranking son's influence to keep the army at bay. And the option of calling on the PCS to set up a defence squad would be bound to prompt swift military retaliation, which was the last thing the mayor wished for his people. But individuals, and especially an out-of-towner like Jasmine, might not expect to enjoy the same level of shelter.

And Chachi thought it was such a pity when Jasmine cracked. The mischievous grin that had been surfacing so readily that afternoon had vanished. Once again a child with the world on her shoulders, she confessed to the pact into which she had entered with Anastasio. One that entailed her delivering the whereabouts of Radio Venceremos into hands that had ripped her dress off her back. A deal which Chachi calculated was dependent on the fulfilling of her part to the letter lest terrible consequences befall her.

'You shouldn't have agreed to it' he said, forgetting that the alternative had been a bullet through the head. 'Firstly, even if I was stupid enough to betray Radio Venceremos, which for the record I'm not, I don't know where it operates from; and even if I thought Leonel would betray Radio Venceremos, which for the same record he would not, it's not like he lives at the green house opposite the grocer's shop and I could go knock on his door and say "Hey, Bro, I've got a rather treacherous favour to ask of you". To minimize the chances of the Guard mounting a coordinated assault, Leonel's column moves camp every few days. And he certainly doesn't come running to tell me where they move to. I sometimes don't see or hear from him in months. Is this sinking in, Jasmine?'

A remote nod said that it was.

'And fourthly,' he resumed with mounting distress, primarily on her behalf, 'and most importantly, they will never give up the transmitter. It's their voice, their most powerful and *effective* weapon. Through it the FMLN informs, mobilizes, recruits, and warns its listeners of up-coming military operations. The transmitter is worth ten thousand AKs...more than ten thousand.'

She had confided in him. And for her efforts had earned herself a harsh reality check, an insight into the tricky relationship between a farmer and his brother the guerrilla; and between a mayor and his son – a major in what Chachi strongly suspected was the very same battalion responsible for the recent *matanza*.

With an expectant expression in her large eyes, she gazed up to him. Now surely he had some helpful suggestions in response to the frank confidence she had entrusted to him.

'What am I to do, Chachi?'

'Hmm,' he replied, finding his mind wanting. 'Before

Anastasio returns for his information, you need to have left not only Casa Menesses, but Nejapa also.'

Expectancy turned to dismay. 'But where would I go, Chachi?'

'Hmm. Tricky.' He could invite her to stay with him at his plantation cabin, but that would place him in peril. Unless of course, her presence there went unpublicised. But no, it was far too risky. If Nancy Portillo didn't spot her, someone else would, and word would leak out, and Anastasio and his goons would be along to finish her off, and send him to paradise by way of hell while they were about it.

'I don't know, Jasmine.'

CHAPTER FIVE

HE MUST HAVE USED his mum's key to access my room, Jasmine registered. Harsh punching sobs wracked her body, sending her lurching up the pebbly footpath towards Chachi's plantation. Not for the first time she had a sense of lurching between nightmare and reality. How come she could remember the panic, the suffocation, the struggling? Then the guilt trip opened up the participants' roles in the episode for her reluctant scrutiny: How come *los patrones* didn't hear raised voices in my quarters? Their son enquiring after Serafin's whereabouts, railing at my unsatisfactory answers?

'Only Leonel can lead me to Serafin. And Leonel has called off the radio interview. But that's good for you, isn't it?' she'd made a stab at persuasion, 'because it means no witness to counter the military's account of El Zacate.'

'Of no consequence now,' was Anastasio's laconic reply. 'In its wisdom the National Congress charged the military to carry out the investigation. Appreciate irony do we…yes? Well a bunch of Hammer and Nail agents are amongst those detailed to track down witnesses. You can also appreciate how well I've sheltered you from those investigators. One month ago you promised me something. Remember what that was, Jasmine? What you promised me was the Venceremos hideout.'

She couldn't give it to him. But it was never going to be quite that simple because Anastasio, eyeing a consolation prize, now wanted something that she *could* give and with his eyes

70

stricken with a haunted madness and Doña Elsa's favoured meat carver appearing from nowhere in his hand he clipped the elasticised cord in her pyjama bottoms.

And had *los patrones* turned a deaf ear when their son pinned her down on her bed with a weight so oppressive that she'd screamed pleading for help from any quarter? Or when he'd driven the carver down hilt-deep between her clenched knees and twisted? Or when the blade sent her right knee springing outwards on pure reflex? Surely every Nejapan had heard when her virginity broke to astonishing pain flaring through her body, up into her brain to explode in her skull in a blinding whiteness. Even now she could smell her own vomit, feel its slippery coldness on her pyjama top.

CHAPTER SIX

August 1984

EVER SINCE JASMINE HAD hobbled bleeding into his hilltop cabin eight days ago, and told him a story that made him loathe Anastasio even more than he had when they were schoolmates, Chachi had taken the part of doting father.

She slept on his single mattress inside his shack. He slept on a reed mat watchman-like outside the only door, his fairly new and gleaming six-shooter tucked into his jeans beneath his smock.

Sure, it was unsafe for her – and for him for that matter – to take up residence on his isolated coffee plantation, but she had ended up here anyway, convalescing after what must have been the most appalling attack for a woman of any age, let alone a fourteen-year-old; an attack that, had he acted decisively when first he'd recognised her highly perilous tightrope trip between Anastasio and Radio Venceremos, was wholly avoidable. Even now as she sat taciturn and withdrawn on a stool beside him, slurping at a ripe mango in her new blue denim dungarees – which had been her favoured choice of replacement garment for both the bloodied pyjamas she'd arrived in and the meagre wardrobe she'd left behind at Casa Menesses – he was painfully aware that her presence here must remain a closely guarded secret. Jasmine had hacked off her long tresses which she had felt, for some inexplicable feminine reason, somehow contributed to Anastasio's sickening behaviour towards her. The result was a bunch of twirls that barely fell to her shoulders, which, in the half-light from the pungent kerosene lamp that filtered out through the cabin's single shuttered window, made her head profile disproportionately large for her elfin stature.

Padre José Maria Melgar, his only confidant, had smuggled in a Dutch volunteer medic from one of the FMLN's mobile hospitals, to administer to Jasmine's wounds both physical and emotional, while the good Padre himself had paid no less than seven surreptitious visits to administer to her spiritual wounds with gentle assurances that in the eyes of God and all good Christian believers, she was perfectly renewed in body and in spirit, and remained as lily innocent as the very day her mother, God rest her soul, had given her birth.

'It's a huge mark of trust that she has come to you – a man – following her ordeal,' Melgar had confided on his first visit.

Trust? thought Chachi. Or simply nowhere else to go?

But it had been nine months since the orchard had sparkled with sweet-scented star-like flowers, and it was now November. So the winds were late this year, but the coffee cherries were ripening on time. He would have to cancel the temporary pickers. They were good married fellows, all six of them, but hardly the sort you'd trust with a secret. News of Jasmine's presence on the plantation would be bound to find its way to their wives who, naturally, would whisper it, on the under-standing that it was said in the strictest confidence and it would travel from ear to ear until it hit Mrs Brigadier.

So how would he cope without his regular team of pickers? He had no idea. While he scampered round his orchards on his merry own, coffee cherries would ripen and rot on the branches before he could get to them. Unless of course he started early and mixed the greens with the reds which, wishing to conserve the high quality that *El Beneficio* had come to expect from him and the resulting elevated prices he had come to expect from the Cooperative, he had hitherto never even considered.

Yes, start the harvest early, he determined. Tomorrow he would sweep the drying patio of its puddles and dead leaves. He would turn the twenty-five soaking troughs hollow-side up, and he would grease the *despulpadora*. And he would begin to strip the orchard of all its cherries – be they red or green or anywhere between.

* * *

During an eleven-day absence of sick leave Anastasio wallowed inconsolably in a hotel bed. Eleven full days of self-imposed detox and having his conscience flay him for everything and in particular for the El Zacate operation and Jasmine's rape. But that was another person. I'm not capable of such things. But if not, where was the stop button for the excruciating scenes that played through his memory of their own accord? 'I'm so sorry, Jasmine,' he wailed as he knelt before a tiny wall picture of the Virgin Mary. 'Can you ever forgive me?' And Jasmine, being the only survivor from El Zacate, was by default the only person qualified to forgive him any of it. Then he laughed at such forlorn hope because his conscience was speaking again: *You kill her mother, then you rape her, and now you think she's going to forgive you.*

In the end it was the memory of Jasmine's nakedness that did the trick: by firing up his loins it dampened the remorse and in the moments before the remorse would return he pulled himself together enough to go in search of some Party Dust. Feeling more like one of his more-together selves, Anastasio checked out of the hotel and reported for work. Only to be told that Colonel Rubén Santamaria was looking for him, because he had another Hammer and Something operation planned.

But to Anastasio's relief, *Hammer and Machete* promised to be an altogether new type of operation.

First by jeep to Ilopango Airbase. Then on to Cuscatlán Province by a Salvadoran Air Force Hughes gunship that had been stripped of its guns and spot lamp in a thoughtful attempt to make it look meek and unthreatening.

Belted into a canvas seat, a full head and shoulders taller than the squat colonel beside him, Anastasio was in no doubt that his height advantage and university education more than compensated for his lower rank. Dark-skinned, high-cheeked, prominent hooked-nose, and eyes of volcanic blackness, his colonel was nothing but a full-blooded *Indio* trumped up to military man by his smartly-pressed fatigues and shaven back and sides, and who he secretly aspired one day, in the not too distant future – *ojala*, to replace at the helm of *Batallón Liberación*.

'Foodstuffs,' Santamaria explained the presence of crates of frijol, rice and coffee, assembled along the cabin deck.

'You mean comestibles,' Anastasio said, upgrading the terminology to a standard befitting a man of his culture.

'I mean *foodstuffs*,' Santamaria insisted. 'Every new day we lose a few more *campesinos* to the rebels who are doing an impressive job of posing as their bosom buddies. Eighty-nine per cent of our population is *campesino*. We can't cleanse them all away, so we'll win their black hearts and simple minds, and convert them back to the path of modernisation.' To this end, he added, by way of foot soldiers I have sent an invitation ahead of us into the local communities, one that should appeal to poor and needy and rich and greedy alike.

Flight Lieutenant José Martin Cabrera, a veteran SAF pilot of too few words for Anastasio's liking, set the helicopter down smack in the middle of a field of cropped granary grass, within sight of two rather muddled-looking valley towns. And together the three men unloaded the crates and set up an unlikely market stall in the centre of the otherwise vacant field.

Whether the invitation had been warmly received or not was debatable, but it had been received nonetheless, which was its remit. And throughout that morning the *converts* arrived. In trickles at first, but as the word spread, in their numbers. Stout ladies smiling coyly gathered up the freebees and said polite thank-yous and waddled hurriedly away. Pretty girls followed sour-faced fathers up the hill to receive their share. The stout ladies returned with huge wicker baskets, the pretty girls and their chaperones with clusters of carrier bags. And Santamaria subjected all his valued customers to a speech of such sentimentality as to curl the hairs on the back of Anastasio's

75

neck: We completely understand the terrible hardships endured by our beloved people…We are truly concerned for your health and wellbeing…These gifts of the highest-quality American produce are given to you *free*, courtesy of the Salvadoran Army, which is here to serve, protect and care for you….Tell your families and friends that ours is a nationwide campaign of food distribution…

'They'll smile, take your charity, say thanks, and serve it up to their rebel sons.' To Anastasio, this was not the road to victory.

'You have always been a cynic, major. I, on the other hand, am an optimist.'

And when an ancient with skin like dry tobacco and a face that folded in half every time he closed his toothless mouth introduced himself as Santiago Benavides, ex-military man, at your service, and presented a fever-stricken boy wrapped in Mayan weave, Anastasio sent him packing because only comestibles were on offer, but Santamaria called him back and ushered the pair to the helicopter. He ordered Cabrera to fly them to the military hospital in the capital with a directive that the child be afforded the very best in medical care, and then he issued a whispered instruction to Cabrera to hurry back lest they be set upon by a posse of rebel bastards.

By the time Cabrera returned, *Hammer and Machete's* stocks were thoroughly depleted. The empty crates were bundled into the helicopter. Anastasio climbed aboard, subsided into the canvas seat beside the colonel and threw the safety straps loosely around his waist.

'Tell me, major,' Santamaria began, with a pat on Anastasio's knee as soon as they were airborne, en-route to Ilopango. By his tone he might have been enquiring after the wellbeing of Anastasio's grandmother. But he wasn't. 'Have you discovered Serafin Romero's hideout?'

Anastasio stiffened. Much to his own regret, he had made no gains to speak of where Radio Venceremos was concerned. Irked by having to report to this unrefined farm boy, Anastasio disguised his unease by yawning in the casual manner of the future man he intended to become. 'The men you assigned me have scoured Santa Ana, Chalatenango and Cuscatlán, and beyond to the disputed zones west of the Rio Lempa. So far the transmitter's location has eluded their best efforts.'

'Have you penetrated further east…Morazán for example?' Santamaria rattled off, clearly having anticipated excuses.

'The logistics of searching an entirely militant-held zone would require more resources than you have allowed. Adonai Limeño would pick us off like *that*,' – snapping fingers. 'His cunning is well documented in our libraries.'

'So you've not searched Morazán,' Santamaria suggested, as if to make certain.

'Where in Morazán were you thinking of?' It was easy to say "search Morazán", but it was a sizable department with lots of rebel-infested jungle.

'If squeezed where it hurts, the man Flint may tell you. Don't you think?'

'Squeezed? How?'

'*Squeezed? How?*' Santamaria aped with naked scorn. 'You used to be a bright spark. But recently you've become distracted to the point of stupidity. And I think I know why.'

Anastasio balked inwardly, but with the self-discipline his lower rank demanded, he selected a suitable verbal response in keeping with his sleeve-badge and epaulettes: 'What would *you* suggest, colonel?'

Santamaria adjusted his position, turning to face Anastasio. 'You failed to *disappear* the girl as instructed, yes? You let her go on the understanding that she'd lead you to Venceremos. She's since gone into hiding. So you lied to me, yes? And you failed to persuade her to be interviewed for our side too, yes?'

Why he'd ever imagined he could keep his secret from Santamaria's many ears to the ground was suddenly beyond him. Embarrassed, he was not. But if promotion depended, as his father had quite poignantly pointed out, on impressing the high rankers, this was not the way to go about it. 'She failed to persuade Leonel...'

'Whatever,' Santamaria interrupted irritably. 'This time you *will* obey my order, and to the letter. Are we agreed?'

They were agreed, albeit through one set of gritted teeth.

'Forget the girl, leave well alone; she only fuddles your mind. Focus your energies instead on Leonel's brother. Easy target. Lives alone on an isolated farm. Spends most of his time boozed up in the cantinas. Squeeze him to get to Leonel to get to Venceremos. It may work, it may not, but it's worth a bloody good try.'

CHAPTER SEVEN

The October winds were still gusting in November, and behind conical indigo volcano peaks, ribbons of magenta and pink were slowly bursting upon the morning sky.

Without prompting, Jasmine volunteered to help bring in the harvest, which made Chachi breathe a huge sigh of relief, though chivalry pressed him to enquire if she was up to it, but she dismissed this with a petulant wave of her small hand and told him that in her opinion there wouldn't be time to separate the reds from the greens, which reflected Chachi's principal concern over the logistics of harvesting seven and a half acres of ripening coffee orchard with two hands – well, now that Jasmine was on board, four.

'So we'd better get a move on,' she suggested gamely.

Using his pocket-knife he poked half a dozen additional holes into one of his dog-eared leather belts to accommodate her smaller waist, and then helped her secure the wicker collection basket to her navel, making her stagger into him when he tugged the belt hard to secure the buckle, and earning himself a reproachful scowl for his troubles. When he had belted a similar basket to his own waist, he instructed Jasmine to fetch her holding hook. The metre-long rod was propped up against the outer wall of the hut. It had a wire hook at one end, and a length of twine gripping a wire loop at the other.

'Where's yours, Chachi?' she enquired, still regarding the holding hook with open hostility.

'I can reach the upper branches…' He raised his eyebrows in a blunt assertion that she couldn't.

That frown was already on her face. 'I don't need one either,' she retorted, and pushed past him and set off across the drying patio towards the plantation, her basket bouncing to every determined stride.

Smiling, Chachi followed the daughter he'd never had.

'One hundred rubies per branch,' he guesstimated, hoisting a two-metre-long branch that stooped under its clusters of cherries, each smooth red skin reflecting a single drop of morning sunlight. He plucked one of the ripe fruit and bit into it. But he kept any connoisseur's comment to himself. 'We'll work by rows,' he declared. With the seed between index finger and thumb he pointed out across the orchard. 'You start from the left, me from the right; we'll cross over in the middle and rake each other's leftovers.'

'A race,' Jasmine proposed, widening her eyes at him in candid enthusiasm.

Given that two were doing the job that eight would ordinarily undertake, why not encourage speed? 'Yes, if you like, a race.'

She headed off to her corner of the orchard and Chachi to his. It did not escape his notice that once his back was turned, Jasmine dashed over to the shack, snatched up the holding hook, and sped back across the patio and into the orchard.

'Don't bend the branches to breaking point with that hook,' he yelled, but received no response. He pictured her tossing the wire hook over a high branch and tugging on the rod thus lowering the branch to within reach. Sliding her sandaled foot through the wire loop she was securing the rod to the ground, and with both hands free to pick cherries, her chances of winning the race were greatly enhanced. He caught himself smiling again as he set to work, tweaking off and dropping handfuls of cherries into the collection basket.

Over eight full days they worked flat out to bring in a decent crop. To transport the cherries by wheelbarrow to what were originally livery troughs, but served very well as water-filled basins, for the cherries to ferment in for a day and a night. From the troughs by the bucket-load to the mechanical *despulpadora* to be stripped of the lucent flesh and mostly-red skins. And after arduously hand-picking the residue pulp that the *despulpadora* had failed to glean away, they tossed the slimy seeds on to the drying patio for the sun to smile benignly upon.

In the mornings Jasmine raked the drying beans into rows separated by aisles wide enough to walk along. In the afternoons she raked them in to the aisles thereby allowing the vacated stretches of cement time to dry. In the evenings she raked the beans back to their original rows.

And on the eleventh morning, Chachi squatted at the edge of the patio and scooped up a handful of beans and held them to his nose, and after popping one into his mouth, biting through, he spat the two halves into his hand, inspected them closely, and declared them dry enough.

Beginning with the rows nearest the hut – these had spent longest in the sun – they set about scooping trowel-loads of dry beans into burlap sacks and, by loan of Ignacio Molina's mule-drawn cart, they made no less than nine bone-jarring journeys down the hillside to *El Beneficio* to hand over the yield and get paid.

So it was with a sense of satisfied achievement that beneath a heaven laden with stars Chachi settled in for the night with a couple of shots of Botrán rum glowing in his belly. He took up his customary position, flat on his back, upon his reed mat at the door to his hut and drifted off to the encouraging notion that Jasmine's doldrums had, over the past eleven days, shown clear signs of lifting.

But his satisfaction was short-lived. He had hardly shut his eyes when a hot acrid flow began pelting into his open mouth. He inadvertently swallowed and with a jolt he opened his eyes and spat out another mouthful that had somehow replaced the one he'd swallowed. Partially silhouetted against the spangled sky, Anastasio Menesses in full military garb was standing astride him, urinating copiously over his face. Chachi sprang out from beneath him, only to find Anastasio's calloused grip smack around his throat, hoist him to his feet and ram him back into the hut wall.

'*Watchiman*,' Anastasio called in his phoney elitist brogue, drawing his sneer up confrontationally close, while he continued to piss, now over Chachi's bare feet. 'Where is your cowardly brother? Why won't he come out of the woods and face me like a man?'

But Chachi had his revolver muzzle hard into Anastasio's liver, and by the abrupt change of expression, the guy knew it.

'Make me kill you,' he pleaded, while the fear within screamed for him to just get on and shoot the bastard. Anastasio hesitated.

Faint sounds of hilarity against a ranchera ballad from Nejapa's *cantina*. Wind rushing through the starlit plantation. Somewhere an owl hooted.

'Your corpse can easily be hidden in these hills,' said Chachi.

'You think I came alone, *Chach*?' Anastasio retorted, after a moment's further deliberation.

Part recklessness, part considered assumption, Chachi decided to call his bluff. 'You are certainly stupid enough to do so.'

Anastasio released Chachi's neck as if it had burnt his hand and took a sharp step back, both hands up, palms forward in a surrender of sorts, his bulky penis, now out of fuel, crooking out of his flies.

It was at this point that Jasmine emerged from the hut wielding one of Chachi's machetes.

The obvious occurred to Chachi: let her have her pound of flesh, an eye for an eye at the blade of a machete. But no sooner had sweet vengeance surfaced than he submerged it on the grounds that neither he nor Jasmine was up to mutilation.

'Get back inside,' Chachi ordered her severely, without either his gaze or his aim straying from Anastasio's alert and watchful black eyes. He was painfully aware that, with the least waver in concentration on his part, his temporary prisoner would instantly reverse their roles.

He sensed rather than saw Jasmine obey his instruction. He was thankful that she had, but bitterly regretful that Anastasio had discovered her whereabouts.

Life from this point on would never be the same.

'*Chach*,' said Anastasio, 'I want that transmitter. No, let's be honest, it's Colonel Rubén Santamaria who wants that transmitter. *I* want the promotion that comes with finding it. So I'll be generous, and allow – let's say – till Friday evening for you to contact Leonel and extract from him, without giving away our little deal, the precise whereabouts of Radio Venceremos.'

'Keep your hands up and back away,' Chachi instructed, taking a firm step forward.

For Chachi this midnight tête-à-tête was at an end. But Anastasio was not quite done yet:

'If you fail me, *Chach*, I shall not make the same mistake as I did tonight. I will return with a *full* battalion, and we'll take our turns with you and your little wench, and leave your burnt cadavers, not hidden in the hills as you so helpfully suggest, but in the middle of Nejapa Town, for the sublime pleasure of its inquisitive residents.'

* * *

Stay away from the plantation until I return.

Or with words to that effect Chachi had cautioned Jasmine before catching the dawn *colectivo* headed for the nation's capital San Salvador, to enlist the dubious services of Sión the Coyote. Because, as Chachi had expressively pointed out, this surname that he shared with his brother the rebel leader carried an Anglo-Saxon ring that would instantly be clocked at the American Embassy, who would in all likelihood, given the fraternal connection, refuse him an entry visa. Besides, Jasmine's hurriedly issued passport recorded her true age, and if she were to apply for a tourist visa, the gringo interviewer was bound to enquire sourly, with whom will you be travelling to the US of A, señorita? Evidence of significant funds in your bank account, please? Printout of flight reservations?

So, for a nominal fee – probably equal to the net profit from the harvest – Sión the Coyote would act as tour guide for a bunch of escapees, some looking for streets of gold, others to get the hell out of the mayhem.

Inside the hut, on a timber dais that Chachi had hammered together, Jasmine left a covered plate of boiled plantain for him to lunch on later. After stringing two hollowed-out halves of a sizeable calabash around her waist, she selected the smallest of his machetes, sliced off a smooth-leafed branch from one of the plantain trees that stood behind the hut, and set off into the woods to the startled rustlings of shy rodents, and bird chatter she fancied she could understand.

Steering clear of the paths she dragged her plantain branch among giant callas of flushing crimsons and yellows that gaped down at her from lofty stems. A pause now to admire hosts of pink zephyr lilies and pompom-like dahlia, and the cacaloxuchitl, which were particularly pearly this morning. She pushed through flowering vines where dragon flies buzzed on a blur of wings and when she emerged she resisted a familiar urge to chase the monarch butterflies fluttering ahead of her through the trees. Here she stood on tiptoe to pluck supple leaves from the saplings, there she squatted beneath the ferns and gathered twigs and thimble-sized pinecones from the forest floor. She wrapped these treasures in her collection of leaves and tucked the parcel under her arm before resuming her expedition, craning her head to gaze up through shafts of bluish sunlight at the cathedral arches through whose interlinking branches the sky glinted in pale shards. The thought of turning foreigner in some glitzy concrete jungle far from all that was home was stressing her. Not to be overlooked was Chachi's blunt assertion that this so-called Haven of the Free – known colloquially as Gringolandia – had happily trained the very soldiers who, in the coldest of blood, had

84

murdered her mother, savaged her and her school friends and massacred El Zacate to bloody smithereens. So it was with mixed feelings that she roamed, as if for the last time, these her forests before a tomorrow when she and Chachi would embark on a journey by way of Guatemala and Mexico to the good ol' *Estados Unidos de Norteamérica.*

Eventually she heard the bees in the distance. An excited hum that guided her to the honeycomb. Reminiscent of a bulging burlap sack, the comb clung beneath a branch half way up a pinkish-barked tree that sprouted a gorgeous feathery crown. At first glance the colouring of the bees camouflaged them against their wax-walled sweet-home, but their black markings gave them away, and Jasmine realised that the comb's surface was crawling with them.

She cleared a space at the foot of the tree where she laid her carefully packed foliage bundle, and set it alight on the second strike of a match from her matchbox. When the bitter smoke was clouding upwards she kicked off her sandals, tucked the machete down the back of her dungarees and, gripping with hands and bare feet, shinned up the trunk. The drone of her quarry grew louder as she climbed, but the smoke was confusing them, disorientating them, and Jasmine drifted upwards with it, partially concealed in its blue-grey cloak. It wasn't long before she could see the bees clearly, thronging in their hundreds upon the intricate weave of hexagonal cells. But she had not come to study their habits. Two swift hacks of the machete were enough to send almost half the nest plummeting to the ground where it landed with a dull squelch, shaking off a cloud of dazed bees. She sent the machete after it. Now the bees were livid: they swirled about her with a clamour like a chainsaw at high revs, flicking against her head and body like mountain hail. Keeping her arms away from her body so as to avoid trapping an angry bee under her armpit, she slid down the trunk, gritting her teeth at each sting to her exposed skin.

Once on the ground, she tucked the machete behind her dungaree breast piece and hurriedly re-sandaled her feet while frenzied bees orbited her head. Then, using the rest of the plantain leaf as mittens, she gathered up the sloppy segment of honeycomb. Spilling golden syrup crawling with bees, she ran through the chest-high ferns to the path that would lead her out of the valley.

By the time she arrived at the riverbank, the bees had given up the pursuit. She squatted on the yielding sand to inspect her prize. It was a decent chunk, enough for two at a sitting with leftovers besides. She plucked away the trapped bees and dismembered bee body parts, and decanted the syrup into her calabash bowls. After cleaning up with river water, she cut a slice of aloe leaf and anointed her stings with the sap.

She thought it only fitting that she and Chachi should dine that night on honeycomb, and that tomorrow they travel abroad with the sweetness of their homeland still on their tongues.

* * *

Anastasio Menesses slid on to a cushioned seat in his favourite air-conditioned Pollo Campero diner. This was his sunrise sanctuary, his recess from Military Headquarters. One of the leggy waitresses with a pony-tail was already hovering to take his order. On another day he would have flirted, but his flirtatious feathers lay as lank as his self esteem.

'Café negro, por favor.' And she swanned off, her smile lost on Anastasio.

Something Santamaria had said was bothering Anastasio. Something not unrelated to the post Hammer and Machete guilt trip the colonel had so ineloquently guided him down, yet on another level entirely unconnected to it. Something that had been pushing its head up through his subconscious with such persistence that he could no longer suppress it. Jasmine fuddles my mind, the colonel had suggested. What was most unsettling about this suggestion was the nugget of truth because, in the short time he'd known this latest household servant, he'd stumbled on a purity that distinguished her from the plastic beauty of the uptown girls. Stumbled on, not discovered, because he'd been completely unprepared for the imprint it would leave on his soul.

'Gracias,' he muttered at the arrival of his coffee. Hot coffee touched his lips. He sipped, vaguely aware that he'd neglected to sugar it.

Hitherto he'd known two types of women: the one he'd never had – but aspired to be worthy of – those uptown girls whose power walks and air of superiority had excited his country boy innards and prompted all manner of wild fantasies, scenarios which he'd paid good money to play out with the other – those poverty-ridden wretches desperate to put a crust on their child's plate; the poorer the wretch the more compliant. But Jasmine was neither of these. Disgracefully unaware of her charms and the power she could wield over men, she was the pure angel of his childhood daydreams.

Fearful that he was obsessing, and obsessing is a step towards insanity, the prospect of which was his greatest fear, it was with reluctance that Anastasio took the decision to follow his colonel's advice: forget the girl, and focus on Flint!

CHAPTER EIGHT

WELL BEFORE FIRST LIGHT an ancient Isuzu bus grumbled into San Salvador. From a hectic bus stop an equally ancient yellow cab whisked Jasmine and Chachi to Terminal Puertobus – the international bus terminus.

Drowning in a sterile undertaker's suit, Sión the *coyote*, who was all of five-foot-three, was standing in the cold of the poorly lit coach park, notebook in hand, marking off his illegal-crossing hopefuls as they arrived with their worldly possessions stuffed to bursting in huge sausage bags.

Once Sión had dished out tickets upon proof of payment and identity, his party bid last farewells to weeping relatives who'd come to see them off. With a blast of impatient babbling from Sión they un-clinched each other and boarded while their homes were being tossed into the bus's hold by the youthful driver.

Scarcely twenty minutes later and bang on time, the bus set off along a well-lit avenue lined with lofty palms whose lower sections were painted white. A speaker above the driver's head was piping out a salsa classic, to which Jasmine, who had selected a window seat for this first leg of the journey as far as Guatemala City, rocked her shoulders.

Chachi promptly informed her that he would catch up on lost sleep.

'Will you take me dancing when we get there, Chachi?' she asked, still see-sawing her shoulders and adding finger clicks to the offbeat.

He stirred, murmured something about chicken feed, and swallowed.

Jasmine sighed and turned to study the cityscape. Sleek office towers pitched high against the dawn, scruffy shop fronts advertising all the wares under the sun, re-treaded tyres at bargain prices, battered pickup trucks pumping out clouds of noxious smoke, and musical car horns warning lamp-less bicycles to get out of the way – *pendejo!* Huddled in sandy gullies, squashed up beside bridges, scattered on scraps of hillside, the corrugated marginal dwellings of San Salvador's shame reflected a pinkish sheen as the first sunlight seeped into the Valley of Hammocks. And a spanking Panhard AML-90 military car lay in wait with its rear-end tucked into a hedge. Loitering beside it, three soldiers in fatigues dangled grease guns by their black grips.

Jasmine turned to Chachi for reassurance. His eyes still shut, a bubble of saliva had worked its way down to the end of his unshaven chin. She wiped it up then wiped her finger on his shirtsleeve.

The bus lugged itself north on to the Pan-American Highway and with a series of roars and cranks the driver made a respectable pace, considering the state of the road.

They passed other settlements and vendors dawdling inside palm-thatched lean-tos, huge white ceramic swans for sale, hundreds of mouth-watering watermelons stacked in pyramids, green fields where cattle grazed, and distant foothills blue as the haze into which they faded.

Jasmine laid her head back and decided she too would catch up on lost sleep.

* * *

The sun was almost at its zenith when she was awoken by an escalation in the thudding of the wheels. Sugarcane stems, inadvertently shed by some overloaded lorry. Jasmine turned to Chachi. Beneath half-dipped lids his eyes were bloodshot with sleepiness. She returned his smile and rubbed the goose

89

bumps on his forearm.

He shut his eyes and wriggled briefly, as if trying to nestle into a more comfortable groove. 'We've been climbing for almost two hours,' he burbled.

And his burble sounded oddly faint, so she began yawning repeatedly, trying to unblock her altitude-affected hearing. He then embarked on a raucous bout of snoring that sounded far too forced to ring true. Sensing one of his games coming on, she faced forward but kept him in her vision. He was baiting her with his continued fake snoring. Or was he? She swivelled her head and stuck her tongue out at him, at which his eyes popped open, prompting a spontaneous chuckle.

'Again,' she pleaded, and turned fully round in her seat to face him.

Chachi rolled his eyes and sighed, but he obliged nonetheless.

She glared closely into his crinkled eyelids. 'No cheating,' she warned, and hooked her index fingers into her mouth and pulled outwards, sticking out her tongue and rolling her eyeballs in what she hoped was a truly ghastly grimace. Chachi's eyes shot open, and she shrieked and clapped her hands, delighted at having been caught out.

'Again,' she laughed.

But he was tired, he said. He was going to sleep now.

The bus ploughed into thick cloud, and Jasmine heard the driver change down through the gears until they were crawling. Shortly afterwards a dark green hatchback made an attempt at accelerating past, which was not easy given it had to negotiate hard-edged potholes and mortar craters, and it was foiled in its attempt by the sudden appearance of blazing fog lamps followed by a mammoth container lorry which not only forced the hatchback to swerve evasively back behind the bus, but obliged the bus to adopt a snail's pace while the two massive vehicles crawled gingerly past one another and the passengers on the nearside peered from their windows at what Jasmine guessed, from their gasps, to be a precipitous drop.

She realised there must be a frustrated convoy of smaller, swifter vehicles trapped behind.

Then, for no apparent reason, their driver slammed on the brakes, cut the engine and switched off the radio, all of which had the effect of snuffing out every conversation in the cabin. Turning round he yelled, 'Roadblock. Have passports and identity carnets ready.'

* * *

While the passengers set about delving into their pockets and hand luggage, a schoolboy in a slack National Guard twinset and a helmet that dwarfed his head clomped up the steps, and stood at the head of the aisle, hands behind back, chin up, eyes drifting. He stopped whistling.

'Have passports or carnets ready for inspection,' he called out loudly enough, but in a voice that had yet to fully break. His order issued, he embarked on a stroll up the aisle, scrutinising the identity document of each passenger and spitting out comments.

Jasmine turned to stare through the window. Several nebulous military shapes had arranged themselves along the kerbside, rifles hugged diagonally across midriffs. Beneath helmets their faces were so diluted that recognition was impossible.

The guardsman gazed upon Chachi, at his passport and then back to Chachi. The gleaming nozzle of an M16 peeked antennae-like above his left epaulette, a stiff leather pistol holster and bulky canvas pouches clinched his broad waist belt.

'*Americano?*' he enquired casually.

'Salvadoran.'

'You have a gringo name,' he pointed out, as if Chachi might not be aware of this.

'Granddad was a gringo.'

While black-knuckled fingers sifted through the pages, Jasmine sensed a tension grip Chachi's body, and she held her breath and sent up a silent prayer.

The guardsman handed back Chachi's passport and gave

Jasmine's a less lengthy examination, and on returning it, actually mumbled a *thank you* and *have a safe journey,* before shuffling on to the row behind. Jasmine exhaled slowly, exchanging a glance with Chachi, and restored the passport to his palm for safekeeping.

After what felt like an age to Jasmine, the nerve-racking inspection concluded, and the guardsman joined his colleagues on the roadside. The diesel engine fired up, blaring harshly after the fraught hush. With a succession of surging roars the driver shifted back up through the gears, but was obliged to change down again as he pulled through a series of sharp climbing turns.

Jasmine laid her head on Chachi's arm, wishing it was her mother's, but feeling closer to him than ever. He responded by putting a protective arm round her and pulling her close.

'Half an hour to the Guatemalan border. Then it's free sailing till we hit Mexico,' he murmured. But any optimism was short-lived. Five minutes and again Jasmine felt the bus shuddering on its slippery brakes.

'Roadblock!' and the driver flung up both hands in a show of resignation. It was likely that he submitted to such delays on all his trips this way. With an irritated flurry Chachi produced the passports and cradled them in his lap. The bus door hissed open. Steeped in silence the fidgeting passengers waited to see who would whistle up those stairs this time. Jasmine craned her head to peer above the headrests.

Their new inspector was older than the last, moustachioed, with a self-assured swagger, a flat cap with visor shadowing his eyes. With hands clasped behind his back, he stood beside the driver and took a few unhurried eternities to cast his eyes over the interior of the bus, not just the passengers but also the walls and ceiling. He even dropped to a squat and gave the floor beneath the seats a cursory scan, before standing again to resume his initial posture.

'Listen up,' he said rather quietly, for there was no need to raise his voice in such attentive stillness. 'When I pass your seat you will deposit your identity documents into this bag. Each passenger will be called individually to exit the bus, identify his luggage and open it for inspection by my extremely professional colleague.' He broke off as if to allow this instruction to sink in. 'On satisfactory completion of the inspection, your document will be returned and you may return to your seat. Anyone refusing to comply with these instructions, or found to be in possession of prohibited articles, will be detained for questioning.' Another pause to show he had done with banalities. 'If any luggage remains unclaimed, we have orders to remove the whole bus to a place of questioning where every passenger will be subjected to additional procedures designed to identify the owner.'

He set off between the seats at a leisurely stroll, swinging the bag from side to side, and into it the wary passengers deposited their various IDs. Chachi secured his passport to Jasmine's with a rubber band and dropped them into the bag. When the final passenger had relinquished her ID, the bag swung back to the front of the bus. A navy blue passport was withdrawn and a name read out:

'Don Juan Antonio García García. Please identify yourself and your luggage.'

A dishevelled youth with one earring and a striped shirt hanging over faded jeans slipped into the aisle and made his way to the front of the bus. The driver stepped out of his seat and followed Juan Antonio down the stairs. Hushed conversations resumed under the military gaze.

Jasmine heard a clunk beneath her. She put her forehead to the window and saw the driver swing up the lid of the luggage compartment and secure it flat to the bus's side panelling. Beside him another soldier beckoned towards the front of the bus. A pallid Juan Antonio came into view and squatted in front of the open compartment. With an effort he heaved out a large suitcase and let it thump to the road. He flicked the latches and lifted the lid, pushing it right back for extra accessibility. The "extremely professional colleague" nudged his rifle further behind his back, squatted beside Juan Antonio, planted a hand in the suitcase and upturned the neatly folded contents. The driver, who had been stooping over the proceedings as if to ensure fair play, stood back now, fished a packet of cigarettes from his breast pocket, lit up, and sucked short drags that plainly implied he was in a hurry to resume the journey.

Juan Antonio slapped shut his suitcase and hefted it back into the luggage compartment. Seconds later he reappeared and as promised received his passport. Conversation petered out as he made his way to take up his seat.

'Niña Alma Gloria Benítez de Palomar.'

A hefty middle-aged woman in a headscarf and floral dress fastened both hands on the headrest in front of her and winched herself to her feet before squeezing past the contrastingly miniature male passenger, presumably Mr Palomar, who did little more than lean back in his seat until she burst into the aisle. She, like Juan Antonio before her, made her way off the bus.

Jasmine in a whisper told Chachi that there were more than forty passengers on the bus. 'This is going to take *forever.*'

'Don Sión will have taken delays into consideration,' he whispered back for reassurance.

She put her forehead to the window and shut her eyes. She heard the hushed voices of the other passengers, the occasional clunk and scrape beneath her, faint conversation outside, and the deep, rapid rhythm of her own apprehension.

'An hour has passed and we still haven't been called.' Chachi nudged her and angled his wrist so she could consult his watch.

She rubbed her eyes and blinked past him. The two women in the row opposite were now dozing, scarf-clad heads back, mouths ajar, relaxing in the knowledge that their inspection was over.

'Don Sasha Emmanuel Flint.'

Chachi started at the sound of his own name. He climbed stiffly out of his seat. Jasmine stared after him, shivering with

94

the cold. Or was it dread? The problem with her premonitions was that they were too vague. 'Chachi,' she blurted suddenly. 'Don't go.'

'Don't worry, I'll be back in no time,' he said with an unconvincing smile.

'Be careful,' she offered lamely, and stood up to follow him. When he had disappeared down the stairwell, she sat down and pressed her face to the window and saw him emerge beyond the front of the bus. But she also saw the officer from the bus stride past him, bark a terse but incoherent order through the driver's window and then give an impatient arm wave.

The passenger door shut with a long hiss.

'*Hombre!*' Jasmine exclaimed, shooting to her feet. 'What are you doing?'

With a roar the engine ignited, the bus lurched forward, toppling Jasmine back into her seat by the window. Forelock dangling over his face, hands forced behind his back, she saw Chachi on both knees at the gravelled kerbside having gleaming handcuffs fitted to his wrists.

CHAPTER NINE

October 1984

The hum of murmured conversations, the clatter of metal on metal, leafy fronds swishing overhead, humidity beading on her upper lip, whiffs of urine and charred wood. But it was the reek of stale sweat on the woollen blanket that finally woke her, and she shoved it away in disgust, sat up in her hammock and supported herself on both elbows.

'Chachi?'

But those same pervasive odours, which had served her acute sense of smell as a homing-guide to a camp that lurked in the midnight black of last night, now reminded her where she was: deep in Cuscatlán's timbered valleys known to locals as Tecomatepe. If it hadn't been for the crude trip wire of tin cans, she might have wandered right into the middle of camp before her presence was announced. She recalled with a little shudder how fortunate it was that Leonel had recognised her before the promptly assembled circle of rifles and revolvers could open fire.

Daybreak had arrived: she could tell by the quality of the light. She climbed out of the hammock and back-stepped into it, swinging it up to support her back. Nibbling at her thumbnail, elbow cradled in spare hand, she proceeded to take stock of her new surroundings. Dozens more hammocks were threaded between the trees, angling randomly one from the other like an unfinished puzzle, the original colours of the henequen cords anyone's guess. Above each hammock a length of twine knotted to the same two trees supported a pitched nylon roof of stained mushroom-colours, their four corners moored to shrub stems by guy lines draped with drying laundry. On threadbare blankets spread out beneath each hammock lay backpacks of nylon duck and webbing, coils of bandoliers – some housing 12 gauge shells, others regular cartridges, and one even bristled with grenades – and there were spare rifle magazines with a distinct curvature that Jasmine likened to that of a banana, quite dissimilar to the military-issued brands.

Plastic water pitchers of purple and blue, eating utensils – mostly calabash-based, carpentry tools, and standing candles of varying heights and thicknesses – several of which were suspiciously akin to the church variety – were cluttered upon two tabletops fashioned from sapling branches lashed together with henequen. And underneath, heavy-duty batteries, wood-handled picks and shovels and other paraphernalia mingled with the shadows.

Two tents, their puckered corners fastened to branches, sheltered shoulder-high stacks of crates draped in blankets, and where one blanket had slipped Jasmine could see the slogan "M-16" with a series of apparently arbitrary numbers stamped neatly in white upon army green timber.

She scanned the forty or so faces in the camp and settled on a knot of women gathered in the only part of the camp that, with the presence of a small wood fire, might reasonably be described as the centre point. One of the women, apparently in the middle stages of pregnancy, was fanning the fire and feeding the flames with kindling. Beside her an austere-faced girl in a military tunic buttoned to the neck was sliding husk-wrapped corn cobs into a large steel cauldron of steaming water. The fire provided a focal point of sorts: several of the male combatants sporting equipment belts clipped to Y-shaped braces were milling behind its tower of muddy smoke. A little to the right of them, two men sat either side of a radio box, one listening and dictating while the other jotted notes into an exercise book. With her eyes Jasmine tracked a man, for no reason other than he wore an attractive garland of leaves and flowers around his neck. He disappeared behind a tree and emerged on the other side, but on slipping behind another he failed to emerge as expected, and when Jasmine sidestepped to get a view behind the tree, he had vanished.

With a leap of her heart she spotted Leonel's four-day beard. Stumbling across the clutter in a jungle suit tucked into black ankle-boots he advanced on her with a tin mug in his stout fist. He fixed her with his gaze and flicked his head up a notch – which today she took as a greeting, although at La Molienda he'd used that particular gesture to invite speech, if she remembered correctly.

He shoved the half-empty mug at her and enquired after her wellbeing.

'Fine. Just fine, thank you. And you?' she replied, discovering her own awkwardness.

'Tina will come to settle you in. You can ask her about women's things,' he told her crisply.

She nodded, sipped the coffee and felt better for it. 'Are you going somewhere?' she enquired, while inwardly pleading with him to stay close, if only to speak more of Chachi.

'When I get back we'll see what we do with you,' he replied, sounding quite unwelcoming. 'In the meantime, if you need anything, ask Tina.'

Jasmine shied away from telling him how very uncomfortably full her bladder felt, and hoping Tina would turn up sooner rather than later she nodded her reply to Leonel who then about-turned and made off at a stride so purposeful that perhaps he meant never to return. A couple of his men, slinging backpacks over their shoulders and clutching rifles, sprang from nowhere, fell in briskly beside him and together they faded into the undergrowth.

Peering into the mug, Jasmine studied a revolving cloud of maize flour that had been mixed in to thicken the brew, and slowly the revolving cloud went out of focus. 'Where are you, Chachito?' she murmured, and tears welled as her thoughts went back to the bus trip. On seeing Chachi manacled at the roadside she had leapt from her seat and pleaded with the driver to stop and let her off. But he'd refused because his express directive from the Guard on pain of death was to keep going no matter what and not look back. Had he understood what would happen to him if he disobeyed? He certainly had. Only once he'd pushed past several sharp bends did he irritably agree to open the door, allowing her – on the understanding that he was not hanging around for her – to jump from the slowly advancing bus. By the time she had sprinted full-pelt back to the place where she'd last seen Chachi, the road was deserted. She'd hunted the woods above and below the highway for him – or his corpse. She had scrutinised more than a kilometre of kerbside and grass-choked ditch. She had only given up when an old timer and his wife, both bending under a stack of lumber, had coaxed her away from her search to their hut for food and respite. She had awoken yesterday morning with a certainty that she wanted to become a *compa*. But now she wasn't quite so certain.

'Are you the *comandante's* woman?' a grunt gate-crashed her reverie. The grunt belonged to a skinny tramp with a dreadlocked beard and dark skin smudged with dirt.

'No,' she sniffed, and lifting her chin retorted, 'Are you?'

The man's eyes narrowed for extra scorn, but the pregnant woman came to the rescue and told him to leave her alone, *pendejo*, and proceeded to physically drive him back by kicking his scrawny sock-less shins. 'Go on, get lost, motherless bastard,' she added.

Eventually he slunk off, but not before making several bizarre lunges, as if trying to assault Jasmine but being restrained in his efforts by powerful invisible hands.

The woman turned to Jasmine and the hostile scowl she had bestowed on the tramp turned to a bright grin. 'Kick the bastards. It's the only language some of them understand,' she advised cheerily. 'I'm Tina, by the way.'

'Jasmine. I need the lavatory.'

Five minutes' walk from the camp, crystal clear waters bubbled out of a series of crevices in rocks of solidified lava. Tina assured her the water was quite potable and that it was used for all their needs, these two crevices for drinking, that one for washing.

Back at camp, Tina rustled up a calabash of *atol* and yet more coffee; and Jasmine, relieved of the burden in her bladder and feeling fresher for the quick bathe she had taken, listened while her pregnant host introduced her to camp rules, codes and protocol, centring on some rather bitter criticism of the general chauvinistic attitude of her male comrades. Tina went to the trouble of naming the principle culprits and covertly pointing them out for Jasmine's benefit. A lean young captain with lazy-pleasure eyes and an impish grin was singled out for particularly venomous treatment. Emilio was his name, and why *el comandante* had ever promoted him was simply beyond her. Thinks he's God's gift to women. Leonel, on the other hand, was singled out as the exception, kindling, for some unfathomable reason, a glow of pride in Jasmine's breast, as if of *her* Leonel it was that Tina was now speaking so highly. 'The others are motherless bastards, every last one of them. They'll try it on. Cute girl like you…got to look out for yourself.' And in the spirit of feminine complicity she introduced Jasmine to the two other women *compa's* in camp that day: Anabela Segovia and Marta Lilian Montes. Given the presence of the newcomer, conversation fired up with enthusiastic personal recollections of joining *el Movimiento Revolucionario*.

Marta Lilian had dark eyes, black hair severely cropped at back and sides and Jasmine put her age at early twenties. When she spoke she chewed on a necklace looping down from the corners of her mouth, and somehow managed to avoid breaking the delicate links. She spoke a lot, admitting to missing her friends back home and sometimes regretting having abandoned her academic studies. Her parents' anguish over her decision to join the Revolution prompted her to tears, but the moment passed when she relayed the reasons for joining up. Reasons not far removed from Jasmine's own.

Anabela was a similar age to Jasmine, and hers was the army tunic buttoned chastely to the neck. She said very little, and when spoken to she had a curious habit of raising one shoulder and peering down at it, thus presenting a profile of her unsmiling face as she muttered her answers. The gesture gave the impression of acute shyness, although in her green eyes lurked a certain pitilessness that Jasmine found a little unsettling. She wore her sandy hair tied back, but wisps had escaped to frame her adolescent face.

'Did your parents try to stop you from joining up?' Jasmine asked Anabela, feeling it was time to put in a little talk of her own.

They did not, she told her tunic-clad shoulder.

'They didn't know where she was,' Marta Lilian darted in on Anabela's behalf. 'We practically forced her to send a letter, to let them know she was all right.' She sidetracked into a friendly warning that *Teniente* Adrian read all correspondence. 'Just a precaution, you understand, to make sure you haven't written anything that might compromise our whereabouts.'

And as for Tina, she would soon be sent to a safe house in Cojutepeque for having got herself pregnant by one of the motherless bastards, who she refused to name on the grounds that Leonel would punish him by confiscating his rifle and sending him on an unarmed mission to replace his weapon at the expense of a soldier. She had no feelings for the father of her child. Her audience must understand. It was the principle of the thing. She just didn't agree with that type of punishment, full stop!

After a decidedly unromantic candlelit supper of boiled corn on the cob served with sachets of ketchup purloined from a well-known hamburger joint, the three women took themselves off to their hammocks, and Jasmine gravitated back to hers. The camp population appeared to have multiplied, perhaps numbering sixty members now. She noticed a tendency towards elaborate hand signals in the exchanges between the combatants, supposedly to cut down on noise. A curious sort of sign language. Silhouetted in the candlelight the gesticulating figures looked like characters from some early animated movie. For a while she followed the flipping hands and springing fingers with her eyes, guessing at their meanings. She gave up when one particularly ambidextrous comrade met her eyes, and paused to shoot her a long stare that was as illegible to her as his sign language.

She became aware of a thin tickling on the side of her neck, and she slapped the spot before plucking away a tiny ant squashed between her fingertips. Where was Leonel, anyway? She ducked beneath her hammock and wandered into the darkness. She heard a cooing rising by semiquavers and gave far too little thought as to what manner of bird it might be. There was no blackness as absolute as the blackness of the forest night, and tonight it was as uninviting as the light she'd left behind. She hesitated, and looked back over her shoulder. The guerrilla camp was a remote orange glow broken up by the undergrowth. She turned again to face the blackness. She allowed pent up sobs to bubble and heave and spill tears down her cheeks. An erratic torch beam sprung from nowhere and lit up a trio of tree trunks directly ahead. Startled, she wiped her eyes on her upper arm.

Tina drew up quietly beside her and began stroking her back, not unlike the way her mother sometimes had to send her to sleep. 'Lost, yeah? Scared too? We all felt the same way when we arrived.'

The admission triggered powerful emotions that had Jasmine bawling into her cupped hands, and Tina gentled her into the sort of motherly embrace she would soon bestow to her own child.

'*El comandante* wants you to stay close,' Tina mentioned eventually. 'He will spend some time with you this evening, to explain things…you know. If you want to stay with us, engage in his conversation, question his reasoning, he likes to see that from newcomers.'

102

Leonel stowed away the hurt of Chachi's death in a familiar and desolate place. He would deal with it later, alone. But right now, he should speak to the girl with whom he shared this latest grief.

Over the last four years Leonel had seen around seventy women put in to join the column. Their reasons were various: fleeing a miserable marriage, anticipating an FMLN-funded education, basic needs as a square meal on the assumption that the PCS ran a fine jungle restaurant or displacement by the ongoing conflict. Jasmine fell into this final category, he decided as he plucked a freshly laundered blanket from a canvas sack in the stores tent and flung it over his shoulder. Beside the stores tent stood both munitions tents, and beside them drooped his personal hammock, a reassuring arrangement for his keen sense of security. He knelt down and dug around in his backpack until he found his weather-beaten Banco Agricola five-year-diary with biro slotted into the hardback binding. He slid the biro out and tucked it behind his right ear. As with the other entrants, he would catalogue Jasmine's progress or lack thereof. Initially, newcomers wanted for what he didactically termed *An Insightful Grasp of Our Revolution*, and he was keen to test their resolve and make clear to these youthful and often vengeful souls what exactly they were letting themselves in for. He could hardly afford to feed the uncommitted: the PCS was no sanctuary, nor was it a charity. Neither did he wish to lead a rabble of ambivalent peasants into battle – they would promptly abandon the field and leave him well *jodido*. With decades of anti-left propaganda assiduously proliferated by way of local and world media he must assume that at least some of it had rubbed off on even the most individually minded newcomers. It was imperative, therefore, that they be re-indoctrinated early on – this was the accepted view of the FMLN command.

Then there was the question of women guerrillas and pregnancy. He would send them home to embark on their motherhood; but Jasmine was effectively homeless. If it should happen to her, he would have to arrange a safe house. And safe houses were tricky to come by and not the sort of resource you wanted to squander on the amorous carelessness of your combatants. If you come to fight, then make war not love!

It was yet early days to determine to what roles she would be best suited. If she turned out to be ineffective or difficult, there was always Citalá. Citalá – a guerrilla-held outpost in the far north of Chalatenango Province where the columns sent their incompetents, those who – for whatever reason – could not return home, or lacked sufficient skills or education to gainfully contribute on behalf of the Party's political wing, or who might, in the *comandancia's* estimation, compromise the security of a safe house. Citalá, a remote border village offering negligible strategic clout to either side, stood as a safe haven. Furthermore, the resident FMLN sympathiser, Francisca González, fed and armed the posted defence squad out of her widow's inheritance.

Leonel considered the potential for a plant, sent by the military to spy. In Jasmine's case he shrugged this off as a most unlikely scenario. After the El Zacate tragedy, she'd have to be inhuman to side with the military. With Chachi gone, there was no-one left against whom to blackmail her.

He set off across camp towards Jasmine's hammock, through a still cool air that had blended the charred odours of the doused campfire, cheap tobacco smoke and composting leaves into a spicy fusion. Beneath pitched tent roofs, candle flames glowed. Snoring bodies cocooned in hammocks. Four compas huddled on ammunition crates, whispered conversation dampening each "s" with a "th", cigarette-ends kindling with every draw, exhaled smoke hanging about like patches of mist. Tina was quietly humming a lullaby, probably stroking that swollen belly as she'd taken to doing of late.

On reaching Jasmine he told her to put her sandals back on even for sleeping because the column sometimes needs to move out in a hurry. When she had fastened them to her small feet and was lying back with hands by her sides, he billowed the fresh blanket over her. She was so slight in build that as Leonel watched the blanket seemed to settle into the very bottom of the hammock with hardly a bulge to tell she was there.

'More fragrant than the last?' he asked, plucking the biro from behind his ear and tapping the stiff diary cover with its cap.

She nodded and managed a smile before pulling the edge of the blanket up for a gingerly sniff. 'Much better.'

'*Now*,' he began, 'when you arrived, first thing you said was you came to join the *compas*. Remember?'

A nod.

'Joining *El Frente* isn't an escape, Jasmine, it's confrontation, I need you to understand that. It's living rough and going hungry with the constant terror of discovery, it's also a commitment to the death. Why?' – shaking his head – 'why would you want all that?'

She pushed back the blanket to get her answer out clearly. 'Mum didn't deserve to die. Neither did the rest of El Zacate, or Chachi. What's left now? El Zacate was neutral, that didn't work. Forced to take sides, I'm not exactly going to side with Mum's killers. So here I am.'

'I hear you,' said Leonel, although what he heard was a kid in a corner. 'But that's hardly patriot talk. Other, more proactive ingredients complete the commitment.'

'That's all I've got right now,' she said, remoter still.

'Of course,' he agreed at once. He was getting ahead of himself. Give the girl time, fill her in on those wedges of history the National Curriculum overlooked, then stand back. A deep breath later he was off: 'Yours is a repeated story going back to before we took up arms in 1980, going back fifty years earlier, to the eruption of Izalco.'

'The volcano?'

'The eruption was the trigger, you see, coming as it did after centuries of a Creole-imposed economic model that favoured the Creoles at the expense of the majority meztizo and Indian populations. The eruption decimated the *campesinos'* lands. Our peasant fathers took it upon themselves to march in demand of improved conditions. Unfortunately no-one told them you don't make demands of a military dictatorship, and of course, the military responded with a *matanza*.'

'Like in El Zacate.'

'Scale-wise, far worse.'

'Worse?' she repeated faintly.

How could it be worse? she must be thinking. He would come to that later. He waved a hand over her to chase away a mosquito, and resumed, using layman's terms in consideration of her tender age. 'If a century's worth of minority rich growing richer and majority poor growing poorer isn't evidence enough to suggest that your Western economic model could do with replacing, then you're either politically in the dark or yours is one of the mansions gleaming in the lush Creole suburbs. And in their efforts to keep such ideas from being voiced by the majority, the military regimes have designed a brain-numbing National Curriculum served up with reasonably-phrased propaganda followed by a lots-of-guns dessert, while building a support base by enriching their buddies, mistresses, and arse-lickers, and pandering to the corrupt will of the oligarchs' Creole remnants.'

'But the military aren't in power now,' she reminded him. She was more up on her current affairs than many of her tender age.

'Right,' he pronounced with assurance. 'They lost their dictatorial grip on Congress back in 1979, when the Junta led a successful coup d'état that overthrew the military government and promised fair elections. But hey, those military goons are slippery bastards – sorry – criminals.'

'Bastards,' she declared a little too loudly and with the childish relish that comes with previously forbidden words.

Leonel stifled a chuckle, and bid her keep her voice down because there were people trying to sleep.

'Sorry,' she whispered.

'In a move to return political power to the army, Aristides Saravia – you heard of him?'

Vaguely.

'Head of Military Intelligence.'

'That's him.'

'Murderous bastard formed what we know today as ARENA, the same party which he led into the 1982 general election.'

'But the Partido Demócrata Cristiano won, didn't they?' she recalled. Who could forget such a flamboyant campaign? A nationwide fiesta full of promise of better times ahead.

'Uh-huh. Martin Aragón – good sort actually – led the PDC, was elected to government. Elected, mind, no coup d'état this time round, no dictatorship – military or otherwise. And so here we have the Salvadoran dilemma.'

Jasmine looked up, enquiring eyes meeting his stare. 'I'm listening.'

'As one might expect,' Leonel went on, cautiously encouraged by her responses, 'given our long history of military governments, loads of high ranking officers feel their loyalty lies with ARENA and not with the elected Democrat government. What do you suppose that means?'

But this time he'd caught her out, because although she searched the canopy for the answer, it was not there to be found. So he moved swiftly in to save her further embarrassment: 'As a result, the army and the National Guard have become riddled with rogue units.'

'Death squads,' she spouted, grappling back into the conversation.

'When they're of battalion-size like *Liberación*, I like to call them rogue units. Rogue units bent on returning the country to military rule, making every effort to disrupt the elected government's endeavours to bring about stability. It was your same Aristides Saravia who ordered the assassinations of the Archbishop of San Salvador and the American churchwomen.'

'He's not *my* Aristides Saravia,' she objected. '*Wacala!*'

107

He stumbled into an apology for the slip of the tongue. But felt it only right to remind her of hero and protector Archbishop Oscar Romero, who had been gunned down while delivering the Eucharist, a decisive act of repression igniting a furious backlash which the then government had declared to be the start of the conflict. The churchwomen had fared no better, having been raped and murdered by Protectors and Servers of the Peace.

'That was on the news for weeks,' she murmured sorrowfully.

'You watched it?'

'Mother always watched the news. I waited for Heidi to come on afterwards.'

'Of course,' he conceded. What did he expect?

'Dilemma,' she prompted.

'Yes...dilemma...well, unlike our good neighbours in Nicaragua, where the Sandinistas fought to overthrow Somoza's military dictatorship, our armed struggle doesn't seek to overthrow our democratically elected government, but to stand with our peasants and the proletariat against an insubordinate military which the government has little power to control.'

'What about elections?' Jasmine asked brightly, before meeting his eyes again. 'The FMLN could run for government, and none of this hiding in the forest like *this*' – nodding abstractedly at the canopy – 'would be necessary.'

'We'd love to,' he responded, gripping the edge of the hammock. 'But our Party isn't recognised by the present government, so we can't participate in the electoral process.'

She made as if to speak, but gnawed her thumbnail before committing herself: 'In that case, you have no way of knowing what FMLN support there is out there. I mean, if the mayor of El Zacate didn't want you, what makes you think others do?'

'With respect, Jasmine, look what happened to El Zacate.' He winced as he saw a shadow dampen her eyes, and he hurried on: 'It's a catch twenty-two situation not of our making. Being denied democratic participation means we have no official way of measuring our support. So our popularity indicator comes from the support we receive on the ground. Through their elected mayors or committee reps or community leaders, the peasants approach the FMLN command when seeking protection against the National Guard, protection being something the government is unable to provide. Besides,' he waved his hand impatiently, 'people are fed up with this failing economy and tattered infrastructure. At the rural level we have a lot of support, and we've invited the PDC to allow us to participate in the electoral process so that our support can be democratically evidenced. But they still refuse. Did I hear you ask why?'

'Why?' – rising to his game.

'My guess is they fear democracy itself,' he said, giving the air a little prod with his index finger. 'They fear the vote might upstage them and install the FMLN in power.'

'Not what I heard,' she challenged. 'I heard it's because you refuse to disarm.' So she had a harder nose than he'd anticipated. But that was heartening too – she testing his basis for testing her resolve.

'We cannot disarm while the PDC – or whichever party comes to power – remains unable to control its own armed forces.'

'How do you engage in armed struggle against an enemy who's bound to destroy you?'

'We are heavily outnumbered,' he admitted. He should have left this question time for the morning when his energies had recovered. 'So progress does take time. The armed forces are salaried, receiving millions in military aid from Washington, and are supported by the most sophisticated weaponry and technology. We, on the other hand, earn no salary for what we do; we lack such basics as shoes. Homemade rifles, as you will no doubt observe, are commonplace.' But he thought it only proper to admit that some money was donated to the FMLN by the *comités de solidaridad.* 'And we receive popular support, too. Still, such assistance, though very gratefully received, is negligible when compared to the massive aid channelled to the military. Are you all right to continue? You look tired.'

'I'm fine. You're the one who's looking tired.'

'I'm just fine. Feeling good, actually,' Leonel assured her behind a stifled yawn. So, having briefly covered the justifications for armed struggle as he saw them, Leonel went on to summarise the Organization's history: the PCS was once an independent political organisation, he told her, 'but had joined four other movements-for-change, two of which – insurrectionist in character – by 1980 were already cultivating an armed wing. The new coalition organisation became known as the Frente Farabundo Martí para la Liberación Nacional. Farabundo Martí was the rebel leader who led farmers and workers on a peaceful demonstration in protest at mistreatment and dire working conditions, both of which worsened after the Izalco eruption in 1932. The military regime responded by butchering over 30,000 of the protesters in what was not the first and would not be the last act of government-sponsored genocide against unarmed civilians in our national territory. A year later they raised that number by 10,000.' His voice quivered and he paused to swallow, because to Leonel they weren't numbers but names. 'Abraham Gadala is the FMLN's current *Comandante en Jefe.* Once the newly formed coalition had agreed that armed struggle was an essential element of their work towards democratic inclusion, they expanded their guerrilla tendency. That tendency increased its membership, recruiting eager combatants from the peasantry for column deployment. After fifty years of repression they were more than eager to enlist, and thus empower themselves. If they were to die, better to die fighting than begging a green beret for clemency in front of your raped wife and kids. The FMLN stood as a voice through which they might finally be heard, even if getting heard meant shoving their message down the Oligarchs' throat. Besides combatants we also recruited intellectuals and poets, to operate directly with Abraham on the unofficial political wing. These operatives continue to distribute propaganda leaflets and liaise with the *comités de solidaridad* which, with considerable help and support of exiles, were set up abroad – in Costa Rica, Mexico, Canada, even the US. Their work has produced important gains, such as securing political recognition for the FMLN from both the French and Mexican governments.

'Okay, let's see if I've got this right,' Jasmine broke in to make a summary of her history lesson. 'So you look after the rural areas.'

'That's not all we do,' Leonel protested, alarmed that this was all she had gleaned from his lengthy memoirs.

'But that's a lot of what you do. Conceded?'

'Go on,' he coaxed, conceding nothing.

'So what about San Salvador? Does anyone stand up for its marginal zones?'

Astonishingly, she was one step ahead of him.

'The capital is home to the Creole descendents of the original oligarchy – rich and powerful families and institutions the military has traditionally protected – and it remains firmly in military hands. It's where the army barracks and headquarters are housed, the foreign embassies, diplomats, *la Casa Presidencial,* and Congress. The place is crawling with National and Hacienda Police, and more soldiers than we can realistically confront. San Salvador will not fall, nor will we attempt to take her.'

'Though you have tried. Twice, according to my...'

'History teacher, yeah?' he forestalled. So he ploughed bravely into a painful admission: 'Back in eighty-one and eighty-two we launched unsuccessful offensives against San Salvador. Sure, it was fool-hardy, but it forced us to reassess our objectives. Currently our aim is the total liberation of the rural areas while conducting sporadic incursions on the outskirts of the capital, thereby stepping up the pressure on the PDC to concede to our proposed terms for a peace settlement. The more rural zones that swing our way, the more pressure subsequently comes to bear on the PDC.'

111

'And what are those proposed demands?'

'Oh, human rights, land distribution, the role of the armed forces, things like that.'

'And of course political recognition for the FMLN,' – as if to remind him of a forgotten agenda. 'So you could be defeated militarily, yeah? But what if you're defeated in a general election too?'

He tried another answer: 'Unlike some revolutionary movements, we believe in the democratic right to vote. But it's not a matter of win-all or lose-all. Even the party that loses in a general election can represent its voters before parliament. While we remain outlawed, we can't even do that.'

She appeared to reflect on this, and then half nodded. 'What would happen *if*,' she began eventually, 'due to the *matanzas* and awful things that happen, the people got fed up with the Democrats, and in the next elections voted instead for ARENA?'

Despite his fatigue brought on by a successful but fraught afternoon raid to snatch CAR 15s, mortar and artillery fuses, and plastic cord explosives from an army transport convoy on route to Santa Ana, during which he had lost four combatants, he felt uplifted by her keen line of questioning. All too often, newcomers' eyes glazed over during his preamble, and when it came to taking up arms they did so without an adequate appreciation of the reasons. Vengeance alone was not reason enough. In fact it was a hindrance to their performance.

'You are astute beyond your years,' he complimented her sincerely. 'You have identified the scenario that we all dread. A scenario whereby the military would effectively have its political clout totally restored, this time under a seal of legitimacy. A bloodbath would follow, bloodier even than anything we have seen so far, and our hopes for competing in a democratic arena would be dashed.'

CHAPTER TEN

IN JASMINE'S EYES SUCHITOTO lived up to its Nahuatle name: A Place of Flowers and Birds. A hilltop town of colonial arches for its colonnades, of pink tiles for its tree-shaded roofs, of fountains for bougainvillea-clad courtyards, and of layer upon layer of birdsong.

It was also home to Leonel's treasured red Toyota pickup: battered, scratched and dented, not to mention the hole in the floor that allowed the driver to watch the potholes slide beneath as he drove. But Leonel's love for the pickup was blind.

With a wink and a nod and the passing of a few American bucks, they secured replacement ID papers for Jasmine, adding an unlikely three years to her age on her new birth certificate thus enabling her to legally buy a full driving licence and thereby receive tuition on the pebbled streets of Suchitoto, because, as Leonel informed her mysteriously, he had just the job for her. 'But first things first. Drive me to Cerén. Time for you to make friends with Serafin Romero.'

By contrast to the Place of Flowers and Birds, Cerén was a dump of a village with wandering goats, and litter by the bucketful. No birds. No flowers to speak of. Cerén owed its saving grace to a World Heritage archaeological site. It was to the bearded one-legged warden of this ancient site that Leonel entrusted his beloved pickup until they returned in a couple of days.

A hard trek from Cerén through prairie swirling with

patches of purple mistflower, across the Rio el Desague by a plank bridge, a night in their hammocks in the wooded hills of Masahuat, and a sweaty morning picking their way through woodlands that were as familiar to Jasmine as they were to Leonel.

The metal antenna was concealed high in the branches of an old conacaste. And although the muffled hum of a generator issuing from somewhere underground announced their proximity to the bunker, the entrance blended in so naturally with the surrounding vegetation that Jasmine was taken aback when Leonel began prodding the ground with a fallen branch, a trap door with a full shaggy head of ferns opened, and from a dark recess a pale hand bid them make haste.

Hesitantly Jasmine dipped her foot into the cavity and the hand guided it on to a ledge of hard soil, and as she descended she realised the ledge was the first in a series of steps that led her down into the earth until she found herself inside a hot and stuffy underground bunker just as Leonel had described. Buttressed with bamboo, the walls and ceiling of Radio Venceremos's temporary hideout were covered with canvas sheets. A canvas sheet for a carpet too, which had become rumpled with boot-prints.

Judging by the way the two *compadres* stooped beneath the ceiling to make an arch of their embrace, Serafin Romero was as tall as Leonel, slimmer though, with sunken cheeks and a beard greying at the tips. He wore multi-pocketed combat trousers, and a sleeveless safari jacket over a T-shirt with Radio Venceremos blazoned in revolutionary red across the front.

At last Serafin unclasped Leonel and, in the pale glow of two halogen lamps strung across the ceiling, turned to scrutinise Jasmine. 'So, you're the pretty little starling from El Zacate that everyone's talking about,' he declared. 'Leonel here was most put out that a recreational tracker should have discovered his secret hideout with such ease. Reckon you could have found mine too, do you?' Serafin challenged. 'Mind, you'll keep it hush-hush now you've been allowed to the inner sanctum. Or

114

I'll have you down here with us forever,' – rupture of hilarity –
'Are you hungry? Got some nice tinned spam.'

'No, thanks.'

'Come, come.' He beckoned Jasmine forward to a wood desk shoved up to one wall. It was cluttered with microphones, a couple of heavy duty batteries, a portable tape recorder, an intriguing wedge-shaped panel of buttons and sliders, biro pens – lined paper sheets covered in tidy blue manuscript, and a cardboard box packed with cassette tapes. 'I want to show you what all the fuss is about,' he announced, like a birthday boy eager to show off his new Lego set. He sprang a big-knuckled index finger which he used to hammer the panelled roof of a metal case that took pride of place on a timber shelf directly above the desk.

'Santamaria would sell both his shrivelled bollocks for my transmitter,' Serafin declared proudly. 'I bought it from a Mexican radio amateur. It was originally designed to transmit telegraph signals, but the clever bastard modified it to broadcast on a forty-metre band. This humble transmitter as you see it, together with one hand-held recorder, one microphone, one cassette, and one bloody noisy generator, *si, señor*, was all I had to start up with. Wasn't it, Leo?'

'It was.'

Serafin suddenly raised his finger, plonked himself on a rustic stool, clapped on a headset that parted his bush of brown curls, and introduced the next track through the microphone: '*Mi Pais.*'

After their initial enthusiastic greeting, Leonel and Serafin began to argue about something, and Jasmine picked up a newspaper from a tray on Serafin's desk and went to sit in a corner while the two goats had it out. Same news, different day, she thought as she read through the pages. A mother bludgeoned to death in her bed by unknown assailants, signs of multiple rape, her five-year-old son survived. The naked bodies of a dozen men discovered at the entrance to Atiquizaya, mouths stuffed with their own genitalia. The corpses of three young men discovered in a ditch, faces melted by battery acid.

Eventually the two grownup children stopped arguing and while Leonel sulkily manned the radio, Serafin took time out to alert Jasmine to a number of key questions he would be putting to her in interview. Unashamedly he also provided answers to several of these.

A while later a young woman wearing a T-shirt just like Serafin's and a severe business-like air, descended upon Radio Venceremos. She handed Serafin an exercise book of the kind school teachers routinely sell to their pupils, and he read from its pages into the microphone, using his fact-stating monologue to detail what turned out to be a lengthy list of the day's murderous events which the reporter had diligently catalogued together with gory descriptions. A number of these incidents were bound to appear in tomorrow's national newspapers, thought Jasmine. But with a very different slant, no doubt.

Going out on live radio an up-beat Serafin referred to the survivor of El Zacate by her unmodified age of fifteen tender years, and was pleased to welcome our very special guest who we shall aptly refer to as "Xochitl-toto" in order to protect her identity until such time as she can be heard before a formal tribunal. 'Nahuatle for Flower-bird,' he added, turning to wink at a stunned Jasmine. She was seated stiffly on a stool beside him. Her mind had journeyed back to La Molienda, and she made nothing of his wink, and heard little of the brief introduction Serafin delivered. She struggled to keep her voice steady because fresh surges of resentment were shuddering through her entire being. She soon realised that her bitterness, rather than dwindling in the three and a half months since the day El Zacate fell apart, had actually escalated to alarming proportions. And it was developing a focus: the army, the Americans for training and arming the army, Major Anastasio Menesses, Colonel Rubén Santamaria, *Batallón Liberación* – in that order. A shortness of breath delivered every sentence with an annoying pant. An acidic lump was forcing its way up to her throat, a thumping headache coming on. She accepted a paper tissue from the business-like reporter, and held it to her nose while tears welled to overflowing. Now her distress rushed at her, threatening to gag her if she didn't break down. She accepted a beaker of warm water from the mellowing reporter. She sipped. It went down the wrong way and she spluttered. Serafin patted her back, and left his splayed hand there, in a sort of embrace. She shrugged it off, sipped more water, tilted her head back and drew in a couple of steadying breaths. She knew that her lungs lacked the capacity to cry out so much grief. That her sobs would suffocate her if she even tried. So she doggedly resumed her account: a halting recollection of El Zacate as seen from La Molienda.

And when she had concluded, Serafin – accustomed to broadcasting tragedy on a daily basis which explained why he appeared unmoved by it all – asked – for the benefit of our esteemed listeners, please – whether you could identify the men who did the killing?

Thus cued, she delivered herself of the answer she had been primed to give, the only part of her story that was not hers: 'I can identify the soldier that shouted the orders. He is Major Anastasio Menesses, of *Batallón Liberación*.'

'Are you willing and able to provide his full name and rank and all your evidence with regards the *matanza* in El Zacate to an independent enquiry?'

'I am.'

Serafin gave her the thumbs-up, slid the button on his microphone, and whispered for extra confidentiality, 'That'll have their shitty arses twitching.' Again the wink, before switching the mike back on for his follow-up: 'Understandably, this interview has been extremely distressing for you Xochitl-toto, but one last question, if I may. The army's own enquiry team turned up evidence they say confirms beyond all possible doubt that the El Zacate *matanza* was the exclusive work of guerrilla forces. How do you respond to this accusation?'

Another of Serafin's answers, but it was hers too: 'When the helicopter flew in to land, the uniformed men in El Zacate did not run away or hide as you'd expect guerrillas to.' And she promptly collapsed into Leonel's arms.

* * *

Three days later during a live interview on Radio Nacional the military press officer dismissed the claims of witness Xochitl-toto as, "unhelpful" and "reopening old wounds".

'They're rattled,' Leonel said, switching channels to get Serafin's response.

'That they saw fit to hold a press conference at all illustrates their concern,' Serafin intoned from his hole in the ground. 'And if the UN should ever decide to investigate this *matanza*, they will find a willing and intelligent witness in Xochitl-toto.'

CHAPTER ELEVEN

November 1984

LEONEL LISTENED TO HER plan for Santamaria, appraised it, and dismissed it as wholly unworkable. Good try, but Santamaria would never fall for such novice subterfuge. Now that you've put that idea out of your head, I have just the job for you.

Jasmine was instructed to receive her weekly detail from Adrian Cruz, and to report back to him at the conclusion of each mission. The lieutenant, a sinuous rogue with an Aztec profile, well defined lips and a poor excuse for a moustache, passed for camp medic and was referred to by some as The Witchdoctor. Marvellous accounts of his resourcefulness in the face of limited medical kit were routinely retold with awe round the campfire. Like the time he intravenously fed a badly wounded combatant with coconut water. Like when he plunged his hand into a shattered ribcage to jumpstart a stopped heart. And when he had Chamba the carpenter fashion a prosthesis for that amputee who pleaded to rejoin the column? Adrian the concerned podiatrist who, if asked nicely, would make you special insoles out of coconut husk because, given the frequent laden marches undertaken, coming down with chronic plantar fasciitis can be a right pain. Adrian had a smutty sense of humour which Jasmine didn't much care for, but he was also an exceedingly emotional sort. Whenever the touchy subject of the military or the gringos cropped up, he was liable to work himself into such a breathless fury that he literally became speechless, and would have to take himself off to his medicine cabinet, still choking on his unfinished sentence. As he did when Leonel announced, over a subdued campfire, cigars, and cinnamon coffee, that the gringos were considering an invasion, because despite squandering US Military Aid the Salvadoran government had been slack in stemming the Red Dread; in fact, to all observant congressmen, the redness was spreading across their table map of El Salvador. 'You see, Jasmine,' Leonel explained to a rapt audience of one, because the others had heard it all before, 'General McCarthy's grooming of gringo hearts and minds to oppose communism was so successful that the groomed now believe with sincerity that their opposition derives from independent and informed thought. That grooming served to shanghai the supple-brained citizenry into a global witch-hunt for any poor oppressed soul irresponsible enough to lean towards the Red Dread, while failing to offer the witches an alternative exit from decades and in some cases centuries of poverty and oppression. Thereafter the gringo beast, wielding its witch-hunt as an attention deflector, has through economic manipulation of worldly banks and cowardly governments, and behind the scenes pressure on the UN and an impressively faithful marriage to warmongering, plundered earth's God-given riches to feed its insatiable avarice.'

Old Wenceslou was already shaking his silvery head. 'It appears that avarice encouraged,' he put in, 'which in effect capitalism achieves fabulously, is to erode communal bonds leaving happy haves regulating unhappy have-nots. Don't bother relying on the happy have to self regulate or even abide by imposed controls on the lengths allowed to achieve each new height his addiction demands. This little irregularity, while lurking beyond the gringo's belief range, is commonly evident to the Third World victims of capitalism who turn to the alternative only after their homeland's assets have found their way into foreign pockets, and their homes have been bashed and their loved-ones butchered by the capitalist gun.'

'There has never been such a feat of mass brainwashing,' Leonel reclaimed the baton to finish his earlier point, 'as that propagandised by McCarthy. Currently in gringo circles, if you have the cheek to consider alternative exits for those living under oppressive military regimes, at best you're dismissed as a communist lunatic, and at worst reported to the authorities.'

Now Adrian was on his feet, flinging out his arms and screeching like the communist lunatic whose existence Leonel was trying to disprove. 'And if you're the bastard born under a tin roof in a crumbling nation governed by thieves, and dare to question your lot, the gringo braves will unleash their tanks and gunships and airborne bombers and warships on you in their efforts to silence your hungry mouth. So if their Rambo comes saying, "Instead of hiding in the jungle like cowards, come out and fight us like men, face to face," remember there's precious little face to face about gringo warfare, so shout over their high-walled green zones and tell them like it is, "Will you come out to play without your tank support, bombers, helicopters, satellites, warships, top-notch technology and your beloved deniable napalm?" You'll soon be witness to their rank cowardice when their answer returns as a resounding *no,* with excuses attached. So I whisper,' although he wasn't whispering but screaming while Leonel patted the air in an attempt at noise reduction, 'shame on them for outnumbering us, for outgunning us, for outdoing us in terms of illegal war practices and every conceivable advantage their dollars can buy, and still not beating us.' At which he promptly dissolved into a choking fit and took himself off to raid his medicine chest for a suitable injection.

Adrian handed over documents containing instructions in minute manuscript, and had Jasmine roll these up tightly and slide them into empty cigar cylinders, which he then slid into the legs of toy dolls or soft toys before carefully stitching the seams back together. He entrusted her with cassettes; to go by their covers you'd be treated to popular cumbia classics, but in fact they carried recorded messages for column leaders' ears

121

only.

At the wheel of Leonel's pickup she covered hundreds of kilometres to make her deliveries, from Abraham Gadala's office in San Salvador's rundown Ilopango district to the guerrilla columns encamped throughout the national territory. She grew familiar with the highways tunnelling beneath frangipani arches, the dodgy escarpment tracks where cattle herders on horseback drove their emaciated beasts, with negotiating fast-flowing streams while silt-laden waters spat in through the hole in the floor, and with approaches to towns where carved up corpses with their intestines still burning and clusters of severed heads were displayed for the curiosity of travellers. Objectionable as some of the PCS's methods of furthering the Cause had appeared to Jasmine, beheading and mutilation were not in the guerrillas' repertoire: these macabre roadside displays were exclusively the work of military hands. However humane it purported to be, no cause could justify the cold-blooded murder of her mother and a thousand other Zacateans, or the ruination of her entire village.

After six successful weeks without a scratch added to his pickup, Leonel was moved to entrust her with cash – several thousands of US dollars at a time. It came packaged in brown paper wrapping, stuffed into suitcases fitted with false bottoms, which Jasmine collected from skulking men and women at deserted points along the banks of the Rio Torola.

After cash came munitions. Adrian bid her travel to the border with Guatemala, then Nicaragua, to receive consignments from exiled Salvadorans and smiling foreign sympathisers. Because these journeys entailed high levels of risk they required advanced planning. Working on the best intelligence they could gather, Adrian and Jasmine plotted the routes she should take in order to avoid as many National Guard check points as possible and reach a rebel-held zone through which she might travel relatively freely. Nevertheless, as Jasmine soon discovered to her alarm, the Guard routinely moved their roadblocks, cropping up where she least expected.

Invariably, at some point during each journey, she found herself steering directly towards an avenue of bright cones siphoning off traffic for inspection and questioning by heavily armed soldiers. She would tuck in behind the car ahead, hoping that the guardsmen had their hands full, and that to call over another vehicle would be to clog up the avenue of cones. She would proceed innocently at cruise pace on the outer lane, wincing with every rut in the road that rattled her cargo of weapons.

All this travelling afforded her the privilege of meeting with the other FMLN columns and their leaders. All except for Adonai Limeño, the *comandante* of liberated Morazán Province, of whom she had heard Leonel speak with considerable regard. The author of *Reliable Intelligence* – a manual that was considered essential reading for guerrillas throughout the world, and of eight highly sought after but locally banned volumes of poetry – as romantic as they were insurrectionist, and winner of Mexico's prestigious *Casa de la Cultura* prize for Creative Contemporary Literature. Back in the schooldays of Spanish Literature classes Jasmine had enthusiastically produced a handful of awkwardly constructed sonnets which she had in her own time managed to tidy up with some brutal trimming, so the knowledge that a renowned poet inhabited FMLN ranks rekindled that enthusiasm. To her profound disappointment however, Adonai was absent on each of the four occasions Jasmine visited Morazán, and she was met instead by well-mannered lieutenants, one of whom was happy to downgrade her disappointment by presenting her with a brand new volume of Adonai's *Desperate Yearnings,* which she determined to have signed whenever they should finally meet. No matter where they met up in the relative safety of this Red Zone, Adonai's troops regaled Jasmine with song. A warrior choir of powerful bass voices overlaid with harmonising tenors chanting revolutionary anthems of such exquisite beauty that Jasmine was as much roused to battle as moved to tears.

On those rare weeks back in Cuscatlán when there were no couriering duties to perform, she joined in the rush to welcome and make a fuss of the squads on their return from assignments. When a mission had gone well, the combatants described in animated detail the raids in which they had participated: the storming of a high-society party and the taking hostage of a minister's son, who was returned in exchange for a substantial ransom or the release of a comrade from military custody; or the wresting of a hamlet from the clutches of the National Guard; or an ambush on a convoy transporting a consignment of munitions from Ilopango Air Field to the military base in Santa Ana. Each victory, however small, stood as grounds for celebration.

But when an offensive turned out badly, survivors returned to be comforted by their comrades while Adrian attended to their wounds and the squad captains briefed Leonel in private. Each loss of a comrade brought about collective mourning. The time spent away from camp meant that Jasmine regularly missed out on the ongoing military training that Leonel or one of his lieutenants – commitments permitting – put the column through three times a week. To correct this deficit, Adrian issued her with her very own AK47 from the armoury. It was heavy, impersonal, mechanical, and old enough to have had a hundred previous owners; and she doubted its capacity to do more than break apart. She told Adrian that she was displeased with it, so he grudgingly issued her with another, of the same brand, but going by the shine on the wood, a significant improvement on the first. The lieutenant gave her a hurried lesson in dismantling, cleaning, and oiling the weapon, and then he strapped a spare magazine to the barrel, tore away a side of cardboard box, and led her on a trek to a glade full of butterflies where several uprooted trees, like toppled columns of some ruined Aztec temple, snuggled in the towering pampas grass. He selected one of the trees and slotted the cardboard amid its upwardly pointing roots, and counting aloud he backed up sixty-five paces.

'Single shot from here. We don't want to make too much noise,' he said sternly.

She stood exactly where he indicated, poised just as he told her to, slid the selector lever to the lowest position, yanked back and released the charging handle, and trained the sights on the cardboard. Startled by a blistering slam to her eardrums and the recoil punching her shoulder, she allowed the barrel an insignificant sideways jolt. The butterflies rose like a cloud from the grove, up above the canopy to be swept away against an overcast sky. The target remained conspicuously intact. She had expected to be disgusted with the weapon, but instead she was disgusted with herself for having missed the target.

'Not to worry, Jaz,' Adrian offered reassurance. 'An AK's sights are positioned too close together to allow great accuracy. But overcome that design flaw, and you'll be good.'

'I'll do it again,' she snapped, briskly chambering another round, adrenalin pumping within her ribcage, a sense of power at her fingertips, and a determination to improve a skill that might soon be called upon. She lined up the target, shuffled her feet to steady herself, and composed her shoulder for the recoil. She squeezed the trigger and held it down. With a muzzle velocity of 710 metres per second, the rifle sent the bullet socking through the cardboard and into the woods beyond. But she was not one to bask in her success. 'Now I'll practice with a moving target,' she informed a drop-jawed Adrian.

CHAPTER TWELVE

WHEN JASMINE AWOKE to ear-splitting automatic rifle fire, the camp was already ablaze with muzzle flashes. Male voices gabbled instructions like "West," "Northwest," and "Get down." Bullets socked into tin and timber. She leapt from her hammock, scooped up her AK, squatted behind one of the tree trunks to which her hammock was rigged, and glared at flickering human silhouettes half buried in shadows, a single blinding flash followed by a glimmering spray of sparks, tents and tree stems illuminated by stages, bullets spitting across her line of vision, rain drizzling down it. She dropped on one knee and with a quivering hand notched the selector up into the middle position, cradling the weapon as she had been taught. She applied her concentration, trying to make sense of the bedlam. Then the bedlam began to revolve until it had turned upside down, and she stuck out her hand and slumped against the tree trunk. Three swift deep breaths and the scene righted itself just as warm wetness slopped on to the side of her face, and instinctively she pursed her lips against it entering her mouth. She heard, or felt, it was hard to tell which, something weighty slump right beside her. She looked down and recognised Jonas the tailor stretched out on his side, facing her with a fretful stare in his youthful features, head resting on his arm. In a splattering of flashes, she could see that the upper side of his head was open. Now blood was seeping from his tear ducts into his staring eyes, turning them into dark pools that spilled over. There was blood on the tree trunk, blood on the grass, and when she pushed herself into a kneeling position and gathered up the rifle, she saw it was also on her hands. Gulping back an urge to scream, she used the cleanest of her trembling hands to wipe her face.

Now she saw the gleam of a helmet gliding away. Guardsmen: they must have sneaked past the tripwire under the noise of the squall-battered trees. 'Kill or be killed,' she told herself. She took aim at the helmet. The gun awoke in her grip, automatically cycling fresh rounds into the chamber. She did not see the impacts, but the helmet swooped earthwards. She released the trigger and the weapon rested still, warm, and comforting. With the camp revealed merely by flashes, identifying the enemy would have been far trickier had it not been for their distinctive protective headgear. Perhaps her eyes were learning, because now several helmets appeared at once, and now an ashen face at which she fired. A string of missiles ploughed into neck and shoulder. Was that figure hunched over a rifle directly ahead a guardsman or a comrade? His head blended into the same shadow in which his rifle was just a rifle, and dashes of olive green alone didn't constitute a military uniform. She lifted her finger away from the trigger, which was just as well because it was that figure who fired next, illuminating his own squint of concentration that told her she had almost shot Emilio, the second lieutenant. Although his was the first of the final shots, it took a full hour for the skirmish to peter out as hidden and wounded guardsmen were rooted out and executed. By the time Leonel was satisfied that no more surprises lurked in the undergrowth, moonlit mist was gliding through the canopy.

* * *

Businesslike and brave-faced the comrades soaked blankets in stream water, bashed out the last of the fires, and hurriedly buried their eleven dead in shallow graves. Two escorts shouldering a hammock rigged up to a branch stretchered the only severely wounded survivor to Suchitoto, from where he was to be whisked by pickup to the FMLN's field hospital in Sihuatán, in the north of the Province. With steam-heated sewing needles, monofilament fishing line and Betadine antiseptic over everything including his hands, Adrian patched up those who needed it while swift work was made of dismantling the camp.

With gunfire still echoing in her ears, Jasmine stole a look at her two victims. The first lay face down in the grass, hands splayed beside his close cropped head, his helmet hollow-side-up a couple of feet away. No apparent wounds, but she wasn't about to turn him over for closer inspection. Her second victim sprawled belly-down, his neck in shreds. She wondered whether those remote flutterings in her breast were in fact the first rumours of guilt.

'Quit dithering and check his pockets for cash,' Emilio growled as he shuffled past under a burden of rolled up canvass in his arms.

The body was still so warm that despite its dreadful wounds, she fancied it might wake up at any moment. She discovered seven one-hundred Colon bills in a Velcro wallet and stuffed them into her dungaree pocket. From the pocket of his breeches she wheedled out a transparent sachet which rattled, and when she held her torch to it, she saw it contained a dozen or so small white pills. Intrigued, she rummaged around in the dead man's pockets and drew out a matchbox tightly bound in adhesive tape. When she shook it beside her ear it sounded as if it contained sand. She pocketed both items before prising the man's rifle from his fingers.

Laden with backpacks and crates a column of fifty-four PCS guerrillas abandoned the compromised campsite and set off for a new home. With a weighty rucksack and her AK47 perched on her back, her personal backpack swinging forward from her neck, and sharing an ammunitions crate with Emilio, Jasmine maintained the punishing pace that Leonel was setting. An advanced guard scouted ahead while two flankers shadowed, and Adrian Cruz and Anabela Segovia disguised the trail left by the marchers. Silence was ordered, only the most necessary conversation permitted. Hand signals were for daylight, and to be kept to an absolute minimum lest they promote distraction. Meanwhile volcanic rock crunched underfoot, slippery leaves cracked, mud squelched and sucked.

Only the scantest skylight hinted at their surroundings, but as the sun gained altitude, the forest was revealed. The trees, utterly straight, trunks wrapped in creepers, soared to impossible heights from where lianas as thick as a man's arm reached down to the forest bed. All about in this lush, humid, bitter and pungent ecosystem insects buzzed, giant blossoms broke open and spread ragged flamboyant petals and long tailed torogoces were wisps of iridescence. The gargled retching of a dozen drunkards started up, and as Jasmine peered up through the curtains of light she made out not drunkards but howler monkeys, some scuttling along branches with babies clinging to their backs; others silhouetted amid splayed leaves. Jasmine trudged on, tugging each step from the mud that was caking her sandals.

She spotted deer slipping behind fan-like thickets and heard busy woodpeckers drumming eerily. If the column made too much noise, the disrupted fauna might betray its presence to the enemy: squirrels jabbered from above, and squadrons of pigeons flushed from their roosts as the combatants passed. Leonel stopped in his tracks and raised a clenched fist. The column halted obediently, and as Leonel lowered his fist so everyone squatted low, setting down burdens and stealthily drawing weapons. They scanned, pitching their ears for any alarming sound. Everything from ground-level to about fifteen metres high was crystal-clear verdant foliage dotted with magenta and yellow flower clusters. A fraught ten minutes drew by, and then several versions of the canopy birds' *pee-wit* piped up. After responding with a *pee-wit-oh*, Leonel stood up and beckoned. Shortly before midday they arrived at the Rio Titihuapa: a fifty-metre wide fast-flowing tributary from whose stony banks steep pined hillsides soared towards a hazy sky.

'We'll have to make two crossings,' Leonel announced, pointing across spume-capped rapids. 'The province of Cabañas is an island surrounded by river. Rio Titihuapa splits away from the Lempa at the Big Forest and rejoins it north of San Vicente – our destination.'

'We could camp here and move out at first light,' Adrian suggested, but Leonel was impatient to put as much distance between them and their compromised site as quickly as possible. The shallowest part of the river was about eighty metres downstream in sight of a single lane plank-bridge. They scrambled for cover while an Isuzu bus clattered over the bridge, and then splashed across and entered yet another contested zone.

By now tendrils of sweaty hair clung to Jasmine's face and neck, and her entire body pleaded to be released from its burdens, the weight of which made her normally comfortable sandals wear like hard wooden slabs that had the soles of her feet smarting. With both hands occupied she was unable to pluck away the pebbles that lodged themselves beneath the arches of her feet, and when she halted to shake them free, Emilio, with sweat dripping off him, complained that she was holding up the column. Her thighs swelled with fire and a throbbing hurt inched its way up her back and concentrated just below her shoulder blades. Nor was she able to reach up to wipe away the stinging perspiration from her eyes, or the cobwebs that stuck to her face after she'd walked into them. On an intake of breath she sucked in a small green maggot at a loose end, and spat it out in disgust. Still there was no letup in the marching, save for when Leonel allowed the occasional minute-long break to quench their thirst from fast depleting water flasks.

They skirted the riverbank for ten kilometres until they came to an arc of sandy embankment upon which the forest extended into the river. At last Leonel bowed to pressure from Adrian:

'We camp here tonight,' he declared, to a chorus of relieved groans.

That evening tempers flared and Adrian darted in to break up a vicious knife brawl between a pair of aggrieved comrades. After the patching up he'd done that morning he was keen to avoid unnecessary raids on his medicine box. Too worn out to prepare supper or to eat any, they settled down on the yielding sand and drifted off to the sound of the river. All too soon, that witchdoctor Adrian was robbing them of much needed sleep by tapping the backs of their hands. 'Push hard and we'll reach San Vicente by nightfall,' the lieutenant said, by way of encouragement.

After they had replenished their flasks from the river and bolted down a frugal breakfast of cold tortillas and black coffee, they loaded up and set off. Jasmine's thoughts turned to the two men she had killed yesterday, and she waited for the guilt to strike. But it did not come as the column marched inland, nor in the cool shadows of serrated rock crests looming overhead; it was absent when, with packs and crates hoisted overhead, they waded across the Rio Titihuapa, and later in the wooded hills in the north of San Vicente Province. Still she felt nothing remotely akin to guilt when she gazed across a valley where sheep grazed to pine-covered mountains. Nor when, having helped spring the new camp well before Adrian's nightfall prediction, she swung at last in the comfy belly of her own hammock, and against camp protocol, peeled off her mud-caked sandals to massage her smarting feet.

'How you doing'?' Totally unexpected, it was Leonel's rumble above her.

She looked up into his bearded smile. He did his goat nod.

'Good, yeah, nice. Thanks,' she gabbled, strapping on her sandals.

'I've been thinking about your plan for Santamaria.'

'Really,' Jasmine said, surprised that he'd reconsidered it at all. Hadn't he dismissed such novice subterfuge as unworkable?

'It may help me kill two birds with one stone,' he continued mysteriously.

'How d'you mean?'

'For about a fortnight I've suspected we're harbouring a mole. I've good reason to believe he was responsible for leaking our whereabouts to the Guard, which led to the attack on our camp.'

'No,' Jasmine exclaimed in wonderment. 'Do you know who?'

'Suspicions at the moment, but your idea may flush him out. We'll tell him about it.'

'But…wouldn't that subvert the outcome?' Jasmine suddenly felt protective of her novice subterfuge.

'He will hear only what he needs to hear.' And unless Leonel was a bit more forthcoming, so would she.

'Who do you *think* it is?' she pressed.

'Later, Jasmine. When we reach San Vicente, you and I will discuss the matter in detail with my lieutenants.'

Jasmine blinked, and tried to look modest about this privileged invitation. Then she remembered her spoils of war and hurriedly dug out the sachet and matchbox from her pocket. 'I found these on a dead soldier.' She held them out.

'Go-pills,' he said in English, picking up the sachet and turning it over. 'Dextroamphetamine, a psycho-stimulant routinely handed out to soldiers. Totally legal.'

'What's it do?'

'Keeps you awake, quells inhibitions, can make you feel invincible.'

'What's in the matchbox?' Intrigued, she watched as he stripped away the tape, and prodded open the tray.

'Cocaine powder. Now that's illegal,' he lowered the tray for her to make her own assessment of the contents.

'A bit like maize flour, isn't it?' she suggested.

'Well, don't go sprinkling the stuff on our tortillas, will you,' he said with a feeble smile, slipping the sachet of dextroamphetamine into his hip pocket.

'Those greens that invaded El Zacate might have taken dextro…'

'…amphetamine,' he completed.

'The white pills,' she confirmed, 'and the cocaine, yeah?'

'You bet.'

'What will you do with them?'

'The Witchdoctor can have them for his medicine chest.'

'I also found money,' she said, scooping out the wad of folded Colon bills.

'Keep it.' He overwhelmed her hand in his and folded her fingers over the notes. 'Unexpected expenses often crop up for our trusty couriers.'

She fell silent, the silence drew out, and she began fiddling with the edge of the blanket. She glanced up. 'What's on your mind, Jasmine?' Leonel asked quietly, and waited, seemingly aware that his most recent entrant to the PCS fraternity required a moment to gather herself for a confession.

'Yesterday I killed two men,' she blurted.

'They were soldiers,' he stated, as if to refute their right to be classed as men. 'But you feel bad, yeah? Well, don't.'

'No, you see, Don Leonel, that's just it. I don't feel bad... at least not yet...though I'm sure I will, because...how do I kill the enemy? Because Jesus said to love him. At this point I don't even feel guilty for not feeling guilty... if that makes any sense...'

Leonel saved her from her rambling: 'No-one's suggesting armed struggle's a guiltless road to bring about change,' he began, settling into his ever-ready philosophy. At least he hadn't brushed aside her concern as he had so many others. 'But faced with a life and death choice between the enemy you love and the friend you love, save the one you love most.'

'Do you feel guilty?' she enquired, wincing inwardly at what must sound childish to a veteran guerrilla leader.

Childish or not, he made a noncommittal motion with his hand. 'It comes and goes,' he admitted. 'But I'd feel far guiltier if I stood aside and did nothing about the military operations in our villages.'

With relief she agreed wholeheartedly, and suddenly felt very tired indeed.

CHAPTER THIRTEEN

WITH THREE BRISK SWIPES of his pointer Colonel Rubén Santamaria outlined a triangle on the patchwork of aerial black-and-whites stencilled to the wall. 'The Forest of Visions, the Forest of Masahuat; two forests running together, spreading across three departments: Santa Ana,' a thwack of the pointer, 'Chalatenango,' – thwack – 'and this' – thwack – 'the northern tip of La Libertad.' A pause to allow comment.

Anastasio approached and circled the triply thwacked area with a wave of his cap. 'And a hidden river dividing them. No doubt the *muchachos* are using it as a thoroughfare to and from Guatemala.'

Santamaria selected another photograph and thwacked the starting point of a meandering path of red ink over the treetops. 'The Guatemalan supply line runs from Nicaragua all the way through El Salvador. Makes no sense running it back via a different route to El Salvador, does it? He left Anastasio squinting at the photograph and went over to the water cooler in the corner. He filled a paper cup and tossed the water down his throat. I'll send playboy here with a detachment kitted in civvies to report on river traffic along the Desague.

A rapping at the door made him look up, and upon invitation one of Liberación's captains stepped forward with a crisp salute.

Santamaria crushed the cup and bowled it cricket-style into the waste bin. 'Captain Sinisterra,' he declared, stifling a smile.

'To what do we owe this interruption?' He was warming to the captain. Hardly out of his teens, properly committed; puts in, not like this leech of a playboy.

'Your visitor has arrived, colonel,' Sinisterra announced.

* * *

Sunsin Rivera had come to the point, and now the grin pushing ripples into his gaunt cheeks suggested he was very pleased with himself indeed. Grin he might, but nervous eyes shifted from Anastasio to Santamaria and back while he waited for a response.

'You appear very confident of your intel?' Santamaria said, and exchanged raised eyebrows with Anastasio.

'Would I come to you if I weren't?' he replied, and dropping his voice he added, 'I bring you *exactly* what you asked for.'

'*What* do you bring, exactly, Don Sunsin? Please, clarify,' Santamaria demanded. Besides, he wanted Anastasio to hear it from the horse's mouth.

But evidently Sunsin's greedy little mind was enjoying his new-found power. 'What have you been pestering me for these past four years?' he teased, which didn't go down well with Anastasio who donned his cap for the reply:

'I don't know, Sunsin, you snivelling turd, what have we been pestering you for?'

Sunsin wisely decided the guessing game was over before it had started. 'The rebel radio, its location, *and* the transmitter's location.'

'And you have this?' Anastasio asked, making a stab at scepticism to conceal, Santamaria surmised, chagrin at his own failure to acquire the information.

Sunsin was speaking again; he knew exactly where the transmitter was hidden. But it wouldn't remain put for long because as they knew only too well – didn't they? – Serafin moves house every few days. Of course, if they were no longer interested in his information, keener parties with cash in hand were raring to go.

Santamaria strolled over to the window that was letting in

135

all the traffic fanfare from the Santa Tecla Highway. He clasped his hands behind his back and gazed out at the sprinkler that sprayed the cropped lawn. He was moved to admit privately that Sunsin's sporadic verbal snippets had over the past three years shown reliability. Five years waiting for this one, and a day, two at the most, to act on it: could he afford to call his bluff? 'Sunsin, you're a businessman, and understand that we make deals to suit both our ends. If not, our partnership would have concluded years ago in your violent death. The information you offer me today, however, is of an extraordinarily sensitive nature. Naturally, you will understand my caution when I tell you that payment will be arranged only after we have captured the transmitter.'

Sunsin was already shaking his head. '*Coronel,* as you say, I'm a businessman. I trade in the genuine article. Exclusively, and my terms are payment on delivery of goods. Fair's fair. The success of your operation depends, not on the quality of my info, but on your boys not fucking up.'

Impulsive Anastasio reacted, bearing in, but Santamaria raised a silencing hand.

'The man is right, major,' Santamaria declared with a sigh, bowing to his own compulsion to deny the rebels their most effective instrument. Besides alerting *los indios* to planned military incursions and wording those incursions in despicably negative terms likely to turn sympathetic ears towards the FMLN and spiteful tongues on the military, Serafin and his team of actors had their little soap opera thing going, featuring a caricature of a blundering Colonel Rubencito Santa-Amariíta, that by several leaked accounts even had the President of the Republic in stitches. A personal affront like that required a proportionate response. Besides, the strategic advantage the army would gain by depriving El Frente of its voice! So the nod to pay as many American dollars as required for information leading to the whereabouts of the transmitter had been given at the highest military level, four years ago, by General Simón Levi himself. Now all that concerned Santamaria was getting his money's worth.

'Tomorrow morning I will have your money and a detachment ready to move on your instructions. You will come along for the ride, of course.'

* * *

All they could do that afternoon was select twenty-two hardy team players from *Liberación* to make up a *Sección*. It wasn't until the following morning when, acting on Sunsin's impressively concise information, they could formalise a manoeuvre applicable to the geography of the target location. The Caves of the Siguanava, as local folklore had dubbed them, penetrate a limestone cliff that cuts through the middle of Moncagua, a town sitting on natural springs eight kilometres north of San Miguel city. There you'll find three caves half submerged in the resulting pool. Follow the cliff west – a ten minute walk, no more because I've done it myself – and if your goons don't keep their bloodshot eyes open they'll walk straight into three other caves opening into the woods, and wake up Serafin and his ladies.

The tactic Santamaria came up with was to line the crest above the dry caves with a company of eleven headed by Anastasio. Santamaria, Sinisterra and another eleven would gain the cliff face through the forest from the opposite direction. If the rebels dared surface they would be fired upon from above; if they attempted to flee into the woods they would meet Santamaria and his men head-on and be clamped against the cliff by artillery fire. Hammer from above. Clamp from ahead. Never miss an opportunity to make an example of your victims – Santamaria recalled nostalgically from his stint at the US Army's School of the Americas – that others might witness the fate of those savages naïve enough to side with the communists. The only departure from the regular team today was that in his stead silent-type Flight Lieutenant José Martin Cabrera, citing training commitments in Panama, had sent – and very much recommended too – a rooky pilot who admitted that his mother had named him Watson after some British detective's sidekick. Why a mother would name her son after the sidekick and not the main man was suspect, but the eager eyes in his broad face eased Santamaria's initial misgivings. So when the *Sección* set off from San Salvador with Operation Hammer and Clamp on their minds, Santamaria's mood was one of cautious optimism.

'Fly over Morazán and approach San Miguel from the north,' he instructed Watson, preferring to avoid a path directly over Moncagua lest he alert his quarry. The more at ease they were, the greater his chances of springing a surprise party. Watson nodded his earphone-clad helmet and banked the ship to his left.

With his finger Santamaria traced meandering lanes across a map, debating for the umpteenth time the escape alternatives open to Serafín should he, by some fluke, break free of the clamp. Run to the east and I'll cut you down while you cross the Río Grande. To the south, I'll net you in San Miguel. You'd flee west to Usulután or north-east to Morazán, he mused, coming to the same conclusion as before, and as before he retraced a red arrow in both these directions with a biro, before folding the map and sliding it into his pocket.

He peered down at the range: a straight line of volcanoes connected by swooping ridges running for over a hundred kilometres, like the spinal column of some colossal prehistoric monster partially buried in the earth. South of the ridge, cotton fields and maize plantations opened out towards the mountains of El Mono, beyond which the Pacific Ocean was a faint blue line. The Hughes gunship sped northwards across the range and then over jungle where as many transmitters could be concealed as guerrillas. Gradually the pilot swept round on a southerly heading and Santamaria could see the discoloured terracotta roofs of San Miguel contrasting with the pink one topping the city's newly finished cathedral.

Watson brought the helicopter in to land on an air strip on the outskirts of the city's El Prado district. Santamaria left him doing his post-flight stuff, and went to wait in the terminal building for the convoy of trucks to arrive from San Salvador with his *Sección*. The wall clock in the airport's air-conditioned conference hall must have been wrong because it took an eternity for an hour and a half to tick by and herald the anticipated arrival. They ate tamales and drank copious amounts of water, for the San Miguel heat is like no other. Refreshed, they rehearsed key details of Operation Hammer and Clamp. Santamaria had each man repeat aloud the role expected of him, and they obeyed without the faintest smirk of derision. He was a god to them, and *Liberación* was their faith. He issued a few final words of caution: 'Eyes open for trip wires. Serafín's *culeros* are always on red alert. Even a twig snapping underfoot or a branch swinging back will put the shits up them. So please, swift and silent, gentlemen. Swift and silent.'

Two AM General trucks blared down the Pan-American Highway at breakneck speed. Without touching the brake the lead, carrying Santamaria and his devoted zealots, swerved on to a dirt track signposted for Moncagua, while the other pelted on. Santamaria rolled up his green sleeves and surveyed the approach to this small town he had only ever visited once, in his youth, on a school swimming outing. On either side, upon patchy scrubland, tamarind and flowering coral trees spread meandering branches above clumps of dust coated vegetation and adobe shacks. The trail rose and then dipped through a high walled crevice and a central plaza where the driver pinned his elbow to the horn while the huge steering wheel juddered in his hands. A scowling woman balancing a toddler on her hip shuffled to the kerbside, and a boy caught a thrown ball and tucked it under his arm as he watched the honking intruder with a sullen brown stare.

With the plaza behind, they followed the road as it levelled out beside a stream. Santamaria stuck his head out of the window and traced the watercourse back to a row of three arches – like a viaduct, each arch a half-waterlogged cave penetrating a vertical rock face. He pulled his head back inside. The track ahead had narrowed to little more than a footpath with tufts of grass lining the middle. Running parallel, the stream tumbled over a low rocky cascade beyond which a dozen women with skirts rucked up above water-level were assiduously scrubbing bed linen.

'Stop here,' Santamaria commanded because he judged that they had travelled the right distance beyond the cliff to adequately perform the clamp manoeuvre. Time was of the essence, because no doubt the rebels had their informers, and even now one of them might be hot footing it to sound the alarm.

The soldiers piled out and, while Santamaria conferred with Anastasio via radio, they turned their attention and wolf whistles towards the lovelies bending to their washing. 'Are you in position?' Santamaria sought clarification that playboy and his lot were in position over the crest. From here on, for the sake of a silent approach, radio volume to be muted until first sign of enemy. Correct?

'Affirmative.'

'Sinisterra?'

Another affirmative, but without the radio because he was standing right beside him.

Santamaria instructed the driver to turn the truck around because they may be in a hurry to move out, and then he called his men away from the river and its distractions and led them into the woods. They fanned out and formed an arrowhead of which Santamaria was the point, and he trotted forward with his M16, faithfully imitated by his disciples on either side. Swift and silent, he urged them in his mind, and was checking his wristwatch when an over-ripe mango thudded to the leafy carpet and he curtailed a startled reflex to shoot it dead.

Nineteen minutes in and they had covered a kilometre. Twenty-one minutes and to his disbelief he was hearing gunfire up ahead. Given their meticulous preparation, gunfire was not what he expected, not yet. But there it was, as erratic as firecrackers, perhaps that's what it was. But his disbelief was short-lived, giving way to dismay, and with heart banging he abandoned the formation and set off at a sprint towards the unpromising sound.

'What's happening?' he screeched into his radio. 'Speak to me.'

'The radio staff,' came Anastasio's breathless reply. 'Scrambling.'

'Scrambling? Which way?' he barked. Who the fuck alerted them?

'...cliff face...Cut 'em off to...west...Can't get down the cliff to chase...'

Santamaria veered to the right, and to his colleagues he bellowed Anastasio's appeal to cut the rebels off to the west. And through the trees he got his first fleeting glimpse of grey-white wall up ahead.

'Along the cliff face to your right,' he urged Sinisterra who was pulling ahead together with most of the others, warping the staggered formation as each man sprinted to his own ability. The wall came at him out of the blue and slammed into his left shoulder. He was catching his breath on a pathway of crushed limestone that traced the cliff base in both directions. He peered up towards the crest and screwed up his face in disgust as he saw why his plan had been flawed from the outset. Flawed for lack of local knowledge and because in the rush to catch the rebels before they took flight, he hadn't taken adequate time to acquaint himself with the target terrain. The pitted cliff face belled outwards the higher up he looked, thus snagging Anastasio's team's efforts on the crest, aiming down at the escapers who would have been amply sheltered by the overhang. You couldn't even blind-fire because the lip of the crest was too broad.

'Did they have the transmitter with them?' he radioed Anastasio. 'Negative. No sight of Matter.'

He breathed again, although he felt no relief. Now he was alone, vaguely aware of the fading stampede and his own

141

laboured breathing. In the shadow of the cliff he stole along the pathway eastwards. The first cavern gaped at him. A fractured aperture folding in on wrinkled lips, wide enough at the bottom to park a family saloon sideways, and tapering over three metres above ground to a sharp toothed Gothic arch. In response to his radioed call to Anastasio advising of his intention to enter the cave he received only a fart of static.

He crossed the threshold into the cool dimness, paused and held his breath, anticipating a sudden rush of bats. It didn't come. Perhaps they've given way to Serafin and his radio gear? Placing each careful step on the channelled floor he advanced while checking out the white ceiling from whose pitted surface dangled countless helictites, sculpted from calcium deposits over the centuries and bunched together in clusters, each sprouting its own bunch of fangs and spiral tentacle-like projections. Driven by his fixated obsession to claim the hitherto elusive prize, and sensing that prize at his fingertips, he pressed on into the darker, cooler depths, and was rewarded with a pungent whiff of petrol, yes, petrol, no mistaking. With no difficulty he also detected the smoky scent of charred wood and that other smoky – if stale – smell of the ten-a-cent cigars on sale in every market. He squeezed the button on his torch and moved the beam about, picking out calcium gullies and alleyways that forked away from the main cavern; and as he advanced so the shadows in the recesses drew aside like curtains. Now the tunnel curved to the right, now it descended deeper into the earth. He edged his way past rock barriers jutting from the walls which drew inwards, and the ceiling narrowed to become a crevice so deep and narrow that not even his torch light could penetrate it. He skirted thigh-high slabs of limestone that a more superstitious mind might have likened to ancient sarcophagi. Now the cave widened and the gash in the ceiling opened out and flattened into a pockmarked surface which, as he continued cautiously, began to droop lower until it hung inches above the floor. He crouched down and put his torch beam through the gap, and realised that the cave continued beyond. He could see vague edges. Fallen boulders, except that as his eyes adjusted to the dimness one of the boulders took on an unlikely rectangular contour, which, when his torchlight hit it, turned into a grey steel box the size of a small suitcase, lying on its side in an attitude of hurried abandonment. Anticipation quivered down his arm and into his hand, dislodging the torchlight from his find. He got on hands and knees and with rifle in one hand and torch in the other, crawled forward along a natural trough. Another vague object beckoned from the periphery, and his torch went to it, and – hey, presto! – the mechanical bulges and bright red paint of a small petrol generator tipped on its side and shoved up against the wall.

'Yes!' he exclaimed, hitting his head on the low ceiling in his excitement. He swivelled the torch back to the steel box and scrambled up to it. 'Viking Valiant,' he whispered, reading off the silver plaque set into the chassis, and he picked out three dials on the semicircular metre-band display. 'The transmitter?' he asked himself, fully expecting verification from some part of his being. Yet that part was reluctant to provide absolute confirmation, despite the evidence before his eyes. He hunted over the box and discovered no less than seven more dials evenly spaced upon a grey panel. 'Oscillator,' he declared with conviction, and he rotated the variable frequency dial and cocked his head like a thief cracking the code to a safe. When no reply was forthcoming, he grunted, and fluttered his fingers across to the next dial, and turned it, expecting at least a click. But the box made no sound, so he rolled it over. This side was smooth and featureless, and he brushed away the sand before rolling it again. A wire mesh below which ran a series of sockets stretched across this side; the fourth wall featured a narrow panel of dials and sockets along one edge. Still kneeling, he bent over the prize. It must be the transmitter. Why else would a Viking Valiant radio box be hiding in the depths of the cave? Yet he could scarcely believe he finally had possession of the rebels' treasure. Hereafter, the nature and course of the

143

conflict would alter dramatically, and a brighter future was already beaming at him.

As if cradling a child he conveyed the transmitter out of the cave and set it gently on the path. It was touch and go whether he spent a few extra minutes with his prize. But he was eager to present her – for it was now a she – for General Simón Levi's pleasure and abundant gratitude.

'I have the matter. The matter is secured,' he spoke reverently into the radio. He discovered a profound regard for Radio Venceremos' propaganda box. He could have shouted out triumphantly, but that, somehow, before such distinguished company, would be the uncouth thing to do.

'What about the rebels?' Anastasio cracked back through static.

'Kill any you have, and stand down. We have what we came for.'

* * *

From the arid slopes of Chaparrastique, Jasmine Gavidia gazed across the land as the helicopter climbed into the twilight, its blades glinting like snapper scales. It had been a close call, a narrow escape and Serafin was in mourning. His darling transmitter in the hands of the enemy. She shaded her eyes and followed the helicopter as it levelled, swung towards the north east, dipped its nose and surged across the sky. Left thumb over right thumb she sank the red button into the handheld detonator. Brilliant light flooded the sky and vanished. A thunderclap pummelled her eardrums. She watched the helicopter break in two and plummet towards the cotton field. Before it landed, she had turned and was jogging down the slope to the village of Las Placitas where Leonel, Serafin and the others waited for her. Novice subterfuge or not, her plan had worked.

144

CHAPTER FOURTEEN

ANASTASIO MENESSES WAS BACK at the Pollo Campero diner, spreading the tabloids on the table, away from the hue and cry over Santamaria's demise that was gripping Military Headquarters. A waitress with a pony-tail and a familiar face swooped in to take his order.

'Cafecito negro, por fa',' he muttered, and to eat he would have the full breakfast, please, and yes, a side order of tortillas, thank you.

She was off, leaving her smile and her floral scent on his mind. He turned to his papers. He couldn't recall having previously seen the photo of the youthful Sinisterra which was sharing the front page of La Prensa with a colour portrait of the highly decorated Colonel. SAF's General Horacio Rodriguez had promptly dispatched a team of accident investigators to the crash site. Once in possession of the "facts" he had called a press conference in the Hotel Atlacatl, and this is what he had to say: 'Our Helicopter Squadron is maintained in tip-top condition. Preceding every flight, our team of dedicated American-trained engineers carries out a meticulous routine of maintenance checks coupled with a thorough search of the aircraft. Moreover, the pilot has a regime of checks to complete of which he informs Base Control and duly records in the onboard logbook before takeoff. And that logbook, ladies and gentlemen of the press, recovered from the crash site, confirms that all the checks were performed to the letter, as do the records held at Ilopango and San Miguel. Base Control received no distress signal from the helicopter. We have decoded the black box and again no indication of any alarm was recorded prior to the explosion, or indeed at any other time during the flight. There is no question of mechanical failure. This brings me to how one of our newest helicopters burst into flames in midair. From the crash site our investigators recovered the remains of an explosive device. I can assure you of two things: one: that bomb was not present on the helicopter before the colonel boarded. Two: airport personnel at San Miguel have assisted in our investigation by providing written declarations in which several describe seeing Colonel Santamaria board the helicopter carrying a metal box in his arms. It appears from these statements that the colonel announced that this box was in fact the very radio transmitter used by the rebels to broadcast their lies and propaganda. Given our findings, we shall be seeking compensation from the military for the loss we have sustained due to their negligence.'

Horacio Rodríguez had, from a great height, dumped on the army's camp. And over the page La Prensa had more: General Simón Levi had called his own press conference to answer Rodríguez's allegation. 'We have no dispute with the findings of our SAF friends,' Levi conceded with uncharacteristic humility, even if he delegated the blame: 'I have identified the officer in charge of the operation and he has been relieved of duty with no right to pension or benefits. This morning I spoke by telephone to el Presidente de la República, and he is of the opinion that following the state funeral to honour the late Colonel, this matter can be brought to a close.'

Such an admission went only half way to appeasing a wily General Rodríguez, who insisted that the matter of compensation had yet to be addressed. That was yesterday. Today full appeasement was on its way: Washington undertakes to fly in a replacement helicopter from Panama. So there you have it, mused Anastasio. Same old routine: we fuck up; Washington consoles with a Vietnam hand-me-down.

The scented waitress set breakfast before Anastasio and then stood back and shifted all her weight on to one leg, accentuating one rather curvy hip. 'Is there anything else I can get for you, sir?'

'I'm sure it's not on the menu,' he probed, pulling his number-one smile. She promptly coloured, and her smile just held. 'Perhaps later,' he said, 'Thank you.'

Now, where was I? Ah, here it is: The assassination of Colonel Rubén Santamaria has rocked the nation, and sent shockwaves throughout the Salvadoran Army. It is the strongest message yet from the guerrillas who have succeeded in eliminating the most effective commander our military has ever fielded. No other man of Santamaria's rank has been prepared to muddy his hands with the lower echelons, and his untimely demise has left a void that will be hard to fill.

Anastasio took a sip of coffee, and pondered this assertion. He had known the Colonel since their attendance at military school, where *el tandón* had united them in its brotherhood. As a major, Anastasio ranked two rungs down, which placed him out of the bidding. But Santamaria had slated him for lieutenant colonel – verbally at any rate. Now, with him gone, gone too were Anastasio's hopes of promotion. Loyalty to Batallón Liberación had depended on Santamaria's unique style of command. None of the smooth-handed, soft bellied, office-bound candidates who had rushed to apply for the newly-vacant position were capable of commanding anywhere near the same respect or loyalty. Which effectively spelt the end of Batallón Liberación as he knew it. And the end of an era! Now, without Santamaria, the once mighty Battalion would go the way of the others: an undisciplined rabble that in its spare time traded munitions for cash in the back rooms of the city's furniture stores.

It was now time to look after Number One. Time to recruit such disenfranchised souls as ex-captains Guillermo Sinisterra and his old running mate Trinidad Llull.

147

Sunsin Rivera was executed military style. This, despite pleas by Jasmine to exonerate him on grounds of Christianity, pleas that were spurned by embittered comrades.

Trussed up, wrists behind back, he was dragged screaming across a glade of eucalyptus trees by Adrian, Emilio and four others who bound him to a stump of a tree while he pleaded for clemency, pity, compassion. He had a wife, four children; he had money, whatever they wanted.

The firing squad comprised nine men and one woman, all rookies, recent recruits selected to give them their first taste at spilling blood. Their noses and mouths covered by red scarves, they snapped to attention on Emilio's command. Leonel strode up to Sunsin and waved a blindfold in his face, but when Sunsin insisted on tearfully beseeching his *comandante* for forgiveness instead of paying attention to the blindfold Leonel took up position at the sideline with the rest of the spectators. Jasmine wondered why it was that she felt compelled to witness such unforgiving brutally. Guilt that as a consequence of her subterfuge, Sunsin stood to lose his life?

The firing squad levelled rifles. Sunsin fell silent and gazed about him for the last time, casting stunned eyes at his executioners before hanging his head and waiting for his own death. The shooting popped. Sunsin threw back his head, screwing up a face that flooded with deep colour. He slumped in his bindings and his head dropped forward, dislodging his cap into the grass. Leonel strode over to inspect the firing squad's work. He grabbed a handful of Sunsin's greying hair and yanked up his face.

'The son of a bitch is still alive,' Anabela muttered beside Jasmine. '*Tiro de gracia,*' she yelled at Leonel, and was immediately chorused by all except Jasmine.

Leonel let the head flop back, drew his revolver and fired point-blank into the side of Sunsin's head.

CHAPTER FIFTEEN

'FUNDAMENTAL.' David rapped his knuckles on the bar. 'We never, *ever* let slip our identities to the employer,' he railed. 'You broker my jobs, I broker yours. The *patrón* and we never meet; anonymity for both sides *at all costs.*'

'Be reasonable, David. There's a war on,' his brother Alejandro reminded unnecessarily. 'I'm raking it in, got eight contracts lined up this week. Don't want to be in this game forever, do you? Make what we can while it's up for grabs, which means adapting *imaginatively* to increased demand. In our line it's not like we can go advertise for new staff, is it? A family business, that's what this is.' He poured two large measures of Botrán rum from a smoky bottle. The ice chimed as the liquid swelled towards the brims. 'Davy, this is strictly a courier job; no guns, no knives, no endless hours skulking in shit waiting for the mark to show.' He pressed the mist-clad glass on David and waited for him to take a sip. 'All you do is carry the stuff to Honduras,' he resumed, switching to his reasonable voice. 'Drop off in San Pedro Sula, return, and hey bloody presto! – it's payday again.' He put a hand on David's shoulder and led him through to the balcony. David squinted up at the huge dome of San Salvador's cathedral rising above the city into a purple-grey dusk.

'What's the load?' he asked eventually, more compliant now.

'It's your job, so I suppose you ought to know. *Coca.*'

'Why doesn't the supplier run it?'

'Building up staff, you know how it is. Needs to get rolling first.'

'Staff?' David took a thoughtful kiss of rum. 'The guy's military then.'

He guessed right. Military associates routinely spoke of staffing their operations from internal networks. But these days some, like Anastasio Menesses, had supplemented their teams with disgruntled ex-agents and civilian operators. Besides, Anastasio was no pushover. Engaging civvies doubled as a security measure. The civilian foolhardy enough to double-cross him would turn several military guns on himself, whereas should the double-crossers rise from within the army, Anastasio's options of recovering lost assets were limited.

'We don't need to know, just as long as his money's green, right?' Alejandro said, conceding as much as his junior partner needed to know.

'But he'll know me,' David pointed out, 'He'll see my face, won't he?'

Alejandro downed his triple-shot in one and sucked a sharp intake of breath. 'He won't suspect you to be the courier unless you tell him, which you won't. You'll make a point of reminding him that we don't meet our employers, tell him you're making the collection, but that the actual run will be undertaken by the courier. Okay, so it's not the most glamorous of jobs,' Alejandro admitted. 'But it's *safe money, bro*. Take the wife. A trip to Honduras and a free night in a swish hotel – hey, Maria would love that. Just because you plonked a bun in her oven doesn't mean you got to tie a knot in your dick.' Alejandro nudged his brother and made a series of suggestive pumping actions with a clenched fist, all designed to snap David from his glum mood. 'A plush air-conditioned hotel room with a view over the city, no worries about waking neighbours with all that huffing and puffing. Go on, take her with you. Besides, you'll need someone you can trust when you get to El Poy.'

* * *

With a supportive hand from her husband, Maria climbed on to the front passenger seat of the Toyota Landcruiser, and when she was settled, his hand played over her tummy's expectant curve. In the novelty of pregnancy she had treated herself to no less than seven ample ankle-length frocks, one for each day, and today she wore the pastel blue sprinkled with daisies, and a pair of Italian flat-soled sandals from *Simán* that David had bought for her only yesterday.

'Does it show?' she asked demurely. Not for the first time David marvelled at how she could have fallen for his rough-edged self. He was prouder of her business administration degree than she was. If he thought she might apply that degree to the betterment of his and Alejandro's business efforts, he might let her fully in on them. Being an ex-uni girl she wasn't averse to a little dabble with the loco-weed when the fancy took her, but if she ever got wind of smuggled kids, she'd absolutely hit the roof. She'd abandon him. So Alejandro had insisted she be allowed in on the loco-weed only, but kept in the dark on the more sinister trade.

Trailing a dust cloud they roared north. As Alejandro had promised, they were waved on at each National Guard checkpoint. They gained Chalatenango Province and embarked on a series of climbs through pine-ridged escarpments. An impressive three hours after leaving San Salvador they began their descent from La Palma towards the frontier. They came off the cordillera and levelled out along a stretch of deserted road that ran the final kilometres to the frontier town of El Poy. It was on this road that David pulled to the verge, jumped down and consulted his wristwatch. Almost half past one. He hurried round to the tailgate, whacked it open, and grimaced as he hefted the first of three hard shell suitcases to the gravel.

'Gun's in the glove pocket,' he grunted. 'Key in the ignition. Anyone approaches, drive off or shoot. I'll be back, two hours max.'

Maria nodded and slid across to the driver's seat. 'Take care, *mi amor.*'

151

'Those border guards won't get a sniff of me,' he retorted, up-beat.

'For our child's sake,' was her final plea which was enough to launch second thoughts. But he quashed those thoughts before they could become a distraction.

David lugged the suitcase across a roadside ditch, found the farmers' trail and headed into a fringe of pine trees and beyond on to steeply rising farmland enclosed by barbed wire fences. At first he skirted these with relative ease, but the higher he climbed the more uneven the terrain became. He slipped and fell into a seated position, and slid down a pebbled bank with his heavy cargo on his lap before puffing his way up the grassy rise on the other side. Making for ever higher ground, but avoiding ridges for fear of silhouetting on the skyline, he slogged up hill while bracing winds tried to wrench him off stride, and he slit his eyes against blasts of grit. He waded across a brook, hooting at the icy water pouring into his trainers, squelched up a meadow and paused short of the crest for a badly needed breather. Ahead of him, puffs of cloud clung to the flanks of intensely blue mountain peaks. To his left he could see the main road slicing through a cluster of tin-roofed shacks that was El Poy, on between the squat blue and white Immigration Control on this side and Customs Offices the far side, and on again through two blue border gates set a good fifty strides apart. A couple of heavy-goods trucks had pulled up alongside Customs. Ambling money changers with waist pouches and snack-sellers with large aluminium bowls beckoned to travellers while shirtless kids pestered rucksack laden gringos for coins.

David spared a thought for Maria – alone on the deserted road with two suitcases packed with sachets of finest Colombian, and if the authorities or the bandits were to get curious, they'd soon discover that it wasn't coffee. Leaning into the biting wind he sidled off the track and followed a gully that developed into a fast descending ravine where he began to slide on the loose scree and found himself being borne along giddily downhill and into the darkness of the pine forest. Here the ravine petered out and he relied on the slope of the land to usher him towards the road. Having skirted the legitimate border crossing, he was now in Honduran territory, in the department of Ocotepeque.

He selected a particularly grand white pine, intending to rely on its height over its neighbouring trees for navigational purposes when he returned with the second and third cases. He knelt beside it and, shielding his eyes from the clusters of needle-like leaves, slid the first suitcase beneath the lower branches and tucked it up against the base of the trunk. He flicked open his penknife and carved a capital "X" into the grey, fissured bark, and then crawled out from beneath the branches. He arched his back and stretched, before checking his progress by his watch. Two-fifty-three. Running late. Two more runs to go.

* * *

By the time David arrived knackered at the Landcruiser to collect the third and final suitcase, the sun was slipping behind a crest, and a solitary Maria had the radio on.

'The border closes in twenty-five minutes,' she warned him, not that he needed reminding.

He flung himself on to the rear seat and lay on his back, hand over his brow while he recovered his breath with minutes he could hardly afford to waste. Maria turned in her seat, removed his hand from his forehead and dabbed away the sweat with a handkerchief.

'I'll meet you on the other side,' he told her, when at last his breathing had regulated and he was feeling a bit cold.

She agreed, clearly relieved to be getting off the lonely road before nightfall.

David launched himself into the woods one last time, ears tuned to the Landcruiser crunching the gravel as it accelerated towards the Immigration authorities and Honduras.

Once he had nestled the final suitcase beside the other two at the base of his chosen pine, he slumped down on the carpet of leaves and lay flat on his back. He flicked the switch on his watch. Seven-forty-one. Grabbing a handy branch he hoisted himself to his feet and, with his shirt cooling on his skin, hobbled into the road. A dazzling light smacked the left side of his face, and he squinted in its direction. Perhaps fifty to sixty metres away, between him and the frontier gate, the Landcruiser was parked at the wayside – as expected. What was unexpected was the police jeep double-parked alongside it. He could make out men, uniforms, and torchlight.

'Honduran police,' David muttered. He managed to break into a jog, heading for the knot of uniforms who clearly had nothing better to do than pester young women in Landcruisers but were never around when needed. 'Hey, *caballeros*, what's all the fuss?' he yelled, trying for jocular but sounding stressed.

All torches swung to him and he raised an arm to shield his eyes.

'You the husband?' the sergeant enquired from behind the glare of his torch. 'Wouldn't catch me leaving the wife in a lonely spot like this, not at night, not any time. Bandits, these hills' – the torch swung off David's face to move to and fro quite pointlessly about the hills – 'are crawling with them. Come down here and find a pretty woman alone in a smart car...' He stood back and straightened, allowing David to guess the rest.

Behind the concerned sergeant, two bored juniors were angling light through the rear windows, checking out the luggage compartment.

'I told the officer you'd gone for a pee,' Maria piped up, nodding her head significantly.

'When nature calls who can resist her?' David bestowed a tepid smile on the sergeant and strutted round to the front passenger door and climbed in beside Maria.

'Where've you come from?' the sergeant asked, examining the pages of Maria's well-worn passport.

'El Salvador,' she informed him with habitual civility where David in his current frame of mind might have added, where

154

else *tonto*?

'The border's been closed for at least an hour, señora. Please, explain where you've been since?' the sergeant came back with heaps of professional civility.

'We stopped for a bite to eat,' Maria told him. 'I'd made sandwiches for the journey.'

The sergeant handed the passport back to Maria.

Painfully aware that his particular travel document lacked the immigration stamp Maria's had, David held his breath. But fortune smiled because with a wave and instruction to have a safe journey, they were released. Unlike the mortar-cratered roads of El Salvador, Honduras boasted broad highways of smooth tarmac, and as the Landcruiser glided along the unlit kilometres between the frontier and the village of Ocotopeque, David laid his uneasy head on the headrest and shut his eyes.

'Where are the cases?' Maria asked.

'Had to leave them beside a tree.' He turned in his seat to look back.

'I can still see police torches,' she said, glancing at the rear-view mirror.

'Me too.'

'What do we do?' She reached across and switched off the radio.

'Park up when we get to the outskirts of Ocotepeque Town. I'll leg it back for the stuff.'

Maria pulled up beside a prairie of swaying grass. David set off at a hard jog back towards the frontier, but it took far longer to locate his white pine than it should have, despite its superior height, which was not so much in evidence in the darkness. Eventually he did track it down, and with a sigh of relief got down on weary hands and knees and crawled beneath the bottom branches. Although his torch readily picked out the carved capital X, it failed to reveal any suitcases. His heart was already buffeting against his ribs as a result of jogging. Unrelated to jogging was his stomach knotting up into his throat. The mattress of pine leaves was bare. Bare! This *is* the right tree, he insisted, revisiting the X with a tremulous torch beam. He sent his hands scampering over ground, beneath fallen leaves, up and around the base of the pine. 'Where are you?' he whimpered. He began scraping the turf with his fingernails as if he might discover the cases buried with the roots. 'No!' – his mind already weighing the appalling consequences of this loss – 'No! No! No! No!' – his hands now patting the tree bark while he had a notion of the questions Alejandro would have for him, not to mention those the *patrón* was liable to put in his own particularly unsavoury style. All three cases had gone, and thin air had played no part in their disappearance. At last his frantic hands joined together and rested as if in supplication at the foot of the big tree, and he subsided, flat on his stomach, peering into the damp carpet of prickly leaves. '*Catracho* Police bastards!'

CHAPTER SIXTEEN

July 1985

LEONEL DID HIS BEST to persuade Jasmine to consider her enrolment in Campamento Sandino's three month training course as much a reward for her plan to rid The Cause of Santamaria as a resource for developing her unexploited reserves of talent for guerrilla thinking. But I could train in-house, she suggested. You would inevitably be called to perform tasks. But what about my couriering duties? It's taken care of, was his reply. So, with assigned codename *Xochil* and feeling like she'd been lumbered, she packed and bussed to Nicaragua.

Amid the disarray of Managua's international bus station an athletic woman with her hair trussed up in a bandana was holding aloft a cardboard plaque bearing the most secret codename scribbled in bright lipstick. Jasmine singled her out and claimed to be Xochil. The woman was Mariana Turcios, an instructor who told Jasmine to wait. Within minutes eight strangers – four male and four female – also claiming to be Xochil turned up, after which they reverted to real names.

A minibus across country to the coastal hamlet of Potosi, and a two-day hike over volcanic fields and plantation-scattered prairie to a dais-like plateau in the rainforests of Chinandega Province – rainforests that, to believe Mariana, who had the relentless energy of a robot, were second only to Brazil's in terms of flora diversity. Arriving midmorning at Campamento Sandino, muddy and ready to drop, they were

157

promptly treated to a guided tour of their accommodation by Mariana.

'Intakes arrive every six weeks and overlap with the previous intake,' she informed them, adding that identifying intakes was a simple matter of Juniors and Seniors. 'Junior girls dormitory,' she declared, and like a matron sending a rascal early to bed, thrust a finger at a rectangular structure of clay-block walls topped with sandbags, and upon the sandbags rested a brace of cedar wood beams that supported a mesh of dried palm branches. Perhaps the women freshers were being shown special favour, because the other three dormitories were simple marquees of green tarpaulin. The Main Hall, doubling as a refectory, was an open-sided pavilion, its palm-thatch roof held up by eucalyptus pillars and rafters. On a couple of schoolroom blackboards were pinned sketches of urban maps cluttered with scribbles and arrows pointing at nothing that Jasmine could make out. Seating and desks came as six rows of timber planks alternately elevated on truncated log-legs, with an aisle down the middle. Along one side of the hall hung an off-white cotton banner on which "*Escuela de Comandantes Heroes de la Patria*" was proclaimed in communistic-red. A male instructor in navy blue overalls was imparting a lesson to a dozen similarly uniformed students who turned to ogle the newcomers and received a dressing-down from their instructor for having succumbed to distraction.

Mariana led her party swiftly past the Main Hall. 'Our *campamento* is remote,' she assured them, just in case they hadn't cottoned on from the protracted travel required. 'Our watch can see across the plains to the ocean in the south, to Cosiguina Volcano in the north – and to the Gulf of Fonseca where the borders of El Salvador, Honduras and Nicaragua converge.' She shrugged her shoulders. 'Given our common history with Nicaragua we are tolerated, if not condoned, by the Sandinista government. The threat comes not from the armed forces but from the Contras – the American-supplied criminals paid to overthrow Nicaragua's democratically elected government. Meanwhile the Contras, with their ties to drug trafficking, use supply planes generously provided by Washington to fly cocaine into the US. Last year the NICA air force shot down a Contra supply plane, and the pilot was captured together with highly sensitive documents that reveal the gringos were illegally selling arms to Iran in order to fund the Contras. Imperialists' minds, corrupted to the point of insanity, continue to dream up perfect failures. Remember their Bay of Pigs debacle?' Mumbled agreement from the audience. 'These days the Nica-army is pushing the Contras back to their camps in Honduras, and the government is exposing the gringo treachery. Our camp here is not a priority for anyone. Please, introduce yourselves to our chefs – Alfonso and his daughter Ruth.'

Beneath the branches of an old silk cotton a pot-bellied scruff in a chef's hat and his trim teenage daughter in a head scarf and ankle-length skirt paused from their labours to offer welcome.

'This kitchen is *their domain*,' Mariana stated severely. 'No-one but the chefs are to tamper with food preparation.' Their domain: rising flames from a fire under a makeshift hob of even-sided rocks, an assortment of earthenware flagons and stainless steel urns, a row of giant baskets of green wicker, a huge plastic tub of water and floating leaves; and running above it all a sagging clothesline clutching strings of garlic, onion and a variety of wood, calabash, and coconut shell utensils.

The tour over, they were released, but only to fetch bucket-loads of water from a stream that wasn't half as close as Mariana had promised.

They bathed.

They slept.

They breakfasted on strong black coffee and fruit salad.

General Americo Merino, a solidly built man from Santiago de Cuba provided by the Cuban Revolutionary Army to direct this clandestine training outfit, delivered an up-beat induction in the Main Hall, letting his new scholars know just how very fortunate they were to be here, that only those who showed particular promise received instruction in the purpose-built compound of Campamento Sandino; the rest must make do with the extensive but not as comprehensive preparation imparted at local level. He cracked on with a moving dedicatory to a list of fallen comrades who had participated in various armed struggles throughout Central and South America. He celebrated their feats with the same fervour that Jasmine had seen in television evangelists. She listened as the General described in nauseating detail hideous methods of torture and execution employed by Washington-backed military governments throughout the Americas; he went on to stress the need for revolutionary participation. 'Those of us wanting to see justice upheld in our national territories must do whatever we are able.' He concluded the induction by running through Campamento rules, and inviting the students to don Wellingtons which could be issued from the store because, as he pointed out needlessly, much of the forest floor was exceedingly muddy.

The camp was staffed by four Cuban military personnel and two retired Sandinista generals, and classes started promptly at seven a.m., Monday to Friday. A Guerrilla Manual, Author: Adonai Limeño, launched each chapter on the back of a root definition: *Chapter One – The Urban Guerrilla: A friend who, through non-conventional means, fights against imperialist imposition or despot governments. A political revolutionary, a patriot, a liberator of peoples subjected to tyranny. His battlefields are psychological, urban and political.*

Jasmine's enthusiasm for examining yet more of Adonai's literature was matched by the devotion with which she submitted to after-class-swatting instead of crashing exhausted in the dormitory with her colleagues. To her mind, by digesting the guerrilla legend's works she was digesting his very thoughts and feelings, and she was stirred by the definition that launched the second chapter, because it appealed to her own moral convictions:

160

The urban guerrilla differs radically from the criminal. The criminal benefits personally from his actions and attacks indiscriminately without distinguishing between exploiter and the exploited. The urban guerrilla, however, realising that he may never benefit personally from his actions rather that such procured benefit may be reaped by others, seeks a political goal, exclusively attacking governments, government forces and those of los imperialistas.

Similarly, the urban guerrilla differs from the terrorist. Terrorists, whether governmental or insurgent-led, direct their attacks towards civilians, indiscriminately wiping out innocents, showing no regard for the lives they purport to seek to protect and enhance. On the other hand, the urban guerrilla's targets are exclusively military and infrastructural.

Jasmine would later claim that the fourth morning at Campamento Sandino changed her life. A man wrapped in a blanket of Izalco weave over peasant's cottons, who, if she'd passed in the street she would have taken for an old farm labourer, opened the lesson by introducing himself simply as Adonai.

Jasmine stargazed.

Adonai Limeño was not a resident member of staff, rather a visiting lecturer. But his weekly two-day visits were eagerly anticipated, even drawing other staff from their commitments elsewhere to sit in on his lectures. Perhaps his regular trips to Nicaragua explained his frequent absences from his column back in El Salvador's Morazán Province. But here in Campamento Sandino, Jasmine worshipped at his altar, interrogating him during lectures, digesting his meticulous explanations, and seeking him out after class to grill him about his column's push-back and defeat of the National Guard that had led to the liberation of Morazán. His patience was immeasurable, and his unhurried blinks disguised the easy way his ancient eyes fluttered into your very soul. He singled Jasmine out one evening and bestowed on her a volume of his Reliable Intelligence Manual. Swelling with pride she dictated a message to herself which he obligingly scribbled and signed inside the front cover.

She was in love.

Working their way through Adonai's Guerrilla Manual, the other instructors explored such chapters as *Logistics of Urban Warfare; Territorial Knowledge; Armed Propaganda; Popular Support;* and *War of Nerves,* all of which were reinforced by field exercises where Juniors were put through their paces in the use, adaptation, speed-dismantling, and cleaning of a range of weaponry, and given grounding in the components, construction, and application of all explosives known to man. And Chapter 101. Jasmine loved Chapter 101, or The Debate, as it was more generally referred to. After offering several sub-chapters on *How to Counter the Advantage Air Strikes Award to Conventional Air Forces,* and ending on an inconclusive upside-down question mark, the author challenged readers to write their own chapter in place of the question mark. Friday afternoons were given over to debating the issue. These debates were so hotly contested that the casual observer might have doubted whether both sides were seeking the same outcome: a viable solution to a common problem.

As if they didn't have enough to fill their time, what with intensely methodical classes, physically demanding field exercises, and revision sessions, the students were set the task of carving their own replica rifles out of rough timber. 'To emotionally engage with a weapon that you will burn once your term here is complete,' Americo explained to his bemused audience, adding that this would help those of you who do not wish to pursue a career in the revolutionary army to "psychologically disengage from arms-dependence once the political objective has been achieved." This rather superfluous task provided light entertainment as the lack of carpentry skills soon became evident and sculptures resembling batons, guitars or abstract art began to emerge.

Another addition to their burdensome work load was the requirement to gather the ingredients for all meals, which entailed raiding maize plantations as long as these were situated well away from Campamento Sandino. Manuela Rendón, a comedienne from El Salvador's Eastern Zone, who had a gift for turning the most mundane event into hilarity, became Jasmine's soul-mate. After Jasmine's objection to what she bluntly described to Americo as "theft", she and Manuela were granted dispensation to gather avocado pears, lemon grass, and berries, all of which grew wild. On one of their wanderings they were drawn to a spread of delicate mauve at the foot of the plateau which, on inspection, turned out to be a soccer-pitch-sized meadow of mistflower, and while picking their way through it instead of hunting for ingredients for tomorrow's vegetable broth, they happened upon a vine-choked gully that cut a straight course of over ten kilometres to pass by Cosiguina's sloping southern flank. This discovery was to prove fortuitous by the end of the three month term.

* * *

In his rented office down a side street off Santa Tecla's market square, Anastasio was contemplating an appalling turn of events. Close to bankrupt at the first turn! What's more, Trinidad's contact – the courier – may have gone to ground. It was anyone's guess how close the kinship was between them. In a display of contrition, Trinidad had left ten minutes ago promising to make the courier's sister pay the debt with her life, unless she came up with the money or the consignment, both of which, to Anastasio's enraged mind, were highly unlikely. So it was with raised eyebrows that he looked up from behind his desk when the flack-jacketed guard ushered the courier's messenger into the office.

'Too ashamed to face me himself, eh?' Anastasio suggested and leaned back in the swivel chair, hands interlinked over his chest while he waited for the visitor to deliver himself of his patrón's bunch of lies.

'I have a message…from the courier,' David mumbled, unassuming.

'I'd be interested to learn what that is,' said Anastasio. He listened to the message, nodding at each excuse that tumbled from the humble messenger's mouth. When all excuses had been conveyed together with the courier's most sincere apologies on the back of an undertaking to replenish the lost items as soon as he was able, Anastasio kept silence. But the simmering rage now shaking his hands erupted. Leaping to his feet he hurled the desk with everything on it right across the room, sending paperwork, lamp, telephone and work tray into the air and the desk crashing against the wall. 'Fifty thousand dollars of stock and your boss lost it all?' he screamed. 'Who the *fuck, fuck, fuck* does he think he's dealing with?'

Behind a rainfall of loose A4 sheets David stood his ground, holding up peaceable hands. 'Señor, it was not entirely the courier's fault. Those *Catracho* police caught him. They're to blame, actually.'

Anastasio struck him open palmed across one cheek and followed with a backhander across the other. 'Do you take me for an imbecile?' he bellowed. 'The *Catracho* police were doing their job. Your man clearly wasn't doing his. So I *refuse* to lose that amount of dollars. Understand? I *refuse!*'

David was stroking a reddening cheek. 'It couldn't be helped,' he replied.

Anastasio grabbed David's collar and hurled him against the wall. 'Listen to me carefully,' he said, grinding his voice to keep it steady. 'I contracted your boss because Trinidad assured me he was competent and discreet. With my stock in his butter-fingers he has shown neither of those qualities.'

'It couldn't be helped,' David persisted with a composure that was supplanting Anastasio's exasperation with confusion.

He lugged David away from the wall only to slam him back. 'Tell me, Señor Whoever-you-are, when exactly does your patrón intend to reimburse me?'

'Well,' David began, 'he would need a month or so to replenish that sort of consignment. Of course, if you were in a hurry, perhaps a lower-grade product could be acquired sooner.'

'Lower-grade product,' Anastasio mimicked. 'What the fuck are you talking about? You take me for an amateur.' He narrowed his eyes. Something was definitely not kosher. The servile manner was slipping and his answers were absurdly assertive for a mere servant's. At last the rage subsided to a manageable level, and he recovered control of his faculties. He strolled over to gaze out of the window, kicking aside the upturned table. He looked out across a sloping lawn at a line of cars parked end-to-end along the kerb. He needed a moment to collect his thoughts. A courier remains anonymous, screened by his messenger. A nameless courier with a not particularly large consignment, but enough to fetch a pretty penny if broken down and sold to your average battalion or your less than average university party. 'Where is the courier now?' he asked without turning round.

'I don't know, señor.'

Of course you don't. And if you did, you're not saying. What will the sister tell Trinidad? Even if we find the courier, I can't *disappear* him or I'll lose my money forever. Got to send him a persuasive message, one that will prompt him to return what's mine to me lest I devote my extensive resources to visit calamity upon him. As he pondered, he cast his eyes appreciatively over a black Toyota Landcruiser. Through the open window he saw the profile of a young woman seated in the front passenger seat.

'Tell me, Messenger Boy, is that your Landcruiser parked outside?' he asked.

'It's my *patrón*'s.'

'Your *patrón*'s. I see. And who's the woman in your patrón's car?'

'What woman?' David made his first fatal reply. Alarm bells ringing, Anastasio turned to face him. 'Oh...that woman... She's the courier's...childminder. He sent me to take her shopping,' David stammered, digging himself deeper into his hole.

'Guard,' Anastasio barked.

165

The guard stepped in.

'Parked in the street you will find a black Landcruiser. Inside it you will find a young woman. Please escort her to my office.'

After a nod the guard about turned to carry out the order.

Anastasio to David: 'Can I be frank with you?' No answer. 'I'm reluctant to believe any of your excuses. I want you to be clear in your mind that I hold your *patrón* personally responsible for my loss. Had he done his job properly, I would by now be a wealthy man instead of broke. Moreover, I would be earning interest on my money. However, being fair-minded, I have decided to allow him one opportunity to rectify his mistake. Today is Monday, yes?' Still no acknowledgement. 'He has until Thursday, nine p.m. to deliver into my hands fifty thousand American dollars in bills – used or unused, it doesn't matter to me. In the meantime I will take from him a substitute for the lost interest I mentioned. Do you get my meaning?'

It was not clear if he did before the guard interrupted, ushering Maria through the door. The guard was about to leave but Anastasio, who was already appraising the girl close up, bid him stay put. Her profile had correctly suggested alluring good looks. Beneath a forehead puckered with questions, brown eyes queried the messenger.

'*Que pasa aqui?*' she asked softly, but David wasn't replying, so she quizzed Anastasio. 'What's going on?'

'You tell me,' Anastasio proposed. 'This man' – a nod in David's direction – 'tells me that you are his *patrón*'s wife. Is this accurate?'

Clearly taken aback, she sought to engage David's eyes, but he was staring out through the window. Meanwhile Anastasio observed the couple's every movement. What *patrón* gives his servant a luxury car in which to run errands? As far as he was aware, only chauffeurs drove their bosses' vehicles, and rarely without the boss or members of his family aboard. Servants were awarded old bangers that would hardly attract the

166

attention of ransom-seeking kidnappers who might use them as Trojan horses to access the wealthy owner's mansion. But a Landcruiser might be a courier's vehicle of choice for those journeys where speed over rough roads was of the essence.

'Are you the wife of this man's *patron*?' he asked again. 'Because if I think you might be, I will have to keep you until he returns what he owes me.'

Finally his question prompted the remotest shake of her head.

'Cuff the man and drive him to his house,' he ordered the guard. 'If no-one knows him there, *disappear* him. The girl stays here.'

'She does not,' David blurted, dropping the servant act altogether, and taking hold of her wrist as if to whisk her away.

Anastasio whipped out his pistol and rammed the nozzle into David's neck while the guard cuffed his hands behind his back.

* * *

When Anastasio was alone with Maria he locked the door and pocketed the key. He yanked the leg of the desk and stood it upright. Then he sat on the desk and beckoned for her to approach.

'What are you going to do?' she asked warily, staying rooted to her spot. 'You said I could go if I wasn't the *patrón's* wife.'

'No,' he contradicted politely. 'What I said was *if I think* that you might be, I would keep you. And I *do* think you may very well be his wife. But listen now; you haven't a thing to worry about, long as you tell me the truth. Are we clear?'

She nodded.

'The courier mentioned you ran into one or two snags in Honduras,' he lied, idly spinning the pistol on his middle finger.

She nodded again. 'The *Catracho* police…stopped us. Took everything.'

'That's my girl,' he purred, his suspicions confirmed. He caressed Maria's cheek and his thumb sought to prise open her pursed lips. 'Do you sing? he asked, no longer in temper but with a familiar exhilaration that harkened back to Santamaria's Hammer and Whatever missions. He and the lads, reaping the spoils of war, would lead the youngest girls into a nearby plantation. For unfathomable reasons each girl sang a hymn while the lads took turns, even while the bayonet was being driven into her chest. But by the time the last man had had his way, the girl was silent. 'Sing, pretty woman, sing!' Now his arousal was so overwhelming that he would have gladly parted with his consignment.

* * *

The feel of loaded firearms soon became familiar to Jasmine's hands. Under a rock-laden backpack and wielding a rifle she ran elaborate assault courses through Chinandega's rainforests, thrusting the bayonet into punch bags suspended from branches and makeshift scaffolding along the route. Lengths of nylon rope were strung taut across plunging passes and, dangling way above a trickling rivulet, she would cross – hand over hand – from one rock cliff to the other.

There were team games too.

Clutching their wooden rifles close to their bodies, the students undertook such involved simulacrums as Ambush, Assault and Occupation, Liberation of Prisoners, Penetration, and Kidnapping. They took turns to be the National Guard, or the screaming toddler caught up in crossfire. With ambitious perseverance they tracked surreptitiously placed clues that would lead them to a vital witness held captive by a ruthless foe. The rescue attempt could be made through encirclement and negotiation, siege or surprise attack. Students' choice.

Consensus had it that the easiest simulacrum to perform was the kidnapping of a secretary who might provide useful intelligence or keys to secret places. Just barge into her home at the dead of night, frighten the wits out of her lover with a pistol to his bollocks, and hey presto, here, have the keys, they're yours.

The hardest – that of the sniper. Clad in a suit and crown

of leaves and lying amid the foliage and shadow of secondary branches, the acting sniper was tricky to spot from the ground. The students could be discovered army-crawling over the muddy forest floor, or creeping stealthily through dew-dappled ferns, now darting for the cover of a Maya nut tree, now ducking behind a thicket; and yet the sniper invariably spotted his approaching adversary way before they spotted him, and he shot them dead with his wooden rifle. Yet on those rare occasions when the sniper was spotted, his chances of escape – which should have rated zero – were greatly enhanced by the trackers falling about laughing. Nothing like watching a shaggy, man-sized shrub sliding down a tree trunk in a hurry and shambling away through the woods to put you off your aim.

The final test of their suitability for guerrilla-hood required them to carry those same wooden rifles across eleven kilometres of varying terrain to Cosiguina, deposit them on the summit, and report back to camp in the shortest time stamina would allow. It all sounded straightforward enough until Americo added that *comandantes* – who would remain anonymous – had been called in from El Salvador to conceal themselves along the route and fire at will upon the contestants. The singular constraint being they make reasonable efforts to place their gunfire no lower than half a metre above ground level, which effectively meant that the students – by now thoroughly intimidated by the task ahead – rather than doing the course at a run would be obliged to crawl on their bellies. Unsurprisingly the event turned out to be as nerve-racking as it was physically draining, and required the participants to keep their wits fully switched on for a day and night without sleep. It was Jasmine and her *Amiga Del Alma* Manuela Rendón who, making good use of their gully, pressed ahead at a walking crouch through a tangle of vines, and scaled the volcano while their battered colleagues were still crawling across the prairie at a snail's pace. And despite having been spotted by a ranging sniper on the return, the bullets passed harmlessly above the level of the gully walls.

One day to go at Campamento Sandino, and an air of achievement at having graduated was tempered by the melancholy of impending goodbyes, and by an awareness that henceforth much would be expected of Sandino's privileged graduates.

Jasmine could be found in the main hall, foisting her summary of Karl Marx's *Concept of Relative Surplus-Value* on a weary looking Americo Merino over afternoon coffee. Here she received an impromptu visit from her beloved mentor *Comandante* Adonai Limeño, who arrived gripping a blue and white sports holdall as if for dear life. Having sought permission to interrupt her, he announced that not only had the Gavidia girl graduated with flying colours, but that her grades stood as the highest hitherto recorded at Campamento Sandino. It was his great honour, therefore, as it was Americo's, to offer his congratulations for this remarkable achievement.

When Jasmine found her speech it came in one relentless surge. 'Thank you, thank you,' and still thanking him, she was seized by a compulsion to impress him even further, and she discovered herself uttering nervous sentences on impulse: 'I've read all your poetry, and your manual on Reliable Intelligence, which opened my eyes to truths one would never consider in a million years of deciphering.' And then, to her vast annoyance, she embarked on an aimless monologue which somehow got strung out to intolerable lengths, until Adonai mercifully stopped her rambling:

'Come,' he interrupted. 'Let's take a walk.'

She snapped shut. Mortified and inwardly vowing to never, ever again embark on a sentence without having first conceived its ending, she strolled at his side, lengthening her pace to match his. She was soon oblivious to her surroundings, focusing on her hero who was muttering about colleagues – those who drew their strength from the convictions of others were invariably less dependable than those who drew their convictions from their own heart, a notion with which she agreed unequivocally. She agreed also that the First World's working classes still managed to keep their sweaty heads above water, but when your Westerner foists his standard economic model with its rigid three-tier social structure upon a troubled Third World state, the bottom tier slips beneath the waves into intolerable poverty. So in his ivory tower your First World lay-politician will debate isms and schisms over doughnuts and finest Salvadoran coffee, while for your average Third World majority the redistribution of wealth becomes the glaring essential. Now he had jumped to the apparently unrelated matter of children here and there and children that he didn't have, and she was saying 'really?' to it all, even though it was he who had taken to stringing together sentences that lacked apparent reason.

'Tell me, Gavidia, is there anything I could say to dissuade you from the Revolution?'

With a start Jasmine awoke as if from a dream. Adonai had paused, set the holdall at his feet and now was casually raking her soul. She glared back, appalled by his question.

'I believe in revolution, not submission,' she told him. 'Nothing you or anyone could say would turn me away, not now…not ever.'

'I'm getting old, you see,' he went on, as if he'd heard not a word of her spirited declaration, 'and have no heirs to the sum of my labours.'

'Bequeath your money to the FMLN,' she suggested, striving to come to terms with where he was going with all this. First you applaud my grades then you discourage their good use.

Adonai roused his pebbly chuckle. 'Daughter, I'm not speaking here of fleeting riches, but of the accumulated knowledge of a tired old man.' With a downward glance he indicated the holdall. 'These are personal notes and original manuscripts, observations and notions on battle strategy and tactics that I've compiled over the years. The earlier work is in print, the later stuff – untested theories and hypotheses – as

171

yet unpublished. If you'd like to have them, they're yours to do with as you wish. Perhaps you could write the definitive chapter on overcoming attacks from the air?'

'*If I'd like to have them*?' she repeated in amazement, her adulation for the old man soaring to new heights while her eyes filled with tears. By addressing her always by her surname, he had managed to maintain a platonic distance between them that legitimised their mutual love. She flung herself at him, and after a moment's rigid surprise, his lean body relaxed in her arms, and gingerly he returned her embrace.

After she received her heirloom she set it gently beside her feet, took up Adonai's warrior hand in both her own and, following the *campesino* custom when expressing profound gratitude, planted a kiss on his gnarled knuckles.

CHAPTER SEVENTEEN

PUNTA EL CHIQUIRIN.

Three communards gathered round one tattered map of the Central American isthmus. The map was pinned by glass ashtrays to the table. Leonel standing over the map, Jasmine imitating her *comandante*. Adrian lounging on a bench, admiring his frosted bottle of Corona Beer.

'That's us here, at the easternmost point of the Salvadoran mainland.' Leonel's forefinger prodded the spot exactly.

'Punta El Chiquirin,' Jasmine read aloud. 'I could see it from across the Gulf of Fonseca when I stood on Cosiguina's summit.'

'You would do,' Leonel agreed. 'Now listen up. Four of you will arrive on Meanguera and liaise with Serafin...that's the island you see in the distance.' Without looking up he pointed across the Gulf of Fonseca towards the east. 'Behind and to the left of Conchaguita Island, Jasmine, you'll see a Prussian-blue island, that's Meanguera. Got it?'

Perhaps a kilometre out a volcano rose from glittering waters. She had it. But it wasn't blue – Prussian or any other kind. It was distinctly green.

'Naturally the armed forces will expect Venceremos to acquire a new transmitter,' Leonel resumed. 'I can tell you for free – these things aren't sold discreetly in El Salvador. For concealment, Serafin will dismantle it into manageable sections. Each party will take possession of various component parts and return via separate routes to El Salvador. Besides being easier to transport this way, if one party is caught, all is not lost.' Leonel's fingertip was now describing a slow arc round to the right of the closest island to the mainland. 'On your way out, navigate south and circle Conchaguita,' he proposed, giving meaning to the arc he was now retracing.

'Or we could cross to the left of Conchaguita,' Jasmine drew her own invisible line on a direct route to their assigned destination.

'Negative,' Leonel stalled her.

'Why?'

'Naval commandos,' Adrian chipped in, tilting his beer bottle at the map.

'You bet,' agreed Leonel. 'Jasmine, Adrian, keep an eye out for frogmen and patrol boats. Why? Because over the last eleven days we've observed their patrols, and they've got a couple of teams moving round the western side of the Gulf, another couple focusing their attentions on the mangroves, coconut forests and beaches along our coast. There's no risk free way for you to travel to Meanguera, but where we can lessen those risks we should. So approach the island from the east, as if coming in from Nicaragua, concealed from observation from the areas where we've spotted naval patrols. Besides, look here, three countries – El Salvador, Honduras, Nicaragua – all sharing the same Gulf; we can take advantage of the continuing dispute over sea borders.' A pause to consult his watch. 'Emilio and Jonah will have left Lislique four hours ago. They'll be half way to Meanguera and they've got outboard motors, whereas you haven't. If there're no more questions, *que vayan con Dios*, and I'll expect you home tomorrow evening.'

Lolling on black sands, the skiff was a sturdy craft of overlapping hardwood staves painted in three solid stem-to-stern bands: black, blue, yellow. Two paddles with spade-like handles were propped inside the hammock-shaped hull.

Somewhat intimidated by the lack of an outboard motor, Jasmine regarded their transportation. 'I've never rowed before,' she admitted. But Adrian was swift to offer encouragement. She would soon take to it. Sure, she would!

They bent to the skiff, putting their backs into driving it forward. A wave swept in and scooped it up, and they used the backwash to carry it out. It stuck, but with the next wave it unstuck and rode free, and Jasmine staggered after it and clambered aboard. After scrambling over the fish-box and settling herself on the bow seat, she reached for the paddle and spent a while trying to get the hang of the hardwood shaft, but it felt fat and cumbersome in her grip, and hesitantly she dipped the blade into the water and practiced swishing it around. Annoyingly Adrian vaulted aboard which prompted the bow to leap sharply and send Jasmine toppling backwards. She sprung the paddle free, allowing it to slide into a breaker and wash ashore while she grappled desperately for the gunwale. Adrian nearly choked on his own laughter. Jasmine yanked herself upright and climbed overboard, recovered her paddle and sloshed back towards the bow. She hauled herself aboard, applying far more pressure on the gunwale than was absolutely necessary, but regretfully to no effect on Adrian's stability or his stupid grin.

Bracing her sandaled feet on one of the raised ribs that spanned the hull, Jasmine wrenched at her paddle. They pushed south with the wind buffeting their backs. Ghostly jellyfish hovered inches beneath the surface. A group of dolphins arrived to sweep alongside the skiff. But in her mind Jasmine had made a race of this journey, with Emilio and Jonah as unwitting contestants. So there was little time to admire marine curiosities. Punta El Chiquirin receded and their destination – Meanguera Island to their left – slipped behind the island volcano of Conchaguita. Rounding the southern slopes of Meanguera, Jasmine could see white walls and corrugated roofs that shared the hillside with a green down of ferns and the odd coconut palm. Fishing canoes basked on sandy brown beaches. Shallow inlets and coves presided over by the hills that screened your innocent fishermen's view of the

175

Salvadoran mainland, and hopefully the naval commandos' view of your average radio transmitter smuggler. They pressed on.

A black fishing trawler with a box-like deckhouse on the foredeck chugged by in the opposite direction. With every plunge of the steep bows, great fountains sprayed high to be gathered up by the wind and dashed against the hull with such force that Jasmine could hear the clatter of it across a hundred metres of sea.

'Where's he going?' she yelled over her shoulder.

'Who knows? Who cares?' was Adrian's laconic reply.

Jasmine steered the skiff towards the east, making a wide semicircle that took them half a kilometre beyond Meanguera until Adrian called to her that it was time to double back. Working together they guided the triangular end-deck steadily to the left, until they had it tidily lined up with the centre of the target island. Now they were coasting past huddled mangroves – islets of green foliage and white flowers poised above the water on tangled roots. Birdcalls filled the air, and Jasmine sighted a yellow-breasted warbler balancing on a mangrove branch. It tucked in tidy green tail feathers and swivelled its minute head sideways, accusing the intruders as they closed in on Meanguera. Gullied and creviced terrain swelled inland under a sparse feathery canopy. This unpromising shoreline gave way to a thirty-metre stretch of brown sand beach strewn with overlapping arcs of dead mangrove stems left there by high tide. Partially obscured beneath a crown of branches lurked a shack of adobe walls, its orange tile roof pitching over its colonnaded hard-mud veranda. Minutes later Jasmine felt the skip ground on the sand. She grinned when she saw Serafin Romero emerge from the hut and come striding down the beach in flamboyant Bermuda shorts and white singlet. With arms outstretched for balance she stood up and allowed Serafin to lift her off and set her gently on the sand. But she staggered and fell against him, her sense of balance still at sea. Serafin caught her up and held her – unnecessarily tightly – to his body, which reeked of burnt wood.

'Whoa, there, *capitana*,' he blurted. 'I've got you. – Just relax.' She unfastened his hands and backed out of his embrace. 'Just trying to save you from falling,' he assured her. Suddenly he darted past her to help Adrian rescue the skiff from being washed back into the sea. When they had wriggled the boat beyond the high-tide mark, Serafin pronounced the formal reception: 'Welcome to *Meanguera del Golfo*.'

Raising herself on tiptoes and twisting interlinked hands together, Jasmine enquired casually if the others were here yet.

'A race was it?' Serafin guessed. 'Well, you're the first to arrive, so I hereby declare you our official *winner*.' And instead of hoisting her arm in victory, he seized her jaw and squeezed until her lips puckered which caused him great amusement.

* * *

'Freshly gathered herbs, that's my secret.' Serafin created a scrumptious dinner of barbecued corvina accompanied by avocado and tomato salad and seasoned with his herbs. There were second and third helpings and had it not been for the lamentable shortage of lemon and coriander, fourths might well have followed. Something about the sea always piques the appetite, Jasmine agreed with Adrian as they rigged up their hammocks in the shade of the veranda. There was no way they were going to sleep indoors, not in that heat.

Jasmine and Adrian had the veranda to themselves while Serafin set out to comb the hillside for more herbs. Jasmine swung in silence for an hour or so, mulling over a chain of events not entirely unrelated to Leonel. If only he weren't such a goat. Eventually she turned to gaze out across the ocean. Aside from the odd moonlit wave crest it was Prussian-blue all the way to the horizon. She shut her eyes and sighed under the burden of what it might be like to have a proper relationship with a man, a good man. One who wasn't so fussed about a woman's virginity, as *campesinos* generally were, she thought.

* * *

177

She woke to the dawn. Emilio and Jonah were now encased in their veranda hammocks. Their arrival hadn't disturbed her sleep.

She padded along the beach, stooping to pick up shells and rinsing them in puddles before stuffing them into her pockets, but before she had enough for the necklace she intended to make she saw Serafin squatting on a platform of pebbles cemented together, and stoking a small fire.

Over black coffee and watermelon he suggested they went fishing.

With her at the bow and him at the stern and a crumpled nylon castnet at their feet, they paddled deep into the Gulf, and when their island was a thin slice in the distance Serafin tucked his paddle beneath his seat and began gathering up the net. Jasmine leaned forward to observe.

'How do you know there's fish here?' she enquired.

'Bubbles on the surface.'

With a brisk twist Serafin flung the net overboard. The wind caught the mesh and whipped it into a cone before allowing it to drop. With a long hiss it slipped beneath the surface leaving a cloud of even more bubbles. Serafin sat down with the end of the throwing line clutched in his hands. He must have read the question in Jasmine's stare because he assured her that soon she would have more fish than she could eat, and that he had collected ripe lemons and coriander to garnish a new fish recipe he was working on. She turned round in her seat and allowed the flight of an osprey to distract her mind from her grumbling tummy. Its oval body as white as sea spray, under-wings mottled with shadowy patches, it reared up, climbing the wind vertically before allowing itself to be borne high across the bow of the boat and back towards the string of conical islands deep within the Gulf.

Serafin finally announced it was time to pull in the net, at which he donned a pair of rough suede gloves and tossed a second pair across the fish box. Jasmine pulled on the huge gloves and gripped the insides to prevent them from sliding off.

'Help me,' Serafin grunted, as he worked the throwing line, feeding it through his gloved hands. 'Take the end, Jaz, and pull hard.'

She secured her footing on one of the inner hull ribs, leaned back, and added her efforts to his. 'It's heavy,' she said hopefully.

And as they toiled, creamy-white seagulls flocked in, announcing the feast with excited shrieks. The mouth of the net, around which the throwing rope had now tightened, surfaced amid a fizz fountain at which several of the hovering birds promptly set about pecking. Now comes the hard part, Serafin told his hungry apprentice, and urged her to pull even harder than before, but please try not to rock the boat so much, okay?

She bent to it, feeling the muscles in her back, arms and thighs pull taut. The mouth of the net set a circular wake in motion, and she felt the jolt when the bulk of it nudged the hull. And Serafin, between wheezes, was pleading with her to *keep pulling, keep pulling*, and she kept pulling and as the sack-like net climbed up the side of the hull, seawater squirted out of the weave, lightening the load, and Jasmine could now see scales, translucent eyes, fluttering gills and violent tailfins trapped in the nylon.

'Grab it,' Serafin huffed, and together they strained at the line until the whole lot flopped over the gunwale and rolled like a single kicking animal at their feet. Serafin whipped open the net and plunged his arm inside. 'What about this, eh?' he said triumphantly, yanked out a huge yellow snapper and held it aloft by its tailfin in the classical proud fisherman's pose.

Jasmine smiled her agreement.

They set about transferring the catch from the net to the fish box and when the net was empty Serafin suggested they head back for a very late breakfast.

* * *

179

By the time Jasmine awoke from her siesta, the sun was behind the roof, Emilio and Jonah were absent and Serafin was on the beach with a plastic bucket in his hand.

She nudged Adrian awake and then stuffed her hammock into her backpack. At the water's edge Serafin gave her two large envelopes of cloudy plastic.

'Your comrades have left with the rest of my new box,' he told her bitterly, as if it were an accusation. Jasmine held up the envelopes, and peering through the film could tell merely that the contents were metallic. 'They contain three sides of the chassis, the filter and bypass caps, screen resistor and rectifier tube sockets,' Serafin itemised. 'My precious, precious thing. You guys, take care of her for me, please?'

Jasmine climbed aboard the skiff, reached into the slender space beneath the fish box and extracted a shallow tray with the whole of the forward-facing panel attached. Into the tray she deposited Serafin's precious, precious thing. She pushed the tray shut, Serafin handed her a hammer and a dozen stout nails, and she did a fair job of sinking the nails all the way up both sides of the panel. When she stood up and peered into the fish box it was innocently empty and only the most acute scrutiny might detect that the floor was perhaps an iota higher than similar box floors in other skiffs. There was only one bucket so it was Adrian who transferred half a dozen bucket loads of squid, langoustine and snapper from Serafin's boat to Jasmine's doctored fish box.

Serafin helped them float the skiff and, knee-deep in water, hugged first Adrian and then Jasmine. '*Vayan con Dios,*' he bid them solemnly.

The tide was against them and made heavy work of the journey westwards. They skirted Conchaguita's olive green western shores. Although from this angle Jasmine couldn't see Punta El Chiquirin, which lay behind Conchaguita, she could make out El Salvador's coastline further east within the Gulf. Sandy beaches fringed with coconut palms behind which that distinctive volcanic landscape flushed into the haze. Seeing her homeland from a distance triggered a rush of protective tenderness. There was so much work to do. She put fresh vigour into her shoulders and arms as she powered the paddle through the waters.

Shrieking seagulls, waves slapping at the bows, spray clattering into the hull. Now a low throbbing hum roused Jasmine, and she looked round to identify its source. Leaping from wave to wave, a white Piranha speedboat hurtled towards them. Four crew in navy blue and dark glasses swaying in a huddle. On the short foredeck a mounted M60 machine gun pursued the skiff, never straying from its target despite the changing position of the boats.

She glanced across at Adrian, who had decked his paddle and was idly rubbing his naked shoulder. They exchanged nods and she drew in her paddle. The Piranha sliced across their path and keeled round sharply, just as its wake arrived to rock the skiff.

'You are Salvadorans?' a chubby captain hollered from behind the gun.

'Of course,' Adrian, appointing himself spokesperson, answered.

'Carnets.'

Jasmine extracted her identity card from her pocket and held it out in readiness.

'Take the gun, Chepe. I'm going aboard.' The captain nodded to one of his unsmiling crewmen.

Jasmine squinted while he straddled the two boats, and for a moment it seemed they must drift apart and drop him into the slopping waves. But Adrian guided the skiff in closer, until the port gunwale was gently nudging the Piranha's taller hull. The captain pushed off with a booted foot and stepped into the fishing boat, directly in front of Jasmine. He examined her upheld carnet without removing his sunglasses. Dumpling features, a small chin sunken into rolls of other chins, and a sort of sagging pear-shape, so much so that the appellation *Mr Sag-man* immediately sprung to Jasmine's mind. It was the sort of thing Manuela Rendón would have said.

'Señorita Jasmine Maria Gavidia, it says here you were born in Nejapa.'

'Nejapa,' she repeated, feeling as if she was betraying her birthplace by admitting to the bogus details declared on her *Carné de Identidad.*

'What does a plantation girl do in a fishing boat?' he asked, and peeled off his sunglasses to peruse her with a stony brown gaze.

'Fish.' For an obvious question an obvious answer.

The captain kneaded his forehead and shut his eyes to show his forbearance had limits. 'Let's see how well you've adjusted to fishing, shall we?' He handed back her carnet and tipped his head towards the fish box. She didn't budge. But Adrian, playing obliging host, moved forward, opened the shutters, and invited the captain to inspect the day's catch. Not surprisingly the captain accepted this hospitable offer, and while Jasmine looked on with rising fury, Mr Sag-man helped himself to a huge snapper, and because it was caught up in the flaccid embrace of a squid he might as well have the squid as well, and he and his crew just love langoustine, don't we Chepe? But Chepe was too busy dodging the tossed langoustines that came winging his way to answer. Has anyone seen a flying squid before? Ha, ha, ha, ha.

Yeah, ha, ha, ha, thought Jasmine, boiling with the injustice of it all. So what if she had no use for the fish other than as a decoy? It was the principle! Policemen and soldiers routinely encouraged the giving of *propinas.* There was no reason to suppose that naval officers were any different. But how much of her catch did Mr Sag-man and his thieves intend to wangle on the pretext of a *propina*? Answer: the whole lot.

Jasmine's sense of justice got the better of her. 'That'll be ten thousand Colons,' she blurted recklessly, and to show she meant business she stood up and held out one open palm. 'Cash.' Behind the captain a fretful-faced Adrian had both palms towards her, patting the air to advocate self control. And if there was comedy to be had, it was Mr Sag-man whose sense of humour was up for it. To show how amusing he found her upturned hand, he took one look at it, threw back his head and hooted at the sky. Dutifully his crew matched him hoot for hoot. But the captain soon curbed his amusement, and turning his back on Jasmine he whisked up the last snapper and tossed it cleanly on to the speedboat.

Jasmine sat down and buried her face in her hands. It wasn't until the Piranha's engine noise was fading that she opened a gap between her fingers and stared through at Adrian, who nodded at her from the bow seat. Together they approached the box and leaned in to stare down at its bare interior. But the floor, although ringing wet and slopping with detached langoustine tentacles, remained safely intact.

'Why did you let them do that?' she snapped at Adrian across the box.

'What do you expect me to do against guns? Wallop their heads with a squid?'

Still smarting from the indignity of it all, Jasmine brooded silently as they paddled back to Punta El Chiquirin.

CHAPTER EIGHTEEN

October 1986

IT WAS DAWN WHEN the boy runner stole into camp and, despite his stealth, woke Jasmine. A kid's silhouette being guided by a man's. Leonel was in Olocuilta to attend one of the *Comandancia General*'s eternal assemblies, so the pair sought out Adrian and the boy spoke close to his ear, after which he was handed a calabash of drinking water. Adrian woke three men from their hammocks and dispatched them into the forest. Doubling up the watch, Jasmine guessed. The boy must have seen a Guard patrol soundlessly combing the forest, probably not close enough for alarm but enough to merit extra vigilance.

Jasmine couldn't get back to sleep. She was pining for a coffee but knew that building a fire was out of the question until after the alert had passed. So she did what any true addict would have done: she took her calabash to last night's urn and from the cold dregs scooped up enough caffeine to quell the persistent pang. Happy now, she climbed back into her hammock, lying on her back and sipping her coffee pretending to herself it was steaming hot. She noticed that the morning air was still, humid and unnatural.

About an hour later, a second runner arrived and, like the first, reported to Adrian. This time Adrian went from hammock to hammock gently rousing the occupants with a tap on the back of their hands.

He had taken the decision to move camp.

As Jasmine joined in the hurried dismantling and pack-up of the camp, she became aware of inexplicable anxiety knotting her stomach. The runners and scouts were practiced and acutely vigilant, and she had grown accustomed to their regular reported sightings of potential danger, and the *comandancia's* assessment of the column's vulnerability. But she had not experienced a sense of foreboding of the kind she did this morning. When she had finished packing her backpack, she went to assist with making a corridor of the crates in readiness for carrying. Although she applied herself to the task the sensation remained. I must speak to someone about this, she concluded eventually. She strolled over to a bamboo hut where beneath a canvas roof Adrian was attending to a dengue-stricken *compañera* who lay pale and shivering in a hammock.

'You'll faint again if you exert yourself,' he warned his patient. 'Rest now; allow the medicine to take effect. I'll call you the moment we're ready to move out.' On sensing Jasmine behind him, he turned round. 'What is it, Jasmine?'

She smiled lamely. 'Not sure, actually, *teniente*.' She glanced across at the laid up comrade who was sobbing quietly. 'I just feel something awful is about to happen.' She turned back to Adrian and shrugged at her own vagueness. 'That's all.'

At column level feminine intuition had earned tentative esteem. But guerrillas were not creatures of superstition and it was to be listened to, consulted even, but always with a pinch of salt. So under Adrian's gaze Jasmine lifted her neckerchief and wiped away perspiration that had beaded on her face.

'Isn't it hot?' she struggled on. 'I mean, unusually hot, don't you think?'

Adrian stepped up to the hut's edge and peered upwards. 'Thick cloud in the sky.'

'Yes, there is,' she agreed eagerly, as if his was a significant observation.

He had obliged her enough, and with a tilt of his head told her to get moving, and turned to cast an eye over his patient, after which he stalked off leaving Jasmine with her uncertainty intact.

'Yes,' she stated to the vacant space Adrian had left. 'There is no more to say.' She walked back to where her backpack and weaponry lay sunken in the grass.

Less than half an hour later she heard low rumblings on the air, and felt a vibration gathering beneath her feet. She looked up and held her breath, heart racing, and waited for the tremor to subside, as invariably they did. But the rumbling soared to thunder pitch and the ground lunged up at her, buckling her knees and sending her flat on her stomach. She shook her head and stared up at the trees; they were in a creaking frenzy, branches shaking off leaves that floated down on the muggy air. The neatly positioned crates shunted each other through the grass. The shadowy interior of the bamboo hut...the fever-stricken comrade, her brow furrowed with the effort of trying to climb out of a swinging hammock...a creaking whoosh... the hut collapsed on top of her. Now the ground everywhere was undulating weirdly. As Jasmine came unsteadily up on all fours she had the distinct sensation that the normally hard land had melted into an ocean of surging swells upon which she rode high and low. Her ribcage tightened in panic and she screamed.

And as swiftly as it had arrived, the earthquake subsided.

* * *

The aftermath of the quake brought about a lull in hostilities. Guerrillas, members of the emergency services and soldiers worked side by side to pull survivors and corpses from the rubble of San Salvador's many satellite villages, where often the only thing left standing was a lopsided signpost welcoming the arriving traveller and another on his departure bidding him a safe journey. In one continuous bulletin Venceremos reported the news of a 7.6 quake, the tireless newsreaders updating the grim death toll as fast as new details emerged: one hundred, five hundred, one thousand, two thousand, and rising. The number of those who had lost their homes rose to one million.

Bidden by Leonel to report to the Red Cross's office and offer her assistance, Jasmine headed through San Salvador's ruptured streets, a lump in her throat, tears never far away. Solid tower blocks had dropped into the ground as if they'd been founded on quicksand. Converted mansions teetered on the brink of collapse. Mountains of bricks and twisted wire signalled where tenements had succumbed. Water spouted from gaping rifts in the roads, and half-naked children played in the resulting rivulets. Cars and buses bore the dents of having been tossed together. Toppled electricity posts, their cables entangled, were being attended to by helmeted firemen.

Joining forces with thousands of volunteers, Jasmine spent eleven days clearing away bricks and smashed masonry and salvaging furniture, squeezing through slender gaps in the perilous masonry to reach trapped and thirsty citizens.

Segundo and Marta Lilian announced they were to tie the knot. A simple beige knee-length dress for the bride. Segundo borrowed Leonel's navy-blue conference blazer. Padre José Maria Melgar arrived to preside over the happy ceremony. Leonel relinquished the keys to his beloved pickup so that the newlyweds could honeymoon at one of the guest cabins on Lake Coatepeque's turquoise shores. Meanwhile, to the tinny music of Radio Cumbia, the wedding guests took to the floor, their outlines cast in candlelight. Jasmine danced a relentless salsa, darkening her T-shirt and dungarees with perspiration, and made Leonel promise to take her dancing to 'a proper nightclub one day', and she got sufficiently carried away to extract similar commitments from Adrian and Emilio and several other dance partners before dawn.

* * *

Pollo Campero. Avenida Roosevelt – as always, Anastasio in his favourite seat with his tabloids – old and new for catch-up because he'd been busy ramping up his private enterprise. Carlota the pretty pony-tailed waitress saying she hardly recognised him in civvies. You'll be joining the *muchachos* next.

187

'Coffee, please, and my usual for breakfast.'

The elections of March 1988 had installed ARENA's new boy Alberto Sorrentino on the presidential throne. And how?

Though no longer a whole-hearted soldier, Anastasio still liked to keep abreast of current affairs. Not that he'd changed his opinion on The Game. Survival was still where it's at. He may be out of uniform today, but joining the *muchachos* has never crossed his mind, because everyone knows that the gringo might is unbeatable, their money ever-flowing. And they will continue backing the Army whatever and for as long as it takes until the *muchachos* and their supporters are ground into the earth or every last one of them is killed.

La Prensa's Sunday supplement was carrying a feature on how the relative calm following the earthquake was unlikely to last because Herberto Ernesto Anaya Sanabria, President of the United Nations Human Rights Commission to El Salvador, has been shot dead. The correspondent was linking the assassination to the disapproval in certain quarters to the PDC's persistence in meeting with the terrorists for such radical engagements as dialogue.

Old tensions will reignite, thought Anastasio, and it'll be back to war as usual.

ARENA to the right of the nation's Magna Flag, the FMLN to the illegal left, and ex-President Martin Aragón in the unenviable, precarious, ineffective middle. Perhaps a pity because as politicians go Martin Aragón was generally considered to be honourable, but corruption scandals involving several of his closest ministers had damaged the Party's reputation in the eyes of the electorate. The nation's infrastructure, already in tatters from decades of light-fingered regimes and conflict, and further eroded by the earthquake, was at the threshold of total collapse, and the population pleaded for solutions to their woes.

So, limbering up for the March election, ARENA had ditched the death-squad mastermind Aristides Saravia and selected from their ranks a replacement leader – the strictly

188

non-militaristic Alberto Sorrentino. Anastasio had to laugh at the mudslinging and slogans that had characterised the run up.

In the unenviable, precarious, ineffective middle corner: "Invest your vote in the Partido Demócrata Cristiano, and reap a brighter future for all who live in our national territory."

In the extremely right corner: "Liken the PDC to a watermelon: green on the outside but red within. Vote, instead, for ARENA."

Not surprisingly perhaps, Alberto Sorrentino's affable manner and air of decency had won the day by taking the majority vote, propelling ARENA into legitimate government.

'Get ready FMLN for a hammering, both politically and militarily.'

* * *

Silent lightning flared in the dark clouds above the plains of San Andrés, where forty-two compatriots were assembling around a picnic of bunches of ripe banana and a cluster of sugarcane.

Minutes ago Leonel had returned from Sonsonate. The word from Adrian was that the big man would shortly deliver a briefing, and he expected full attendance. If there had been any doubts as to the position the newly-elected government would take with respect to the FMLN, this was the briefing that would dispel or confirm those doubts. Because in Sonsonate, Leonel, together with *la Comandancia General*, including Party Chief Abraham Gadala, had round-tabled with a delegation from ARENA as well as military dignitaries headed by the Army's highly decorated General Simón Levi.

Having taken a side-saddle perch on a comfy hackberry branch Jasmine was well pleased with this high seat because from it she could observe the whole group and avoid further encounters with Serafin, who'd developed a roaming right hand.

Leonel strode into the midst of his warriors and arranged a crate of ammo as a bench.

'I have good news and bad news. Secretary General Pérez

de Cuellar's recommendation to the Security Council has been approved,' – pushing his hair back with both hands and tucking it behind his ears. 'The UN will launch a preparatory office in San Salvador, and regional offices in several towns throughout the national territory.'

'The UN panders to its most powerful members.' Emilio doubted the goodness of this news.

'Let's see,' Leonel came back. 'International observers in our back yard may mollify the army's actions.'

'Or hamper ours.' Adrian's counter triggered a ripple of agreement, which Leonel, all for continuing the briefing, ignored.

'Nevertheless, ONUSAL – as the office is to be named – will, together with the Catholics and the Organization of American States, observe the peace negotiations from here on.'

Observe! Observe what? By Emilio's reckoning, thus far the OAS had observed and done sweet FA. The Jesuits were the only outfit making constructive peace efforts. 'Besides us, that is. Yes?'

A dozen agreed.

So what did ARENA want this time? The same bullshit as the PDC no doubt. Our unconditional disarmament? Adrian again.

The briefing dissolved into general conversation.

'We too will insist on a select number of unreasonable demands to use as bargaining tools.' This was Wenceslau, swatting a mosquito against his crinkled neck. No one ever disagreed with Wenceslau because besides Leonel he was the only PCS combatant to have trained in Cuba. And well, Cuba was Cuba.

Leonel continued, 'Besides our unconditional unilateral disarmament – like Adrian says, ARENA has renewed calls for an amnesty, and added what they say is a generous concession to us.'

Characteristically, Adrian had worked himself swiftly up to yelling pitch. 'Bullshit!' – springing to his feet – 'Those *hijos de putas* wouldn't concede a…' which was as much as he could manage before breathlessly resuming his seat.

'What is this supposed concession, Don Leonel?' Wenceslau invited.

'We already know that the general amnesty from prosecution for war crimes, which they seek, is to cover the armed forces. Their concession is that it be extended to the guerrillas also.'

'We don't need an amnesty,' Emilio came in. 'Justice for what they've done…The people want justice.'

This led to an argument involving virtually everyone, talking over each other with raised voices.

'Okay. Okay. That's enough,' Leonel called out, and when the competing voices had simmered down he forged ahead with the good news: 'ARENA flatly refuses to discuss our concerns regarding land distribution, a human rights commission, and electoral participation, until we at least decommission our weapons and agree to the amnesty.'

'Then we persevere. We fight on.' Emilio threw up his hands. Leonel now delivered the bad news:

'They've stuck a new demand on their list. Doing his customary show of concern over our credentials for the benefit of the UN visitors, Simón Levi dealt the first real low-blow, accusing the FMLN of carrying out contraband activities… drug smuggling to fund our campaigns and he capped it by likening us to Colombia's FARC guerrillas. And he made the *oh-so-reasonable* demand that we ditch the practice.'

A pause – stunned but reflective. Lightning was still webbing above the plains. The smell of rain hit Jasmine's nostrils. Adrian broke the pause by pointing out that at least the PCS and, as far as he was aware, the FMLN collectively was not and had never been involved in peddling drugs. Not directly anyway. 'We may have one or two marihuana smokers here…but cocaine…' he shook his head, '…no way, man. That's an army thing. Everyone knows they feed their boys dextroamphetamine and cocaine.'

191

Leonel thanked him for that. 'The Interior Minister chipped in, saying that by funding our campaigns with drug money the FMLN had lost all political credibility. Which is exactly what ARENA wants because it distances us from our goal of political legitimacy.'

'We may get a smidgen of financial assistance from folks involved in that sort of thing, but that's as far as it goes,' Adrian conceded under pressure from no one.

'How can we give up doing something we've never done?' said Emilio.

'What difference does it make?' Adrian back to fever pitch. 'We've always said it's not important where our money comes from, so long as it buys food and bullets and builds schools and hospitals, and that's exactly what we're doing with it.'

'I agree,' – now Serafin, calmingly, perhaps for Adrian's benefit. 'Government money is no cleaner than ours.'

Leonel wagged a finger at Serafin. 'The National Guard's blue-eyed boy director Carlos Araujo claimed that FMLN columns are actively engaged in drug trafficking. To prove it he whisked us through a slide show of cocaine shipments he assured us his men had confiscated from our members.' Leonel cracked his knuckles one by one. 'I didn't let on that I recognised two of the miserable *cabrones*. Not PCS men, not even ex-PCS, I'm glad to say, but they've been around, so after the meeting I spoke with the *comandante* from the zone implicated, although he says the men featured were no longer with his column. All the same, the UN envoy agreed that the government's demand for the FMLN to purge itself of drug contraband was a fair one, and of course the ministers went away smiling.'

'When this news gets out, and you can bet that ARENA will publicise it widely, our *comités de solidaridad* will wonder what the fuck they're funding,' Adrian said.

'All commands are instructing their columns with the same message. If anyone has been engaged in drug contraband, it stops now. Is that understood?'

'Yes, *comandante*,' they chorused in ragged overlaps, some repeating themselves.

'Now,' Leonel resumed, 'since ARENA has no interest in disproving the allegation against us, it falls on us to do so. I have assigned the mission to Comrade Jasmine Gavidia.'

A spontaneous round of applause greeted Jasmine's ears, which was the way of guerrillas when important missions were assigned. Well done, Jasmine. If you need anything, don't hesitate. *Vaya con Dios!*

'What about smuggling arms?' Adrian questioned with a smirk.

On his way over to the hackberry tree Leonel told Adrian to fuck off, and the collective laughter this prompted lightened the mood in the camp.

'Well, I must be heading off,' Serafin's voice surfaced somewhere, and Jasmine scanned the darkness for him, catching his lanky profile as he came to his feet. 'Got to get back and put this news on air.' Of the four who had smuggled in the radio components, he sought out only Jasmine to thank personally; and from her elevated position she accepted his thanks graciously enough by her standards but not for Leonel's, because he ordered her to come down from up there and show the man proper respect. Miserably she submitted to Serafin's manipulation of her face until her lips puckered, to his tireless amusement.

'He's got the hots for you,' Leonel chuckled. When they had watched Serafin vanish into the night, Leonel bid her come, he wanted to show her something, and he led her to a break in the bush where they could gaze across the plain. For some reason thousands of lighted candles arranged in clusters covered the plain, turning it into a vast altar of ghostly blue-violet flames glowing beneath the heavens.

'St Elmo's fire on the maize,' Leonel saved her from guesswork.

'Our political participation may some day depend on the evidence your mission turns up,' said Leonel returning to the subject at hand. 'As soon as you have good data and a traceable lead based not merely on reliable witnesses but on your personal observations, report back to me, and together we'll assess your evidence and decide what back-up you require to get a closer look.' He stooped to peer into her eyes. 'No heroics. No barging in by yourself. You with me?'

She told him that she understood fine. When she again looked across the plain, St Elmo had put out all but a few of his candles.

CHAPTER NINETEEN

PANCHIMALCO VILLAGE ROOSTED HIGH in the cordillera south of the capital, and to get there in Leonel's pickup involved a steep second-gear toil into damp clouds and beyond Los Planes de Renderos through woodlands so florid and teaming with birdsong that it had an otherworld feel. When Jasmine finally arrived at Panchimalco, she felt that her mission started in the Garden of Eden. Whether its remoteness was an advantage or disadvantage for a cocaine cash-and-carry outfit was a matter she debated only briefly. Her lead was straightforward enough. Seek and find *La Mujer de Canela*; set up static obs; keep an eye out for *coca* peddlers and slap a surreptitious tail on any and all iffy vehicles that engage in iffy-looking deliveries with the target premises. Simple!

A diner would be a good place to casually enquire about the precise whereabouts of La Mujer de Canela; it was also a good place to chase away the midmorning chill. Rubbing together hands clad in fingerless mittens, Jasmine ordered a mug of strong black coffee spiked with cinnamon.

The waitress bustled off towards the kitchen and Jasmine turned to gaze through the canopied window. Somewhere out of sight the purest of voices was singing the repetitive stanzas of a peasants' lament. Against this soundtrack Jasmine watched a boy and girl in the bliss of childhood play scampering across the plaza. On arrival at the church steps, the boy tapped the girl's shoulder before dashing off, the girl hot on his heels, her bright skirts billowing around slender brown legs. The boy ducked behind a pillar, keeping it between them, dodging his sister's attempts to tap his shoulder. A stout, fierce-eyed matron waddled up behind and clobbered him over the head with a length of cane, which she then used to point at him threateningly. He submitted to a scolding which he tried to deflect by pointing accusingly at his sister. The siblings then fell in line behind their mother and were marshalled down the hill and into the residential area.

The waitress served up the coffee. Sunlight glaring off the cobbles prompted Jasmine to reach for her backpack which lay heavier than ever at her feet. Leonel had thoroughly kitted it out for her mission and, if memory served her, a pair of sunglasses was amongst the paraphernalia. There was reading material for those long lonely hours when absolutely nothing happens: *People's War People's Army* by Vo Nguyen Giap (due back at The National University library by Jan. 18, 1979 – so accused a faded purple stamp inside the front cover), a hand held radio, cans of condensed milk, tinned pilchards, packs of beef jerky, a tub of gun oil, another of penicillin, a cigarette lighter, a camera, a pack of Kodak Tri-X film and a pen torch with batteries included. There was more: a Smith & Wesson 686 double action revolver with a stainless steel cylinder and polished zebrawood grip. With a barrel length of only 2.5 inches the gun was dinky enough for Jasmine to tuck inside her dungaree's waistband. And at her hip, sheathed in burgundy leather, hung a steel-bladed machete with a snug handle of smooth poui wood. While foraging for her sunglasses she heard the distinctive thudding of a helicopter approaching from the south. She froze on instinct, hand in her backpack, heart racing. The hated sound escalated, bellowed overhead and then receded to the north. She put on her sunglasses and called over the waitress. 'Where can I find La Mujer de Canela?' Jasmine asked, paying her bill and including a generous *propina*.

'Follow the road till its end.' The waitress pocketed the coins in her apron and wiped the table. 'Panchimalco has only one road. You can't miss it.'

La Mujer de Canela turned out to be a bakery run from the last in a line of coloured townhouses terraced down a cobbled, abruptly ending cul-de-sac. In the narrow corridor between cars parked nose to tail, Jasmine made a three-point turn. On the same kerb as the bakery, she managed to reverse into a tight gap between a moped and a wheel-less car suspended on brick stacks. Excellent position; driver's side to the pavement; good visibility through side mirror of target premises; and facing away from the cul-de-sac she was poised to pursue shady-looking delivery men making hasty getaways in iffy vehicles. She adjusted the rear-view mirror to give her another angle on the bakery. Grateful for tinted windows that allowed her to observe without being observed, she settled down with optimism that this would be a shortish wait.

There were distractions, however. Nosy kids on the roam, squinting through car windows. A vendor with a push-cart selling syrup-capped shaved ice in styrofoam cups. On the pavement beyond the bonnet a frowning girl seated in a child's plastic chair, clutching the armrests and rocking forward, eyeing the pickup, perhaps wondering when the occupant might finally alight.

A white Ford van pulled up, double parked outside the bakery and took delivery of six trays swathed in chequered cloths. Jasmine agonised over whether this constituted a suspicious delivery, but the driver left the van's rear doors wide open and hung around chatting in the bakery doorway. Surely a *coca* retailer would be anxious to lock up and be away. A tall father with two young kids in tow left the bakery, all three clutching brown paper bags into which they dipped their hands and snuck out fat chocolate chip biscuits, biting off chunks as they walked.

Jasmine studiously catalogued all comings and goings from La Mujer de Canela in her Banco Agricola year diary. By seven p.m. the bakery had shut its doors and pulled down its steel shutters, and although Jasmine was no longer entirely certain what it was she was looking for nor of recognising it when it arrived or occurred, no particularly devious operation had today prompted her to suspect that La Mujer de Canela was anything but a legitimate family enterprise.

* * *

Nightfall on Panchimalco's lamp-less streets. Jasmine alighted, put on her backpack, approached the end of the cul-de-sac and was met by a plunging vertical escarpment, hundreds of feet deep, its foot sweeping out to cradle San Salvador's winking metropolis in the Valley of Hammocks. Centuries ago, before the advent of the motorcar, Lenca farmers had carved a staircase into the rock face leading from Panchimalco down to the valley. Tonight, Jasmine would take to this staircase, thus saving her parking space by reason of occupation and being conspicuously absent should snooping Guard patrols shine torches through blacked-out pickup truck windows.

Over time the passage of the farmers had worn a curved dip into the forward edge of each step, effectively channelling a tricky-to-negotiate convex slide down the centre of the staircase. Acutely aware of the yawning void to her left, Jasmine embarked on a halting descent, pressing in close to the sheer wall, palms sliding flat upon it, fingers hunting every nook and cranny for purchase. After twenty minutes she came to the first of four dog-leg turns. She eased herself round it in a seated position, grasping above the junction at the steps' outer edges. Then again she stood up, embraced the wall and resumed her gradual downward journey. She treated the next dog-leg junction with similar respect, but by the third and fourth she was gathering confidence, as much from experience as from the knowledge that the drop beside her was less dramatic than at the start, and although she still shuffled round them on her behind, she did so with greater speed. By the time the steps had petered out altogether, a half moon was high in the heavens.

Jasmine swung left into the woods beneath the escarpment of La Puerta del Diablo, picking her way round thickets and ducking beneath long tresses of tree moss that dangled from the branches. Presently she came to a brook burbling over a bed of pebbles. Charmed by the hush of a waterfall she traced the brook and came to a rocky cove folded into the escarpment where a slender cascade formed a series of pools spilling one into the next before meandering away through the trees. She took off her backpack and rigged up her hammock in a grove of pink poui. Satisfied with her sleeping arrangements, she undressed, dug out a cake of hotel soap from her backpack, and stepped through a fringe of water hyacinth into the smallest of the pools. Teeth chattering, she lowered herself until she sat with the chilly waters up to her breasts. With some splashing around the shivering abated, and she lathered herself down and washed her hair, then reclined and allowed the clear flow to rinse over her. The water hyacinth's lavender-blue and gold caught her eye and she began plucking the dainty flowers, tracing the peacock feather-like markings with her little finger before launching the petals and watching them spirited away through ripples glinting in the soft moonlight.

Finally, she took to her hammock and, with the odd distant report of gunfire to startle her, embarked on reducing to zero the backlog of undelivered prayers.

* * *

By 6.30 a.m. Jasmine was back at her observation point in the Toyota. Her Banco Agricola diary received a scattering of new entries: one van taking delivery of dozens of hot cross buns. Another of a three-storey iced wedding cake topped with a role-reversed bride-carrying-the-groom statue crossing the threshold beneath an arch of marzipan leaves. No less than sixty-nine walk-in clients. At midday a woman with a clear shower cap that presumably doubled as a baker's cap crowning a cascade of auburn curls emerged pushing an empty supermarket trolley from La Mujer de Canela. An iffy vehicle perhaps, but not exactly what Jasmine had in mind for your average drug peddler. When the auburn lady returned a little over an hour later, her transportation was juggling pineapples in its wire pit. Nevertheless, Jasmine faithfully catalogued this event in her Banco Agricola diary.

At noon on the fourth day since arriving in Panchimalco, Jasmine's patience was rewarded when a black Nissan Pathfinder pulled up, double parked right beside the Toyota and blared its horn. A tall, sallow youth with a beard and a fancy cowboy hat alighted and stalked like a praying mantis, not to the bakery – which should have put Jasmine off the scent – but to the very house outside which she was parked. Another giant in a black anorak, mantis-like enough to have been the other's twin, answered the door, nodded without speaking, disappeared back into the house while the driver, spinning his key ring on a middle finger, loped round to the rear of his vehicle and opened up the boot, leaving it gaping while he slid bottom-first back into the cabin. The anorak reappeared and peered furtively about without spotting Jasmine. Satisfied that the coast was clear, he reached inside the boot and tugged out a wooden crate, which he hefted on to his shoulder and carried indoors. He returned and repeated the procedure three times before the driver resurfaced, shut the boot and then, resuming his place in the cabin, started the engine and let it tick over. The anorak re-emerged with a brick-sized brown-paper package in each hand. Jasmine saw him clap them together once before he crammed himself into the Pathfinder's back seat, where he remained for a good while behind blackened windows. When he eventually got out his hands were tucked into his anorak pockets.

The last twelve minutes of activity were the iffiest she'd witnessed since taking up observations, and she decided that the sombrero-clad mantis qualified for pursuit.

The Pathfinder managed a five-point turn and roared past. The pickup spluttered to life and hobbled after it. The Pathfinder signalled right out of Panchimalco. Jasmine followed downhill at a calculated distance. Thick foliage closed above, shutting out the sky. Between trees to the right danced shards of a great city far below. Her quarry led her into that city, to La Colonia Escalón – a desirable neighborhood with bored security guards to chase away the riffraff and clean walled defences topped with rolls of razor wire. The mantis parked outside the lofty fortifications of a private mansion, and Jasmine pulled to the kerb a fair way back but within spying range. She observed two maids in spotless uniforms carry a single crate between them from the SUV's boot and through a black iron door that was set into a larger iron entryway. The mantis stooped in after them but didn't hang around and was again at the wheel in less than a minute.

Jasmine resumed the trail out of the city and down a dual carriageway signposted for Comalapa and the coast. Here the larger vehicle glided away. Jasmine was obliged to jam her foot to the floor in order to keep up, the rushing wind and the smoke-blowing engine howled jointly and with every pothole the pickup clanged like a toolbox landing on loose scaffolding from on high.

They abandoned the dual carriageway for the Costa del Sol road, and by mid afternoon were tanking alongside squat dagger plants perched on sand flats that rippled to an unbroken belt of leaning coconut palms through which glimmered the Pacific Ocean. Four times Jasmine decelerated and crawled past checkpoints in the wake of an obliging freight lorry or overloaded ex-American school bus. Shortly after the bridge that crosses the Rio Jiboa's cloudy waters, the Pathfinder veered without indicating on to the sands. Jasmine nudged the brake pedal and changed down into third but rattled on regardless, because to stop here would be to conspicuously expose the pickup on the level ground. A good two hundred metres ahead and Jasmine caught the flicker of roofs off to the right. A dozen fishermen's huts of bamboo and palm-thatch lurked amid the palms. She swung on to the sands, and parked in the shelter of the grove. The quiet was deafening and it took several seconds for the swish of breakers and wind-tussled branches to register. She looked back across the flats, and picked out the Pathfinder reversing into the palm belt.

What to do? Jasmine wondered. The black SUV had come

to a halt, its rear screened behind coconut palms while its bonnet and cabin protruded roadside. An hour passed without activity from the target. Jasmine hadn't eaten all day and the smell of the sea was doing its work on her appetite. She set off on foot through the grove on to the beach and approached an ancient fisherman hunched over his nets in one of the beached canoes, introducing herself *a-la-campesina*: full name, town and province of origin – true version.

'Esteban Santos, at your service, señorita,' he mumbled in return – lots of missing teeth for an otherwise engaging smile. He agreed to part with a couple of fresh corvina for next to nothing, and after an indulgent Señora Santos had fried them crisp in a pan of African palm oil, Jasmine reclined happily in the pickup's carrier, picking fish bones from her teeth. A puffy dark cloud skated from east to west. The tide greyed and receded. Jasmine returned to the cab as the first warm rain arrived.

* * *

Three canoes driving westwards on rain-darkened waters, powerful oarsmen, wake igniting like sparklers at the bows.

They must be soaked through, Jasmine reasoned, watching them idly. With a sudden jolt she recognised their trajectory: one that would land them neatly down from the stationary Pathfinder's semi-concealed position. She sat up and opened the window. The canoes powered so low against the tide that they were possibly taking in water.

She climbed down from the pickup and, crouching low, scurried across the flats towards the smudge of a Pathfinder's bonnet. The convoy rode the breakers easily, the oarsmen guiding with deft strokes that took them ashore. Stick-like occupants leapt overboard and set about hauling their boats up the beach beyond the reach of the surf. Jasmine dropped flat on her stomach and crawled up behind a ground-creeping plant. With rain pelting her back she stared through the trees, motionless, all senses alert.

The painted head of a stylised quetzal graced the bow of the

202

leading canoe, while blue and white waves along the panelling behind supposedly represented the bird's plumage. Both the other canoes were unremarkable, even drab on a rainy day.

She heard a clunk and darted her eyes back to the Pathfinder, its rear end seemingly wedged between two trees. The mantis was at large, his sombrero and shoulders visible across the roof moving towards the tailgate. After some fumbling of keys he opened the boot, stood aside and adjusted his hat. Jasmine checked on the fishermen, who were now swiftly unloading slim rectangular objects from the canoes. From the shape and handle-position I'd say those are rifle cases. There was something familiar about the gait of the tall leader of the gang who made his way up the beach empty handed, while his four comrades filed up behind lugging a case in each hand. A sixth man dallied briefly at the canoes before making a listing advance with one hand winging out to counterbalance the rifle case in his other. Whatever's in those rifle cases is heavier than a rifle. The leader slipped into the grove and became a shadow that went up to the driver and together they made a single, confused blur. Jasmine dared crawl closer for a clearer view; close enough at the edge of the trees to even hear a remote mumble of conversation. The followers arrived and one by one they slid their cargoes into the open boot, shoving and arranging to their satisfaction. And when they were done one of them folded both halves of the tailgate shut, snatched the keys – apparently tossed to him by the driver – out of the air, and locked up.

Jasmine observed the fishermen slink off back to their canoes. The Pathfinder powered up and rumbled to its right, and Jasmine ducked beneath the sweeping headlight beams, pressing her cheek into the damp sand while great rubber tyres went past before, with a roar from the engine and a tight wheel spin, they accelerated towards the coast road. She waited long enough to see the spray shooting into the air as the canoes smashed through the oncoming surf, and when they were convoying eastwards parallel to the coast she leapt to her feet and sprinted back to Esteban's hut.

But hers was an irresponsible request. Mumbling through gums yellowed by lamplight, Esteban explained that the currents and the tide are very strong tonight, señorita. Not even the most experienced fisherman should take to the ocean now.

She pointed out to sea, although the three teams were lost to the downpour. 'I have to follow those boats. I'm willing to take the risk.'

But Esteban flatly refused to plague his conscience with the perils the señorita would encounter on those turbulent waters. Just look at them!

Jasmine pleaded. He shook his head resolutely. Jasmine insisted. Sorry, but no, he could not allow her to be so foolhardy. She showed him the colour of her money: a grand total of three hundred and seventy-one Colons plus a handful of coins, all of which he was welcome to. He showed signs of yielding. She insisted all the more. He scratched his chin thoughtfully and the bristles rasped like a shaken maraca.

'Tell you what,' he said, heaving a sigh to show that relenting didn't come easily – or cheaply. 'Why don't you keep your money? Frankly, it's not worth a day's fishing, and there's no way I'm playing tourist guide to a kid bent on pursuing shady characters on a stormy sea in the dead of night. I could use a pickup, though.' He stopped scratching and noticed her sudden dismay.

She squatted down and, sifting damp sand through her fingers, considered the fisherman's proposal. He was clearly taking advantage of her; but she could ill afford to lose her lead. Bigger things, more costly things than Leonel's pickup, depended on her mission succeeding. 'I'll swap the pickup for a boat,' she agreed, coming to her feet and brushing her hands together.

'Small. No outboard motor. Still interested?'

'Okay.'

Esteban resumed his scratching, lifting his chin and shifting his claws down his neck. 'I'll fetch it at first light.'

'No,' Jasmine wailed, now feeling totally duped. 'I must follow them *tonight*,' – stamping one foot.

He cleared his throat noisily. Not daring to look Jasmine turned away when finally he leaned to one side and spat it all out in the sand.

'I don't know who you work for, child,' he said, his mouth duly purged. 'Perhaps you're military. Perhaps you're in league with the *muchachos*. Don't know. Don't want to know. But I can tell you this: those men have been landing on this beach regularly for the past six and a half months. I'd seen that quetzal canoe before – in Tehuacán – about half a day's travel up the Rio Lempa. No roads to the place, so unless you want to foot it through the woods, I suggest you take the river. Tomorrow, at first light, you'll find your way.'

'How will I recognise Tehuacán if the quetzal's not there?'

Esteban chuckled. 'Two hillocks, just like a pair of *chiches*. And the church of Santa Rita hasn't been repaired since it was bombed last year. You can't miss it,' he assured her, before calling to Señora Santos to stretch out the spare reed mat for their guest.

CHAPTER TWENTY

FEELING A SEASONED BOATWOMAN, Jasmine tugged confidently at the paddle. She rounded the tip of El Estero Jaltepeque into the mouth of the River Lempa. On a sunny beach to her left a sprawl of palm shacks welcomed out-of-towners who sought sun, sea, and *Mamacita*'s fried *bacalao*. Kids with wet matted hair splashed at the water's edge, bigger swimmers further out. To her right, wind-whipped waves curled on to the sugary sands of Tasajera Island. A stone's throw up the beach, clusters of coconut palms shaded a carpet of taro leaves – one tree featured a divided trunk that sprouted two separate crowns. Thickets populated the interior of this uninhabited islet.

The hubbub of beachside huts gave way to the burble her bow wave. On a strip of sandbank a spindly-legged roseate spoonbill, its wings a beautiful rosy-pink, swivelled its spatula-like bill and pursued Jasmine with one beady red eye. She was now driving up the river proper: a clay brown highway winding between overhanging vegetation crammed with heron and where flashes of iridescence were glimpses of macaw and yellow naped parrot. Other canoes, several boasting Yamaha outboard motors, slid downriver on the back of the current, their occupants acknowledging Jasmine with a courteous *'Que le vaya bien!'* Twisting and turning, the Lempa led her northwards and displayed for her scrutiny rickety planked jetties leading to beaches where canoes with colourful art down their sides were parked alongside old-time dugouts, and where women sat bent over buckets hand-raking milk into curds, and where the huts were by and large bamboo and palm-thatch, though some families had upgraded to unpainted adobe blocks roofed over by a shell of pink tiles.

By early afternoon the river was wriggling out of its twists, and after a particularly lengthy stretch of straight highway, the foliage unwrapped yet another village. It took little imagination to recognise the peculiar land feature to which Esteban had referred. Two thickly wooded hillocks – the larger hulking beyond the first – both swelling inland from the shoreline. At the foot of the first, a couple of dozen huts horseshoed a sandy plaza that fed on to the riverbank. At its crown, a compact white church with twin bell towers huddled amid a sweep of trees. Jasmine, slowing to a crawl, narrowed her eyes for enhanced scrutiny of the church. Single pilasters stood on either side of the round arched entrance and supported a horizontal entablature. Upon this pedestal stood a diminutive rectangular niche that housed a statue whose features Jasmine could not make out.

'Tehuacán,' she breathed, and confirmation came a skipped heartbeat later when she spotted the painted quetzal sweeping along curved planking. She pushed on past the village to cast an eye over the second knoll. Like its smaller neighbour, it was remarkably conical in shape and the two were united by a swooping pass. Beyond the hills, the river widened and was laced with low-lying sandbanks. By now Tehuacán had receded behind the slope of the second hillock, and Jasmine swung in towards an inlet strewn with brushwood and coconut husks, where she put to shore. With arms leaden with fatigue, she wrestled the canoe across the beach and left it upside down beneath an outcrop of vegetation.

* * *

Jasmine picked her way up the steep incline, employing her machete only when the way ahead became heavily obstructed. A parade of pink flecks bobbed into view. She blinked them

207

into focus. Almond blossom. The bark on this side of the tree had been stripped away, and lined up with precision one above the other was a trio of perfectly round holes, courtesy of busy woodpeckers. An air plant nestled in the branches. Jasmine scaled the tree to have a look into the air plant's red vase-like leaves. As expected they were cradles of rainwater, so she quenched her thirst and replenished her flask before helping herself to a couple of almond fruit.

Her ascent took thirty-five minutes before she topped the rise and gazed at a boulder-strewn lawn shaded by more almond trees and several floss silks whose branches were festooned with crimson star-shaped flowers.

'*Que bonito!*' she exclaimed, and ran forward. She clambered on to a boulder and sprang feet-together across to another, before raising her arms and leaping to the ground. She arrived at the other side of the summit and found a break in the foliage through which she peered down upon a sea of forest canopy. Here and there the shaggy head of a giant coconut palm or bushy water beech soared above the lesser trees. The jungle ended abruptly in a distant flat line beyond which the glittering Pacific Ocean marked the end of the world.

Directly below her the forest swooped away before climbing the smaller hillock. Two hundred metres from summit to summit, by Jasmine's approximation. This was a first-rate spy point. She commenced a critical analysis of the target. Inset with small deep windows, the church's northern wall was visible through a scattering of branches. Most of the terracotta tiles were missing, exposing a ribcage of rafters. A path cut through an overgrown yard and led down the hill into the sandy village plaza. Tehuacán was not so much a village, more a sprawl of adobe-walled huts in the sandy folds of the forest. No roads, just a hint of a path here and there between the trees. Women clad in happy colours gutting fish, others bent over plastic basins sifting milk into curds. Naked brown kids with tousled sun bleached hair doddering on uncertain legs. One baby girl seated alone in nappies and pigtails was clapping a pair of cuttlefish shells together and Jasmine fancied she could hear the noise of it. A dog to warn of – or off – visitors, a tethered mule to do the donkeywork. No fishing neighbourhood would be without its goats and chickens to add a little variety to its diet. Where the plaza met the river, fishermen hunched in canoes mending nets, and more kids cavorted and splashed. There was the quetzal canoe, with no-one in attendance.

It might be days or even weeks before Jasmine could stray any significant distance from the mount, and the small rations in her backpack would soon run out. There was an abundant supply of nuts at hand, river water too, some rainwater could be collected from air plants and fresh coconut water was plentiful. But she should survey her surroundings, assess security, and identify further food and water sources.

She emptied her backpack, concealing the contents under a pile of dead leaves and kindling which she intended to use later for building a campfire. With the flaccid sack riding on her back she did a spiralling downhill inspection of the ground and leaves for signs of human incursion. The odd hacked banana stem – browning; remnants of custard apple peel – again several days old; a pile of faeces – whether human or hound was not worth further inspection, and an empty Marlboro pack. The odd human may stray this way, but there was little to suggest regular use.

She rambled, coming across sour sop, custard apple and guava within the first half hour, and stuffing a couple of each into her backpack.

* * *

Was Tehuacán the manufacturer of whatever those rifle cases contained? Or was it merely the canoeists' yard? Or perhaps it served as a storage facility, which would mean another link in the lead had to be identified and followed. Jasmine was painfully aware that in keeping Tehuacán under twenty-four hour scrutiny she would have to manage without a comrade to share shifts. If she missed the quetzal's departure, she would high-tail it back to the coast – which her best guess suggested would be its destiny; and if she lost it altogether, she would return to Don Esteban's village and pick up the lead when it next paid one of its regular visits.

In the evening mouth-watering wafts of frying garlic and onions and fish almost tempted Jasmine down from the hill. When the sun went down over Tehuacán, darkness prevailed, pierced by the amber smudges from kerosene lanterns above doorways and the flicker of candlelight through un-shuttered windows. Tonight a knot of diehards stayed up late to share a bottle of the hard stuff.

Once midnight had ticked by and the final lamp had been doused Jasmine turned to her hammock for rest.

Rising before the first of the fishermen, she crept down to the inlet where she'd left her canoe, and here she bathed and topped up her water supply which she later boiled, allowed the silt to settle in the bottom of the pan, and then filtered through a wedge of coconut husk. With the west moon above San Vicente's balsam forests, and the remotest paling over Usulután's serrated peaks in the east, she resumed her observations with binoculars, Banco Agrícola diary, Nikon camera, and Radio Venceremos' sporadic transmissions of news and stirring revolutionary anthems for company. Women emerged from their huts to light fires on which they prepared coffee in hardy iron pots and boiled corn in great stainless steel cauldrons. Girls who should have been at school took to bending knee deep in the river to wash great swathes of linen. At the sweetness of boiling corn fishermen, young and old, put in an appearance, some lighting cigarettes and coughing their way over to their canoes while others hovered behind for a caffeine fix and a spot of breakfast before setting their boats afloat. By seven-thirty a.m., the tardiest of the crews had pushed off and were paddling hard downriver.

At mid-afternoon the women gathered on the riverbank and the children swam out to meet the returning canoes. The catch may have been depleted by merchants on the piers along the coast between La Libertad and Jiquilisco bay, but it was nonetheless happily received.

But half a dozen boats, including the quetzal, remained conspicuously idle, and Jasmine recorded this in her diary which by Saturday was crammed with her neatly lettered observations and addendums scurrying around all four edges of each page.

Sunday was a lazy day for everyone. Although doleful church bells could be heard from afar, there were none to rally Tehuacán's faithful. The church of Santa Rita remained silent and joyless.

She'd been on the mount a week and a day when she received her first visitors. In the dead of night, a couple of shirtless blokes in their forties, presumably from down there, arrived uninvited on the summit, waking her with rowdy banter. She watched them from a safe distance as their exhaustion from their ascent coupled with the two litre bottle of *guarro* took effect. But a peaceful night's sleep was to elude them, because they snored so loudly – great reverberating snorts – that they kept waking each other and telling the other to shut the fuck up. Jasmine was obliged to relinquish the hilltop to her unwelcome guests for a whole day while she watched the village from further down, until finally, late afternoon, the duo roused themselves and hobbled away. The visit had, however, served as a blunt reminder to Jasmine to observe caution at all times, especially when it came to erasing the evidence of her habitation, such as the charred cluster of rocks and powdery white ash that were the remains of last night's campfire.

* * *

Late evening on the fifteenth day on the hill, and Jasmine was scanning Tehuacán through her lenses yet again, and yet again after everyone else had gone indoors five good buddies remained in the plaza under the hazy amber of kerosene lamps.

Another knot of diehards, Jasmine thought, eyeing them with no great interest. But no sooner had the last lantern faded than the men got up and went smartly over to the row of parked canoes, and now it was evident that these were no diehards on

211

a binge because two of them were throwing their weight at the quetzal, another two were doing the same to a second boat, and the fifth handled a long slender craft all by himself. Now three boats were on the water, their oarsmen steering swiftly on the current, out into the middle of the river.

Backpack on, Jasmine pelted down the hillside and came out at the inlet. She rolled her canoe on to its hull and, hands on stern and feet ploughing up the sand, pushed it into the water. There was some splashing because the small craft winged out broadside to the current, but once she had embarked it responded eagerly to her paddle, and she swung in close to the banks and the shadow afforded by the overhanging shrubs. In her anxious rush to recover her lead she had become short of breath, but when thankfully the moonlit convoy reappeared she felt her breathing regulate into a steady rhythm in time with her paddling.

The convoy set a punishing pace, and Jasmine found herself uttering little whimpers as she wrenched at the paddle in her efforts to match their speed. But she realised that silence must rank high on their list of concerns, otherwise they would have resorted to outboard motors and left her standing. As it was, she managed to keep them in view for a good two hours. But the meandering course of the river and the stamina of the men began to tell, and although she pushed her burning arms she could only watch as her quarry, pulling steadily away, disappeared for minutes on end and grew fainter with every reappearance. Having pounded past Tasajera Island they faded into the night with a finality that seemed irrevocable.

They've gone out to sea. Jasmine peered ahead into the expansive blackness, heavy with disappointment and fatigue. Determined to recover visual contact, she threw all her weight behind the paddle, hacking and hauling with desperation. She and the canoe rode a swell and then a low and then she saw a silver-capped breaker billow up and wash towards her. It kicked up the bow, sending a veil of spray hissing over her while she whisked in the paddle and grabbed for but missed the gunwales, and for an eternal airborne second Jasmine and the canoe and the sea became separated. The canoe thudded into the backwash and here Jasmine joined it with a hard thump, and together they wallowed momentarily only to be gathered up by the succeeding breaker. Frantically Jasmine began paddling again and managed to push over the back of the wave.

In the calmer waters beyond the breakers she held the paddle still, and looked about her. Now the ocean seemed an ominous place. She imagined the depths below her and the creatures that would be lurking in them, and she shuddered involuntarily. By contrast, looking behind, she could easily pick out the friendly unbroken belt of palms, the odd flickering lantern in a beachfront shack, and the canoes parked along silvery beaches.

But there was no sign anywhere of the three canoes she had pursued down the Lempa. She looked around feeling desperate. This was a crucial solo mission, and she couldn't bear to return to Leonel empty-handed. He would reassign the mission and she would be back to couriering, or worse – to Citalá.

Putting these thoughts aside, she turned again to the ocean, narrowed her eyes and scanned the surface.

Her heart quickened. This time she saw something, perhaps two kilometres out, a fleck swelling and fading beneath dim greyish-blue cloud.

'A light...perhaps,' she speculated excitedly. 'No...a reflection – of metal.'

Her eyes, accustomed now to picking out the finest detail, fixed themselves on that weak glimmer and it grew stronger. It was a fishing trawler, anchored offshore.

Could that be where the canoes were heading? She stared doubtfully across the waters towards the other boat, conscious that the longer she dithered, the further away her quarry.

'Must get closer, but in this canoe I'll be spotted before I can get near enough.'

CHAPTER TWENTY-ONE

HAVING MADE THE DECISION to see the trawler up close, Jasmine spun the canoe until Tasajera was directly ahead. She mounted a breaker in full tumble and surfed towards the beach. As soon as the keel began catching in the shallows she vaulted overboard and then heaved the canoe up to where the taro leaves grew. In her hurry she tried to kick off her sandals but they were strapped fast to her feet.

'Poochica, not now!' she dropped down and peeled them off – straps still fastened. She stuffed the Smith & Wesson, wristwatch and camera into her backpack. She regretted having to leave them behind but seawater would only ruin them. Kneeling beside a spiky maguey she scraped away the sand with her hands and when she had laid the backpack at the bottom of the shallow pit she filled it once more before roughing the surface with her fingers so that the smooth sand would not be conspicuous. She stood up and retied the machete scabbard around her waist before running into the sea. She dived beneath a breaker and felt it surge over her as she propelled herself forward with powerful leg strokes. She touched the seabed with her fingertips and felt them ploughing the soft sand leftwards. A sturdy current was pushing to the east. She adjusted her direction to counter the current, and when her back no longer felt the waves rolling above, she came up for air and trod water, giving her eyes time to find the trawler.

She drew in a long breath and struck out for the faint outline of the mysterious vessel, swimming inches below the surface. She drove forward with a steady breast stroke that took her swiftly towards the south-west and counted sixty seconds before surfacing to refill her lungs. Each time she surfaced, the trawler was nearer. After half an hour she paused to tread water again. The ship was riding at anchor and Jasmine could now make out some detail. A yellowish glow in the deckhouse and against its rear wall the deck cabin stood a foot or so lower down on the main deck. A wooden life dinghy was on the roof of the cabin, its nose by the aft mast. She spotted the three canoes, lying low alongside the trawler's black hull.

When next Jasmine paused to tread water, the trawler rocked easily no more than fifty metres away. *Hija de la Luna*, she read from the bow. I've seen you before in these waters. She scanned the hull, but there was no sign of an anchor on this side.

She submerged, going deep this time, spun over and swam facing upwards. The three canoes drifted into view, warping and splintering into crystalline patterns. Then the hull of the trawler appeared above her. She came up beneath the steel keel and ran her fingers across its barnacle encrusted paintwork, jerking her hand away from the razor-sharp shells. The anchor cable materialised in the dimness ahead and she kicked out towards it, coming up for air between the cable and the port side. She looked up towards the deck, following the line of the cable until it reached the cathead that jutted out a metre from the gunwale to where it disappeared on to the deck through the hawsehole.

No-one peering over the side, she noted with satisfaction. The crew are probably busy with their visitors. Reaching up she seized the cable with both hands, clasped it between her thighs and climbed hand over hand towards the deck while water drizzled from her dungarees. The machete scabbard pressed against her waist and each time she gripped with her thighs, the blade end swung outwards. Twisting upon the axis of leather thong, it sent the handle end clubbing her right elbow, brushing across her breasts and knocking the cable beneath her stomach. It was an awkward movement which she decided to rectify. She paused. Twisting the belt chord she adjusted the scabbard until it rested diagonally across the anchor cable beneath her navel. Now she could move upwards with greater ease. But she had only advanced a foot higher when, with a sharp hiss, the machete slid from its scabbard. She shot out her hand but the end of the blade kissed her fingertip before plunging, handle first, into the water. With only the faintest splash, it slid beneath the surface.

Pursing her lips she continued grimly up the cable. She reached the cathead and, grasping the shaft with both hands, swung her feet on to the gunwale before pushing herself beneath the railing and on to the deck. Up here the wind was strong, coming in warm punches that diluted the odours of fish and grease. She glanced about her. The railing ran from the forecastle all the way to the stern, dropping a couple of feet where the foredeck met the main deck. The deck plating was surprisingly warm and seemed to grip the soles of her feet, giving her purchase as she stepped across the gangway and crouched beside the deckhouse wall. Above her the window leaned outwards. To her right she could see a bulbous white funnel, its oval mouth gaping seaward.

She looked to her left across the foredeck and towards the raised whaleback forecastle. A step away from the portside bulwark was a stool-sized capstan with the anchor cable wound around it a dozen or so times.

The steel wall beside her felt rough beneath her fingers as, gradually, she stood up. A darting wide-eyed peep through the window into the softly lit deckhouse interior told her that no-one was at the helm. She breathed a sigh of relief. Nevertheless, she ducked down before edging forward to peer round the corner. Against the forward facing deckhouse wall clung a red and white life-ring with rope untidily coiled around it. Now she could hear voices – staccato syllables mangling with the hollow clanking of the outriggers and the hooting of the wind. She skipped past the life-ring and risked a peek round the deckhouse's starboard corner. Five men were gathered on the gangway beneath the overhang of the main cabin's roof. The ship rolled and Jasmine flattened her palm hard to the wall to prevent herself from being pitched forward. She crouched down, and in her eagerness to take in the scene she was only vaguely aware of the water draining from her saturated dungarees and trickling across the deck.

With their backs towards the cabin wall, three of the men were kneeling over a plywood crate. A missile container. Jasmine recalled seeing similar crates in the PCS's armoury and she recognised the white foam separators dividing the interior into accommodating sections. From these sections the three were whipping out beige-coloured plastic bags and packing them into a long hard-shell case which lay on top of another of identical dimensions. Twelve-pack weapons transporters: she had used such containers to deliver new rifles to cells to replace their ailing models. Beyond the three packers a brick-house of a man with a huge ginger head, blue-grey sweater rolled up at the sleeves and frayed jeans was jotting notes into a leather-bound register which he was resting precariously on the railing. Without moving his head, he flicked pea-sized black eyes up from the register. Jasmine ducked behind the deckhouse and, holding her breath, wedged her back hard up to the wall. She reached for her Smith and Wesson and then for her machete. She found neither, and suddenly felt very vulnerable indeed.

Biting her bottom lip, she chanced another peep beyond the corner. Mercifully the purser's eyes were once again on his note-taking. There was a fifth man: partially screened by the purser, he wore a high-neck sweater with epaulettes and elbow patches and he was leaning on the starboard railings and gazing towards the distant coastline. Beneath a peaked cap jutted a robust jaw. The end of a cigarette danced before his shadow-dimmed face.

Now the smoker had straightened up and was pointing

towards the mainland. 'Coastguard,' he called out in the outsized voice that comes with shouting orders above the wind.

Jasmine looked in the direction he was pointing and saw a Piranha assault craft parting the water, spreading swept-back wings of curling waves. On the bow deck an unmanned mounted gun listed loosely in its housing, angling down over the low curved windshield.

Now they'll panic.

But there was no panic. As if choreographed the three packers simultaneously raised surly faces, gave the approaching boat a cursory glance, and returned to their labours.

'He's never late, *patrón*,' the ginger purser snorted, turning his wrist to look at his watch. In contrast to the *patrón's*, his was a baritone voice, far too small for his hulking mass.

The speedboat's motor shut down, and the smoking *patrón* fed a rope ladder over the trawler's gunwale.

'You stay in the boat, Chaval. We'll be back in five.'

Jasmine started at the voice, and clung with both hands to the deckhouse wall as if to steady herself from the surprise. Captain Sag-man himself, the very same creep who'd intercepted her and Adrian in the Gulf of Fonseca while they'd been innocently transporting a radio transmitter. Now the pear-shaped oaf squeezed between the railings on to the ship and shook hands with the smoker. Behind him another head emerged above deck-level, and if Sag-man's arrival was a surprise, the bristly flattop hairdo that rose in stages was a total shock to the system, and Jasmine slapped a hand over her mouth, trapping a gasp of revulsion.

Anastasio!

No swirling camouflages tonight, but a loose smock of fine black cotton and golden embroidery spilling over his broad shoulders. As ever his brooding gaze made a stern appraisal of everyone and everything it met, and his jaw muscles were constantly pulsing, like a nervous tick. Unlike Captain Sag-man, Anastasio hitched his long legs over the railings, and when he straightened up he towered above the others.

'What's today's count?' Anastasio demanded with a nodded greeting.

'Fifty-six units. 2.27 kilos in each,' the *patrón* replied, with smoke jetting from his mouth and nostrils. He flicked the cigarette butt overboard, took a fresh one from a crumpled pack and, shielding his lighter from the wind, lit up.

Anastasio stepped across to inspect the packing process which was coming to an end. Sag-man nudged up beside him and began tapping on a calculator. 'I want a copy of the inventory,' Anastasio let him know.

'Three layers.' The purser lifted a page of his register and Anastasio looked briefly at the wind-rattled carbon paper.

'Rounded down to the nearest American Dollar, that comes to one grand and four hundreds,' Sag-man declared jovially, and held up the calculator's panel for inspection by any who might doubt his integrity.

The *patrón* pulled a mocking smirk. 'Your cut is more generous every time, captain.' Turning on Anastasio he extended open hands in a good humoured let's-be-reasonable gesture. 'Talk sense to the man; get him to do something about his exorbitant fees, will you.'

But good humour was wasted on Anastasio. 'Arrangements between you and your Ecuadorian associates have zilch to do with me.'

Shaking his woolly-capped head in mock woe the *patrón* unhooked his waist pouch and foisted it on Sag-man. 'Take. Count it if you must. Just hurry up about it.'

'You anticipated the amount exactly, yet you complain,' Sag-man pointed out.

'I've half a mind to reroute through the Caribbean,' the *patrón* threatened.

Chuckling to himself, Captain Sag-man unzipped the leather pouch and began flicking through the bank notes. 'You're fortunate that Don Anastasio is sourcing from Peru instead of Colombia. Costa Rica has dozens of unsupervised air strips near the Nicaraguan border that could put you out of business, but Don Anastasio prefers not to link up with the remnant Contras gangs. He's got standards, prefers to do deal with respectable tycoons like me and you. Although I'm sure he could be persuaded otherwise, *if* your prices were not to his liking.' He broke off to cast a meaningful stare at his scowling complainant before resuming: 'I charge you a nominal fee to transport your goods through the Gulf; and don't give me any bullshit about you swallowing that cost; you pass it on to our Don Anastasio, isn't that right?' His fingers slotted themselves inside the pouch to mark the count while he fired a question at Anastasio: 'How much are you forking out for this shipment?'

'Less talk, fatso. We haven't got all night.'

Sag-man shrugged and continued to count the notes, again addressing the *patrón*: 'Anyway, the Pacific coast is your cheapest option,' he asserted, plainly defending his turf. 'To get to the Caribbean by boat you'd risk discovery on the Amazon or incur Canal charges and risk being trumped in Panama. You'd also have to pay off a handful of Caribbeans, any one of whom might be on the DEA's payroll. No, my friend,' he concluded, zipped the pouch and clapped the *patrón's* epaulette-capped shoulder, 'I think you know *very well* that you are safer with us.' And to Anastasio. 'You coming?'

'Go on ahead. I'll hitch a ride with my boys and my stuff.'

'Fine by me,' said Sag-man. He ducked through the railings, and his powdery skinhead sank below deck-level. Moments later Jasmine heard the Piranha's outboard motor strike up and throb away, and she watched the craft plough off in a south-easterly direction before it swung round and accelerated towards the dark volcanic highlands that presided over the Salvadoran coast.

'Got you!' Warm breath hit Jasmine's right ear, and she leaped on a heart-rending reflex only to be clamped from behind in a huge pair of arms. First she screamed. Then she kicked out. But her captor leaned backwards, hoisting her clean off the deck, and stepped neatly on to the gangway in full view of the motley assembly.

'*Patrón*, look what I found,' he cried in that soprano voice of his.

Jasmine set to work on his trunk-like wrists, striving to prise them apart. 'Get off me,' she said, panicking as the overwhelming crush triggered a helplessness similar to that she had experienced at the hands of Anastasio in another life. The wrists wouldn't budge, so she jerked her body about, realising now – and now was too late – that for all her knowledge of munitions and explosives she had yet to learn the basic art of unarmed self defence. The massive arms contracted a notch and her burly captor literally bent over backwards until Jasmine saw her own bare feet kicking against a starry sky.

'*A girl!*' The *patrón* flicked his cigarette into the sea and barged past the packers sending them sprawling over their finished work. 'A stowaway? On my ship?'

Behind him, Anastasio whipped round and Jasmine saw the moment recognition dawned. Now he barged past the rising packers sending them sprawling again.

'Get off me,' Jasmine repeated, the menace she intended sounding annoyingly like terror, and she pitched back a clenched fist and struck something fleshy, then threw her arms up and tried to wriggle out of the crush, but the biceps tightened, strapping her up with suffocating rigidity.

'Where on earth did she board?' the *patrón* asked.

'*Patrón*, I thought I saw movement when I was taking the inventory,' the purser shrieked triumphantly. 'And while she was busy admiring the *beautiful* speedboat, I went round the deckhouse and snuck up behind her. *Patrón*, you should have seen her jump,' he paused to cackle from deep within his chest, taking Jasmine on a bumpy ride, 'but I got a tight hold of her. *Patrón*, I don't think she's a stowaway because she's soaked through. Must have swum here.'

'All right, Marlon, let her down, but hold her fast,' the *patrón* said, as Anastasio stood, blinking in disbelief. The *patrón* lit up. Jasmine got a whiff of vanilla-scented smoke.

'*Hijo de puta*! What the hell are you doing here?' Anastasio had found his voice.

'You know this girl?' The *patrón* turned to Anastasio and demanded that he should please explain.

Anastasio heaved a great sigh, after which he got round to admitting that she was a *muchacha*, worked for my mum. Now she's an *hija de puta guerrillera*.

The *patrón* bent forwards and examined his unexpected catch at close quarters. When he spoke his square stubbly jaw jutted out taking his bottom lip with it. 'Where is her boat? Or are we to assume that she swam all the way from the mainland?'

'Ask her,' Anastasio suggested, brightening.

'Where have you come from, girl? What have you come here to do?' The *patrón* carefully enunciated as if addressing a non-Spanish speaker. Instead of replying she fastened her teeth on Marlon's great wrist, biting hard on salty skin. Satisfied she had a good purchase she pulled back, raising the pinched skin. But the skin did not break nor did Marlon offer the remotest expression of discomfort. She became aware of chuckling coming from her audience, and with her mouth still fastened to Marlon's wrist, she looked up, glancing from face to face. Realising there was actually amusement in their eyes she unclamped the skin and spat out a couple of wiry hairs that had come away. At least she'd left teeth marks.

Suddenly Anastasio seized her jaw and squeezed. 'Where are the others? Speak, Jasmine.'

'Take your filthy hands off me.'

He pulled a puzzled frown.

'Obviously she can't speak with you clawing her face like that,' the *patrón* pointed out. 'Let her go, man!'

Anastasio relinquished his grip, and for a while the semicircle of repugnant spectators rubbed their chins and exchanged glances, evidently wondering what the hell to do about her. Meanwhile Jasmine's hands had one of Marlon's thumbs in a vice-like grip and she was making progress in bending back the thumb when the *patrón* made the admission that in fact she was more of a liability to Anastasio than to him. 'So what do *you* propose we do with her?'

Tut-tutting as if in regret Anastasio gazed directly into Jasmine's eyes. 'We could have been very good together, me and you. But you had to mess things up. Because of you, Santamaria is dead and so are my chances of promotion. And now out of the blue you turn up here, trying to disrupt our legitimate enterprise. What for, Jasmine? What for? To go telling tales to ONUSAL?' He tipped his head as if ONUSAL was just up the road. 'That's what you're here for, isn't it?' He went silent for such a long while that the *patrón* told him to get a bloody move on and decide or he would simply chuck her overboard and she could swim back the way she'd come. But Anastasio was not to be hurried. He had self-interested plans up his sleeve. Supporting his weight with hands on knees, he leaned in and spoke low but steadily right beside Jasmine's left ear. 'Leave the guerrillas, Jasmine. Be my woman again. What do you want? Money? A house?' – pause for reflection – 'Marriage? Okay, we can talk about that too. You'll want for nothing.' Hesitant now, 'I've thought about you so often since our night together. I was a bit rough, I know, and I regret that. But next time I'll be gentle, I promise.' Now he stood back and nodded at her encouragingly.

Jasmine didn't know where her laugh came from. It just erupted out of her mouth of its own accord. '*Never*,' she screamed. 'Do you hear me? *Never!*'

Anastasio swallowed hard and his face darkened. 'A dangerous girl,' he declared under composure for the benefit of the *patrón*. 'If we don't get rid of her once and for all she'll be back, cropping up where we least expect her. Leave the bitch where no-one can find her.'

The *patrón* preferred plain language. 'Weigh her down and chuck her overboard.'

'No,' Jasmine implored, while lunging in her human straightjacket at Anastasio. 'You'll regret this.' She shot out her foot, but with him hopping back and Marlon the bursar swinging her aside, she missed his crotch by a long chalk. 'It'll all come back to you, every bad thing you ever did,' she assured him as Marlon swung her away.

'Until then why don't we all have a bit of fun?' Anastasio proposed, and made a show of unbuckling his belt and tugging the strap. By way of encouragement he listed her assets for the benefit of *Hija de la Luna*'s crew: 'Don't be fooled by those baggy dungarees, beneath them she's got the tightest, shapeliest butt you're ever likely to see,' he assured, to growing interest from all quarters except the *patrón*.

'No!' the *patrón* snapped, clearly irritated by now. 'I'm not having that sort of thing happening on *my* ship. 'Besides,' he added as if on reflection he was after all one of the lads, 'you'll all want a go and we just haven't got the time. Our operation's like a relay race; can't let the baton rest long enough for the law to pick it up, know what I mean?' If they did, they weren't admitting. The *patrón* turned swiftly to his boatswain – a fair-haired youth who had appeared from the direction of the port-side gangway and who was now staring drop-jawed at Jasmine. 'Fetch the spare anchor from the hold and bring some rope.'

The boatswain scampered back along the gangway and the *patrón* rolled his eyes at the sound of the lad tumbling down the companionway.

'That will have hurt,' he muttered dryly, before addressing Marlon: 'Take her to the aft deck. Bind her wrists and ankles to the anchor and drop her overboard.'

'*Si, patrón.*' Marlon nodded. He set off down the gangway with Jasmine thrusting out her hand, trying for purchase on the deckhouse, but her fingernails scraped along the wall as she was borne along. Each time she whipped up her legs and aimed for a foothold on the bitts or railing, he twisted his whole body to bring her out of reach. When they emerged on to the aft deck she was in tears. There was no way she would be able to resist an anchor's weight, and the very thought of drowning, of water flooding her lungs, of the suffocation that would eventually lead to death, drove her to thrash about and scream with unbridled hysteria. The *patrón* approached, drew back his huge fist and smashed it into the side of her chin.

When she came to, she felt the hard deck plating beneath her shoulders. She opened her eyes to blurred human shapes moving across a hazy blackness that she presumed was night sky. 'Ouch,' she groaned. But when she tried to touch her throbbing chin, harsh unyielding cord cut into her wrists, and she realised they were trussed severely together behind her back. She was bound at the ankles, too.

Marlon stepped over her and she watched him squat astride the anchor and feed a length of rope through the iron ring at the end, and with a whipping hand-over-hand action he fastened some kind of knot. He turned and nodded to someone behind her and she craned her head backwards.

'Monster,' she muttered, seeing Anastasio stoop over her and feeling him tuck his hands beneath her shoulders and lift her up.

He sniggered. 'While you were dozing so peacefully we all had a peak at those fine little titties, brought back sweet memories.'

She swallowed dryly and turned away. Beside her, Marlon gathered up the curved fluke of the anchor, while the boatswain, who Jasmine noticed was now nursing a scratch above his left eye, raised the shank end in cupped hands. The *patrón* took hold of her ankles, and together the two teams moved towards the port bulwark.

She groaned and shook her head while wriggling feebly in her bindings. Now the men laid her flat on the taffrail.

'We chuck her first,' the *patrón* advised Anastasio. 'In the seconds it takes for the cable to feed out we dash over and help the others toss the anchor as far from the side as possible. Got it?'

Jasmine descended to the sound of rushing wind. The anchor cable trailed out above her. Her back hit the water with a loud clap and the air was driven from her lungs. She went under but surfaced almost immediately and rocked for a short while on the choppy surface. She drew in a lungful of air, knowing that she would need it once the anchor hit water. Above her she could see the pallid faces of Anastasio and the young boatswain peering after her. Anastasio waved a hand and spat over the side. Somewhere close she heard the anchor splash and Anastasio's spittle was lost in spray. She felt the rope yank taut and she was dragged under. After the first metre the temperature dropped considerably. She pursed her lips but kept her eyes open. The ship faded gradually into darkness. She gritted her teeth as a sting hit through the burble in her ears and intensified the deeper she plunged. Then there was total blackness. Only the constant pull of the knots at her ankles and wrists and the even pressure against her back gave her any sensation of motion.

* * *

The anchor must have landed because the downward pull gave a little, and she wondered whether on account of the air she held in her lungs her fall had broken somewhere above the seabed, leaving her suspended in the blackness. Her lungs were beginning to hunt for air, and it took nothing more than a single bubble to seep between her lips for her to drift the rest of the way down, or at least that's what she reckoned made the difference.

The sand was cold and soft to the touch when finally she bounced almost weightlessly on the seabed. She twisted over and buoyed to her feet, feeling her hair drifting across her face. She shuffled forwards, aimlessly, and when her foot skimmed on a layer of sand over cold metal she realised she had landed beside the anchor. She wriggled her toes over its surface, seeking out the anchor ring and the halyard knot.

Then she heard the sudden acceleration in her own heartbeat. This was no anchor.

'My machete,' she exclaimed, expelling a mouthful of precious air bubbles. She floated down until she lay on her side with her back to the machete. With desperate fingers she located the blade, turned it over so that the sharp side settled on the knot between her wrists. With a series of short, jerky slices she cut through the strands of halyard, feeling first one, then the other fray and give under the blade. Suddenly her wrists were free. She sat up and swiftly set about the rope that held her ankles and soon she kicked the clinging strands away. If she wished to use arms and legs for a speedy swim to the surface she should leave the machete behind, but surely it was better to keep an instrument of such apparent providence. So, gripping the machete above her head, point upwards, she pushed off the seabed, and using only her legs to propel herself she soared towards the surface, her ribcage already convulsing. And though she clamped her lips together yet her lungs sucked at the water through her nose and she felt a salty trickle run down the back of her throat. She knew she could hold out no longer, for all her lung muscles were working against her. When her mouth shot open involuntarily, she felt an abrupt weightlessness grip the machete. Air! A moment later she exploded through the surface and sucked in a desperate lungful of sweet, sweet air.

Hija de la Luna was already well underway, the stern churning up the sea behind it. Treading water, gasping and wiping her eyes Jasmine watched the trawler swing its way round, and when it was heading safely south, she struck out for Tasajera Island.

CHAPTER TWENTY-TWO

MACHETE IN HAND, Jasmine led the way up the mount. 'These hills are referred to by locals as Chinchontepeque, which in Nahuatle means *two bruises*,' she announced in her best tour guide voice.

'Big Tits Hill, actually,' Leonel corrected with undisguised relish.

They topped the rise and Jasmine gave him a whistle-stop tour of their new abode and its gardens, and then marched him over to the look-out spot and pointed out the features of interest.

'The quetzal boat we saw from the river. It and two others row out to the trawler to collect the cargo I told you about.'

'Peruvian you say?'

'Peruvian cargo, Ecuadorian crew. Afterwards...well, I didn't see where they went but I'm guessing they rendezvous with Señor Mantis the Pathfinder driver, who then distributes the stuff to his clients.' She dropped down on the grass and sat cross-legged. 'Now we wait and watch.'

'What about a store?' he – the fascinated tourist – now questioned.

'What *about* a store?'

'*Los contrabandistas* would need to store those goods – whatever they are – before embarking on a round of deliveries. Don't you think?'

'I realise that,' Jasmine agreed. 'They wouldn't have gone

directly from the trawler to the rendezvous.'

'So where would such a store be located?' he pushed.

'Somewhere in Tehuacán, I guess.'

'Where in Tehuacán?'

She frowned up at him. Hadn't he issued instructions not to go barging in alone but to involve him the minute she had a firm lead? And isn't that exactly what she'd done?

'That's what we're here to find out,' he murmured, and settled his binoculars over his eyes. 'Have you seen the church? Shocking bad way, isn't it?'

She left him surveying the village and went to build a fire and set coffee brewing. While dusk was fallng, the *Comandante* and his promising underling sat on rocks facing each other and dined on pawpaw with an exotic filling of chopped almonds coated in comb-clotted honey. For afters, black coffee sweetened with yet more honey. Having been deprived of conversation for nearly three weeks, Jasmine found herself chatting away non-stop while Leonel seemed content to watch her over the rim of his coffee mug.

'I'm rambling, aren't I?' she stalled, aware that he hadn't uttered a word for half an hour. The firelight was gilding the contours of his face and dancing in his eyes, eyes that, though he pulled his familiar confident grin, hinted at some inner anxiety.

'I have some bad news, Jasmine,' he said eventually, setting his cup in the grass. 'I attended another week of talks with the Ministry, after which I had a chat with Ivan…Ivan Saavedra. Ivan mentioned that one of his comrades had been your classmate at *el Campamento*. Apparently she spoke very highly of you. Jasmine this, Jasmine that.'

'That would be Manuelita,' she blurted happily, and was about to embark on fond reminiscence when foreboding dawned, and she raised a hand to her lips.

'Manuela Rendón was killed last Saturday. I'm sorry.'

'How?' she whispered.

'During combat duties, that's all I heard.'

She held his stare for a long while, willing – not for the first time in recent years – that events would undo themselves. 'These things…' But she couldn't finish the sentence, and she hung her head.

'I know,' Leonel murmured, leaning forward and patting her knee.

* * *

Leonel was not a sedentary man, Jasmine was soon reminded. He stared down at Tehuacán, stalked the grove like a caged jaguar, and returned to stare again.

'We may be up here for days…weeks even,' she warned him.

'I've got things to do in Cuscatlán.'

'Your *things to do in Cuscatlán* are undermined by all this business with *el contrabando*. From what you say ONUSAL takes the accusations seriously. Or perhaps you were exaggerating?'

'I know, I know the reasons,' he snapped. 'I just don't like sitting around doing nothing.'

'Don Leonel,' she said, lowering the binoculars, 'teach me self-defence.' A lesson or two in unarmed combat could come in handy, besides serving as a distraction for Leonel.

He whipped off his shirt to reveal well-defined pectorals, flung down the shirt and began circling her, fingers beckoning her to the challenge. She grinned, leapt off the boulder and faced him in the formal stance, right leg forward.

He pushed one vertical palm towards her while curving his other arm over his head. She told him she'd seen Chinese fighters do that on TV, and she hoisted her hands too, and turned sideways-on, as he was now doing.

'The main thing to remember about self defence is that it's for defending, not attacking,' he asserted, rising to his new role as instructor.

He sidled past, his hands describing elaborate patterns in the air. 'I'll teach you to strike with every part of your anatomy. Your entire body will become a lethal weapon.'

'Is that karate?'

'It is. In fact in my karate class I was known as Señor Dexterous,' he advised her solemnly, as if to say, *so don't mess with me!*

'*Señor Dexterous!*' She erupted with laughter. 'What kind of name is that?'

'Concentrate, Jasmine, now do as I do.'

She put her legs together and stood with palms on hips, elbows out. Not exactly as he was doing, but close enough.

'Legs slightly apart,' he prompted. 'Now drop your body weight' – bouncing easily on bended knees and bunching his fists – 'and pull your right hand back to your side.'

She obeyed, enthralled.

Leonel lunged forward and in slow motion drove a clenched fist towards her jaw. 'Step back and angle yourself to your right.'

She twisted her body as his knuckles glided towards her chin, which she obligingly lifted for the encounter.

'Use that hand there to deflect the blow…yes, that's right.'

She sliced her left hand across his wrist and shoved the oncoming blow aside.

'Now counter punch with your right fist.'

'In slow motion, like you?'

'Of course.'

She thrust her right fist on to the side of his jaw. 'Raspy.'

'Don't sidetrack. Now pivot on your left foot and kick me in the bollocks,' hastily adding, 'in slow motion.'

'I can see it coming together,' she admitted, discovering that she was landing her fist on his raspy jaw while simultaneously delivering a kick to his groin.

'Good. Now let's do it again,' Leonel said, standing back and recomposing himself. But he'd let himself in for more than he'd bargained because four and a half hours later when he called a halt, Jasmine insisted they continue training. A new moon rose in the east before finally the pupil allowed the instructor respite.

They slept.

They rose.

After a hurried breakfast and a scan of Tehuacán, they resumed the training programme for an entire day. Pauses every other minute while one or the other darted over to the look-out point to check on the canoes, before rushing back to resume the close physical engagements that training demanded.

'Don't pit your strength against that of a man,' Leonel told her severely. 'Trade your speed and technique against his weaknesses.'

'You can stop that slow motion nonsense,' she replied. She would never learn if he continued to take it easy on her. 'I want you to treat me like a man.'

But of course she wasn't a man. If every now and then in a tangle of arms they hesitated mere seconds longer than was strictly necessary before disengaging, laughter was employed as a sort of release valve to resolve some mild embarrassment. But on Sunday morning of the fourth week of entanglements, laughter no longer worked. With Leonel flat on his back Jasmine found herself sitting astride his waist and despite his instruction to avoid pitting her inadequate strength against that of a man she was trying to push down his hands, and he was resisting but not hard enough, and gradually she managed to drive his hands to the ground, pinning them beside his ears. But the angle brought them face to face and she was laughing in triumph when on an impulse he raised his head and kissed her full on the lips. She wasn't at all taken aback, which she thought was strange but in a pleasing way. Affection swelled in her breast and she sank flat on top of him and returned his kiss. He rolled over, taking her under him but raising himself on vein-ridged arms, and although she felt a wash of desire, she also felt something rallying against it. Am I ready for this – with Leonel?

He peeled off his singlet and helped her out of her dungarees and then he told her that her eyes were like sunflowers floating on dewponds, which she thought was very poetic, and left her thinking yes, perhaps she was ready for this. With who better than Leonel, even if they weren't married? So she told him that she was now a woman and to prove it she sat up and pulled off her T-shirt, unclipped her bra and lay back down again in apprehensive invitation. He fastened his mouth to one nipple then the other which sent delightful shivers to trigger other parts of her body to quiver of their own accord. But when his hand reached down and crept into her briefs the escalating fires of desire unaccountably went out, and she felt so disappointed with herself that she refused to kiss him any more, scrambled out from beneath him and wept with bitter frustration. Leonel approached from behind, slid his arms around her in a cosy embrace, kissed the top of her head and apologised for being such a goat. She planted a kiss on his forearm and rubbed it in with her palm.

CHAPTER TWENTY-THREE

'THE QUETZAL HAS FLOWN,' announced Jasmine. 'And two others besides.'

An unspoken agreement that martial arts training be suspended had Leonel reading Alfredo Espino's *Jicaras Tristes*, but on Jasmine's announcement he came over to look for himself. 'When do you suppose they'll be back?'

At dawn, she was almost certain. She would take first watch.

After Leonel had turned in, Jasmine trained her binoculars on the village. But Leonel found little sleep, and coming up to one a.m. he joined her, which was just as well because no sooner had they settled than he nudged her and pointed across Tehuacán's roofs. 'Three boats on the water. Earlier than you anticipated.'

Jasmine reached up and snatched the binoculars. 'Yes, they're back. Too dark to make out the quetzal, but it must be them. No-one else arrives so deep into curfew.'

Three canoes put to shore. Six figures alighted, and from the hulls each hauled out two dark cases like those Jasmine had seen on Don Estaban's beach and again on *Hija de la Luna*. The figures raced through the village and hurried into the church.

'I should have guessed,' Leonel exclaimed. For a long while nothing else happened. Jasmine's ever-ripe competitive streak was eager to be first to declare the visitors' emergence.

'They're coming out now,' Leonel got in first – just.

So Jasmine pointed out the detail: 'Empty handed.'

The six had slipped out of the church and while one held back perhaps to lock the door the others slunk downhill, through the plaza and began launching their canoes on the Lempa. The last man jogged through the village to join his team-mates.

'That's Anastasio,' Jasmine said, cringing.

'I can just about make out more cases in the canoes,' Leonel murmured.

'Immediate deliveries,' Jasmine suggested.

'What, without checking their consignment?'

'Anastasio goes through it with Captain Sag-man on the trawler.'

'And the consignment is Peruvian?'

'*Yes*, I *told* you that, like *three times* already.'

'Very quick turn-around, wouldn't you say?'

'Once they get rolling, yes,' Jasmine agreed, monitoring the third canoe until it slid from view behind the curtain of trees. 'Let's go.'

* * *

Kerosene fumes drifted on the night even though Tehuacán's lamps had long been doused. Way above them three small round-arched windows evenly spaced along a white wall came into view. Jasmine shuddered. Surrounded by a frame of foliage the church's north wall floated eerily. It wasn't until they pushed through on to the grassy churchyard that she could see where the looming wall met the earth.

Leonel suggested she check the side door to the chancel while he went round to the front door. 'If they're both locked, we go in through the roof.'

The dark timber door was set deep in the limed wall. Jasmine tugged at the wrought iron ring, but the door wouldn't budge.

'The main entrance is locked too,' Leonel confirmed seconds later. 'Plan B: scale the wall...but where?'

Such obstacles were trifles for Jasmine. She selected a suitable tree, shinned up it and used one of its sturdy branches as a bridge to cross to a rafter beam along which she walked tight-rope-style to the top of the wall. She seated herself between two beams, dangling her legs over the wall's edge, and waited for the show.

'You little monkey,' Leonel accused, before appraising the tree with a frown.

'Hurry up, Señor Dexterous,' she called from her perch.

'I'm twice your weight, señorita,' he assured her, putting a boot to a knobbly root and giving the tree trunk a full embrace while his boot slid up and down the root like a motorcyclist's starting up on a frosty morning.

Jasmine let out a satisfied chuckle.

Leonel glared up at her. 'Well don't just sit there; see if there's something inside for me to stand on.'

Jasmine dropped down into the church and wandered through the nave, gazing round the austere interior. Aside for broken pews, scattered timbers, and dead leaves, it was bare, with high-set, glassless windows. Against the sky the rafters looked sturdy enough, and in places boasted the remains of gold-coloured paintwork. From the beams hung scraps of cloth, rotted into shabby ribbons which still bore the faded colours of the original dyes. She heard Leonel whistling his bird impression to remind her of his presence outside, so she checked the side door but it was bolted with a chunky padlock that she suspected from its condition to be newer than anything else in the church. She levered up a pew, laying one end slantwise on the wall's crest, stood back and fed it upwards, and when she ran out of arm length and still the pew hadn't see-sawed, she squatted low and then sprang up.

Lots of busy footprints which she stooped to inspect with her torchlight – large, male, running in all directions. The fine curved stripes of track shoes, and the thicker jagged tread of jungle boots.

She went up the three steps to the chancel to a stone altar a couple of metres back from the top step. She heard Leonel drop heavily and turned to address him as he straightened up.

'You notice something?' she said.

236

'Notice what?'

'The rifle cases…they're not here.'

'Uh-huh. So where did they stash them?'

'There are footprints all over the place.' She gestured with a forefinger while Leonel crunched down the nave to the double doors of the main entrance, which he discovered unsurprisingly were also locked from the inside. 'But they lead in no particular direction.'

They set about hunting for the rifle cases. Jasmine went up the narrow spiral staircase to the north bell tower. The bronze bell was still hanging from its holding. She stared between the slender windows, across the missing roof, to where the south tower stood, its lower half ashen against the forest blackness. Like a Jack-in-the-box Leonel popped up in the south bell tower, and looked across at her. She shook her head.

Shoulders hunched, he thrust both upturned hands forwards and then outwards.

She shrugged, and then started back down the stairs.

'They've disappeared,' he said, when they were again in the gloom of the nave.

'We're just not looking in the right place,' she reasoned. They'd searched the church from top to bottom. She began clucking her tongue abstractly. Where would I stash rifle cases in a place like this? She was watching her foot scrape a pattern in the dusty floor when something caught her eye: a straight line. Faint and broken up, but a straight line nonetheless, one that continued between each scuff and footprint and might have been obliterated completely by her foot-art if she hadn't paused to consider its significance. She called Leonel over to have a look.

'There's dust everywhere,' she began.

'*That's what you called me over to see?*' he snapped.

'Everywhere…except here.' The line was vague, a ridge of gathered dust that angled away from the foot of the altar. 'See that?' She ran her fingertip along the delicate ridge, obliterating it but illustrating its continuity.

'Below the altar,' they chorused.

Wasting no time they put their combined weight to the side of the altar, and to Jasmine's delight it responded, grinding across the flagstones.

'Look,' she huffed, pointing towards a rift in the floor; a rift that was widening to a dark rectangular hollow a shade larger than a manhole.

'An undercroft!' Leonel declared, and he knelt down, dug out his diving torch, and shot the slender beam into the opening.

'What do you see?' Leonel's broad shoulders were screening Jasmine's view. He stood up and handed over the torch.

Lying flat on her stomach, her head and right arm inside the cavity, she penetrated the darkness with the light beam, picking out two opposing walls of good stone masonry, and a sandy floor. 'I don't know about an undercroft. It looks more like a tunnel to me,' she said. She jumped to her feet and brushed the dust from her hands. 'We've got to go down there.'

Leonel manoeuvred feet-first through the hole. Jasmine watched his fingers relinquish their grip and heard the thud of boots landing. When she followed, she felt his hands grab her waist and lower her, setting her gently on the floor. They were indeed in a tunnel, its roof perfectly domed and proportioned, and like the walls it was of dressed limestone blocks fitted together with precision. The floor of limestone slabs was covered with fine sand which showed countless footprints.

'Which way shall we try first?'

'Towards the river,' he said decisively, and set off at a smart pace, his torch lighting the way ahead. 'When Chachi and I were kids, Granddad told us fabulous bedtime stories about the Nahua, Maya, and Lenca People and their obsession for tunnelling. I remember one about the conquistadors erecting a church over a burial ground as a sign of their conquest, but later on in the story it turned out that the Spaniards' true reason for choosing the site was their discovery of gold deposits, and the church served as a smoke screen for smuggling it out under the Indigenes' noses.'

He was still talking about his granddad and Jasmine was only half listening when he stopped.

'What is it? Why have you stopped?' she demanded.

'Dead end.'

She squeezed up beside him and stared ahead. To her disappointment a blank wall ended the tunnel. But her disappointment turned into alarm when she realised how close Leonel had come to falling down a rectangular stone-walled shaft that plunged almost vertically into the ground.

* * *

'We could slide down.'

'It'll be a tricky climb back up.' Leonel directed his torchlight downwards. But she knew that he, like her, was too keyed up to contemplate going back. But he needed encouragement before taking the plunge, so she squeezed his bicep. 'You've got big muscles,' she appealed to his vanity, 'I know you can do it.'

Leonel seated himself on the flagged ledge, bit down on his torch and eased his body into the shaft. Arms bent at the elbows and palms flattened against either wall, he began a cautious descent into the black depths. But Jasmine couldn't reach. Sitting on the ledge as he had done, arms fully outstretched, her fingertips were a hand's breadth short of the walls.

'Stand on my shoulder,' Leonel mumbled over the torch.

She did as bid and allowed herself to be lowered through the shaft. Hands free she was able to time him, and it was a good eleven minutes before she felt a jolt as he landed. Leonel's torch explored the walls, curved roof and paved floor of a tunnel identical to the other.

'This way.' He ventured forward, Jasmine tagged hold of his shirt tail, and together they proceeded until Leonel halted and in a tight whisper declared: 'Bingo!'

He held the torch vertically, allowing the beam to start at his feet, and moved it forward to settle upon a stack of olive green rifle containers shoved up against one wall. More rifle

239

containers beyond, and others beyond those. Jasmine pushed past Leonel and sidled into the resulting corridor to take a closer look at the find.

'Eight stacks and six high…that's forty-eight cases. Let's see what's in them.' Leonel flicked a latch but it was locked. He drew his chunky Swiss Army knife and began to saw at the hard resin casing.

'This will take for ever,' Jasmine said and yanked one of the cases on to the floor, whipped out her machete and put the blade tip to the casing. One hand over the other, she bore down on the handle. With a *thuth* she pierced the resin shell, and proceeded to carve out a rough opening. Leonel abandoned his efforts and, kneeling beside the case Jasmine had by now successfully breached, stuck his hand through the hole and winkled out a handbag-sized slab tightly packaged in polythene film.

'Well, it's not ammunition. Best guess – this is *coca*.'

Jasmine agreed on the presumption that Leonel knew what he was talking about.

'These rifle cases are airtight, watertight and heat-resistant. They even have a humidity indicator. They're ideal for storing cocaine.' Leonel extracted a second bag.

'Aren't you going to taste it, to make sure, like they do in the movies?'

'Uh-uh,' he declined. 'The smallest amount will send you *en onda*, and I'll need all my wits about me for the climb out of here.'

Jasmine raised herself on tiptoe and peered over the rows of rifle cases. 'That's a lot of cocaine.'

'With a dozen such stashes you could pay off our military's US aid bill.'

'I thought the US gives the stuff to our military for free.' Jasmine was aware she was naive. But Leonel wasn't the sort to hold that against her.

'If by charity you refer to an average of US$100 million every fiscal year to be repaid in full plus interest, then yes. For the year that Liberación massacred El Zacate, their charity to our military ran to US$197 million. The sums say our grandchildren's grandchildren will still be paying off this debt.'

The machete blade had accidentally nicked a hole in one of the bags and Leonel sniffed at the contents. 'Peruvian,' he declared with the air of a wine connoisseur.

'You can tell that just by sniffing it?' Jasmine enquired, amazed.

'No. You told me it was.'

'Let's see what's beyond the crates,' she suggested, snatching the torch before advancing past the cases. But scarcely a dozen paces beyond, she was obliged to pull up. 'The roof has collapsed,' she whispered, playing the light over broken masonry that swelled to the ceiling, blocking the way ahead. 'Earthquakes?'

'Possibly. Although these walls look like they were built to withstand anything. We'll go back the other way, where the tunnel runs beneath the church towards the river.'

When they arrived at the shaft they wasted no time or torchlight in peering up it, but carried on regardless.

'The floor's falling away,' she observed, and after a while added, 'and it's slippery,' referring to the way her sandals were skidding over the sand on the downward gradient. Leonel broke into a jog, torchlight leading, and Jasmine easily kept pace behind him.

'There's something up ahead…Bundles,' he was hazarding, '…to the wall.' And he came to a halt, tottering forward like an inexperienced roller-skater.

Again Jasmine squeezed up beside him, and examined this new find. Misted blue plastic sheets…possibly bags… loosely bulked up against the wall as if thrown over a pile of something…possibly boxes.

'Ammunition crates.' Leonel whisked out his penknife, selected a bag and when he had slit through the plastic he drew out the miniature saw and began sawing until the bind parted with a snap, and he ripped the lid from the crate.

241

'Dynamite,' he announced. 'Good old fashioned dynamite.' Leonel was on a roll. 'Let's see what's in those rifle cases.' He stood aside while Jasmine's machete forced a crate lid. He whistled softly. 'M16 rifle…Brand new. Must be fifty here.' He seized one of the guns and inspected it closely. 'I'd like to take you home with me,' he murmured as he turned it over in his hands.

Jasmine pointed to a coffin leaning upright against the wall, and told Leonel that if it wasn't a coffin it had to be a SAM.

Leonel heaved a sigh, tucked his rifle into its bed, moved to the upright crate, pierced the blue plastic sheet and lifted away the lid.

'Strela. Surface-to-air missile.' He whistled again. 'The launcher must be in one of the other crates. Armed with an infrared heat-seeking guidance system, you could bring down a helicopter or a fighter plane with one of these. Very expensive kit.'

'Anastasio is siphoning off army-issue weaponry which he sells to pay for cocaine,' Jasmine put two and two together.

'Then we have a little paradox,' Leonel announced, sidling along to the next stack. 'Anastasio is selling arms to his old enemies…Us.' He threw torchlight on the ceiling. 'The plastic sheeting protects the plywood against dampness. We must be under the river now. The Nahua really knew how to build their tunnels.'

'Let's grab a couple of boxes and come back later for the rest,' Jasmine suggested.

'We'll never get them up the shaft,' Leonel pointed out. 'We'll have to return with some rope and pull them out when we've got more time and manpower.' He glanced at his watch. 'Right, Jasmine, do your stuff, photograph the lot in situ. Get some good close-ups, yeah? – and then let's get the fuck out of here.'

* * *

'One hundred and two highest grade party-dust and your second spanking new surface-to-air big M,' hulking Marlon declared in his unbroken voice. He slapped shut his ledger and offered it to Anastasio. But Anastasio declined because he'd done his sums while the packers had been busy.

'Cold?'

'I was recalling the girl we chucked overboard last month. Just a kid, *man*! How she swam all the way from the shore…?' – shaking his head ruefully – 'Just thinking of her lying there beneath us gives me the creeps.'

'Bah!' Anastasio threw up a hand. 'She was dangerous beyond anything you can imagine.' To drive the point home, he hawked, headed an invisible football over the railings and spat after it. All eyes warily on the airborne spittle until it was whisked safely clear by the wind.

'Well, I've no particular wish to hear this, and since there's no longer any need for me to hang around…' Captain Sag-man raised a hand for a salute which he abandoned halfway through before ducking beneath the rails.

'Hold on,' Anastasio blurted. Sag-man froze on the rope ladder. 'My canoes are so weighed down tonight that the water threatens to flood over the sides, and I've still got over a quarter of the stuff to load.' Anastasio watched comprehension dawn in Sag-man's eyes.

'Don't even think about it, Don Anastasio. I'll give you a lift to shore, but I'm not taking your cargo onboard. Imagine I get clocked with that stuff in my Navy patrol boat. End of my career. End of your business. Sorry!'

'I'd pay cash, of course.' Anastasio winked at the *patrón*.

'Don Anastasio is right,' the *patrón* declared. 'Time is money, and his boats are slow. Silent, which is good, but slow nonetheless. I can't hang around for him to return for the surplus. Everything will move swifter with the help of your speedboat.' Then to Anastasio's displeasure he added: 'You have Don Anastasio by the bollocks. Squeeze hard enough and I imagine you'd exact a reasonable price.' He winked humourlessly back at Anastasio.

There were some sensitive negotiations to play out before a

deal would be struck.

'Tehuacán is beyond my postings zone,' – Sag-man on the squeeze. 'I'd have to give my commander good reason to suspect the presence of rebels in the area, but doing so would bring you attention you might rather do without.'

'How far can you travel up the Lempa?' Anastasio tested.

'For an extra one-hundred cash for me and fifty each for my men – up front – I'll drop your surplus just past the sand banks,' Sag-man conceded. 'You'll have to return from Tehuacán to collect it after you've made your first deposit, but I'm still saving you a good two to three hours.'

'Just get the stuff off my ship and allow me to return to *El Perú*,' the *patrón* barked, in an effort to hurry the negotiators.

Between the sword and the wall, and he knew it, Anastasio rubbed his chin for all of a second before nodding his acceptance of terms. He doubled over the railings and yelled down at his dispatchers: 'Trinidad, go with the captain and keep watch over my cargo which he has so *generously* agreed to transport as far as the sand banks. The rest of us will leave the first load at Tehuacán and return for you and the surplus.'

The Piranha droned away leaving the three canoes wallowing but making steady progress at the hands of the oarsmen towards the black, treeless gap in the coastline that was the mouth of the Lempa. As with all things rushed, their progress was blighted by unforeseen circumstances. The heavier than usual loads stuck one then another of the boats to shoals whose depths on previous trips had allowed the oarsmen to glide cleanly over. This necessitated debarking and shoving to ride the boats free. And when they arrived at the church, further delay was incurred due to the rusted lock in the portal door which, through lack of oiling, was becoming increasingly tricky to engage. After the drop-off had finally been made, Anastasio drove his team back down the river to collect the surplus and Trinidad.

When they put ashore on the sandy strip that angled from the bank like a glistening whaleback into the middle of the

244

river, they found Trinidad rucked up in the bush with eleven rifle cases for company. Because he had plastered his face and shaven head with tattoos – a growing ex-military fad – his expressions, and with them his moods, were not that apparent until he opened his mouth.

Fifty-one minutes, by Anastasio's Rolex, of paddling and putting up with a whinging Trinidad until the teams leapt overboard and lugged the boats up the beach. Dogs barked. Men in shorts appeared in doorways. Mothers were heard hushing infants back to sleep. But none of this worried Anastasio. Working the carrot and stick treatment he had seen to it that every Tehuacanan household received a monthly fistful of dollars for the storage facility their village afforded while apprising them of the accidents that had befallen whistle-blowing *soplones* in the past. Here, nocturnal comings and goings were a lucrative inconvenience. It was, therefore, with the buoyancy of a man fully at home that Anastasio led his crew through the village and up to the church of Santa Rita. If unworried on the approach to the church, once inside he became very worried.

'*Que putas!*'

Why was the altar standing beside the manhole instead of atop it? Anastasio's panic-kindled mind was working overtime. Jaw-dropped, he set down his rifle cases. '*Que putas!*'

When all rifle cases were grounded, Aran, being the slightest of the team, was jostled aside first by Guillermo Sinisterra, then by José Antonio, and finally by Chepito, in their haste to inspect the conspicuous void that should have been inconspicuous.

Then they looked at one another and at last at Anastasio.

Because of their repetitious routine in the church, Anastasio couldn't actually recall having pushed the stone back into place, but was certain he was not so sloppy as to have neglected doing so.

'Careless of you, leaving the opening uncovered like that,' Trinidad was first to try out an explanation.

Lost in his own bewilderment Anastasio barely heard that.

'Don Anastasio,' José spoke up, 'You were the last to leave, right? Did you see any*one* suspicious while you were last here?'

'Of course not,' Anastasio snapped, waking to José's idiocy.

'Did you see any*thing* suspicious when you were last here?' Eyes narrowing for enhanced deciphering powers.

'No. Everything was as normal.'

'Did anyone see *you* leave?'

'José Antonio, will you shut the fuck up!'

But José was only mildly stressed by Anastasio's bark, so he returned to his first statement and turned it into a question: 'You were the last to leave, were you not?'

There was no stopping the bastard, so before the others tried their hands at super-sleuthing, Anastasio fished out his torch and sent the beam through the hole. If unauthorised persons had gone down there, he would see to it that they die in the tunnels together with his secret. 'Trinny, hang back to guard the boxes and the entrance. Aran, Guillermo – Team one, José Antonio and Chepito – Team Two. Fetch the rope and your weapons. *Rapidito!*'

'Why do I always have to be the one to stay behind?' Trinidad whined to Anastasio's escalating exasperation with the man.

'Because you're a habitual whiner and none of us can stand you for it.'

After Trinidad had anchored one end of the knotted rope to the cast iron handle on the sacristy door, the five chosen-ones coiled a section of the rope round their left shoulders as if transporting a giant python between them. Thus encumbered they lowered themselves, one after the other, through the opening in the floor.

Because Chepito brought up the rear he was first to have his coil unravel and be relieved of the burden of it, leaving him clutching his rifle diagonally across his torso while he shuffled along behind José Antonio, who was fast feeding out his bundle as they advanced down the tunnel. By the time they'd arrived at the dead end only Anastasio was left with rope draped over

246

his shoulder, and he unhooked it and tossed it down the shaft. With intermittent knots to provide purchase he climbed down, anxious to check on his precious investment, to satisfy himself that it was all intact and accounted for.

The woman's voice so startled him that he lurched into the rope and hugged it tightly to himself. Thus halted he glared into the blackness below, and listened, and then felt José Antonio's foot on his head.

'Stop and be quiet,' he hissed upwards.

Silence followed, save for the creaking of the rope and his pulse thumping.

I saw her drown, he reminded himself sternly. It can't be her.

Now he heard it a second time – cheerful, inquisitive cadences, at odds with this sombre, dark passage. He had one hand gripping the rope above his head and the other at chest level, and here he could feel his heart lurching. Is it not enough that she haunted my dreams when she lived? Must she haunt them also in death? He shook his head and shrugged off the fear that had been creeping up on him.

But no sooner had he hissed *Vamonos!* than it came again: fragmented now, as if carried on a wind.

'Did you hear some*thing* down below?' José's whisper from above confirmed that this was no phantom of imagination.

He willed away an urge to spring the rope free and drop the rest of the way.

'After her!' he growled, and began to slide down the shaft with only the occasional sharp tug on a knot to check his speed. Still it was a fretful eternity before he and his urban gangsters were assembled in the tunnel below. 'You and you, that way. You and you, follow me.'

On the double he led Sinisterra and Chepito towards the stash of cocaine. He would check on it first because it was a more arduous and costly merchandise to acquire and distribute than the weaponry. Besides, even now two big names in the business awaited delivery of a combined 650 Ks. Good money, even at

247

today's prices, he considered. He was still contemplating profit when he heard yelling from the men he had sent in the other direction. He spun round.

The tunnel was humming with running feet.

'Faster,' he goaded the two men sprinting in front of him. He grabbed hold of Sinisterra's shirt tail and hauled him to one side and told him to get out of the way, fool!

Sinisterra stumbled and rebounded off the wall before crashing to the ground, and Anastasio skipped over him. He dispatched Chepito in similar fashion, but this time remembered to duck his head when he leaped over the sprawling man. Now he could see the way ahead, his torch light spreading the shadow curtains for him to run through; past the shaft in the ceiling, down the gradient, and then the crunching of his feet was suffocated by the stunning decibels of machinegun fire in a confined space.

'Don't shoot! Idiots, stop shooting,' he screamed. 'Whatever you do, do not shoot!'

But his voice was no match for the volume of live rounds.

* * *

Slip-sliding steps put an infuriating lag on Jasmine's progress up the gradient, and behind her Leonel was faring no better in his boots. When she heard male voices up ahead, she flung back a splayed hand to warn Leonel. He doused his torch and they stood motionless in the full darkness.

'Hear them?'

He could.

The rhythm of their own breathing. That yelling – distant, excited, confused. A torch beam emerged flitting up ahead.

'They're coming this way. Back!' She swivelled round and sprinted after Leonel. But whoever was behind had spotted them for seconds later, automatic fire clamoured in their pursuit.

They hurtled along this tunnel that plunged deep beneath the riverbed and when they got to the stockpiles of guns Leonel switched on his torch in second-long flashes, enough to pick their way through the tight corridor and to preview a little way ahead. The crates were behind them now. The firing had stopped. Then everything quaked: the stone slabs beneath their feet, the walls and the arched ceiling, even the air quivered, and it seemed to Jasmine that her heart rattled in her ribcage and then up into her throat.

Leonel glanced over his shoulder, and she saw his horror spotlighted in iridescent white: his mouth a dark elliptical cavity; a child's eyes seeing ghosts. If he was shouting she couldn't hear him. She swivelled about, and it was her turn to gape in disbelief as a scorching heat wave sent her reeling against the wall. The crates had given way to a quivering fireball that to Jasmine's eyes was revolving upon itself while bubbling at the constraints of the tunnel, and perhaps all this was true because it was actually growing and that could only mean that in its search for space it was shifting towards her.

Idiotas!

In their haste the pursuers had fired blindly and erratic rounds had ploughed into the explosives. Jasmine watched, transfixed, as this lesser sun of cavorting flames came rolling her way. Something else was happening. With a sharply ascending whoosh the roof above the crates caved in; and through the fireball Jasmine could see masonry and rocks plummeting from above. She discovered a scream in her throat as she realised the worst was still to come. Over the falling masonry the river gushed in like a colossal brown serpent. It splashed against the walls, curled back on itself and in a blink it had doubled its depth. Having run out of space it gathered itself before plunging up the tunnel. It smothered the fireball in an instant. Once more darkness reigned.

Jasmine turned her scream into a word: 'Run,'

The stone floor levelled then began to rise. Get above river-level or we've had it, she decided, keeping pace with the shadow that pounded ahead. She cursed the sandy floor as her soles slipped back and she stumbled, but she collected herself and pelted forwards. A glance over her shoulder showed nothing, but she could hear the wave – now a rustling thunder whose menace in the blackness was greater for it. Jasmine's foot slid again and – outstretched hands leading – she fell and as Leonel faded ahead so his torchlight faded with him. She scrambled to her feet and raced on, reaching out blindly. A smattering of water on her hair, spray pelting her back, now pinching her bare wrists. The wave swept her off her feet into a storm of energy, tearing her in many directions until she truly believed she would lose her limbs. Her mouth flooded with sand-loaded waters and the whole lot went down her throat. The back of her head whacked a hard object, and she cried out, taking in another mouthful of water and sand. She lost all sense of bearing, unable to tell up from down. As she tried to roll into a ball and shield her head with her arms she was thrashed against one hard surface after another. Then her temple struck stone and even the blackness seemed to fade.

* * *

Balancing like a skateboard rider Anastasio skidded across the floor. He saw the first crate erupt; and a beautiful flame billowed like a white parachute launched from an aircraft. Three men bearing rifles aloft were silhouetted like a child's paper cut-out. In mid momentum Anastasio turned, stooping, scratching the floor with his fingertips, he managed to bring himself to a halt before bounding back towards the shaft. With the first tongues of heat roasting his behind he leapt on to the knotted rope and while the end swung and spun he hauled his body up into the shaft. Once inside the rope steadied. Hand over hand, and punting his feet against each knot, he climbed. Then someone turned out the lights, and turned off the screams of his men besides. And Anastasio was mildly surprised to feel a soothing waft of tepid air on the back of his legs where a moment ago he was being cooked alive. Still the shuddering earth rumbled about him. He had a notion that the shaft was pulsating, and every grind and crack from the walls raised that notion to terrifyingly real. He was crawling through the belly of a writhing serpent, and not daring to pause for breath.

At the end, good old Trinny, for all his tedious sulking, was there to meet him and reach down and pull him up through the manhole and into the chancel and demand to know what the *gran carajo* was happening because there were fish everywhere.

Bending from the waist, left hand on Trinidad's left shoulder for support, Anastasio put him in the picture: 'Imbeciles, shooting shadows. Hit my explosives. The bloody tunnel caved in. Swamped everything. *Every fucking thing!*'

'Everything?' Trinidad repeated, and teetered backwards, leaving Anastasio's hand outstretched towards him.

While Trinidad retreated to the comfort of a mind-stifling sulk, Anastasio glanced at the surplus crates assembled beside the altar and put his own mind to work.

'Listen,' he snapped at Trinidad. 'The others are fucked. Just me and you now. We save what we can. Save ourselves. Let's get this lot back to the boats fast and leave this hole.'

'Fifty-fifty,' Trinidad stalled.

Given the rarity of Trinny's jokes, this one caught Anastasio fully off guard.

'You heard, fifty-fifty.' The obstinate stare implying he was for real.

'Trinidad, you buffoon, now's not the time to open trade negotiations.'

'Then do it yourself.' Trinidad had nothing to lose and all to gain, even if Anastasio's word was as reliable as a sandcastle at high tide.

Anastasio threw up his hands and looked away for support and found none. 'Okay, fifty-bloody-fifty.' But in his mind his fingers were crossed. Unless Trinny became a lot more useful and soon, he may just have signed his own death warrant.

Galvanised into action, the partners in crime grabbed a rifle case in each hand and bolted from the church. Blinking at the new morning's sunlight they hurried down the slope and on to the beach where they pushed through a throng of bewildered villagers. Children squatted and poked their fingers at the fish that littered the water-splattered sands. Elderly men in rough-edged reed hats gazed wistfully at the now vague swirling traces of the gigantic whirlpool that had, only a few minutes previous, sucked at the river.

'There was a fountain as high as the sky,' one brown-skinned boy with sun-coppered hair assured another.

'I saw it too,' agreed the other with happy enthusiasm. 'It was as high as this.' He shot his tiny hand above his golden head, raised himself on tiptoes and then leaped for greater emphasis.

The business tycoons flung their rifle cases into the quetzal and raced back to the church for more, and after they had lowered the missile crate and rested it unfettered on top of the rifle cases, they threw their combined weight at the canoe until it buoyed free, and Anastasio was climbing aboard when he heard the first helicopter. It came in low over the treetops from the west, power plant whining. He craned his head and saw the gunner at his post in the open rear cabin door. He saw also the M60D door gun angled with menacing intent over Tehuacán.

'They'll mistake us for *muchachos*,' he shouted to Trinidad.

Confirmation of this was already on its way. Anastasio saw the machinegun shuddering in the gunner's gloved hands and the dance of muzzle flashes. Screaming broke out. Bullets rained. Running villagers fell. Anastasio saw wrapped in a blur a man and woman holding hands making a dash for the shelter of the trees. The woman went down clutching her side, her husband knelt beside while she writhed and kicked up small jets of sand with her bare heels. He gathered her in his arms, came up on one knee and began, shakily, to push himself to his feet. His left shin erupted and doubled and crimson blood squirted on to the sand as he buckled under his wife. Anastasio tore his eyes from the couple and scanned the plaza. Villagers seeking refuge in the nearest hut, others belting into the forest, and still others with kids in tow were scurrying up the hill and slipping through the church's open doors. A mother in a white pinafore hurtled across Anastasio's vision, going for a pigtailed baby who was digging her own private well with a cuttlefish shell, apparently oblivious to the mayhem around her. With one arm the woman scooped up the digger and raced back towards her hut. The toddler screamed and kicked, and stretched minute fingers towards the shell she had left behind.

Anastasio dithered. We're going to be vulnerable on the river. Way too risky. He unhooked his rifle, abandoned the canoe to drift free, bellowed at Trinidad to return fire, and then made a crouching dash across the plaza and pushed up behind the wall of a hut. He turned his rifle sights skywards, came across a wavering fuselage and as soon as he was over the hole in the wall he triggered. That irregular lump backlit against the starboard window had to be the gunner. The bullets flew away beyond his muzzle flashes and disappeared in a fuzz. The hovering target reacted and took itself down river and out of sight. Anastasio's ears followed the whining of rotors until the gunship re-emerged beyond the treetops above him. Trinidad, crouched on the other side of the plaza, would have a decent shot.

'Good man,' he grunted. Sulky Trinny had opted for good sense by dragging the SAM up the beach and even now was hefting the portable launcher on to his shoulder. On a good day the weapon was a readily manageable piece of kit. In haste it was an unwieldy tree-trunk, and Trinidad, too slow to react when the airborne gunner triggered, crumpled without a fight. But with a muffled clunk the slim rocket was launched and on an almost flat trajectory it whooshed across the plaza before punching into a hut – the adobe variety – with as little fuss as a flung stone slipping into a lake. One…two… The hut's roof ejected upon a bed of sparks ten feet into the air, shaking free its tiles before the almost naked rafter frame succumbed to gravity. There were no longer any walls to speak of, so the roof crashed with a great huff of sparks upon an uneven pedestal of rubble. The blast raked through the village, Anastasio feeling the storm of it across his back as he discovered his reflexes had already sunk him face down in the sand. Sand under his tongue, salty grit between his teeth. When he chanced a peek back at the hut, debris, catching fire as it fell, was heaping up around its wretched remains, and from the heaps sprouted bonfires of blue-crested flames waving like Medusa's locks, licking the forest's overhanging branches.

'This is getting out of hand,' Anastasio understated.

The helicopter was now dwindling as it droned off across the river on a north-westerly heading. He watched it swing wide and slide behind the treetops.

'Trinidad,' he called, though his last remaining partner looked too dead to answer.

The gathering clatter of a second helicopter was closing in from the north east. It drifted overhead and Anastasio looked up at its giant brown belly. To the adrenalin-drunk senses the rotor blades, whooping like the beating wings of some gigantic bat, appeared to extend over the entire village. Anastasio wasted no time. He jumped to his feet, took aim and sprayed the underbelly with gunfire. As if recoiling from the sting of it, the helicopter dipped its nose and surged off towards the river where it banked to its right and decelerated until it lingered just above the larger of the two hillocks. From there its gunner unleashed his weapon into the village, and Anastasio brushed away the sand that spat up into his eyes. The roofs began to fold under the onslaught and the inhabitants that had survived the SAM blast were crippled and killed. As if gaining in confidence the helicopter drew nearer. Anastasio saw the gunner's assistant feeding a belt of NATO cartridges to the gun.

The creaking and snapping timbers, the crackling of burning roofs, the screams of the panicked and the wounded, the helicopter's single power plant and relentless gunfire, all crowded the smoke-filled air in a deafening cacophony. Anastasio gasped in dismay as he surveyed the village he had promised would profit from his business now melting into ruins before his very eyes. Flames from burning huts took hold of surrounding trees with awesome speed. As one tree was enveloped so another began to hiss before it too was engulfed and shared its fire with yet another.

'Got to stick my neck out if I want to hit the bastard,' Anastasio realised none too soon. So he sucked in a huge lungful of air and after almost choking himself on noxious vapours he darted into the centre of the blazing plaza, propped himself on one knee with rifle already angled high, and triggered. Yet he had merely begun when he heard the whining return of the first gunship. He looked to his left and saw that it had approached low over the water, probably having flown upriver screened behind the trees. Now, side-on, it dangled from its blur of rotor blades metres above the sandy shoreline, whipping up the river surface. The bleak gunner was aiming directly at him and as the bullets issued from the muzzle Anastasio abandoned his weapon, tore away across the sand before diving between two towering mantles of fire. He spun over on to his back and, as if backing away from the snapping jaws of an alligator, withdrew deeper into the woods.

For a few moments he glared about him. There was nothing for it but to flee.

* * *

The fractured monologue ailed and came back strongly only to ail again, like some uncanny radio broadcast on a fragile wavelength. 'Jasmine?…Jasmine?…Speak to me…Jasmine?… Can you hear me?' She felt her chest constrict, and water flooded up her throat and burst from her mouth, and she sat bolt upright and retched, and on a groan flopped back and rolled on her side and again on to her back. She opened her eyes to an image framed in darkness of Leonel wiping his mouth with the back of his hand.

'I can hear,' she decided, on the irrational assumption that hearing was unlikely under the circumstances. What circumstances? She scarcely remembered.

Leonel's worry lines reformed themselves into a smile. 'Forgive me. I didn't mean to leave you…I was…'

'What happened?'

'The wave caught me and swept me along until it petered out at river-level. I looked behind me, you were gone. Went

255

back in, found you, carried you out, gave you mouth to mouth, and I think I've just swallowed a mouthful of your vomit.'

She might have said, *serves you right for leaving me*, but frankly he deserved worse. To her right the tunnel sloped beneath still, dark water.

'Our exit that way is cut off,' Leonel answered her un-asked question. 'Let's hope there's another way out this side of the river. Can you move?'

Jasmine wriggled her limbs one by one and then sat up. She could move.

'You've got a nasty bump on your forehead,' he diagnosed, offering his hand. 'You'll soon have a blinding headache, if you haven't one already.'

Pulling on his fingers she came stiffly to her feet. The camera! She began slapping her pockets. Plenty of sand but no camera. 'It's gone. After all our efforts, the evidence, I've lost the evidence.'

'A few minutes ago I thought I'd lost you, so losing the camera is nothing. Besides, it couldn't be helped,' Leonel reassured her. 'Our immediate priority is to find a way out of here.'

Shivering in her damp dungarees Jasmine fell into a stiff-limbed jog behind Leonel, leaving the waterlogged tunnel behind them. But all too soon he shambled to a halt. In the small light of the torch Jasmine could see that here too she was confronted by ceiling-to-floor masonry. 'Makes no sense to build tunnels only to seal them off,' she moaned, thoroughly irritated. 'So we're trapped.'

Leonel studied the ceiling. 'The curved lintel next to the wall is wider than the surrounding blocks,' he murmured, running his fingertips along its edges and into each of the four corners. 'It's the same size as the opening in the undercroft's floor. Perhaps it leads to a ground-level exit. Hold this for me.' After handing over the torch he stood feet apart, with palms flattened on the lintel. Veins rose on his neck and forearms, and he grunted as he heaved against the stone. Jasmine grimaced with him.

'It won't budge,' he gasped at last. 'There must be a thick layer of earth above it. We'll have to go back the way we came.'

Jasmine glared up at him and frowned. 'How?'

'We swim.'

Soon she was peering doubtfully at the black waters. 'We probably ran sixty metres from the explosion,' she thought to mention on the off chance he had some brilliant Plan C up his sleeve.

'If we can swim back to where the crates were, we may be able to get out through the same hole into which the water flooded,' Leonel reasoned quite confidently.

So this was his Plan C, and there was precious little brilliance to see in it. In fact from where she stood, testing the water temperature with her toe, it looked dismal.

'We'll take five minutes to aerate our lungs. Then we go,' he proposed gamely.

'What if the hole is blocked?' she ventured the unthinkable.

'We swim on to the shaft.'

'That's over a hundred and fifty metres from here,' she complained.

'Well, if you have any better suggestions, now would be an excellent time to air them.'

Her shoulders rose and fell as she began to oxygenate her lungs in earnest.

Leonel strode into the water and she followed. She watched him take one last gulp of air before he stretched out flat and drifted away beneath the surface. In the utter darkness she submerged herself and with her eyes wide open she kicked away from the slope. Only the vaguest of shades wafted in the silent blackness ahead. Now powerful surges from Leonel's pumping boots were washing against her face, and she followed them faithfully, counting out the seconds in her mind, her hair bunching and spreading and bunching again.

Sixty seconds counted and no end in sight. At two minutes her lungs were pumping with the compelling urge to breathe.

Her right hand struck a splintered edge of wood, probably from a crate. She fended off another, and soon she swam through as much debris as water and she had to modify her style to a one handed doggy paddle with the other arm bent across her face like a fender, which only slowed her progress, but with Leonel's clumsy boots punching water and wood and whatever else in her direction this was a necessary precaution. At three minutes counted her lungs were burning and forcing a ball of lung-air up into her throat. Still she fought to refuse them while bubbles began seeping out between her lips and stroking her cheeks, and in blind desperation she abandoned the doggy paddle and reverted to full lashing breaststrokes. Her heart skipped a beat because Leonel's boot soles and calves flashed against a misty whiteness. An eddying current nudging her from the left probably meant she was now at the breached ceiling and directly in the river's flow. Leonel's boots stopped kicking, drifted downwards and then like a moonwalker's landed on some dark lumpy mound. From there he pushed off and shot upwards directly into the light. She sprang after him. His boots were overlapped in a high-diver's pose, then his green-clad thighs slid by stages into view, and now his scrunched up face puffing bubbles from nose and clenched teeth. Together they burst into the air and filled their lungs with it. But it was flavoured with wood smoke and metal and the bitterness of scorched leaves. And it was screaming, and thudding with artillery and helicopters. Jasmine blinked the water from her eyes. A UH-1M gunship hovered directly above her observations point; its gunner bent to the mounted gun, hosing Tehuacán with tracer. Huts ablaze, the plaza strewn with twisted and twisting bodies. The helicopter banked at a precarious angle, avoiding a direct hit by a serpentine thread of bullets that Jasmine traced back to Anastasio who from smack in the middle of the plaza was kneeling on one knee, his back arched, his M16 pumping.

'Swim for the shore,' Leonel yelled, tugging her shoulder strap to divert her attention.

Still hunting for breath Jasmine struck out towards the safe side of the river. But the gunner had spotted two desperate swimmers. Little spitting waves danced around them, chopping up the surface. Jasmine dived, going deep until she felt the riverbed sifting between her fingertips. Ploughing her fingers into the sand she propelled herself forward, bearing downriver with the current. Now her lungs refused to hold out longer than thirty hurriedly counted seconds. She surfaced and swept the hair from her eyes and swivelled her head, seeking out Leonel. He was conspicuously absent. She saw the helicopter above, and its busy artillery duo. Alerted by a gathering whine from behind she glanced over her shoulder. Airborne, but only just, another helicopter screamed upriver towards her. She dived again and spun round to look up through the silt's yellowness. A shadow thundered across splintered light. A short amount of time passed. Short, but long enough for her to reckon the shadow's non-reappearance meant the pilot hadn't spotted her. Perhaps he'd been preoccupied with his colleagues in the other gunship. She swam purposefully towards the western bank, pushing herself for as long as she could hold breath before surfacing to refresh her lungs and glance round for Leonel, but still she couldn't see him. Her toes sank into the riverbed and she waded ashore, pausing in the shallows to look back towards Tehuacán, at what was now a full scale battle between military and *contrabandistas*. Whoever won, Tehuacán would lose. With the help of the current she had put some eighty metres between her and the battle, and she scanned that distance for a sign of Leonel. A scrap of sunlit red rippling with the brown. His neckerchief! She charged sloshing over to it and was relieved to find it still attached to Leonel's neck but alarmed because his head was underwater. With cupped hands she raised his head clear. His mouth began gulping at the air, and when she wiped the matted hair from his eyes he opened them and stared up blankly.

'Are you injured, *comandante*?'

'Just get me to land,' he wheezed, and his face contorted in agony.

A tug of war ensued between Jasmine and the river but with Leonel helping out with a feeble one-armed paddle she managed to drag him towards shore while a crimson cloud spread from his left shoulder into the current. Once ashore she knelt beside him while he groaned. She unbuttoned his shirt before inspecting the jagged skin around a very angry wound to his upper left pectoral. It didn't look good. If only Adrian were here!

'The bullet caught you from behind,' she told him. 'And passed through your left shoulder.' A pause to exhale hard. 'I think your shoulder blade is broken. If no blood comes when you cough then perhaps your lung is undamaged. Still, I must get you to a hospital.' After bathing the wound in coconut milk she rummaged in his trouser pocket for his penknife.

'Can you sit up? I need your shirt.' Clasping his hand in both of hers she leaned back and hoisted a wincing Leonel to a seated position, and gingerly he shrugged out of his shirt. She sliced away strips of the green fabric and bound up the wound, securing a knot at his shoulder, and then she wriggled out of her mauve T-shirt, leaving her breasts screened by her bra and dungaree breast flap. She drew the blade through the stretchy fabric and fashioned a sling into which she tucked his elbow, and when she had judged the position to her satisfaction she fastened a knot on his shoulder and another one behind his back, and instructed him to keep his arm close to his body.

'There's an FMLN mobile hospital in San Vicente,' he croaked, easing his back on to the sand.

'The military will be covering the roads,' she thought aloud. 'But there's a tributary that joins the Lempa half way towards the coast. That will take us almost as far as the city.'

'You're leaving me?' he said, almost melting her heart with his defencelessness.

She put her revolver in his good hand and wrapped his fingers round the grip. 'I'm going for a boat.'

* * *

She was pelting along past young palm shoots and leaping over half-submerged fallen trees. Time was short because Leonel was losing blood and would be weaker by the minute. And what if he were discovered by paratroopers? It just didn't bear thinking about.

Tehuacán and anything in its vicinity would soon be humming with government forces. Besides the clear and present danger this posed to Leonel, it meant that going back to Chinchontepeque to fetch her canoe was out of the question.

What about Jaltepeque village? Acquiring a boat there meant a long run to the coast followed by a hard paddle back against the current. On the other hand a few hundred metres to the north the Lempa broadened at a confluence where it was joined by the Jiotique and Titihuapa rivers, and where, she recalled from Leonel's endless maps, a number of fishing hamlets were strung along the shores. She opted for north. There would be precious little time for bargaining pleasantries today.

She adjusted her direction, and within minutes emerged on to a crescent-shaped beach where curled palm pods resembling miniature canoes had washed up with a bunch of tangled fronds. The confluence spread before her like an ocean, funnelling round a slender sandbank into the Lempa to her right before sweeping away on its palm-fringed eastern shores. A dozen canoes buoyed in the bay created by the sandbank, their occupants' mesmerised stares trained downriver on Tehuacán.

While the battle tumult continued to carry up from the south, Jasmine strode into the water. Option One: the canoe nearest the shore was a modern vessel with sturdy planking, capable of transporting a crew of six and a ton of fish. Too heavy, too many occupants to deal with. Option Two: Beyond Option One a small old-style canoe floated at standstill. Only two occupants: a stick-insect of an oarsman topped with a red and white baseball cap, and a forty-odd señora in a skirt of many colours who was clutching a canvas sack. Option Two was Jasmine's.

Invisibility through distraction, ideal conditions already in play because all eyes were thoroughly entertained by helicopters, one of which was loitering over Tehuacán, shedding lead by the bucket load. The other obligingly raced overhead just when she needed it most. Jasmine filled her lungs, lay flat in the shallows and crawled forward until she was in deep enough to swim. The first hull passed overhead. The second was a shadow that firmed up as she closed in on it. She exhaled and sank to the riverbed where she settled herself on her haunches. She exploded upwards and punched through the surface and meeting the *senora's* stricken eyes she clapped hold of the gunwale in both hands and yanked it after her on her way underwater. It wasn't enough to topple the boat, but was enough to panic the woman who toppled it for her. After a double splash the water hummed with kicking limbs and swirling skirts and gurgled shouts of alarm. Jasmine glided upwards, realising with satisfaction that the oarsman had acted as she had hoped. A true *caballero*, he had rushed to his mother's aid, leaving Leonel's prospective transport unattended, at least until he had her safely ashore. Jasmine seized the abandoned paddle, surfaced in the pocket of air trapped in the overturned hull and slid the paddle beneath the bow seat and the end deck. She took hold of a gunwale in each hand and with some vigorous kicking on her part and encouragement from the current she propelled the craft towards the sandbank. When her feet landed she wrested the canoe upright. But it had taken in rather a lot of water by this time and lagged low, and it soon stuck fast on the rise to the bank. She looked round for good ideas. The Lempa was a highway flanked by forests. A windswept curtain of black smoke billowed inland from behind Chinchontepeque. From the sidelines awed spectators watched heavy fusillade lashing their neighbours from above. No good ideas there. But the pause had rested her limbs, and this time when she put her weight to the canoe it slid high enough so that when she let it loll most of the water spilled out. She was rocking it, setting off wakes in the hull to spill the residue water when someone yelled, 'Hey, bitch, that's my boat.'

She spun round. He was wringing wet, T-shirt sagging on him, matted black hair parted down the middle, embittered glower. It was the oarsman and yes, strictly speaking, she had his boat, and he was storming along the tapered sandbank for it, and going by his grimace he didn't strike Jasmine as being in the mood for reasoning.

'I need it,' she said lamely. But the rightful owner took hold of his property and with the paddle clattering in the hull began lugging it back into the water. So naturally Jasmine stomped over and shoved him away, which was one of the hardest things she'd had to do considering the rights and wrongs of this action. But if it's for saving a life, and in this case Leonel's life, it had to be right. Didn't it? Her victim staggered back a couple of steps. 'I've got no time to explain, but I need your boat, *now*. I'll bring it back.' She held up both hands in an attempt at appeasement.

But you can't appease a man when you've dunked his mum in a river and nicked his transport. He rushed at Jasmine and flung out his right fist. Making a conscious effort to be collected, Jasmine took her weight on her right leg and prepared for the block. The bad guy was upon her, not at all collected, and certainly no *caballero* now. Jasmine swung her left hand down and by clouting his inner forearm she deflected the blow, and she struck upwards with her right fist and connected with his floating rib and while the youth folded she dealt him a fisted chop to the back of his neck for good measure.

Clutching his chest under both hands and gagging, the victim curled at her feet, and for a time she stood over him with her fists clenched at her sides, heaving long breaths through her nose to compose herself while feeling not guilt but a mild pride that she had so naturally put Leonel's training into practice.

Leonel!

At first the canoe moved in short shunts that took it no further than a foot at a time, but as she continued to push at the stern, she shortened the moments between each shunt until they ran together, and gradually she was able to build up a steady momentum. When she reached the place where the sandbank joined the beach she paused to glance across the river just as a gunship wrapped in camouflage burst into the wider waterway. Floating downriver past Tehuacán is not an option. I'm going to have to take the canoe overland.

She lined up the prow with a raised gap between two coconut palms and shunted it through and built up speed, weaving between trees, ever conscious of Leonel's precarious position a little over a kilometre away. Soon her legs were filled with something akin to molten lead, and she stumbled and dropped on all fours, heaving each breath with a whimper. She pulled herself to her feet and started again, building short shunts into a steady forward slide.

When eventually she reached Leonel she positioned the bow so that it jutted into the current, and only then did she slump to her knees and catch her breath.

His eyes were shut but he stirred on sand that was stained a darker shade of brown by the blood which, despite the bandage, seeped from his wound. 'Is that you, Jasmine?' he said feebly.

'I have a boat.' Gasp. Heave. 'Can you sit in it?'

'Not sit…lie.'

Jasmine came to her feet and after a fleeting scout round scooped up a large pebble that had been half embedded in damp sand and with it she hammered away the middle seat from its risers before tossing the short plank and the pebble into the woods.

'Come.' She volunteered her hand and shoulder as supports, assisted Leonel to his feet and guided him towards the canoe. He hauled his damaged body aboard and eased it down until he was lying flat across the spacers in the depths of the hull with his eyes tightly shut. Jasmine pushed off, climbed aboard and took up the paddle. With efficient strokes she drove upon the downstream current, the bows sweeping back a wake of clear ripples. The bombardment fast receded behind them.

Battling with fatigue Jasmine steered to her right and entered the tributary. Ploughing a path against the current now, she drove westwards. Military reinforcements sped towards Tehuacán: a Hughes helicopter; a prop-propelled Skymaster followed; two more helicopters for backup; and if that wasn't enough to thoroughly punish a small riverside hamlet for its misdemeanours, a full squadron of A-37 bombers put in an appearance, just to make sure.

'In an hour, there will be nothing left of Tehuacán,' she muttered in disgust.

Cane fields skirted the tributary. Her eyes distrusted the overlapping auburn stems and bent green leaves for the camouflage they provided. She had an impression of an army of scarecrows presenting rather curious arms – feathers instead of bayonets fixed to rifle muzzles. But she saw also, standing amid the cane, scores of peasants with downed cutlasses, taking time off to worry about the persisting bombardment that raged over there to the east.

The stream shrunk and became choked with clusters of yellow water poppies whose trailing stems got entangled with the paddle, and in one of Jasmine's distracted efforts to push forward, the paddle was snatched from her grip leaving her adrift on a current that threatening to carry her back to the Lempa. She climbed overboard, dropped into the stream and dragged the boat towards the muddy bank. She was met by a dozen plantation workers, two of whom splashed over to help haul in the canoe.

'Are you from Tehuacán?' they were asking, eager for news of their neighbours. 'What's happened? Why all the smoke? It is burning?'

'I'll tell you. I'll tell you. Just listen, please.' She managed to stem the flow of questions. 'First help me get this man to the mobile hospital.'

CHAPTER TWENTY-FOUR

'WHAT DO YOU EXPECT me to do, Doctor, fly?' The tall stooping woman, who was probably a lot younger than she looked, grasped both crutches with one hand and with the other lifted her skirt to reveal a weeping sore on the fleshy side of her shin. 'I'm begging you, please, let me in.'

'And I'm begging you, señora, please, understand, we've run out of space,' Dr Lemus lamented from behind the entrance gate which remained padlocked. 'We are occupying the school premises temporarily while it's closed, our time here is limited. Get yourself to Zacamil Hospital where first rate treatment is absolutely free.'

'Doctor, surely we can accommodate the lady here.' Leonel had his good shoulder to the wire boundary fence and his bad shoulder trussed up in bandages. He flicked his head, as much to invite a reply as to clear away his hair from his eyes.

'I thought I told you to remain seated in the playground,' Dr Lemus retorted, his eyes enlarged through spherical glasses. 'Since you dispatched Jasmine to Cuscatlán, you've been as restless as a flea on a mongrel's back.'

'It's my shoulder that's knackered, not my legs,' Leonel chuckled. 'So what d'you say? Go on, let her in.'

Across the fence the woman dropped her hem and regarded both men with a distrustful scowl.

'I have clear guidelines from Abraham…'

'He doesn't have to know, does he?'

'Please, refrain from interrupting. It's considered rude where I come from. Clear guidelines on how to spend the *limited resources* the FMLN has for this field hospital. Can you show me an unoccupied bed? You cannot. There are patients – like yourself – making do on the floor. Tripped over one just this morning. That would be a thing: the only doctor in this hospital becomes one of its patients.'

'You've got other staff,' Leonel failed to prompt even a flicker of a smile.

'We've got two nurses, that's it, one doubles as lab tech and the other – that Dutch girl – qualified as radiology tech but helpfully doubling as nurse. And the cardiologist, Gloria, who seems to have taken a shine to you – a mystery to all but herself – puts in an unpaid day's work as anaesthetist *and* paediatrician. Now if that doesn't sound like overcrowded and understaffed to you, then perhaps you'd like to take the matter up with Abraham yourself. I assure you, I would be most grateful.'

The arguments against were compelling, but so was the imploring gaze the unwell women was now bestowing on Leonel. 'But…'

'No buts. This facility was set up exclusively to treat war casualties. Now hers,' he pointed at the woman, 'is not a war injury. She'll be welcomed in any of the civilian hospitals where treatment is free.' On that note Lemus stalked up the flight of stairs and through the double doors.

Leonel shrugged his shoulders at the woman. 'I tried.'

'You tried, bullshit.' She spat dryly.

Leonel had a curious sense that the guerrillas' isolation had spared them this odd strain of sarcasm that had come to feature in the humour of urban Salvadorians. After so many years in the forest, was he now out of touch with the *real world*?

'You're all the same, you lot,' the snubbed patient started up again. 'Look after your own and to hell with the rest of us.'

Leonel turned his back on the volley of invectives that followed him up the stairs. Once through the entrance he sought out Dr Lemus in the circular main hall. In each of the single beds and two bunks that converged towards a central bay a real casualty of war convalesced, hooked up to an intravenous drip. From behind a green curtain to the operating theatre Dr Lemus's hushed but urgent mumbles punctuated male whimpering and the general low hubbub of the place.

The doctor was right of course. Hospital staff were already run off their feet. The place was overwhelmed by casualties from the military's operations along southern Cabañas and recent surges to retake San Vicente. Leonel had listened to the radio – even the national stations. There wasn't much else to do since Dr Lemus, giving the prognosis for his shoulder, said that without three weeks rest following yesterday's reconstructive surgery its mobility would be severely impaired. Sorrentino's government was asserting itself, and the military was wheeling out its overkill policy for every occasion: bomb first and then send in the infantry.

During the prolonged wait on Chinchontepeque, Leonel had experienced – not for the first time – a conflict of duties. He'd felt anxious to return to the column, yet it was imperative the cocaine issue be resolved by the time ONUSAL became fully participant in the peace talks. He could not, in all conscience, have left Jasmine to tackle the *contrabandistas* on her own. Moreover, given that he was the column's spokesperson for the forthcoming talks, he had determined that he should have first hand involvement in the investigation in order to avoid the possible dismissal of hearsay evidence. Two witnesses were better than one. Now, despite Dr Lemus's prognosis, he was impatient to heal because there would be a great deal of fighting in the months and possibly years ahead while ARENA, with full military backing, did everything in its power to reverse the rural zones' reddening trend.

The woman with the sore leg started wailing hideously, snapping Leonel out of his ponderings. She abandoned the crutches and they fell away as she swooned to the ground with too many adjustments to her final posture to ring true.

'Ignore her,' the pickup driver muttered, 'She does it to get a free meal.'

A voice called Leonel over the Tannoy; please report to the reception to receive an urgent telephone call.

The call was from Abraham Gadala himself, and the news was not good. SAF had got wind that a murderous guerrilla *comandante* featured on their Most Wanted list was receiving field hospital treatment in San Vicente town. Even now bombers were preparing for takeoff. With minutes to spare there was nothing for it but to evacuate the school and take as many patients as possible to the church where Padre Antonio Salazar would receive them. Following the assassination of several men and women of the cloth, churches were strictly no-go for the military. They should be safe there.

* * *

San Vicente's sunlit uphill thoroughfare was deserted, if you overlooked the straggling refugees hugging the cracked white walls in the shadow of the eaves.

Leonel sought to reassure Dr Lemus, 'Padre Antonio will receive us in the Church of San Vicente.'

'Would they bomb the church too?' Dr Lemus asked, far from reassured.

'Unlikely.' He was about to elaborate but a boy interrupted with an entreaty for Leonel to look behind him.

Silent as shadows, two A37 Dragonfly attack planes swept in from the east, one behind the other, each leading with a 7.62 mm Gatling.

From the hillside, Leonel felt the pavement quiver beneath his feet. The bombers, having launched a 750lb bomb apiece, soared overhead. Leonel turned to gaze back at the black cloud that shot high while debris sprang like branches from its pulsating trunk. The cloud boiled and then thinned, leaving in its altering shadow the scattered ruins of the school. The churned earth was like a brown stain over the car park and an adjoining playground where only the merry-go-round remained intact. Over the rush of thudding rubble showering back to earth, the drone of a helicopter heralded the arrival of the paratroopers.

In an alb of priestly whiteness, Padre Antonio held open one of the double doors to the chancel and beckoned to the men and women coming across the plaza. 'Don Leonel,' he exclaimed, and clasped Leonel by the shoulder. But there was no time for elaborate greetings, so he met Leonel's eyes and decreed with suitable solemnity: 'You are all welcome. Enter, and find sanctuary in the house of the Lord.'

From the bell tower, Leonel observed the helicopter put down in the centre of a crossroad that sectioned off four cotton fields. Here it disgorged six heavily armed troopers. These men jogged along the road until they came to the remains of the school where they clambered amid the rubble and where, at point blank range, they executed those survivors they found.

* * *

Major Rene Larios of the Second Light Infantry Battalion attached to Military Detachment 2 had spent the weekend at his holiday lodge on the shores of Lake Coatepeque in the arms of his mistress. To make absolutely certain neither his whinging wife nor his duty to God and country could disturb their passions he had disconnected the telephone and switched off his radio, so it was not until the following Monday morning that word reached him that Leonel Flint, together with an unknown number of bandits and medical personnel, had narrowly escaped Operation Squeeze. Had he heard that they were now ensconced in the Church of San Vicente where they were receiving food, water, and medical attention with the full cooperation of that bastard Padre Antonio?

Seated in their jeep beside a cotton plantation two veterans observed the church that crowned the hill.

Captain Nathan Escobar put forward an idea to Larios: 'I say we bust in, wipe'em out, and stick Leonel's head on a pole.'

Larios stalled before replying. 'You hanker after the old days,' he murmured.

'After results, actually,' Escobar stood his ground. But

politics had got in the way of war.

'We've already played that hand. Sorrentino's getting shafted by foreign nosey-parkers over our methods. You got to fight nice wars these days, got to respect human rights while you kill them, down arms to allow the enemy to take tea and biscuits within firing range.'

'Let's win this thing and the world won't give a shit about how we did it.'

Larios raised his binoculars. 'Vatican eyes and influence all over the shop. Didn't take too kindly to Archbishop Romero's assassination, despite our denials. And after that thing with the Jesuits and their housekeepers, Sorrentino, in his suspect wisdom, invited the dog collars and those gringo embassy fairies to a press conference. To show he cared. Wants the Catholic vote, and with most of our population Catholic, makes sense, don't you think?'

'Umm...'

'So *El Presidente* issued a statement declaring that no act of violence may occur in a Catholic place of worship or against paid members of the Church or their staff. What with the Church's increasing involvement in the peace talks, they got all bases covered. The guerrillas' accusations against us can be discredited anywhere, except under the long nose of the Church with UN observers in its back yard.' Larios felt a pang of remorse at having spelt things out so bluntly. Escobar's heart was in the right place. And it was unfair to expect a foot soldier to think like a politician.

'So we sit around and scratch our arses while our number one most wanted red danger-man struts free? Taking the piss a bit, aren't they?' Escobar lowered his binoculars on to his lap and slumped his shoulders, cutting a very dejected figure.

'I didn't say that.' Larios turned the key and let the engine tick over. 'Have the water company cut off their supply. Take a full platoon and secure the area around the church. You take up station at the main entrance. Prevent food, water, guns and medical supplies from passing through those doors. Every

271

couple of hours, knock and ask to use the shitter. The priest won't refuse. Go in, look around, assess their condition, then leave. No physical aggression, just starve them out. And the moment Flint pokes his head through that door, chop it off. But do it outside. You follow me?'

'Yep, yep,' barked Escobar.

* * *

Check out that nun. But the nun was not a nun, and she hoped no one would be any the wiser. Ignoring the minor modification to the scapular, the four piece habit was a perfect copy of the habit worn by those sympathetic Benedictine sisters of the order of Las Hermanas de Belén, having been skilfully made in dyed cotton by Don Martin, Suchitoto's premier tailor. It was necessary that the black tunic hang close to the ground. Nevertheless, more than once Jasmine tripped on its skirts as she shuffled through San Vicente while the twilight dragged black shadows down bullet-pocked walls and across quiet cobbled streets.

'Evening, sister. Don't forget the curfew.' A soldier-shaped shadow ambled by.

'Thank you, son,' Jasmine replied, tucking her head down. Now she was thankful for the tunic's length because her M16 was well concealed beneath it.

She pinned her left elbow tighter to her side. She had bound the rifle to her waist by feeding a length of twine through the tunic's hip slits, looping it once between the trigger guard and pistol grip, a second time around the bolt and magazine and once more around the hand guard before securing it with a double knot at her right side. The rifle was further held in place by a leather belt and the gun's barrel, which was tucked into the headband of the white coif, was cushioned against her hair. She had arranged the black veil so that it cascaded over her shoulders. Strapped to her navel over her dungarees, and causing less discomfort than the rifle, was another of Don Martin's creations: a neatly folded camouflage uniform with gold coloured star insignia denoting the rank of colonel sewn into the epaulets. Size: XXL.

It was quite an uncomfortable arrangement, especially as the rifle dug into her ribs with every step she took. But the cotton scapular, falling from her shoulders and hanging as did the tunic almost to her feet, helped smooth out the irregular bulges of these and other deadly accoutrements that she wore concealed about her person.

So, clutching the wooden crucifix hanging from her neck to prevent it from swinging, she shuffled along the pavement with the gait of a much older woman.

'Sister, where are you off to at this time of night?'

She looked in the direction of the male voice. A pair of boots and olive-green-clad legs strolled into view and came to a halt directly in front of her, obliging her to stop.

'I'm on my way to see the padre,' she told him brightly. 'I bring him food.' With a hand almost entirely draped in sleeve she held out the clear polythene bag which she had prepared earlier.

The soldier bent low and peered at it closely. 'That's a lot of bread and cheese for one man,' he remarked, as another pair of legs entered Jasmine's field of vision.

'The padre has an excellent appetite.'

'She must be body-searched,' said the newcomer harshly.

Jasmine recoiled. 'Touch me and I shall report you to the Archbishop.'

'Curfew starts in twenty minutes, sister,' the first man advised. 'I'll deliver the food to the padre and you can be on your way.'

'Have you washed your hands in holy water in the last hour?' Jasmine croaked.

The soldier's feet shuffled uncertainly and she went on without her answer, 'Then you cannot touch any holy sustenance, so unless you wish to hinder the work of our Lord, you may step aside.'

Both pairs of legs bustled to her left and she continued her journey up the hill and across the plaza towards the church.

273

The door, which was bordered on either side by fluted half columns, stood on a wide semicircular step across which another pair of black boots clip-clopped towards her.

'What business have you here at this late hour?' The monotone of a man more accustomed to giving orders than taking them.

'And who might you be?'

'Captain Nathan Escobar, in charge of church security. State your business.'

'My business is with the padre,' Jasmine replied, hunching her back as much as the rifle, which clung to her body like a splint, would allow.

'You have deliveries? Books, perhaps? The odd cassette tape?' – and stepping up a semiquaver – 'Guns?'

Jasmine considered a suitably offended expression but decided she lacked the acting skills, so she held up the plastic picnic bag, which Escobar snatched away.

'Bread is not permitted in church,' he declared, apparently at home with such a ridiculous notion.

'But your men down the hill said I could take it to him.'

'They let you pass with *this*?' he blurted in disbelief, and shook the bag at her.

She nodded retiringly. 'I hope I haven't got them into any trouble.'

'No good, useless *hijos de put...*' He cleared his throat and collected himself. 'Sorry, sister.'

She waved his apology away with a benevolent hand.

The studded wooden door creaked open and from the dim interior emerged the black skirts of a priestly cassock.

'I was expecting you, sister. Please, enter the House of the Lord.' In the glow from a kerosene lantern above the door, the stubbled face of Padre Antonio beamed with a sweaty sheen.

'Thank you, padre,' Jasmine said, and before a hesitant Captain Escobar could reach out to manhandle a saintly nun she slipped into the cool of the nave.

With an iron key the size of a ladle Padre Antonio locked

the door and then, taking Jasmine by the elbow, ushered her towards the vestry. Pews had been pushed together to form elongated cradles to rest the convalescents.

'How is he?' Jasmine enquired as to Leonel's health.

'He needs to get out of here, for his sake and for the rest of us,' Padre Antonio told her rather shakily. 'Those greens outside want him dead. Did you hear the news?'

'What news?'

'Well, it was on the radio, apparently once he's out of here, the others will be allowed to leave and seek treatment elsewhere.'

Poor Padre Antonio. The stress was evidently getting to him, for his eyes were bloodshot, and when Jasmine remarked about this out of concern, he said both the water and electricity had been cut off. With a chuckle he nodded towards the tall brass candlesticks set along a wall ledge. 'The only lamp we have is that one outside, which our captain of church security insists should remain there.' Candlelit Bible reading was bound to strain anyone's eyes. He led her up the steps to the chancel and through the arched doorway into the vestry.

In the half-light of a single candle, her first sight of Leonel was of him seated on a stone bench recessed into the wall, one foot up on it, the other flat to the floor, head back and eyes shut as if asleep. He wasn't asleep and was humming softly to himself, and when the padre called to him with a *Leonel, look who's here*, he stopped humming and opened his eyes. He stood up and reached for a towel that had been draped over the backrest of a chair. His upper body was bare save for a tight bandage applied to his shoulder.

'You look well.' Jasmine smiled away her disappointment at his lacklustre greeting while resisting a compulsion to run and fling her arms around him.

'I am well,' he laughed, 'very well.'

Padre Antonio laughed in sympathy.

Jasmine unclipped the safety pins that fixed the veil in place and removed the garment before pulling the velcro clasp at the back of her head and allowing the coif to drop to the floor. Piece by piece she removed her nun's habit. She untied the twine and handed the rifle to Leonel. He took up the weapon, flicked the latch and checked the magazine.

'It's loaded.' When he looked up she saw that his eyes were as bloodshot as the padre's. The penny dropped. She stomped over to Leonel, raised herself on tiptoes, reached up and clutched the back of his neck – an action that he misread because he snuck in a knowing wink to the Padre and puckered his lips for Jasmine. But she yanked his shaggy head down and sniffed his breath.

'*Wacala!*' she cried out in disgust, and turned her head aside while her palm shoved his face away. 'You're drunk!'

But Leonel had recovered swiftly from this manhandling and was nodding with apparent satisfaction, and then, one hand upheld, the other to his chest, as if about to take a solemn oath, he composed himself sufficiently to gulp down several huge mouthfuls of air. 'It's all Antonio's fault,' he burped hard, a feat that prompted in both men a ridiculous attack of the giggles.

Jasmine turned on Padre Antonio and glared. 'How could you do this? How can I take him now?'

With a visible effort Padre Antonio brought his sniggering under control. 'Señorita Jasmine,' he said reasonably, hands spread in pleading, 'please understand, they cut off our water supply and our food. We have been living off the Eucharist and wine.'

'Yes, that's it.' Leonel came forward, pointing an unsteady finger at her. 'Fortunately the sacristy was well stocked.'

'Well,' Padre Antonio started confidently before his words became scattered by spasms of suppressed hilarity, 'it was better stocked with *wine* than with *bread*.'

At which the men erupted in peals of wild laughter. Torsos doubled up, hands flicking from the wrists, feet stamping. If Leonel felt no shame, Jasmine felt it for him, that shame matched by her own disappointment in him. Who would have believed big men could behave like this? – one a guerrilla commander, the other a priest, for goodness sake! Jasmine decided to leave full judgement for another day because all her efforts would fall apart if she didn't get to grips with this situation right now. Willing away despair, she went forward and, tugging at Leonel's elbows, spoke sternly: 'I need you to come with me. I brought a uniform so you can pass for a soldier escorting a nun back to the convent after curfew. Come with me, *comandante*.'

But he shook her off. 'I don't want to go anywhere,' he blurted. 'I want to stay here for the rest of my life.'

'Yes, let him stay, señorita,' Padre Antonio agreed.

Jasmine punched Leonel in the midriff. A belch of rank air whooshed from his mouth and he doubled up and dropped heavily on to hands and knees. She stepped back and watched as he retched and retched again, and great gushes of cherry-red vomit splattered on the flagged floor and over his fingers. While he was coughing up the last of the contents of his stomach, she turned on Padre Antonio who held up his hands and backed away through the sacristy door.

* * *

It was a long wait during which Jasmine gave Leonel time to reflect on his behaviour.

Captain Escobar would knock at the door, he does so like clockwork, Padre Antonio assured her as he gave her the guided tour of the church. You know those types – military precision and all that. Well, tonight perhaps his clock wasn't working because the captain's knocking was conspicuous in its silence. Just when you need him to do his Nosy Parker thing, he decides to slacken off. The guided tour over, Jasmine exchanged small-talk with the two-dozen patients and attending medical staff. But her nerves could only run to small talk, so when the conversation threatened to rise to big talk she excused herself and sat on the chancel steps, unloading and reloading her revolver's chambers with magnum bullets while the young *vigilante* with sunglasses perched on his forehead told her how when he grows up he wants to be a mechanic, just like uncle Fabio. What's your name? she asked. Fabio. Of course it was. When finally the knock did come, it startled her.

'How can I help you, captain?' She held the door ajar with a gap sufficient to speak through but not for him to wedge his boot into.

'Would the sister be so kind as to allow me to use the lavatory?' he said, adopting a civility of posture and voice both of which were betrayed by his uniform.

'There's no flush water. Go poo in the bushes,' she told him tetchily.

Taken aback, he had to compose himself. 'I don't want to *poo*, just to *pee*.'

'Not this time. Patients are convalescing in here, and the stink is unhealthy for them. Unless, of course, you want to have the water reconnected?'

'ANDA – the water company.' He shook his head in cheerful confusion. 'You don't pay your bills, they cut you off. It's out of my hands.'

'Then you'll have to find somewhere else to do your stuff, won't you?' She waited until he made to speak and then cut him off: 'The answer's *no!*'

He scowled at her before hurrying down the steps. He must have needed the lavatory because he sidled off towards a hedgerow that marked the churchyard boundary.

'Now,' Jasmine whispered, yanking a sobering Leonel through the door and starting across the plaza.

With his slim torso discreetly curved into the hedge, Escobar peered over his shoulder and called after them. 'Hey…sister… wait.' Prompted by the sight of the nun and an unknown soldier, he turned inadvertently, and when Jasmine glanced his way she saw his arc of urine glimmering in the moonlight.

'Oh, that's awful,' she called back, as the shadowy figure of Padre Antonio with a raised candlestick stole up behind the captain.

Side by side the nun and the soldier crossed the plaza. They turned down Main Street and hurried beside a long white wall. A row of doused lanterns marked the doorways ahead, each doorway set in a foot-deep niche and flanked by blue shuttered windows. They crossed a junction, resisting a powerful urge to break into a run and headed downhill towards the splattered ruins of the school.

'We're too conspicuous here on the main street. Let's take that alleyway,' Leonel suggested, pointing towards an aperture not forty metres ahead. But from that same alleyway the uniform and skeletal M16 of a guardsman glided into the street. He stood with legs apart and tucked the rifle butt into his shoulder before lazily raising the barrel to a level position. Jasmine tugged on Leonel's sleeve.

'Keep walking, keep walking,' he urged. 'We play our parts.'

Leonel's attempt at reassurance was short-lived. One by one, similarly clad men detached themselves from the shadows and joined the first to form a tidy line right across the street. In all there were eight.

'We're cut off,' said Jasmine, and a check over her shoulder told her that from the junction they had crossed moments before another file of the Guard was in the process of arranging itself: five dropping to one knee while another five gathered behind.

Jasmine came to a halt and Leonel did the same. This seemed to act as a cue for one to take three resolute paces forward. He hollered as if delivering marching orders: 'I know you are the rebel Leonel Flint. Be assured that we have you completely cut off. You will surrender or be shot. Place all your weapons on the ground in front of you, raise your hands high where I can see them, and take three steps back. I will count to ten.'

'He's right,' Leonel mumbled from the corner of his mouth, apparently ready to throw in the towel. 'But he's talking to me, Jasmine. He hasn't cottoned on that you're *not* a nun.'

'Three,' the guard barked, his countdown having skipped a couple of numbers.

'My shoulder won't cope with a gun battle,' Leonel

admitted.

In a glance Jasmine took in walls, recessed doorways, and the electricity cables that swooped from pole to pole beneath a mantle of stars.

'Five.'

'Let the sister go. I'll come quietly,' Leonel yelled, and began to shrug out of his rifle strap.

'Wait,' Jasmine snapped. The drink was still clouding Leonel's judgement. Surrender was certain death. Combat was possible life. And she had come prepared for combat.

'The sister must walk over to us. I will personally escort her to the convent. *Seven.*'

Jasmine's right hand went up her left sleeve, delved into a canvas pouch at her waist and extracted an AN-M8 smoke grenade: its segmented metal casing cool to her touch. 'When I say *now*, run for the doorway to my left.'

Mercifully, Leonel agreed without question or hesitation. She turned to him and raised her left hand as if to administer a benediction, but the habit's sleeve acted as a screen behind which she primed the grenade and with an underarm swing rolled it ten metres downhill. '*Now!*' Jasmine and Leonel pelted for the doorway. Hissing smoke spewed into the street, and thudding repetitious rounds were already thwacking into concrete. Guardsmen inadvertently struck down their colleagues across the swirling clouds, and along with yelps of pain someone was screaming for them to hold your fucking fire, you fucking idiots! Jasmine whipped out a second smoke grenade and tossed it up the street, and soon the smoke was so thick that she could barely see Leonel who huddled in the recess beside her. Now she selected the last two egg-shaped shells from her pouches. These were M-67 antipersonnel fragmentation grenades. She flipped off the pins, lobbed one in each direction and ducked back into the relative safety of the recessed doorway. The handy little bombs rang across the cobbles and came to a standstill, and during the fuse-time Jasmine pulled Leonel in closer to her. Then, almost simultaneously, they exploded. The coils of notched wire shrapnel blasted through the smoke in a thousand deadly shards. Jasmine took out her Smith & Wesson and began picking off the ill-defined human shapes as, screaming, disorientated and confused, they loomed and vanished in the smoke. Out of the corner of her eye she saw Leonel's grimacing face as he cradled the M16 at waist-level to save his injured shoulder.

Within seconds Jasmine's revolver was empty. She reloaded and set about firing, then again she began to reload.

'*Mierda!*' she exploded in frustration. 'This is far too slow.'

Beside her Leonel's face was screwed up in agony. His rifle muzzle was slipping ever lower, kicking up orange sparks where his bullets were cracking the street cobbles. The rifle slipped from his grip and in the uproar bounced seemingly without sound on the step. Jasmine shoved her revolver beneath her habit, stooped, recovered the rifle, elbowed Leonel out of the way and, putting her back to the door, placed sustained fire into the haze. In two minutes the smoke will be gone, she reminded herself, as she popped the empty magazine and slotted in a fresh one. By then we must be away from here. A soldier materialised, bundling forward blindly almost side on to Jasmine; but he must have spotted her because he was now swinging his aim towards the doorway. She made the marginal adjustment and her sustained fire bit away the left side of his face. He turned as if to stroll away but sank into the thinning mist. She heard a single gunshot behind her. Leonel had drawn his revolver and was shooting at the timber panelling beside the doorknob.

'Hurry,' she beseeched, as another soldier came blundering upon her. She placed one shot into his forehead and a second into his chest. The force spun him round and he spiralled to the ground.

Smoke tentacles began eddying past her, and she realised that Leonel had managed to open the front door. With her finger on the trigger she sent a final volley into the street, tracing a semicircle from left to right with the magazine running dry as she stepped back. But the floor wasn't where it should be and she went tumbling down three steps to land heavily on her back. The fall was a blessing in disguise because a stream of fusillade flicked overhead and crashed into pottery or glass or perhaps both. Leonel slammed the heavy door shut, cutting off the smoke which now swirled around the gloom of a fully furnished living room: sofa, TV and the sorts of mod-cons that take you by surprise after four years beneath a forest canopy.

'There's no way to secure the door,' he bellowed.

'Out back,' Jasmine suggested, scrambling to her feet. She led the way through the living room and swung open the first door she came to. A terror-stricken couple in a double bed clung to each other. At their side stood a wooden cradle adorned with colourful playthings. The woman shoved her husband away, turned to the cradle and lifted out a nappy-clad toddler. Nothing was going to part her from her child.

'Please...don't kill us,' the man stammered, holding up both palms.

'Where's the rear exit?' Jasmine demanded.

'Through the courtyard...over the roof. It's the only way.' He pointed to his left.

'Thank you,' Jasmine said in softer tones. There must be little joy in waking to discover a gun-wielding nun and a giant soldier at the end of your bed. As an afterthought, she bid the couple hide themselves because real soldiers have a habit of labelling as communist anyone helping out a fellow citizen on any grounds – which in today's El Salvador earns you a summary death sentence.

She spun round and pushed past Leonel. 'This way.' His heavy footfalls followed as she raced along a short corridor and out into the courtyard. She was surrounded on all sides by spotless limed walls in which doors and shuttered windows were outlined.

Now she heard a crash behind her. The front door, having been kicked in, must have tumbled down the short flight of steps. She surveyed the courtyard. The roof was too high without a ladder. She eyed the clay oven that stood in the far left corner.

'There,' she said, ditching the void magazine and punching in a replacement. 'Use the oven as a step. I'll cover you.'

'No, Jasmine, you go first.'

'There's no time to argue. Just do it, please.' Jasmine turned her back on him and pointed her rifle towards the door through which they had come. 'Go. Now!'

'But...'

She whirled round and jabbed the muzzle into his bandaged shoulder, just where she knew the wound ran. 'Do it. *Now!*'

Leonel staggered backwards, clutching his shoulder, a stricken look in his eyes. But at least he abandoned his misplaced efforts at chivalry and lunged towards the clay oven from which he launched himself on to the roof. He landed awkwardly but managed a clambering ascent towards the apex. She felt for him. His wound must be absolute agony. But the alternative was worse.

Three bouts of automatic rifle fire from the bedroom made Jasmine wince. The occupants had paid the highest price for their assistance-under-duress to the Reds.

She dashed forward and slammed her back to the wall beside the door. Moments later a guardsman stepped into the courtyard. Incited by the compelling image of Leonel crabbing sideways up the pitched roof, he took aim without looking around. Know your terrain! It came back to Jasmine every time. She sent a bullet into the soldier's hip and watched him buckle. A second shot opened a small wound beside his ear and burst out the other side like water from a thumb-regulated hosepipe. The man crashed, his forehead smacking the concrete floor.

Leonel had disappeared over the top of the roof. Thank goodness!

Jasmine listened out for the next soldier. He's seen his colleague fall and won't make the same mistake of strolling mindlessly into the patio. She considered his position, conscious of her own trembling hands clutching the rifle to her heaving breast. She was breathing deeply, not from exhaustion but to fight a temptation towards recklessness. The passage was some fifteen of her paces in length, ten for an average soldier. Once cleared, any pursuit must likely come from the living room, giving her perhaps five seconds to break. She dropped on one knee, blind-aimed round the doorsill, and fired. The advantage: anyone lurking there would be hit or would likely retreat. The disadvantage: she was giving away her position and could not later scan the passageway without incurring an unacceptably high risk of being fired upon with accuracy. She held her breath and listened. Nothing. Seconds drew by and still nothing. Act or wait? Still no sound from the passageway. Act, she decided, and started breathing again. She pushed herself away from the wall and ran across the patio, intending to leap from the clay oven on to the roof. But she tripped on those wretched tunic skirts and fell sprawling beyond the sump hole. The rifle was flung from her hand and slid up against the far wall. She spun over and, supporting herself on both elbows, saw the second guardsman step into the patio. A big man with rifle leading, and he wasn't smiling because he hadn't come to play. With bleak eyes watching he loomed over her and shoved the muzzle hard to her forehead.

'Commie whore,' he muttered and swung his boot viciously into her ribs. She managed to control her shout of pain, releasing it as a throaty grunt. He stepped over her and kicked again, this time from the other side. Now he moved one leg to stand directly astride her head. The muzzle dug harder, forcing her head right back to the floor.

'That's right,' he grunted almost under his breath. 'Die beneath my feet.' And if he'd glanced down behind him, he might have seen the telltale stirring in the bundled disarray of his victim's habit. Jasmine reached behind her dungarees, found the Smith and Wesson, aimed upwards and squeezed the trigger. The bullet erupted through the cotton fabric and she saw the wisp of it vanish into the man's groin. She sent another in after the first before sliding out from beneath

284

him. Her attacker dropped his gun, clutched his groin and embarked on convulsive hip movements before releasing a scream to waken the dead. Jasmine crouched on one knee and watched as the man subsided on to his back, curled up in the foetal position and drew one last breath.

In the brief calm that followed Jasmine could hear dogs all over the city doing their barking. But no human dared raise a voice.

After pulling off her habit and stuffing it into the oven, she slipped the betrothal ring from her finger into her pocket before tucking the cross behind her dungarees. Aware that more soldiers may yet arrive, she clambered on to the oven, and leaped up, gripped the tile ridges and swung her right leg on to the horizontal drainage duck before hauling herself on to the roof. She dropped down the back wall on to a black-earth path that ran between the wall and a grassy bank. Here she found Leonel in a very bad state.

CHAPTER TWENTY-FIVE

June 1988

TEN DAYS AFTER THE bombing of the FMLN's San Vicente field hospital, Leonel Flint was convalescing in a safe house in Ilobasco town, Cabañas Province.

FMLN sympathisers Jeremias and Ria Benavides had, at great risk, provided him with a private room and food and arranged for the Party surgeon to perform a second round of surgery to his shoulder. Nurse Jasmine Gavidia was tasked with the daily bathing of his wound, the administering of ointments and painkillers, and the changing of bandages. Ria herself had cropped Leonel's hair to almost bald, which made him look a lot younger, but also lent him a vulnerability Jasmine had not previously seen.

A succession of idle days followed, and idle days were not good for Leonel, not to Jasmine's reckoning. She read the daily newspapers while he marvelled at random noises entering through his bedroom window: girls playing clapping games, the odd cart hammering by on iron-shod wheels, and snippets of lively conversations about the European football leagues. Was that jasmine blossom he could smell when the midmorning breeze carried the mist away? It's coffee flower, she informed him from behind her newspaper. Coffee flower, he repeated, shutting his eyes and relishing the fragrance. Come to think of it, these days he was speaking less of the war and more about his plans for when it was over. But she put this development down to his need for convalescence, so instead of pulling

286

him up about it she concentrated on nursing him back to full health. The sooner he was back at the helm of the column the better. She considered returning to the PCS herself, and voiced this to Leonel, but he dismissed the idea on the grounds that Jeremias and Ria were sympathisers not combatants, and if unfriendly forces were to discover them harbouring him, all three would be looking at an early grave. So Jasmine remained in Ilobasco town. Lookout, protector, nurse.

Jeremias – or "Jere" as he was known to close friends – and Ria Benavides had gathered at Leonel's bedside and, with doleful church bells pealing through that window to the outside world, spoke with candid bliss of the Palm Sunday mass from which they had only this minute returned. To Jasmine's keen eye, Leonel was on a puzzling high. 'Ria, your skirt is a happy skirt,' he declared as if addressing an auditorium. 'Simply a riot of colour, a sunrise!' Jasmine winced, and cleared her throat to distract him lest our Jere here took umbrage at such a deluge of clumsy compliments directed towards his wife by his Most Wanted houseguest. 'Jere's nicely turned-out too,' Leonel announced, 'very dapper in that pinstripe. How much would a tailor charge to make me such a smart suit?' To which a wary Jere reckoned he could strike a very reasonable bargain.

'I brought an extra one for you, Don Leonel.' Ria navigated the focus back to Palm Sunday and handed him a crucifix of dried palm leaves.

He accepted it and thanked her for such consideration, and apparently at a loss as to what to do with the cross he sniffed it.

'It's not a flower, silly,' Ria laughed, clutching her own cross at her stomach. 'It's to remind you of the humility of Jesus; a king riding into a city on a donkey.'

Leonel's eyes reddened as he came down off his high, and he asked if he and Jasmine could please be left to speak in private. With a sympathetic smile Ria pushed her bewildered husband from the guest room. When they were alone, Jasmine took a perch on the edge of the bed but watched Leonel in silence, allowing him to get whatever was troubling him off his chest. With hooded eyes, seemingly lost in his own dreamy Cuscatlán, he spent a full couple of minutes collecting himself.

'Jasmine,' he opened, finally.

She encouraged him to speak his mind. '*Dígame.*'

'I'm wearying of this war. Over eight years, and still no end in sight.' His idiotic rambling had given way to low, measured speech. 'That's too long to live in a forest, don't you think? I've lost touch with village life; if I see a guy who hasn't lived like an animal or isn't fully preoccupied with the war effort I don't know how to speak to him. I feel like I'm losing my humanity.' He refilled his lungs, stumbling against the pain in his shoulder, and exhaled. 'This bed' – stroking the white linen – 'feels good to sleep in a bed. Don't actually remember what it feels like…you know…but it's good, all the same. It's also good to bathe frequently, to be clean all the time.' He laughed at this comment, although not with a great deal of humour. 'Silly little things that others take for granted.' His reddened eyes now welled up. Jasmine held her breath, alarmed at the prospect of Leonel in tears. She needed him to be strong and focused. 'When I look at Jere and Ria,' he continued, a distinct thickness to his voice now, 'they have this home, a patch of farm…They read poetry to each other, just like you and I do.' Then more firmly, 'This is how we were meant to live. This is how *I* want *us* to live. You and me.'

If that was a proposal it was fittingly lost on Jasmine. 'We are in the midst of a war, c*omandante*,' she reminded him, aiming to gentle him back to the path of righteousness, and privately rebuking herself for not having done so earlier. 'We command over eighty per cent of the national territory, and are making encouraging advances in the central region. The tranquillity that Don Jere and Doña Ria enjoy, the same tranquillity that you're basking in now, was returned to villages like Ilobasco by the collective FMLN effort. Now we surround San Salvador on all sides except the south. We must fight on until victory is complete. Remember…*Hasta la Victoria*?'

'You are young, Jasmine, in love with the revolution. I

remember that first love, that passion, and I still have it, believe me,' he insisted. 'But San Salvador will not fall. We have gained all the territory we are going to gain, and we have some very compelling evidence to counter the cocaine allegations. We have done as much as we can. It is time to concede a little…for the sake of peace, Jasmine, for the sake of peace.'

'We are *winning*,' Jasmine railed, springing to her feet and not liking this reformed Leonel. 'We have the enemy by the throat.' She flung out a hand and caught an invisible throat in a stranglehold. 'We must squeeze a little longer…a little harder, and *they will fall…*'

'No, Jasmine, it is enough already,' he interrupted her, his face screwed up in agony. She fell silent, resumed her perch on the edge of the bed, and looked away, smarting from his outburst.

'Forgive me, *comandante*,' she mustered eventually.

He heaved a heavy sigh. 'I'm sorry too, Jasmine, I didn't mean to shout at you.'

They were both sorry. They had both apologised. But still she couldn't meet his eyes. With a grunt of pain he pushed himself upright. He took her face in his hand, turned it towards him and made her look him in the eye. 'Go to Abraham, reason with him, attend the peace conferences and agree terms. Will you do that for me?'

'You know I will.'

'On Tuesday, I sent Jere to personally deliver a letter to Abraham. Today, I need you to deliver a copy of that same letter to Adrian.'

It was a mysterious request, but a contrite Jasmine did not venture to question it. 'Of course,' she agreed softly, knowing that some measure of decisiveness from him was better than none.

'Do you want to know what's in the letter?' He freed her face and ran his fingers back over his head, a subconscious gesture from a time before Ria had called in the barber. Suddenly he held a crumpled white envelope which he thrust at her as if he never wanted to see it again.

'You'd tell me if you thought I ought to know.' The envelope now in her hand.

'Always pragmatic,' he mused, managing his melt-your-heart smile. But she smiled bleakly. The village sounds flooded back into the guest room and reminded her of a world beyond the window.

'Adrian is a good combatant,' Leonel broke the pause with a startling understatement. Adrian was a great combatant, an outstanding medic; and a more faithful comrade could not be found in all Cuscatlán. 'But he is no leader. The letter you hold is a copy of a statement I sent to Abraham Gadala requesting funds be released to you, to buy you new clothes, and new boots for everyone.'

'It's Palm Sunday, not Christmas,' she laughed, at last breaking free of the sting of his earlier rebuke. 'I don't need new clothes.'

'It is our custom when power passes from one hand to another. The statement appoints you to PCS *comandante* in my place.'

CHAPTER TWENTY-SIX

IF JASMINE HAD THOUGHT she could gently ease into the swing of things as the PCS's new resident leader, she was mistaken.

There was work to do. Endless eavesdropping on army transmissions on a confiscated radio and from this charting the enemy's movements, geographical familiarisation for all without exception, imprisoned comrades to spring, others to safe-house, field hospital duties. There were also schools to set up and then rebuild, military training for combatants, new recruits to interview, food, water and medicines to acquire, weapon and ammo replenishment, fortnightly reports to Abraham Gadala, long camp-moving marches every three to four days, and the planning and execution of campaigns. Planned and revised for every eventuality with a meticulousness that, to quote Adrian, "borders on the fanatical!" Yet despite such fanatical planning, a worrying truth soon dawned on her. She discussed it with her lieutenants. The number of combatants lost during air strikes is unacceptably high, she declared. Reclaiming a town is straightforward. Catch the Guard off guard – pun ignored. Most are kids. Bang, bang! It's over. But it's the reprisals that cost most in terms of lives both to us and to the village that requested the PCS's liberating skills in the first place. Not only must we leave a permanent defence squad behind – eight or nine members – but when coupled with the number of combatants lost during military reprisals,

291

column numbers are fast depleting.

Emilio reminded her that Leonel used to wait until column numbers were up again before embarking on a new recapturing venture. But Jasmine, with a sense of urgency prompted by recollections of El Zacate, felt obliged to undertake the mission as soon after receiving the tape recording as was practicable – allowing for the planning, scouting and intelligence gathering that must come first.

'What can we do to effectively counter the superiority of air strikes?' she asked them in plain Spanish.

'So far there is no guerrilla tactic that can offer a real solution to attacks from the air,' Adrian, who was normally an encyclopaedia, admitted lamely.

* * *

'How did Adrian and the others take the news of your appointment?' Leonel had migrated from the bedroom to an armchair in the living room from where he could watch the 14-inch colour TV. But after reluctantly releasing Jasmine from a stimulating embrace he tactfully bent from the waist as much to switch off the TV as to conceal the unbefitting evidence of his stimulation.

Jasmine threw herself into an armchair opposite him and, interlinking fingers and twirling her thumbs, answered gamely, 'I hope okay.'

Leonel seated himself in the delicate manner of a man still nursing a painful wound and while Ria served up tall glasses of iced *tamarindo*, he regarded his protégé with a contemplative eye. Her skin was darker than ever, the rich reddish-ochre of the Lenca. The sun had been at her hair too: fiery bands of copper and gold coiling with the black, loosely gathered back to spring a plume down to her trim waist. He considered her new attire, purchased with the money Abraham had given for it. She had selected an olive-green boiler suit, zipped to the neck, loose fitting except where it tautened on her thighs. Black hiking boots had finally replaced those beaten up sandals. Not for the first time Leonel had to make mental adjustments to the way he thought of and addressed her, a sort of catch-up to one who was fast maturing.

Ria prudently took herself off to the kitchen to prepare what she promised was going to be a rich *mondongo* soup with cassava so soft it will melt in your mouths.

'There will be confrontation between you and Adrian,' Leonel said. 'But I'm confident you will handle it appropriately. Now listen.' He beckoned, and Jasmine pulled her chair closer and leaned forward. 'Doctor Lemus says I'll never regain full mobility of my arm, so my use to the column as a field combatant is limited.' He held up a hand to silence her protest. 'Were the armed forces to see me weakened like this they would press us harder at the peace table. Abraham Gadala has agreed that from here on you will attend all peace talks as the PCS's rep.' Pause. 'Okay?'

'I'm listening.' She was fidgeting.

'Listening is precisely what I want you to do. Listen and observe. Learn all you can about each attendee's negotiating style. Don't be intimidated by them. Invariably the negotiations break down. You don't need me to remind you there are those in government and in the military who genuinely feel they will lose out big time if we are ever allowed to democratically engage the electorate. But there is also intransigence on our side, bitterness in our hearts that wants to see vengeance before peace. But for the sake of our potential voters, we need to inject a sense of urgency into our diplomatic efforts. Don't interrupt, Jasmine, please.' She had lost none of her impetuousness. In many ways she was so like Adrian, only without his levels of testosterone to fuddle the brain. 'I know, I know. ARENA is allowed to use any means at its disposal with massive backing from the gringos, while we're expected to limit our efforts to diplomacy. But listen, Jasmine, let me finish, yeah? The church is in on the act, as are ONUSAL and the OAS. We have a growing number of sympathisers around the world rooting for us in very practical ways. So speak with Abraham, as I have. Urge him not to allow these fragile opportunities to continue being an exercise in bureaucratic lip-service. Will you do that for me?'

She would, but wanted to know when he was coming back to Cuscatlán. Pause. 'You can still lead us. Even if you don't actively engage in combat, you could participate in other ways, like formulating strategies and tactics.'

'I won't be returning to the column,' he said bluntly. 'I'll be working out of Abraham's office. You are now the leader. Accept it and deliver on your commitment.' He sat back. 'You know, before I went to Santiago de Cuba, I was Adonai's protégé. There's no man on earth whose judgement I'd rather trust. Shortly after I arrived here in Ilobasco, the old fellow came to see how I was doing. It was he who suggested I appoint you to the leadership. I said, "Hey, but she's only eighteen." He said that was the age he first led a column, back in the old days, before the FMLN's formation. He said you and he are made from the same dough.'

* * *

The confrontation that Leonel had predicted turned out to be a dramatic event, but not necessarily in the way he had imagined. The catalyst was an unauthorised raid on a farm – Rancho González – by Adrian and Segundo, during which they had stolen a couple of goats. A challenge to Jasmine's authority, given that she forbade the practice of stealing livestock that Leonel had previously permitted. Since the theft an atmosphere of unresolved tension had been brewing in the column. Jasmine could sense it, and it grew all the more uneasy the longer it went unspoken. Unspoken, yet spoken in apparently insignificant acts of derision: the odd overly-casual reply, loaded quip, back-turned towards her when she approached; and now this flagrant act of disobedience from Adrian and Segundo. Adrian the lieutenant widely slated for the *comandancia*, Segundo Adrian's faithful disciple and long-time pal. She drew the inevitable conclusion as to who had led who.

But she wanted to move camp before broaching the subject

with the lieutenant. Partly because they had been in their present camp for three days already, and partly because she found that leading the column on these long treks gave her time to think. She needed to be clear as to how to approach a lieutenant who was a vital element to the column, and who, it was plain to see from his long membership, rank and accomplishments, would be Leonel's natural successor. Granted, Leonel had summoned Adrian and Emilio to Ilobasco to explain his decision prior to her appointment. Jasmine was curious to know what had been said in that meeting. Emilio had accepted his choice with good grace. But Adrian was another matter. While he continued to be a loose cannon, her leadership would be resented by the others.

Now there were only eighteen combatants (plus two goats) in the column that arrived at the new site. In the forest fringes of Cojutepeque they could, if they wandered to the lip of the escarpment, look over the valley of patchwork farmland, and fend off unwanted approaches from that direction. Cojutepecans could be relied upon to send warning of any military advance up the mountain road on the other side of the village.

Even once they had rigged up hammocks and temporary wooden structures, Jasmine decided to leave it till the following day before speaking with Adrian. Tempers were always fraying by the time they reached a new site, and all everyone wanted to do was to rest their aching bodies and shut fatigued eyes.

So the following afternoon, while the goats were being spit-roasted, Jasmine called Adrian to go with her for a scout round. They went beyond the perimeter wire, and when they were striding through waist-high mimosas triggering their rows of tiny leaves to clap shut, Jasmine paused and called his name. But he drifted on as if he hadn't heard her, ostensibly checking out the scenery. She spoke his name again, and this time he turned back to stand half-facing her.

She just came out with it: 'You have been with the column since the very beginning, haven't you?'

He nodded and dipped his eyes to his hand, apparently to watch his thumbnail flicking his fingernail. She had expected glaring. There was none.

'Do you want command, Adrian? I can arrange it with Don Abraham.'

He hung his head, still grooming his fingernails.

'Well, what did you expect me to do? Refuse?' she snapped, mistaking his silence for reproach. She put her hands on her hips and exhaled sharply. Privately she had already conceded that she was prepared to hand over the reigns of the PCS to Adrian, if that was what the column wished. In her mind she had built up a picture of resentful comrades, she imagined she felt it too – their resentment, Adrian's resentment. But now she saw that his silence was not reproach. It was the silence of weariness, weariness on the threshold of desperation. Her heart sank. Adrian's grimace told her that he was trying to stem the tears that were now streaming down his face.

She discovered her hand operating on its own initiative, and it went up to cup the side of his neck. He stood unbending and awkward-looking. Her hand cradled the side of his jaw from where her thumb swept aside the tears that skated down. His face twisted with inner struggle. She applied enough pressure to coax his head down towards her shoulder. His final resistance expelled itself in a sob, followed by a shuffle of his feet so that he was facing her instead of twisting towards her; and gradually and stiffly he bowed forward, his temple guided in to alight on the upper part of her breast. Then he wept like someone gasping for air. It was a sound that made the fine hairs on the back of Jasmine's neck stand up, and she knew that it came from somewhere unspeakably deep. He dropped to his knees and clung to her thighs as if his very life depended on them. She caught the words *fire* and *tough*. Meanwhile she made sympathetic murmurs and stroked his sweaty scalp through his bristly hair, and lifted her own face to the canopy and blinked back her own tears. After a while it was as though the choking became unblocked and Adrian was free to howl at full voice. He was repeating the same words over and over, a sentence distorted by his howls. *Paw, send*, didn't make sense, but as Jasmine listened his entreaty became clearer. He was saying: 'I want this war to end.'

'We will make it end,' she said. 'But we have a little way to go yet.'

Eventually Adrian cried himself dry and then, looking rather sheepish, asked if Jasmine would mind staying with him until his eyes had shed their redness. And sunken amid the mimosas they sat facing each other and reminisced about *what is it? More than four years – wow! Has it been that long?* they had known each other.

On their return to camp they found everyone in buoyant mood. Sitting two to a crate in their new boots round the doused embers of the fire, the combatants were ravenously tucking into roasted goat, their happy faces glossy with grease, and they were making far too much noise.

Jasmine felt for her combatants. You never get used to hunger; nor do you get used to thirst. On top of that, the news that Leonel was not returning. But the mouth-watering smell of the roast had lifted their appetites as much as their spirits. She joined in, accepting a slab of medium-rare from a hesitant Anabela, and her inclusion was well received.

This was how Jasmine's leadership was ultimately accepted within the column. The loose end had been Adrian, and once he came round, the others fell in line.

* * *

Eighteen months of Jasmine Gavidia running squads to recapture, liberate and uphold towns and cities throughout Cuscatlán, Cabañas and along the frosty south-eastern borders of Chalatenango, fuelled hostilities between ARENA and the FMLN, and Jasmine's name was added to the army's Most Wanted list, even if press photographers had yet to come up with an accompanying polaroid. Her offensives lasted from as little as a few minutes, to hours, and even days. She begged and borrowed combatants from other zones, and campaigned in the red zones for recruits.

Not to be underestimated, the military hit back hard, the fighting spread, soon all FMLN columns were reengaged, and a new wave of disruption gripped the country. The citizenry was swept up in the throes of some of the most ferocious confrontations of the eleven-year conflict. Erupting gunfire would send the crowds diving to the ground. Some lay flat on their stomachs, hands over ears, biting back their screams. Others got up and half crawling, half crouching made off, seeking a safer place. Where an exchange between the army and the guerrillas became prolonged, Jasmine caught glimpses of men coming to their feet, cradling bodies in their arms; and flip-flops and sandals peppered the ground from where their owners had fled. In the cities, around the abandoned footwear, newspaper pages, wrapping paper, plain paper, just paper – hundreds of sheets of it whirled in an unnatural wind.

Advances were liable to be frustratingly gradual. Precious ground gained over many hours of hard combat and tenuously held was abruptly relinquished when a ferocious army fusillade pushed the guerrillas back. In her comrades' eyes, Jasmine saw a savage alertness that reflected her own state of mind. It was exhausting work, both physically and mentally. If she paused to think about it, it was terrifying.

The banging of mortar shells and gunfire continued ringing in her ears long after the battles had died down. An incessant pounding, on occasions even while recumbent in her hammock she reached instinctively for her gun. But over time she grew accustomed to it, falling asleep with the echo of it penetrating her dreams.

The same old problem of air support prevailed: the helicopters swung in overhead, the fighting intensified, and the town suffered heavy structural damage. SAF went into overkill, destroying buildings for the sake of downing a couple of combatants.

'There must be a solution to the problem of the helicopters,' she railed during an evening assembly she had convened with Adrian and Emilio. 'We cannot afford to lose so many villagers, or to provoke such extensive structural damage to their homes, not if we are to retain their support.'

'It's not our collateral damage,' Emilio pointed out.

'Irrelevant!' Adrian countered, matching Jasmine's exasperation. 'It's because of our presence in the villages that SAF resorts to such destructive measures. Let's face it: lately we've been full steam ahead. We've pushed the greens back from her here, from there. They know they're holding on to the very last of the peasant villages. That's why their fighting is fiercer now than it's been for years, and will probably get fiercer, if we continue at this level of intensity.'

'You're both right,' said Jasmine diplomatically. 'But the villages will no longer call on us if we cannot better protect them in the face of this renewed military concentration, and they'll return to the old ways of submission.'

'Still, we are closing in around the capital,' Adrian looked on the bright side. 'Even La Libertad and La Paz are now liberated provinces, apart from a few die-hard villages along the coast that pose no real threat either way.'

Encouraged by Adrian, Emilio also saw the bright side. 'We are slowly strangling the capital.'

'But is it enough to strangle Señor Sorrentino at the negotiating table?' Jasmine looked up at them.

They had no answer for her.

CHAPTER TWENTY-SEVEN

JASMINE SET OFF ON foot to Suchitoto from where she caught the early afternoon trashcan of a bus to San Salvador before riding a smart urban minibus to Abraham Gadala's roadside office in Ilopango. With a coin she clanged the cheerless grille that protected the iron front door, and while she waited in the sweltering city heat for an answer a shirtless street waif tapped her shoulder, a pleading expression on his grubby face and a grubby hand held out in supplication. She pressed the coin into his open palm and was rewarded with a beacon of a smile.

The door swung open and Jasmine was bid wait by a personal assistant who phoned through notice of her arrival. Given the nod from on high, the assistant led Jasmine in to Abraham's office, which resembled a smoky library, with a ceiling fan to circulate the cigarette smoke more effectively. A cordial greeting to begin with, and then to kill time while the assistant served up powerful Turkish coffee and set a brightly painted bowl of fruit on the conference table, Abraham engaged in small talk.

And after Abraham had declined his personal assistant's *will that be all, sir?* and told her there was a curfew on all incoming calls until further notice, the un-smiling secretary left the two FMLN members to their privacy.

'Our combatants grow weary and frustrated with the lack of progress, Don Abraham,' Jasmine cut straight to the chase and added a frank postscript: 'So do I.'

'My Fortnightly Progress Reports suggest that the PCS has been exceedingly active these past eighteen months. Despite the fears we had following the election, instead of succumbing to the intensified military offensives, you have actually prised from their hands those very last villages the ruling party was most keen to command, and,' Abraham folded hairy arms across his safari tunic, 'I am informed by a most reliable source that you have never lost an offensive. Surely, lack of progress is not the cause of the PCS's frustrations.'

But he was missing the point altogether, so she would have to elaborate: 'With every village we take, I must commit combatants there indefinitely to cover military reprisals. New recruits arrive in insufficient numbers to replace the growing deficit. For the past two months we have been so thinly spread that we ran combat operations with no more than three members per squad. I have already redistributed forces. Where there were ten covering a town, there are now six, and where there were six, only four remain.'

Abraham plucked at his beard and nodded approvingly. 'The fact that with only three combatants you wrest entire towns from heavily armed units has also come to my notice. I don't mind admitting to you there were those of us who questioned the wisdom behind Leonel's appointing you to take the PCS forward in his stead. But you proved the doubters amongst us wrong. Judging by FPR reports, you have become the most prolific town-taker in the history of the FMLN. Why do you suppose that is?'

'A sense of urgency,' she retorted, her fervour overriding the protocol for her rank.

'Urgency,' he repeated as if trying to place the word. 'Yes, urgency.' He pointed a finger at her. 'But a man can only run as fast as the legs that carry him. You, on the other hand, because of your sense of urgency, have outrun your resources, particularly your human resources. And the inevitable has happened: you've hit a brick wall. From now on you are to modify your work rate, slow down and regulate it, launch offensives only when you have replenished the members who die or are committed in the villages. Gradually our numbers will increase.'

Perhaps he wasn't exactly missing the point. 'With respect, Don Abraham, if we do as you say, we will be at this forever. Seventy-five thousand deaths, eight thousand others disappeared, and eleven years of war. It's time to stop and to drive ARENA to seriously consider the demands laid out in the FMLN's draft proposal.'

'You come to me with an old debate and expect me to provide a solution?' he suggested, raising unkempt silvery eyebrows. She was young, with a mere eighteen months as column leader and challenging the collective wisdom of the old hands.

Jasmine wagged her finger across the table at Abraham. 'There is no brick wall, as you say, only a stalemate from which neither side can break the other or back down, unless *we* act. Having lost virtually all rural zones to us, the armed forces are now backed up in the capital. We have San Salvador surrounded on all sides, yet this favourable position – favourable to us, not them – together with the findings you presented to ONUSAL last June, still doesn't amount to sufficient motivation to drive ARENA to even consider our proposals with sincerity. In the meantime, the war continues, and under such conditions, Don Abraham, it will continue indefinitely.'

'Indeed,' he replied. 'You will presumably have a suggestion as to how we should proceed, *comandante*, as to how we break this deadlock?'

She recalled her candlelit guerrilla induction patiently delivered by Leonel, and the way he winced when he relayed the times when, eleven years ago now, history had shut doors of opportunity on the then unseasoned FMLN. The Party today was not the Party of eleven years ago. She would answer Abraham by suggesting they knock once more at the most securely shut of those doors. 'You are *Comandante* in Chief,

Don Abraham. Give the order to launch a full scale offensive against San Salvador.'

* * *

Had it not been for the propitious FP Reports and Adonai Limeño's flattering praise of her in Abraham's ear, her proposal might have gone down like a sack of bricks. As it was, having put up some initial resistance, primarily she suspected to test whether she had thought it through at all thoroughly, he authorised her to develop a speculative plan and call for tentative preparations, and recorded such authorisation on a cassette whose label told the casual eye that Jasmine's taste in music ran to Prokofiev's Romeo and Juliet.

Jasmine spent the night at a boarding house in Cuscatancingo, and left early next morning, armed with her cassette, to embark on a round of meetings aimed at securing the backing of the column leaders, although she knew that without Adonai's backing her plan would fall at the first hurdle. So until she made her suggestion directly to the Old Maestro, she would merely allow the others to listen to and act upon Don Abraham's recorded instructions.

First stop: Santa Ana Province, where she met with a bearded Ivan Saavedra on the volcanic slopes of the active Ilamatepec. During the afternoon she outlined her proposal over pots of floral infusions. He listened to the cassette and made no comment or expression to betray his thoughts. Acting on the instruction to allow Jasmine sight of his armoury, he threatened three volunteers from their slumber, and shouldering spades they trekked half a kilometre down the volcano slope into the deeper wooded folds. The crates of munitions lay buried beneath a light covering of black earth and dead leaves. Ivan sliced the plastic sheeting and stood aside while Jasmine inspected the contents of the store by torchlight. In the exercise book she otherwise used to send messages to Leonel, she recorded an inventory of Ivan's considerable arsenal.

'By Monday next week, all this needs to be in the cisterns

at the agreed addresses in Zacamil, Soyapango, 49th Street, and Mejicanos.'

'That will leave us with nothing,' Ivan protested. But he hadn't heard the worst.

'All your combatants should be made available for instant redeployment, Don Ivan. Please start calling them in from the towns and villages.'

* * *

Feeling too ill at ease to stay the night, Jasmine bid an awkward *hasta luego* to a sullen-faced Ivan three hours before curfew lifted. Sensing his fierce black eyes boring into the back of her head, she breathed a huge sigh of relief when out of sight. Ivan had a way of saying far too much with his silence.

While an owl hooted unseen Jasmine hastened through misted orchards, amazed at how slackly they'd been pruned. Her reflective mood broke every time wind stirred the high branches or when the lowing of cattle warned her she was nearing an open space. She arrived in Juayua as the sun was rising through the mists to announce the lifting of the curfew. But with rain clouds gathering, she bussed to Sonsonate City where it was raining in torrents. She took shelter in a cheap motel on the outskirts. When the rain failed to let up, she paid the receptionist for a night's board, and slept fitfully while prostitutes serviced a succession of clients in the neighbouring rooms.

She caught the first bus heading for San Diego, in the province of La Libertad. At every stop along the way vendors by the dozen boarded to peddle their wares to parched travellers: plastic pouches of drinking water, maize cakes, canned soft drinks, and boiled sweets. Those vendors who didn't make it onboard conducted transactions through open windows.

It was late morning when Jasmine met with Carlos Rivera on the black sands close to the wooden pier that stretched into the sea and upon which fishmongers were trading.

'We will have other work for your men,' she told him as they sat on the promenade wall, sipping *colachampán* through a straw and watching his combatants surfing on glittering, curling waves. Their bodies were brown as cinnamon and their hair, like hers, was streaked with the colour of the sun.

It was during the second hour into the curfew that Carlos led Jasmine across railway tracks submerged in hard earth. At this time of night, the market was a ramshackle place of refuse being scattered by warm sea winds, of scavenging dogs, and of a legion of foul-smelling vagrants sleeping beneath boarded up stalls and in the narrow alleys between the shops that backed on to the market square. In one of these alleys, they stepped round such a vagrant who to Jasmine looked more like a bundle of filthy rags. She thought he was asleep, or dead. The last time she had smelt anything so decomposed was amongst the dead when searching for her mother. Suddenly the vagrant stirred and then cried out. With heartache and welling tears she watched him drag his legless torso out into the market square.

'When our combatants are free, we could make time to attend to these men,' she suggested, using her thumbs to flick away the overspill from her eyes.

'I agree,' Carlos replied, having gone a little way further down the alleyway. 'In fact we have a moral obligation to do so, since many of these vagabonds were once *compa's*. You'll even find one or two *ex-comandantes* amongst them, before their wounds precluded them from resuming combat operations.' He jangled a small bunch of keys, bid her make haste and then disappeared into the wall.

When she reached the point of his disappearance, she saw that he was sidling up a crevice of a passage by way of the narrowest flight of steps she had ever seen. She hurried after him and at the top step Carlos unlocked a slender metal door and followed his torchlight through.

'A warehouse?' she asked, stepping on to a wooden scaffold that had been erected like a gallery around the interior of a two storey rectangular brick hall.

'A warehouse…maybe,' he said mysteriously.

Below them and to their right a heavy goods lorry with enclosed trailer was parked alongside the wall. Lined up in the remaining space were three yellow metal containers, each the size of a commercial skip; and arranged on top of these were cardboard cartons and wooden crates which Jasmine saw were filled with vegetables. At the far end of the hall, a steel sliding door barred the entrance.

Carlos led her down a ladder that creaked and curved under their combined weight.

'You cache your weapons here, in a public place?' she asked sceptically when they had landed on solid concrete.

'Not here.' He stamped the floor with his heel. 'But there.'

Perhaps the concrete was not as solid as she had at first reckoned.

'A cellar?' she guessed.

He got down on hands and knees and crawled beneath the trailer. Jasmine edged up beside him as he tapped an iron handle that curved out of a manhole cover.

'This warehouse, as you describe it, used to be a dead-end alleyway between two buildings,' Carlos explained. 'The owner purchased both buildings and somehow,' he rubbed thumb and middle finger together to imply bribery, 'he convinced the municipal authority that the alleyway, being a dead-end, was no longer a public right of way, and that as sole owner of the buildings on either side he was entitled to consider the space in between as his own. So he roofed it over. But it still has the old manhole that housed the water meter. He had the water company install a single meter at the back for the combined premises, leaving this hole free. He cleared it out, had it enlarged and walled properly, and now it serves our purposes quite well.' He grinned smugly . 'Any idea who the owner is?'

She shook her head, obliging his sense of disclosure.

'Guillermo Gadala.'

'Don Abraham's brother?' She was genuinely surprised.

'The same.'

'But the brothers are bitter enemies,' she repeated common

hearsay, never having questioned its authenticity until now.

'A public front,' Carlos chuckled. 'More to protect Guillermo than Abraham. As you know, they come from an affluent immigrant family. Guillermo the well-liked businessman; his brother Abraham the rebel. Guillermo must clearly be seen to disapprove of his brother's insurrectionary activities, but I guess that in their case, blood *is* thicker than water. Of course,' Carlos added with a wry smile, 'Abraham has to pay rent for the space out of his own pocket, but you won't find a safer weapons store anywhere in the national territory.'

She helped him lift aside the manhole cover, and followed him into his munitions store. It was small and in Carlos's torch-light she saw it was stocked floor to ceiling with plywood ammunition crates and hard resin cases.

While compiling the inventory, she helped herself to a Beretta 92F automatic pistol which, chambering a fifteen-round magazine, and with a muzzle velocity of 1,280 feet per second, supplanted the double action revolver beneath her boiler suit.

* * *

With no platforms to demarcate the railway station, the huge diesel locomotive screeched to an eventual halt amid crowds going about their daily affairs. Though the four carriages arrived crammed with sweaty humanity clutching their precarious cloth bundles and chattels, still more travellers piled aboard and clung to the outer walls while others pushed up beside those who were already sitting on the roof.

Jasmine chose the end carriage and nudged up to sit facing backwards on the iron girder that spanned the rear fenders. After twenty minutes' wait in the pitiless heat, the Pride of El Salvador's Railways and Harbours growled off, gradually picking up pace. With the crossties clattering beneath in strict rhythm, it sped eastwards along the coastal plains on an eight hour journey towards Usulután.

* * *

307

Maximiliano Santos looked like a chief, or at least Jasmine's idea of how a chief should look: sloping forehead, high cheekbones, nose like an eagle's beak, pitch-black shoulder-length hair, and the lean physique of the active man who'd only just turned the fifty that he proudly confessed to be.

Max and his clan, collectively titled the Union of Indigenous Cuscatlecos, were encamped a short walk from the shores of the Rio Grande de San Miguel. When Jasmine asked to see his armoury, he showed her to a dugout canoe which had six inches of water swilling in its hull. Untroubled by such matters as seaworthiness, Max paddled out into the Bay of Jiquilisco and put to shore on Bird Island. Under cover of darkness, he discovered beneath the sand a length of henequen twine which he tugged hard and as Jasmine watched a timber-panelled floor shook free a covering of sand and leaves and slid away to uncover a bunker – perhaps an ex-Venceremos hideout. When she had finished adding Max's arsenal to her notebook, she asked that it all be transferred to the capital, and she awarded him a helpful list of designated safe houses.

* * *

'It's a day's journey to Morazán,' Maximiliano told her. 'If you don't mind, I'd like to go with you. It's been a good while since I last saw *El Maestro* in his home town.'

She didn't mind. She would be glad of the company.

They journeyed to Morazán by bus, along roads edged with eucalyptus trees and splashes of crimson bougainvillea. They crossed the stone bridge over the Rio Torola and toiled up boulder-strewn hills which swelled into thickly wooded mountains where the air was bitingly cold.

On a steep and wooded mountainside the picturesque village of San Francisco Gotera was a criss-cross of pebbled streets and a jumble of colourful houses and shops with the red star insignia of the FMLN emblazoned on every wall and lamppost.

When they met on the rear veranda of the parish house Jasmine clung as hard to Adonai as he did to her. Predictably his face was stubble-covered. He wore a flamboyant blanket of Mayan weave over his cream-coloured cottons, and had donned his ubiquitous Wellingtons for the occasion.

At last he unwrapped her from his embrace and held her at arm's length. 'Gavidia,' he exclaimed, and again she had a notion that between each lazy blink he was casually perusing her soul. 'What a joy to meet you again.'

Maximiliano inclined his head reverently and clasped the old warrior's hand in both his own.

'I have studied your works, maestro,' Jasmine said eagerly. She proceeded to declaim from memory her favourite lines: '*With the fake wood of their ammunition crates we wall our houses, and are reminded of our lot. Laughing, our children play clapping games in bomb craters, and are emboldened by theirs. Chanting the odes of their fathers, peasant men bury painful memories in grey fields of ash, and pluck them, red, from the orchards. Singing sweet melodies of motherhood, our virgins wash bloody sheets where blood has flowed yet draw them, white, from the river.*'

'Mild frivolity,' he claimed, and set about arranging three chairs in a semicircle and instructed his guests to sit at either end so that he could sit between them. While he went to rustle up some hot chocolate Jasmine reconsidered the speech she had designed to enlist his support for and leadership of the offensive she had dreamed up. But now, somehow, the much revised overture seemed inappropriate: the naïve scheme of a novice echoing inwardly instead of the learned strategy of a tested *compa* leader. Yes, she was convinced it was the only way forward and yes, she trusted Adonai's leadership capabilities implicitly. All she had to do was state her plan and clearly outline the reasons for it. He would understand. He would divine a strategy and appropriate tactics to see the offensive through, and he would lead, victorious as he always had in Morazán. *Hasta la Victoria y Siempre!*

'Why such a frown?' said Adonai, standing beside her and lowering a tray.

'Just thinking,' she smiled, and selected the purple mug.

He offered the tray to Maximiliano before seating himself with the oiled joints of a much younger man. 'What do you say we head directly to the point before you etch a permanent crease in your forehead?'

That was fine by his audience.

'Let me tell you what I know and then you can correct me. Agreed? Two days ago I received a visit from Abraham Gadala. Now, Abraham's feathers are not easily ruffled, but he was fretful. You must understand something about Abraham. He was pivotal in bringing the revolutionary component factions under a single FMLN umbrella. It was a long and arduous process for him and for others, but having achieved unification and with it constructed a nascent political party, he is rightly nervous of any potentially destabilising factor that might present itself. Now, on the one hand that gives you' – tipping his white head at Jasmine – 'a lever to pull. I'm sure that hasn't escaped your shrewd mind, Gavidia. On the other hand, should you decide to pull that lever, please, I beseech you, be very aware that Abraham and many like him have been to hell and back to build what you in your youth have inherited. In plain language, Gavidia, I'm asking that in your contemplations regarding our collective future, you bear in the forefront of your mind not only your personal loss, which I know is a tragic one, but also the years of toil and sacrifice invested by countless comrades, including yourself, to get us all to this advantageous point. Are you willing to risk undermining such work? More chocolate?'

'No, to the first question, and no thanks to the second.'

'Thank *you*,' he said firmly. It was his way to offer gratitude for merely being understood. 'So naturally, when Abraham called by to say you wished me to lead a coordinated offensive against the capital, I knew he must have misunderstood you. "Surely," I said to him, "you are mistaken." But he was most adamant. Perplexingly so. This is my question to you, Gavidia: is *Comandante* Abraham Gadala mistaken?'

'I believe an offensive on the capital to be necessary,' she struggled to say, inwardly wobbled by his word of warning. Did she think enlisting his support would be a simple matter? Well, think again. But somewhere in that casually browsing gaze, she detected a test to her resolve.

'How so?' he asked, slowly stirring his chocolate.

'The stalemate between us and ARENA will continue indefinitely, leading to more bloodshed. Neither side looks like defeating the other outright.'

'Your combatants are weary,' Adonai stated, and jarred by his assumption she glanced into his serene stare. But it was not an assumption, rather common knowledge, and she should assume that government forces would suspect the same. 'We're all weary,' he added, before sipping his chocolate. Perhaps she was feeling oversensitive now, but that last comment triggered in her a prickle of isolation. This was an uphill battle and she was fighting it on her lonesome.

'But no more so than the soldiers and villagers,' she retorted. 'The only Salvadorans not weary are bigwig civvies and VIP army hotshots who when they're not stealing from the public purse are cowering in fortified mansions in La Zona Militar and sending out conscripts, many of whom are frightened kids, to wield machineguns in the very villages where they were dragged from their classrooms.'

'She reckons a strike against the capital will break the deadlock,' Maximiliano chipped in, bringing the conversation back on track.

'I believe she does reckon that,' Adonai replied and swivelled his head to observe Maximilian. 'Are you convinced of this?'

'I see her point but am unable to conceive a viable procedure for such an offensive.' He gave a non-committal shrug. 'This is not some small town where most of the population is already for us. We are talking here about a heavily guarded city of over one million inhabitants, the majority of whom are ARENA supporters.'

Adonai said he agreed, and then turned to Jasmine. 'Do

you propose we incite a general uprising of the masses? San Salvador's masses are clearly against us, and I doubt the peasantry can be mobilised.'

Jasmine gave a bleak smile. This was a test of her knowledge of his manuscripts – the ones he had 'bequeathed' in Nicaragua. 'The Vietnamese and Nicaraguan experiences taught us that to expect a general uprising is a flawed guerrilla aspiration. Those civilians wishing to participate have already joined the guerrilla columns. Of those supporters who remain in the cities we should expect no more than the provision of food and safe houses.' She turned round in her chair to face Adonai, her confidence rekindled and stirring. He was asking questions, and that was a good sign. 'We should not include a call for a general uprising. The offensive should be carried out exclusively by our members.'

Adonai's neutral expression persisted throughout his next question. 'What action would you suggest employing against such a sizable and handsomely-armed adversary, one that outnumbers us nine-to-one and is backed by infinite American resources and modern technology?'

Now Jasmine swallowed a trace of pride. This was like being back in training camp from which she had graduated six years ago. Yet she reminded herself that, given Adonai's unparalleled experience and deserved reputation, it was essential to get him on her side if the other column leaders were to be won over, that without total inclusion of all FMLN members the plan was a non-starter, so she ploughed on. 'No conventional action. No main force action. As armies eventually discover to their detriment, such tactics are imprecise, leading to heavy civilian casualties, which turns the citizenry against them. Instead, we should apply guerrilla tactics, exclusively.'

'Which tactics exactly?'

'Two,' she declared. 'Adaptable to developing battle conditions. The first is to worry the enemy, niggle at them, fray their nerves with a variety of flash attacks. We choose the time, place and duration of each encounter before disappearing.

Secondly, send a single large squad to flaunt itself to an enemy unit, to flirt with it. When it advances, instead of engaging, our squad withdraws and disappears, as one or separating to regroup – we can work out the details to suit each terrain. The enemy rests or splits up to search the area, conducting house to house, all that stuff. We send forward three squads and snipers to harass – no main force action, just harassment. Conventional armies tire of this sooner rather than later. We send five squads to attack. If the enemy withdraws, seven squads pursue. If not, we select one of the previous stages from which to take up the offensive, making appropriate adjustments identified from the previous pushback.'

'That's all very well,' Adonai suggested, '*if* you are dealing with ground forces. But as you may have noticed from Guerrilla Manual, I placed a question mark at the end of Chapter 101. Do you know why that is?'

'Air strikes,' Jasmine stated. Who could forget? Full debates had been mounted on the back of that question mark's possible meaning.

'Air strikes it is. And if we are to counter the threat from above, 101 must be written. Did you write such a chapter?'

Come to think of it, she had, actually.

'And how did you title it?'

'Raiding beehives.'

* * *

But three outspoken dissenters felt moved to approach Abraham Gadala. Bronzed Carlos Rivera brought a sack of mangoes; Ivan Saavedra had a bag of wild albahaca and basil; and Maximiliano Santos paraded two boxes of Cuban stogies and a funny anecdote of how he came by them. Granted an audience in the Party's Ilopango digs, they pooled their gifts and settled round the table, to voice grave concerns that could not simply be brushed under the carpet. Abraham, vexed at Jasmine for upsetting the congenial balance the FMLN's all male hierarchy had previous enjoyed, was doing his level-best to defuse the tension. Upping his vexation was Adonai's

313

absence, despite a well-coded invitation. Abraham had a notion that the old maestro's serene spirit would have soothed present company, because by the looks on their faces, they could benefit from a lot of soothing.

'About this proposed assault on the capital,' Carlos set the ball rolling, 'the sums say we'll be slaughtered within ninety minutes of entering the outskirts, unless of course we undertake an embarrassing retreat.'

'If we go along with *Comandante* Gavidia's scheme, we stand to lose everything,' Ivan Saavedra added. 'There's no getting away from it: centralising our entire forces and artillery in San Salvador means leaving hundreds of villages undefended, villages our members have fought and died to liberate and to maintain as liberated. All that's taken us eleven years of hard sacrifices to achieve could disappear down the drain. Are you willing to start over from scratch if the scheme fails?'

Abraham had anticipated every objection. He steeled himself to listen without interruption while they got those objections off their chests; and he knew better than to query their resolve, for each had qualified himself beyond question in countless campaigns in remote mountains north and west, and market towns east of the Lempa, and even fishing hamlets where support for the guerrillas was generally low. But like it or not, he couldn't deny that Jasmine made a truly compelling argument.

'But there is truth in what *Comandante* Gavidia says,' he ventured an interruption. 'Although we have liberated every rural zone, Sorrentino still snubs our proposals for peace. Theoretically, at least, I must agree that exerting additional pressure on ARENA implies hitting them on their own turf, where they feel safest, which also happens to be the only un-liberated zone in the national territory.'

'I agree with her, also,' Ivan claimed. 'We all agree with her, *theoretically*.' He looked round and the other dissenters nodded. 'But unlike the rural villages, San Salvador doesn't want to be liberated, does it? We have exerted all possible pressure on ARENA. And we couldn't liberate a metropolis where eighty per cent of military forces are concentrated, even if the population sought liberation, which, as I'm tired of repeating, they certainly do not.'

'Where I disagree on principle,' said Maximiliano, reaching for his second stogie, 'is on withdrawing from our rural positions to concentrate our entire resources on what is, by comparison, a relatively small area.'

Abraham raised a weary hand. The office was thick with smoke, and Carlos, who was the only non-smoker, was making a big deal of it by coughing elaborately and complaining that second-hand smoke was bad for the lungs. He was still waving a cloud away when the phone rang and after Abraham had admonished his personal assistant for breaking the call-curfew he thanked her for breaking it. To Abraham's considerable relief she announced Adonai Limeño's arrival, and even now he was letting himself into the conference hall. It always amazed Abraham how such a giant of a reputation should dress in unassuming white cottons, as if he'd walked straight off a maize field. Aptly his gift was corn boiled in leaves because, as he reminded them, they are people of the maize, because the Mesoamerican variety can be yellow, red, black or white, with all these colours commonly inhabiting a single ear of corn. There was ceremony in Adonai's giving of the corn, and already Abraham could feel the tension receding because of it.

When Adonai seated himself, he seemed to sink into his cottons.

Abraham recovered the line Adonai's entry had interrupted: 'Let's first see what emerges from the peace talks. However, do I have your assurances that should we record – in favour of the offensive – a majority vote rather than a unanimous one, it will nonetheless count on our unanimous support?'

Ivan agreed, leaning in to stub out his stogie in the communal ashtray. 'You need not concern yourself as to our collective loyalty. I'm confident I speak for each of us when I say we are committed to you and the FMLN.'

315

But Abraham was not so sure, because all present readily agreed with Ivan's declaration – all except Adonai, who remained conspicuously wordless on the matter.

'That brings me to a related matter,' Abraham continued. 'And if you' – nodding at Adonai – 'would be so good as to update Jasmine Gavidia, I'd be grateful.'

They waited for the further matter to be disclosed.

'That in the absence of Leonel Flint, you, Don Adonai, should assume over all custody of the planning and realising of the offensive. No one here need be reminded that your record speaks for itself.'

'You are the most qualified, Adonai,' Carlos seconded the motion.

With his white head down and his limbs drowning in those cottons, Adonai might have fallen asleep. His pose remained unaltered when he spoke: 'You are, perhaps, overlooking the obvious, comrades. Consider that the Gavidia girl's knowledge of counter-conventional battle-aspects and their militaristic applications matches ours, that she's a meticulous and farsighted planner. Unlike us, she's young, vigorous, and fresh with revolutionary zest and possesses considerable experience. A closer review of her record will show that she is the most qualified amongst us.'

In the fraught silence it was again Carlos's turn to make his feelings known:

'Her record is impressive, no one doubts that. But she is an emotional creature, given to unwarranted bouts of compassion. The leader of this venture will require uncompromising steel to see it through to the end. Are you willing to risk what is already a risky venture being compromised by her over-sentimentality?'

Abraham thought that a poor stab at Jasmine's credentials.

Now Adonai sat up in his chair and set his forearms on the table edge with hands clasped. 'Comrades, this is how I see it. No-one here is suggesting the proposed offensive comes without risks. We are aware that should it fail, the army will follow up with a nationwide sweep to recover all we've taken eleven years to liberate. When our parties united, you and I were in our prime, but lacking experience. Remember the painful lessons of eighty-one and eighty-two from those failed offensives on the capital? In the years since, we've gained the experience but lost our youth.'

'You mean we're old,' Maximiliano, proud of his half-century, stated with a wry chuckle that went unshared.

'I mean Leonel is the only youngster, in the most liberal sense of the word, among us,' Adonai said. 'Metaphorically and physically he's got balls. He also has enough know-how to take on the challenge under discussion. But the brother went and got himself shot in the shoulder and put out of action. Returning now to the Gavidia girl: Let us also not forget that wily mind of hers brought an end to Santamaria's decade-long reign of terror. From the very beginning she demonstrated uncanny resourcefulness, and since achieving direct combatant status has shown an instinct to foresee and adjust to rapidly changing battle conditions. Hers is the combined experience of having worked alongside Leonel, studied at Campamento Sandino where she achieved the highest grades ever recorded since the camp's establishment in 1979, and six frenetic years of direct combat, besides a very successful eighteen months as column leader. None of us, not even Leonel, has had such favourable credentials all at one time. If her womanhood worries you, and judging by the looks on your faces I think it does, let me add this: the fact that I am a man with field experience does not in itself compensate for all she has to offer this venture.'

Abraham wedged his bristled chin between thumb and forefinger, because that's how he liked to think. But Adonai hadn't finished:

'When I met Gavidia at Campamento Sandino…must've been six years ago now… frankly her attitude impressed me, so much so that I let her have my hand-written manuscripts on the prosecution of guerrilla war – a sort of bequeathing if you like. Having since spent some significant time with her, I am

317

aware that she has committed the entire lot to memory.' He unclasped his hands and spread palms down side by side on the table. 'I haven't fought at her side,' he admitted, 'but I have studied her campaigns: Tazumal, San Juan Opico, Metapán, San Pedro – which the armed forces had jealously guarded for the sake of conserving strategic presence. Yet Gavidia snatched the lot, and these towns remain under PCS protection even today.' He chuckled at the very thought of it. 'Comrades, her curriculum is unsurpassed.'

'She is our most prolific town-snatcher,' Abraham pointed out, warming to Adonai's proposal which suddenly seemed less wacky than when the old warrior had first stunned everyone with it.

Adonai coughed into his fist and sipped some water before he was ready to offer up his final submission: 'Now, gentlemen, she believes it can be done.'

'Do you believe it can be done?' Carlos challenged, and all eyes returned to Adonai as he delivered an answer:

'I believe that before we vote on whether to launch this offensive on the capital, we first consider very thoroughly under whose command rest our best chances of success. Such is the scale of the proposed venture that the difference in physicality between one male overall leader and one female overall leader becomes extraneous. Is Gavidia a specialist in war-craft? Yes. Can she lead large columns into battle? Yes. Has she ever lost a campaign? No.'

Quiet descended. Adonai replenished his glass from the jug and drank.

It was Maximiliano who spoke up at last. 'We still have time to ponder the matter before making a final decision. As Don Abraham says, let's see what the next peace talks throw up.'

'That at least is agreed then.' Abraham closed the meeting.

* * *

No grand edifice for ONUSAL, but a regular two-storey townhouse in a safe-ish San Salvador suburb. If you got past the blue-berets, you'd take a left and step inside an air-conditioned hall with high, barred windows and a fake-wood conference table. In immaculate livery Simón Levi – top general with his greying left parting, laughter lines and shades was seated next to the UN's Chief of Mission, Iqbal Haq, presiding. A powdery moustache, thinning black hair, crescent-shaped shadows beneath stony brown eyes, and a white shirt unbuttoned to his chest, Iqbal – doing his presiding from the head of the table – was mumbling English into a telephone. Arrayed before him in political splendour sat a motley line-up of players who'd rather not touch each other without a bargepole: cabinet bigwigs and their legal bluffers, uniformed generals and theirs; Victor Carranza – the Organization of American States' rep hobnobbing with a robed Archbishop José Maria Coronado like old friends; Interior Minister José Antonio Morales doing his best to turn his pinstriped back on safari-suited Abraham Gadala, who didn't give a toss because he had Jasmine to his right, and if she was aware of the glances she was attracting from around the table, she didn't let on. Studious as ever, she was revising the fat buff-folder previously prepared and supplied by Iqbal that contained amongst other documents the minutes of the previous meeting, a copy of the FMLN's draft proposal, and a copy of J.M. Gavidia's schedule of findings and statements answering the accusation of cocaine contraband. To complete a picture of political will: pinned to the wall behind Iqbal a cloth banner portrayed two white doves winging peacefully over a not so peaceful looking volcano. To Abraham, that ONUSAL flag, hanging from a wooden stand in one corner, aptly reflected the UN's predictable stand against all forms of tyranny. Limp!

Iqbal clunked the telephone back on its cradle. 'Shall we commence with official introductions?'

* * *

By day the strong-willed assembly grappled with the skeleton peace agreement. Attempts to flesh it out with discussion and suspect compromises and precious little substance made such issues as human rights violations, land distribution, the cessation of hostilities, and the setting up of a new national civilian police force, hard going.

By night armed UN peace-keepers ferried Jasmine and Abraham in a bullet-proof SUV to Antiguo Cuscatlán where the University of Central America housed its Jesuits and their visitors and a scattering of employees. In Jasmine's chamber of bare essentials, she and Abraham pored over the minutes of that day's charade, the endless statements and demand schedules from interested and disinterested parties alike, and their own neatly scribbled addendums.

By ten a.m. each morning they were back at the negotiating table to fight their respective corners.

Wednesday a.m. Gustavo Blass, Director of the Hacienda Police, treated the assembly to a slide show. When the lights had been dimmed and even popcorn had been offered – possibly as a joke because no-one accepted to prove otherwise – the show began with stills of likely lads conspicuously clad in communistic red FMLN T-shirts, standing proud beside ranks of plastic bags containing some yellowish substance that Gustavo helpfully claimed his forensic team had identified as cocaine. And yet more likely lads posing over an enviable assortment of weaponry; and if anyone was in any doubt as to the identity of each weapon, Gustavo would be happy to direct them to the relevant page in the file provided. These were probably the very same slides Leonel had seen several years ago during similar talks in Sonsonate when the Comandancia General had met with delegates from the then recently elected ARENA. Jasmine remembered the occasion well, not only because after the briefing that Leonel had delivered to the PCS she was assigned her first solo mission, but also because it was when Leonel had first informed the PCS that Secretary General Pérez de Cuellar's recommendation to the Security Council to open preparatory offices throughout the national territory had been approved. And now here she was, watching that same slide show in one of those very preparatory offices.

In the afternoon a slot was provided for the FMLN to

put forward its case, and it was left to Jasmine to address the assembly on the matter of the Party's alleged involvement in the contraband of controlled drugs.

'Actually we discovered no FMLN participation in the drugs trade up through the Golfo de Fonseca. Although, during our investigations, it became apparent that an army major in collusion with several naval officers was conducting this illicit business with Peruvian and Ecuadorian contrabandistas who were parading as trawler-men. Mistaking the contrabandistas for guerrillas, SAF bombed Tehuacán, destroying the village and killing seventy-four civilians. None of the non-residents discovered amongst the dead in Tehuacán were FMLN members, despite the army's claim to the contrary.'

Iqbal pounded his small fist on the table and called for order as the politicians and generals jeered and shook their heads in amused disbelief.

'Tell us how you know this,' Gustavo Blass demanded on the end of a jolly chortle while cleaning his specs with chamois.

'I saw two of the parties involved,' Jasmine claimed, feeling oddly unruffled despite the gaping lack of photographs in her filed evidence, which was bound to be picked up on sooner rather than later.

'Have you filed photographic evidence of this,' Iqbal enquired.

'I regret that I lost the camera, but I saw them nonetheless.'

'Lost the camera. How very convenient!' Gustavo and sarcasm were a natural team. 'Without photographic evidence you have no case.'

But Iqbal threw her a line. 'Verbal evidence from an eye-witness is valid in these proceedings.'

Blass shrugged this off. Knocked back but not down, he angled his head so that Iqbal was excluded from his glare for Jasmine – and more to the point the menace that glare conveyed. 'But you could not possibly have got so close without being personally involved. These people are highly secretive. The Navy has been trying for decades to get as close to the contrabandistas as you say you did, without any significant measure of success. Yet you manage to waltz your way in and out, unscathed.'

Your time for snuffing my rights through threats and violence is almost at an end, Jasmine answered, having this parallel conversation through stares. 'The Navy has been close for decades, illegally importing controlled drugs, filtering them through the armed forces.'

Another hullabaloo of protestation from the suits and uniforms. Iqbal, who had by now discovered a handy gavel, hammered for quiet.

'*Silencio. Por favor. Silencio!*' Iqbal gripped his mallet and into the resulting lull he dropped his question: '*Comandante* Gavidia, your report mentions the discovery of sachets of dextroamphetamine on…how shall I put this?…fallen soldiers. What's the significance of your comments here, considering this is a legal substance?'

'I make no additional comments in respect of this drug, other than to repeat the conclusion of my essay – which you have there: that despite its current legal status, dextroamphetamine contributes significantly towards irrational and violent behaviour, and in my judgement it should be made illegal. But the findings in my report are confined to cocaine contraband, which is routinely carried out by the army and its death squads, imported from South America and distributed amongst the soldiers.'

By hoisting the mallet Iqbal curtailed the potential furore. 'I see,' he said, somewhat remotely. 'These are rather serious allegations, *comandante*.'

'The same serious allegations levelled against the FMLN, yet it didn't take us decades to close in on the *contrabandistas*. My leads took me close, only to discover it was none other than our accusers who are involved in the trade. And as far as I know, they still are.'

The gavel, back in the air, had the desired effect, even if Jasmine overheard an anonymous whisper accuse Iqbal of bias.

'*Comandante* Gavidia, have you named all the military personnel you saw at Tehuacán on that day?' Iqbal asked. Perhaps concerned that she may be unfamiliar with peace talk culture he was considerately prompting her through her evidence.

'Only one,' she confirmed. 'Major Anastasio Menesses was there. I saw him shooting at a SAF helicopter. My statement and a full report of our findings, including his name, was filed with ONUSAL, and can be found starting at page 148-A of the file in front of you.'

A flutter of page-turning and licking of thumbs as ARENA's participants turned to the right page and began reading quietly to themselves, an admission no doubt that, on the suspect belief that all would go swimmingly their way, none had bothered to read Jasmine's submissions before the meeting.

Iqbal jotted something in his note pad. 'Then we must investigate this Major Menesses. One of ONUSAL's tasks here in your country is to follow up allegations of corruption and human rights abuses. Your application has been noted, *Comandante* Gavidia.'

* * *

Thursday, noon.

'I'm encouraged, cautiously optimistic even, by the progress being made,' Iqbal confessed to a ravenous Jasmine over a lunch adjournment for cold meats and salad charitably provided by ONUSAL in the walled courtyard at the rear of the house. It was no surprise to anyone that the politicians and legal whips had taken themselves off to pull the wool off each others eyes, leaving Abraham Gadala, Archbishop Coronado and Victor Carranza to share the cold buffet with Iqbal and Jasmine.

'Greater readiness by ARENA to concede ground would go a long way towards achieving an agreement,' Abraham suggested, apparently feeling none of the optimism – cautious or otherwise. 'I question their resolve in this respect.'

'Patience, Abraham,' the Archbishop advised. 'I share your

frustration, but we must gently nudge these prehistoric hog-heads into the present day.'

'Drag them,' Carranza adjusted the verb.

'By the scruff of their necks,' Jasmine added through a mouthful of egg salad.

'Now, now,' Iqbal cautioned. 'Our collective aim is to secure a peace agreement. No gain is to be had by dishing out discourtesies to your opposite numbers.'

But when Friday came and Simón Levi exploited his time slot to sum up the strategic battle positions as he saw them, because unlike politicians he was well able to suss out military strategy, Iqbal's well-meaning but sadly green hopes for a peace agreement that would have looked good on his diplomatic CV came crashing down.

'I have it on reliable authority that the FMLN's combatants are tired, on their last legs, no longer able to mount significant military operations,' Simón declared with haughtiness, clearly encouraged by the daily gains his generals were reporting with regards his territorial recovery plan. 'They're all bark and no bite. But' – he thrust forward a forefinger – 'ARENA is a Salvadoran party elected by the people to responsibly protect their interests. To allow even a fringe element of the FMLN to remain militarised would represent an unacceptable threat to our national security. It is, therefore, only right for us, on behalf of the Salvadoran electorate, to continue insisting that the FMLN agree to unilaterally disarm itself under the supervision of the National Guard and,' he turned towards Iqbal, 'ONUSAL's international peace-keeping forces. Once FMLN disarmament is complete and verified, the Salvadoran government will commit to negotiating FMLN participation and inclusion in the political process. If you refuse to disarm,' now he directed his smug attention at a brooding Abraham, 'we will have no alternative but to oblige you to do so by all means at our disposal, including military actions. We demand, therefore, the immediate ceasefire and unconditional surrender of your guerrillas.' He had said his piece, and by the way he was removing his shades to glare at Abraham he was well satisfied with what he evidently considered his strategic battle advantage.

Jasmine glanced up as Abraham rose to his feet beside her, his studied political smile, powerless to countenance further political intransigence, waned while his eyes beheld his audience with a stare that Jasmine could not make out from the angle. But it must have been some stare because Levi wouldn't stop blinking as he sank to his seat, and a profound hush gripped the assembly. Even Iqbal's personal assistant, who had all the while been busily typing up the minutes at the PC, looked up now.

'With Uncle Sam as the master puppeteer, Central America's marionette dictatorships have blithely massacred millions of peasants for having the audacity to voice dissatisfaction at extremes of poverty and exploitation,' Abraham began, low and deliberate. 'And then you scratch your heads when despite your best work to shrink our movement, our numbers swell. So you legislate to set us up as illegal citizens in our own land. But your efforts to silence our pleas either by the gun – naively believing that just causes die with their proponents – or by banning us from democratic participation, only serve to swell our conviction, and our numbers. The silenced oppressed will eventually speak with violence,' – quoting Adonai – 'although this little fact seems to upset your sense of integrity.' He broke off, perhaps to temper a mounting breathlessness that only Jasmine – through familiarity – would detect. 'I came here to talk peace, and yes, we are tired, tired after fifty years of housing orphans, of staring at empty cots, of the Guard's midnight invasions of our homes to drag away our fathers; tired of pulling corpses from our rivers and of washing blood off our walls, and tired of endless queues of coffins and of the sound of widows weeping, tired of the disappearance of our priests and the rape of our daughters, and tired of being punished for asking you nicely to stop doing these things to us. It was because we finally grew tired that eleven years ago we took up arms to defend our campesinos from your military incursions; and now, under further threat of military action, you insist we throw down those very arms that have halted the military in its tracks and brought you to the negotiating table.' He stalled. Jasmine watched the bended knuckle of his freckled forefinger clout the tabletop. 'Your agenda is clear. Because the UN is either unwilling or powerless to stop your violence against our civilians, and with unflinching backing from your Washington allies, you will continue the slaughter in your efforts to rid the region of popular movements. We,' – punching his chest thrice with a closed fist – 'are Salvadorans too, and have sought nothing more than to be included in the democratic process of our homeland instead of excluded from it.' He heaved a long breath and exhaled slowly, composing himself. He resumed, an underlying fervour lifting his monologue. 'We will give you a taste of your own agenda by bringing the war to your city. We'll see how quickly you too take up arms to defend yourselves, and how quickly you too grow tired.'

Iqbal regained his voice just in time to call out, 'Señor Gadala. Wait. Please!'

But it was too late. Leaving his audience well lambasted the FMLN's top man had slammed the door on the charade.

Jasmine rose to her feet, gathered up the loose pages and stuffed them into her folder. 'I think that's my cue to leave,' she said, and hugging the folder to her breast she turned to Iqbal. 'I'm willing to give evidence in any court regarding Major Anastasio Menesses. He led the *matanza* against El Zacate – that was my hometown. With my own eyes I saw him direct the operation known as Hammer and Nail. I saw him take possession of a large shipment of cocaine, and I also saw him shooting at a SAF helicopter. If you're unable to take effective action against the armed forces but want to do something for the campesinos, expose those who were behind the *matanzas*. Then, perhaps finally, they will stop.'

She left.

* * *

326

'Hire the best professional money can buy, and take her out, once and for all,' Anastasio grimaced at Gabriel, his new recruit from the slums of Santa Tecla. The extent of Jasmine's evidence against him had come as a shock. According to The General, she was not the sort to be easily intimidated, even if she could be kidnapped.

'We can do the job ourselves,' the eager youth insisted.

'Nonsense! She's deadlier than a rattlesnake. Play it safe, contract an independent assassin. I want her terminated.'

CHAPTER TWENTY-EIGHT

'I SINCERELY HOPE THIS will not be the last time I see your dirty faces.' Dressed in his ubiquitous khaki pressed just smooth enough to walk amid the likes of politicians but unstarched to depict the wearer as a man of action, the FMLN chief Abraham Gadala spoke with grave intonation as one by one The Five filed in solemn step past the Rights for the Silenced Voices. Seemingly innocuous, the three-page typed document lay open at page three on the Party office's conference table. 'Will you join me in signing our Statement?'

They would, came the unanimous reply.

Hands behind back he stepped back to let them pass, and embarked on a recitation of the Declaration, much of it lifted directly from the USA's Declaration of Independence. 'To protect such basic human rights as Life and Liberty, governments are instituted amongst men, deriving their powers from the consent of the governed. Whenever a government in its preference to serving these ends and their sanctity becomes destructive to these, thereby translating itself as a despot government, it is the Citizens' right and duty to remove such government and institute new government through the democratic process. When, however, the democratic vehicle has been tampered with by the despot government to such ends that by means of the same democratic process or other peaceful measures the despot government's removal from office or at the very least the abolition of its despotism fall beyond the Democratic Power of the People, the right to Revolution by armed resistance is activated. Prudence, indeed, will dictate that governments should not be changed for light or transient reasons; and accordingly all experience has shown that mankind is more disposed to suffer while evil persists than to right itself by abolishing the forms to which it is accustomed. Our *Campesinos*, who make up eighty-two per cent of our nation's population, having for fifty years and more engaged in peaceful marches and demonstrations, and signed petitions to the governments of our homeland and to a succession of UN Secretary Generals, and sought litigation via the courts systems, and delivered appeals to the international community, all in their efforts to curtail the injustices meted upon them by government forces, and having on every occasion been responded to by grotesque levels of violence instead of peaceful negotiations, have thereby exhausted all peaceful and democratic avenues in their efforts to voice their concerns. As a consequence it has become the FMLN's firmly held view that the right to an armed offensive against the despot government on its home territory has been justifiably activated. Accordingly, we the Frente Farabundo Martí para la Liberación Nacional have resolved to conduct such armed incursion as the last and only resort remaining to us in the hope of pressuring the government ARENA into – finally – conceding that parliamentary representation for our nation's majority constitutes a legitimate democratic right and into granting our nation's citizenry that Right. Are we unanimously agreed?'

We were.

When each *comandante* had put his scribble to the document, Abraham turned to Jasmine. 'We are in your hands now, *Comandante* Gavidia. You have our full backing, and we all share in the responsibility.'

* * *

'We strike first at the head,' Jasmine told her bleary-eyed comrades, having woken them from their hammocks immed-

329

iately upon her arrival. Squatting, shivering, peeking out from blankets in which they had swaddled themselves, warming their hands on calabashes of coffee and smoking cheap cigarettes, they were gathered round a campfire to hear the General Command's decision on *La Ofensiva*.

She had confirmed the go-ahead given by Abraham Gadala, authorising the offensive against San Salvador and eleven suburbs. Now she handed photocopied maps to Adrian, Emilio and Anabela, who distributed one to each combatant.

'Casa Presidencial,' she stated, 'takes up half the block, with 28th Street running along its northern wall, 27th at its south, the continuation of Metzi Street at its west side and a factory wall on the east side. The entrance to the factory looks across the continuation of 27th with a view up Colonial Street.' She paused, allowing her comrades to identify the positions mentioned and to familiarise themselves with the map. One by one they looked back at her expectantly, and she carried on. 'Ten greens are positioned at intervals around the high perimeter wall, four along the front of the property, three at the west side, and another four at the north. Others, we don't know how many, are positioned inside the grounds. When Adrian and I surveyed the location, we could see their heads appearing over the wall, so they must be standing on some sort of platform. Clearly, from three sides of the premises they can fire directly on to the street.' Again she broke off, wanting each combatant to consider the logistics of conducting a siege on such a well protected site.

'Furthermore,' she waved her copy of the map while slipping her spare hand into her pocket, 'two soldiers command each junction up from those that corner Colonial, 27th, Metzi and 28th. That makes fourteen more soldiers for us to take care of.'

'In other words the house is guarded at three stations,' Adrian expanded. 'One inside the garden, a second along the outer perimeter wall, and a third a junction up on all approach roads. Despite his doubts about the seriousness of our intentions, Sorrentino has increased his personal security.'

'What about the factory?' Anabela piped up. 'Can we get close from that side?'

'Negative,' Emilio replied. 'The wall is much higher on the factory side, and the factory itself is crawling with workers day and night. Besides, sounding out sympathisers so close to the presidential mansion would be far too risky. We are obliged to concentrate on three fronts only.'

'As you will see from the plans, it's almost a fortress,' said Jasmine. 'Now let's examine what lies behind the walls. The house takes up about half the land area and is built against the south-eastern corner.' She nodded at Adrian, and he went on:

'That rectangle you see on the plan at the north side is a swimming pool. It is surrounded by lawns. Opposite the pool, between the house and the north-eastern corner, are changing rooms and a barbeque area.' He nodded back to Jasmine.

'Once we get through the first checkpoints at the outer junctions, we will approach the mansion from the south and north simultaneously. These two junctions,' Jasmine held up her map for them to see, and indicated the junctions 'will present us with three streets down which to fire.'

Although he was the most senior member, Wenceslou raised his hand like a schoolboy, and was cordially invited to speak. 'Excuse me, *comandante,* but from these plans and from what I recall of the site, Colonial, Metzi, 27th and 28th are long, straight and wide roads. The soldiers will see us coming well before we can take them out. We will undoubtedly sustain heavy losses at the outer junctions only to face a second and heavier defence once we reach the inner junctions.'

'Wenceslou is right,' Segundo agreed. 'And the soldiers positioned in the garden have the advantage of height over the wall and the shield that the wall itself provides. If any of us manages to get past the primary defences, we will be picked off by the immediate defence force stationed close to the target.'

'We will worry about how to get past the first check points later,' Jasmine asserted. 'Right now, I want us to assume that we are within firing range of the target area, and to study phase two of the siege.'

* * *

For the sake of secrecy, which is paramount when planning a combat operation against one of Latin America's most press-sensitive cities, the exact location of each of the various meetings held between the FMLN zone leaders during the following eighteen days was known only to the attending *comandantes* and their lieutenants.

Snow had fallen overnight, and now it lay deep across the Chalatenango mountains. The sky was dazzling, and the air was mulled with fragrances born of pine forests. Along snow-laden branches, grey squirrels scurried, hesitated, sniffed, and scurried again.

Jasmine shivered, paused on the uphill track and turned towards the uninhibited gleeful squealing. On the other side of a plunging gully, kids aged, if she had to guess, between five and sixteen were at blissful play on a hillside behind timber box huts scattered amid slender pines. In eye-catching anoraks they gathered the snow in gloved hands and pressed it into cannonballs. A small girl in a pink woolly hat, brandishing a malformed pancake of a snowball, was on the prowl for a target. On spotting a likely adolescent ruffian kneeling to gather up his own icy missile, she tiptoed towards him, making, as any fine warrior would advise, an approach from the rear. The marked man lurched to his feet and, oblivious to the threat from behind, hurled his perfectly round snowball towards a bushy-haired scruff who in response leapt, straight arms outstretched above his head, to take the catch. But on impact the ball exploded into a puff of white powder, leaving the goalie staring into his empty gloves. Meanwhile the plucky woolly-hat pitched her pancake at her unsuspecting victim's back, but it was a botched effort that lacked strength, and the snowball splashed down his calf. Finally alerted to the rearguard attack, the ruffian twisted round and with a playfully-menacing scowl pounced after his miniature attacker, which only made her scream with delight, and she turned to flee, but perhaps she wanted to be caught because by pausing to check on her pursuer she goaded him to the chase, and she squealed away, wading through the snow, but she got what she deserved when he dived after her, and with one scoop had her cradled in his arms. For several minutes Jasmine lingered on the path, watching cheerful kids do the things all kids love to do, and when they piled on top of one another in a muddled scrum she resisted a fierce longing to forget and forever forsake the Offensive in favour of dashing across to join them at play. She didn't know why tears came to her eyes, but she dabbed at them with her gloved thumb, soaking them into the wool. It took a huge effort of will to turn away. She sidled off the track and headed deep into the pine woods for the first meeting since the signing of the Rights for the Silenced Voices with Chief Max of the Union of Indigenous Cuscatlecos.

'Send three hundred combatants dressed in civilian clothing into San Salvador,' she instructed Maximiliano Santos. 'To spy. Tell them to pay attention to the military build-up, to assess their strength. I want daily updates on the number of their infantry, tanks, and the number of aircraft SAF operates out of Ilopango, their makes and models. I need to know how many guardsmen mark each position and where they are concentrated. Here.' She handed Max a wad of maps of the city, and several bunches of biro pens of varying colours wrapped in elastic bands. 'Have your men mark the military positions: green for infantry, red for tanks or armoured cars, and blue for personnel carriers. When they return, send them immediately to take up positions along the cordillera at the south of the city, from La Puerta del Diablo to the steep escarpment below Los Planes de Renderos. Guardsmen seeking to advance on your position there will be forced to march uphill, giving you the advantage. With Gatlings, Howitzers and surface-to-airs you will be high enough to retaliate against air assaults.'

Just before noon on Tuesday, three hundred UIC guerrillas came up the Valley of Hammocks, between La Puerta del Diablo and the volcano, and began infiltrating the capital.

* * *

"You won't find a safer weapons store anywhere in the national territory," Carlos Rivera had bragged to Jasmine. Accepting his assurance, Jasmine agreed to meet with the sun-polished surfer in a gap crammed with empty ammunition crates.

'Position a thousand combatants along the upper southern flanks of the San Salvador volcano,' she told him. 'We will draw the enemy tanks and helicopters towards the city's northern outskirts, and from the scrubland on the volcano's slopes you'll have superior firing position on to the city and concealment for picking off passing and hovering aircraft.'

'Obviously favourable terrain,' Carlos observed. 'You'd think the military would have already posted platoons along the volcano's ridge and flanks.'

'I've sent scouts ahead; they reported no military presence there yet. If General Levi doubts our intentions or ability to launch an effective offensive, who are we to complain? However, should you come across greens already manning the high ground, do not try and dislodge them through engagement. Rather send a detachment to show itself, and then retreat to entice them away, while the rest of your column moves up the northern flank. I want you to besiege the soldiers from above and below. You must defeat them and command the mountain top.'

'How do you propose to draw tanks and helicopters to this area?' Carlos tapped the map with his finger.

'Public telephones.'

'Telephones?'

She hoisted two plastic bags, apparently of Frijoles Ricos, but when Carlos put the torch to them he saw they were packed with an assortment of coins.

'A hundred of your indirect combatants will be employed in making phone calls to the emergency services,' she instructed. 'Claiming to be residents of the housing estates in front of the *champas* at the foot of the volcano, they will complain of armed guerrillas positioned on their rooftops and in their gardens. We know from experience that such reported sightings warrant air strikes. When SAF dispatches helicopters to the area, you and your men on the volcano will use small arms fire and Howitzers on them, and when you come under fire do not retreat over the crater, rather go down into the city, divide into regular squads and at each infantry-manned corner, engage and disappear, engage and disappear, as normal.'

'What about those with coins, will they not have weapons too? Surely we need every combatant armed. Thanks to our collective stores, there's plenty to go round.'

Jasmine leaned forward over an ammunition case, her fists pressing down on the lid. 'They will continue to make calls and lead the infantry where we want them.'

'And where will that be?'

'Into the multi-storey car parks and the high-rise office blocks and shopping complexes. To those derelict apartment blocks that were abandoned after the earthquake, and away from the government buildings and the wide boulevards and parks. Your people will persist in calling the emergency services, the National and Hacienda Police, the municipal offices; all the various numbers listed for the military are here,' she slapped a bunch of pages on to the crate, 'including those for SAF. Call all these numbers. Tell the National Guard that militants are inside the buildings I have listed below and then ring and tell SAF the same story. SAF and the army can be counted on for overkill, and with several high speed aircraft in the confines of a valley they will be vulnerable to accidents and friendly fire. We will encourage this from them.'

'So that's all those one hundred combatants will do?' Carlos asked as if he were complaining on their behalf.

'It's no small undertaking,' Jasmine insisted. 'You must confuse the armed forces, perplex them, and provide them with contradictory information. I want them running in all directions.'

'Will they do no fighting at all?' Carlos asked, by now looking quite miserable.

'Later, Don Carlos. There will be plenty for everyone to get their teeth into.'

* * *

Late the following night one thousand five hundred combatants, divided into thirty columns of fifty, each led by a newly appointed captain, came over the volcano from the north and trickled down through the farmland. Twenty-eight columns took up positions in the wooded nature reserve, while two carried on, their pockets jingling, down into the corrugated lamina champas on the fringes of the big city.

* * *

She drew aside the foliage that screened the entrance and replaced it after she had passed through, climbed down into the stuffy bunker. Today she felt smothered by Serafin's embrace, and pushed him away. When he tried to pinch her face she slapped his hand.

'Camomile tea?' he suggested, as if the offer of a hot beverage were a common alternative to taking liberties.

'Coffee.'

So while the brew was being spiked with cinnamon, Jasmine told him the reason for her visit: 'Advise your listeners to evacuate the city, to gather their belongings and leave, to go stay with friends and relatives. But they must leave San Salvador.'

'What about those who don't listen to Radio Venceremos?' said Serafin.

'From your broadcasts the word will spread,' she said with a shrug. 'We will give them more warning than El Zacate received.'

'So you're really going through with this?' Serafin sounded awed. 'One or two have said you've bitten off more than you can chew. But I didn't see them volunteering to take your place.' He put out his hand to comfort her but then remembered she wasn't in the mood for his affections and yanked it back. 'I know you can do it, Jasmine. Me and my Radio will give you all the support you need.'

'Good, because I need one of your assistants.'

'Clarification...all the *radio* support. Remember, we are

336

not fighters.'

'Not for fighting. I need someone who can work a radio station.'

Serafin looked over his shoulder at his freckle-faced male assistant who had taken over at the turntable. 'Well, my other two are reporters, and at this moment they're out and about, so I've only got José Sabanetas. That's him talking crap into the mike now. He always wanted to be one of you lot, but they wouldn't take him because a bout of childhood polio has knackered his walking.'

'He can walk, though?'

'Yeah, it's the catching up he'll find difficult when you go dashing for cover under a hail of bullets.'

'Will he agree to come with me?'

'When do you need him?'

'Now.'

'You'd better ask him, then.'

* * *

'Today it's the turn of Chanmico. Confirmed reports of a *matanza* there,' Abraham Gadala said tersely, his normally robust voice sounding thin in the telephone receiver which Jasmine pressed to her ear. 'Ivan Saavedra had left eleven indirect combatants in Chanmico but General Levi, when interviewed this morning on Radio Nacional, claimed that one-hundred and fifty rebels were killed during a Guard operation. I can no longer allow our rural areas to go undefended this way, so I'm authorising our zone *comandantes* to deploy reduced defence forces in the villages.'

'With respect, *comandante*, I need every direct combatant for the Offensive,' Jasmine insisted.

'No, Jasmine, already Chalatenango has been badly compromised. Besides Morazán, Chalate was our most secure province. Chanmico included, we've lost eight villages to the army in under a month. We must not abandon our commitment to the peasants, not after all they've been through, and after the heavy cost in lives to secure liberated

337

zones throughout the national territory. You'll have to find a way to do without some of the combatants or we'll be obliged to reconsider the Offensive.'

Jasmine drew in a deep breath. 'Don Abraham, if we deploy again to the rural areas, the war will continue for decades to come.' She allowed herself a small smile as she came up with blackmail. The lever that Adonai had referred to. 'Besides, Don Adonai will break away from the FMLN, and so will the PCS.'

* * *

Tuesday evening, Jere and Ria's place, Ilobasco Town, a gathering of The Five over a jug of tamarind juice and plates of boiled cassava.

'This housing estate is full of tramps and vagrants, but more importantly for our purposes, it's a labyrinth of alleyways and derelict houses.' Jasmine slid her little finger across the map. 'It'll seem like fighting in a village.'

'I know this area,' Ivan nodded. 'Very central.'

'Precisely. Have your men send the vagrants packing, and when I give the signal you will engage the military by encirclement, but instead of pushing inwards you will spread outwards, drawing their most centralised units with you, making them believe they are pushing you back. Carlos's people will take up positions on the volcano to the north, the UIC will occupy the cordillera at the south, thereby giving us command of the high ground on both sides of the valley.'

'And the east?' Ivan wanted to be certain.

'I'm already camped with nine hundred of my most durable pugilists…'

'*Most durable pugilists*,' cut in Ivan with a derisive laugh. 'Speak plain Spanish man.'

An unruffled Adonai started again. 'I am already camped with nine-hundred of my most durable pugilists along Lake Ilopango's honeymoon shores,' – bestowing a languid blink on Jasmine – 'On your signal we will shell the air force base and landing zones on our way towards the city.'

'So we spread out from the centre and close in from the

outskirts at the same time?' Ivan wanted to be absolutely certain.

'Like a ripple in a coffee cup,' she simplified.

'*Comandante* Gavidia, what sign will you give for us to commence the Offensive?' Carlos Rivera asked.

'You will see three flares go up from Panchimalco,' Jasmine replied. Be vigilant, because once they're fired, the PCS will immediately move into the city for our first phase. There will be no second sign.'

'When will you give the sign?' Ivan Saavedra wanted to know.

'At the coming of mist, storm or high winds.'

CHAPTER TWENTY-NINE

JASMINE WOULD HAVE LIKED to occupy the summit of La Puerta del Diablo's towering crag because it gave panoramic views of the landscape in all directions, but for that very reason it was a popular tourist spot, attracting visitors in their droves and armed police to protect the visitors from those malicious guerrillas. Given that pitching camp atop the peak was therefore a no-go, and that for the timely signalling of the first co-ordinated strikes Jasmine needed to see both the eastern approach to the Valley of Hammocks and the Valley itself, there was nothing for it but to divide the PCS. She'd thought about it long and hard. There simply was no way round it, as much as she loathed the idea, but one must work with the terrain. She could split away a couple of small squads, and leave the main body of the column in one piece.

So the PCS gathered in the woods at the foot of La Puerta del Diablo. When a bunch of them stripped and started larking about in the pools and taking turns to stand beneath the waterfall, she had to remind them to keep silence. She selected two three-man lookout teams and led them up the farmers' staircase to Panchimalco. She posted team one on a sloping grassy ledge a stone's throw from the cul-de-sac which was home to La Mujer de Canela. They would be able to spot any undesirable approach on the waterfall from the valley. Team two moved into a derelict house at the end of a terraced row which had a decent view of the plaza and the entrance to the village

340

and any military that might turn into Panchimalco from the main road. Now for her digs. She walked out of Panchimalco, crossed the main road and plunged into the woods. She could have used the path, but it was a good kilometre up the road towards Los Planes de Renderos, and anyway she knew the way through the woods. The mission house was a prefabricated sprawl amid beautifully kept flower gardens because Padre Carpio loved flowers. From the colonnaded veranda Jasmine could overlook the valley's eastern approach, not for unwanted advances on the PCS's position, but because the mist always drives in from the east. Padre Carpio was a Nicaraguan, an old, bespectacled gentleman of books and poetry and folk music, and Jasmine would love to listen to his collection of Mercedes Sosa over mulled coffee and a friendly debate on the subject of monthly tithes, but she must first check on her people. So once she had laid her metaphorical hat, she returned, first to check on her two lookout teams and then to use her new walkie-talkie. 'Adrian, meet me half way up the staircase.'

In fact they met above the second dogleg turn and together they scanned the bristling basin of city lights with their binoculars. To the left the dark outline of the cordillera undulated away into the night, to the right presided the humpback volcano with a garland of red telephone antennae finishing off its flat summit.

'Cuscatlán,' Jasmine whispered, more than a little taken with the grandeur of the valley that gave its Nahuatle name to the whole province.

She began spouting some of the city's landmarks as she picked them out with her lenses, and Adrian matched her landmark for landmark: La Torre Cuscatlán, Plaza Las Américas, Rubén Darío Street. And the Cathedral, still shrouded in scaffolding. Will they ever complete the repair work? When they had run the list dry, they returned to the waterfall and Jasmine called her comrades forward and handed out yet more photocopied maps of the city upon which she had written a list of sites that she wished them to visit and thoroughly acquaint themselves with. Quiet fell as a meticulous study of the maps was undertaken.

'Why wait so long for the weather to change?' Adrian broke the silence with a question that Jasmine guessed was on all their minds.

'The military outnumber us nine-to-one, and their firepower and technology are vastly superior to ours. We all know from painful experience the threat from the air posed by the Salvadoran Air Force. So I intend to harness every possible advantage, even those nature makes available, in order to redress the balance a little,' she explained. 'SAF has long despised the army for what it sees as a bunch of uneducated ruffians – can't say I disagree. Despite the strained relationship between the two forces, when the chips are down SAF will back up the infantry. But weather such as storms affects the operational ability of conventional armed forces more than it does us. I anticipate that even on home ground, helicopters will become the backbone of SAF's strike force, and these, like the army's tanks and trucks, are noisy machines, even behind a curtain of rain or mist.'

'But SAF pilots will have night vision goggles,' Adrian reminded her.

'Adonai's notes contain a chapter dedicated to this very topic. He somewhat crudely – which is unlike him – likens looking through NVGs to looking through an empty toilet roll tube with the far end covered over with green cellophane. He goes on to say that even in good weather conditions, flying at over one hundred knots leaves very little time for pilots and gunners to react. This, he says, is one of the principal causes of the high number of helicopter accidents reported during war.'

Adrian gazed into the middle distance to think about this. 'Flying low in a built up area with electricity cables, bridges and low trees, must be a nightmare for pilots,' he acknowledged.

'Exactly,' Jasmine agreed. 'Add to that the zero depth perception you get when looking through NVGs and poor weather to contend with and the hazards increase. We will pitch our planning and ears against their NVGs and height advantage. If we conceal ourselves adequately, their noise will alert us to their approach before they can pick us out. We will be able to pinpoint their location with some accuracy while we remain largely silent and invisible to them. This is not one of our peasant hamlets that they care nothing about; this is San Salvador – the capital, their home, their family's home, and that of a lot of people who they consider very important. With poor visibility and the hazards we have mentioned, the effectiveness of air strikes will be significantly reduced. Their gunners will hesitate before firing blindly upon home ground.'

She took a handful of questions from the floor, but it was evident from these that her troops had by now familiarised themselves with the offensive's multifaceted tactical elements. They must now familiarise themselves with the most essential element for the success of guerrilla tactics: the terrain.

'Leave in pairs,' she told them. 'Get your bearings of the city. Visit the places I have marked on the maps. If you have any last minute doubts as to the logistics or feasibility of the operations I have allocated to be carried out at each site, I want to hear your thoughts. I may or may not agree with you, but I will consider your observations carefully.'

It had gone 4 a.m. when Jasmine finally returned to the mission house and waited eagerly for the mist to signal the commencement of the Offensive.

But it didn't come.

* * *

And so the waiting began.

The evenings saw high-spirited communards tune in to Radio Nacional's frequency and learn of rumours that an unconfirmed number of guerrillas – thought to be in their dozens, armed and very dangerous, do not approach or attempt to disarm but call these numbers – had come down from the mountains and were infiltrating San Salvador in a wretched quest to terrorise the law-abiding citizenry. It was conceded that the source of this information was Radio Venceremos, and as such the various broadcasters played

343

down its authenticity, and indeed that of any information that the rebel station provided to its listeners. As a precaution the military has ordered forty thousand soldiers on to the streets of the capital, leaving eleven thousand National Guardsmen to continue routine operations in the countryside.

'Then we're quits,' Adrian blurted, rocketing to his feet in his customary blast of fury at such inflammatory talk. 'You do routine operations on my turf; I'll do routine operations on yours. *Punto!*'

Thunderous trucks ferried soldiers and military hardware to such well-heeled districts as Colonia Escalón, San Benito, Colonia Militar, and to the mansions of bigwig ministers and foreign ambassadors. Static units of three to five men guarded street corners while foot patrols roved the pavements in squads of four. Panhard AML 90s took up mobile street patrols. Like miniature tanks on rubber tractor tyres instead of caterpillar tracks, these were swift, agile machines that bullied their way up busy avenues to their assigned defensive and strategic positions.

Jasmine's days were filled with travel. As overall skipper, she must liaise with her brother columns, keep the intelligence flow circulating, revise tactics to fit unforeseen events or topographical features, to fan the revolutionary flames lest anyone had become distracted by events at home.

'Strike like horsewhips and disappear. Sustained engagements do not interest us, rather silence, invisibility, surprise, and short but blisteringly intense violence,' she reminded a gathering of *comandantes* as she fed the pigeons during an assembly she had called in the bustling Plaza Gerardo Barrios. On every street corner, armed soldiers had gathered, and she was conscious that the meeting must be brief. After all, their grainy black and white photographs that adorned the famed Most Wanted list were now adorning lamp posts and tabloid front pages too.

'My men are growing agitated, *comandante*,' Carlos admitted gravely. 'We have been here for over a week with no

344

sign from you to commence the Offensive. Already guardsmen have discovered five – *five!* – of my weapons caches, and there have been skirmishes between a couple of my members and a persistently nosy military unit. We've had to move a bunch of stock and members to new locations, which is a risky business by daylight and not that easy to do after dark, with the curfew in place.'

'And all the while the military's operations in the rural zones continue,' Ivan added, speaking under his breath lest he be overheard beyond their circle. 'My men had moved their wives and little ones to the safety of the liberated zones, but since we pulled out our forces, the Guard is moving in and targeting anyone they suspect of being related to a guerrilla combatant. We dread listening to Venceremos' bulletins. In this past week the Guard visited the homes of eleven of my men. What did they do? What they always do: dragged their wives and kids from their beds. Shot them in the plazas. Took the pretty ones away in jeeps. You know the score!' He made a squirting sound through his front teeth and shook his head miserably. 'I talk to my men. I try and say comforting words, but it's not easy. They find it difficult to concentrate now. Always anxious to return to their villages, to protect those who still live and to bury their dead.' He looked at the others for support. 'What do you reckon, we get rolling now? Strike tomorrow at dawn?'

'I have every sympathy for our combatants and their families,' Jasmine answered, making a concerted effort to get that sympathy into her voice. But all she heard was her resolute determination, and she feared it sounded like obstinacy. 'But we face an army that outnumbers us on its own territory and among its own supporters. I feel we must wait a little longer.' She knelt down and tossed another edge of tortilla to the thinnest of the pigeons, allowing her fellow-*comandantes* to gather in a huddle and whisper amongst themselves.

'We will await your command, *Comandante* Gavidia.' It was Maximiliano who eventually announced the common verdict.

That night on the mission house veranda Jasmine settled herself on a wooden chair with her rifle across her lap and gazed down the approach to the Valley of Hammocks. The wooded hillside descended towards a sunken volcano with a lake-filled crater beyond which the dark jagged outline of other volcanoes was pitched high against the star-filled heavens.

'The mist always comes at dawn, and always from the east,' she reminded herself, because she was almost ready to doubt common knowledge. She knew all her combatants by name. She'd even met some of their families. She felt confident of the PCS combatants' loyalty to the Revolution and their eagerness to participate in its realisation. She and Adrian, with her trade-mark maps in hand, had taken them through the battle plans until each participant knew precisely what was required of him. They could faithfully recite their parts plus a dozen variations to suit possible changes in circumstances on the ground or in weather conditions. Still, for this offensive against San Salvador, she required a supreme level of commitment, one that meant leaving their families and homes vulnerable to enemy attack. Yesterday and today, fresh reports of "successful missions" and "significant gains against the rebel forces" had been aired by Radio Nacional, while the same incidents had been grimly described by Radio Venceremos as *matanzas*. Perhaps it was easier for her now. With no family of her own to worry about, could she honestly imagine her combatants' private anguish over the fate of their wives, daughters and sons at the hands of guardsmen high on dextroamphetamine and probably cocaine too? After the Offensive was over, when the FMLN combatant men and women hurried home to their villages, what would they find? Their daughters raped, murdered even? Their husbands hanging from trees? Their houses reduced to desolate shells? What if the weather failed to turn? How long could she expect the FMLN to wait? And what if the Offensive should fail?

The cold wind blew her long hair across her face, and

she tied it back with an elastic band. When dawn broke, she looked down the approach to the valley and saw that it was distressingly clear.

* * *

Adrian was right, Jasmine accepted on the following Monday morning. Three weeks in and the combatants were growing increasingly restive. She met them in their huddled groups in the undergrowth, stropping their knives on wet rocks. Their brooding faces unshaven, their eyes flashing in the shadows, talking quietly amongst themselves. No complaints were made. There was no need. She knew them well enough, spotted the restless signs in each member's body language.

Despite their sullen demeanour, however, the combatants greeted Jasmine with a great deal of respect, often coming to their feet when she approached, and soon she was called upon to arbitrate in their squabbles with one another. She knew that, petty as they might seem, in the tense atmosphere that prevailed before battle, the subjects of such wrangles were of vital importance to each man. They argued over everything, from the thickness of the tortillas and the grains of salt to be shared amongst them – which she was able to settle by way of redistributing the portions – to who was the best footballer in the national team, which, being more of a subjective matter, she decided by praising the merits of each of the four candidates put forward, and painstakingly working the men into a general agreement that they were all pretty good. It was a vague decision but one which, coming from the *comandante* herself, left each man feeling that his preferred candidate had come away with high praise indeed when previously his comrades had pointed out only his faults and ridiculed anyone who could possibly believe the player was any good at all.

One evening Emilio returned to the waterfall from a supplies and intelligence gathering outing. On his shoulder he carried a crate of fizzy drinks. No explanation was offered as to where he acquired the welcome refreshments. Jasmine didn't ask. In the tedium of waiting, this mundane event caught everybody's imagination, and the other combatants slipped out of their hammocks and gathered enthusiastically round him. While he was lowering the crate, a pornographic magazine slipped from his inner jacket pocket and fell open on the ground. A moment's hesitation while the moonlight made clear what exactly they were all squinting at, and then fifty plus men pounced on the magazine and a violent scrum ensued. To Jasmine's amazement several combatants actually drew knives while clutching torn pages in their spare hand. Two or three were trying, with outspread arms and much yelling, to keep the aggrieved parties apart.

'Give me those,' Jasmine demanded furiously.

The shouting abated at once, but for a long drawn-out minute the men clutched their ragged pages in quivering hands and glared with such open hostility at one another that murder might very well have been on their minds.

Mindful not to fan any flames but to channel them towards a harmless outlet, Jasmine repeated her demand with a fraction less severity.

This time, one by one, the men hung their heads. Some even chuckled at the ridiculous spectacle they made. Sighing with resignation and unable to meet her eyes, they shuffled forwards to deposit the crumpled pictures in her outstretched hand. Too many for her to hold, the overflow floated to the ground.

'Adrian, will you fetch me some tape and help me put these pages together again?'

Fascinated, the men squatted round her while she, sitting cross-legged, taped the torn page fragments back together, taking care to properly align the photographs.

To Segundo she said, 'Which do you prefer; tits, bum or *pie*?'

Segundo squirmed through a ripple of muffled giggles from his comrades before sheepishly admitting to tits, *comandante*.

With the precision of a tailor cutting out a suit pattern for an eminent client, Jasmine, with Adrian's medical scissors in hand, detached a depiction of a pair of disgracefully huge breasts and handed the cut-out to Segundo. Still squatting, the men drew closer and nodded their approval to one another.

Emilio tried to make out that he wasn't interested, but amid an outburst of heckling from his peers who insisted that he had a weakness for the larger woman he accepted a cut-out of a pair of huge female buttocks on the understanding that he was merely taking part in *the game.*

'Yeah, whatever!' Jasmine muttered, as she flicked through the pages for another likely candidate to appease her frustrated men, who were looking on eagerly and even laughing aloud, a sound that Jasmine had not heard in almost a month. For each man she cut away a slice of photograph that depicted a female body part according to his preference.

'When you are tired of looking at your pictures you may swap them amongst yourselves,' she decreed, 'but I want no fighting over them.'

The men agreed readily and then, under a salvo of verbal abuse from disgusted female comrades, they slunk away into the woods, clutching their scraps of magazine to their chests and looking furtively over their shoulders, as if expecting to be set upon.

On another day, Adrian curtailed the boredom by scraping crosses into the leafy ground and after having marked out boxes within the sketches he set the combatants at playing an ancient form of ludo.

CHAPTER THIRTY

THE AIR CONDITIONING unit in Anastasio's HQ was making a racket, though not as much as the traffic that pelted hell for leather down the Pan-American towards Santa Tecla, which he could see beyond tidy green lawns edged with coconut palms. He checked to satisfy himself that the window was indeed shut. It was.

'A woman has taken Leonel's place,' Captain Nathan Escobar, in his new role as Anastasio's personal intelligence officer, declared.

'You'll have to do a lot better than that,' Anastasio laughed. He hadn't recruited Escobar to spout common knowledge parrot-fashion.

'But did you know that Abraham Gadala assigned her overall charge of his promised offensive against San Salvador?'

Anastasio glared at Escobar. 'Why the hell would he do that?' he asked, privately conceding that this was indeed fresh intelligence.

Escobar shrugged. 'La Libertad, Cuscatlán, Cabañas, San Vicente...you name it, she led the incursions that pushed us out. Fucking amazing!'

'But she must be...what?' Anastasio paused to tot up the years, 'twenty...twenty-one at the most. Surely Gadala wouldn't entrust...'

Escobar interrupted, 'I've studied her work, even started a little compilation for our library. She's a second Adonai. But tell me, how do *you* know her age?'

'Her campaigns are similar to his,' Anastasio admitted, ignoring this latest in a tiresome line of digs and battling a reluctant admiration for the maid's accomplishments. 'Zero conventional fronts, they tell me; lots of chameleon manoeuvres, some of which aren't even documented. Is your source trustworthy?'

'Implicitly.'

'Does the General know?'

'I put it in one of my daily reports to him.'

'What else do you put in your daily reports?'

'Warnings, mostly. Not that he listens. He takes my report and puts it on top of a pile of others and who knows when or even if he gets round to reading it. I've told him about the weapons we've uncovered. You know about them?'

'You faxed me, remember?'

'So I did. Well, it all points to increased guerrilla presence in the city, doesn't it? It's hard to read the General, he makes out like he's all sceptical yet he sets the President up with a fucking private army all for himself. I'm telling you, Major, if someone doesn't act, and I mean take some serious counter insurgency measures, the bastards will catch us with our pants down. Got any cool ideas?'

'Well, going above Levi's head would not be cool. Apparently the President shares his scepticism, even if he has taken the precaution of enhancing his own personal security team at the expense of the army. We'll appeal laterally. It's what the Colonel used to do. Leave it to me. I'll liaise with our SAF buddies and draw up counter strategies to cover a number of scenarios. We, at least, will be prepared for anything that slut throws at us.'

'We'll need an operations base,' Escobar suggested. 'SAF's Ilopango station is bound to be on the rebels' target list. That hardly makes for ideal working conditions, and SAF officers wouldn't be seen dead in an army compound.'

'We'll set up a joint operations base at Comalapa

International Airport,' Anastasio proposed, his mind abuzz with fresh ideas. 'Given the negative publicity they'd incur, the militants won't dare attempt an assault on a civilian airfield.'

* * *

On Friday afternoon Adrian returned to the waterfall in a foul mood. He'd spent the greater part of the day in heated discussions with the four other zone skippers. Solemn-faced, he tossed his pack to the ground beneath his hammock and turned to glare at Jasmine.

'The columns are more restless than ever,' skipping the greeting he panted out the warning. He paused to dig out his water bottle from the string basket that hung from his shoulder. He drained it before shoving the bottle back into the netting. 'Last night a very good sympathiser was discovered harbouring some of our people in his house. The military carted him away.' He made a slicing gesture across his throat. 'There's infighting amongst the members. Two of Ivan's lot were stabbed by their own comrades. They're not to blame, says Ivan. What does he fucking know? And more of our weapons were seized, including a dismantled Gatling hidden in a garage. The garage owner got it in the neck – how? – in front of his missus of course – how else?' He put two fingertips to the back of his own neck to illustrate the point. 'Pow!'

Jasmine observed him impassively, listening to the rising bitterness in his voice and watching him caress his left pectoral – a gesture that to the casual observer might appear relaxed but as she had come to learn over the last seven years, he did only when he was on edge. Ivan Saavedra and his counterparts must have harangued him. This morning he'd gone in her stead to address them; meanwhile she had risked a cross city bus journey to Ilopango to keep Abraham Gadala posted on the current position, and to discuss some last minute details – necessary adjustments that had cropped up due to the lengthy delay to the start of the offensive. Abraham had also expressed his exasperation in no uncertain terms, pointing out that this delay had provided the security forces with "all the time in the world" to ready themselves. Not to mention weakening the FMLN's position with each new weapons cache uncovered and confiscated, events that inevitably led to the disappearance of our generous sympathisers and their kin.

Was she asking too much of the combatants? Cooped up like this, anxious about their families back home, worried that at any moment their waterfall hideout might be discovered: of course they were on edge. Yet they had stuck it out thus far; but how much further could she ask them to go?

Adrian rounded on her. 'We can wait no longer for the weather to change, *comandante;* we must strike now or the whole thing will fall apart.'

The combatants had gathered as they routinely did when the *comandante* was about. They listened silently in an atmosphere that hung somewhere between unease and hunger for gossip. Jasmine might have asked what Leonel would do, but that would undermine her leadership in their eyes and dip their confidence.

'Strike now,' Adrian asserted, perhaps reading the unasked question in her eyes. 'It's been one month since we set up camp here. We've never stayed in one place so long. Never! Here we are, practically on the outskirts of a hostile city, whiling away the time in our hammocks.' Adrian was pacing to and fro and cracking his knuckles noisily. 'Give the order, *comandante,* or let's just pack up and go home.'

'We would then lose all we have so meticulously prepared for. Is that what you want?' she snapped back at him.

'We will lose it all anyway if we are discovered,' Adrian retorted.

'But we haven't been discovered.' She heard her own voice rising.

'Not yet, but we will be,' he shouted back, and whirled round and slammed his fist into a tree trunk, apparently so incensed that he didn't even flinch at the pain.

Jasmine saw that he had reached the limit of his forbearance. With her hands in her boiler suit pockets she strolled over to stand at the pool's edge, and gazed into the waterfall.

'Don Adrian, I still question my own motives, frequently,' she said, now in a matter-of-fact tone.

He made no reply but threw himself to the ground and, sighing deeply, leaned back against the tree he had so poorly treated, and shut his eyes.

'But I ask myself repeatedly, will the *matanzas* stop if we pack up and go home?' She let the question float, allowing silence to fill the prolonged pause. Allowing the entire audience to answer the question for themselves. She gazed up the silvery length of the waterfall and into the darkening sky. A shadow caught her attention; it was elevating itself on outstretched wings, tapping in to the air currents. She recognised the black hawk by its tail feathers. Banded in black and white, they were spread like a Japanese fan and fluttered gently as the bird made delicate adjustments to its course. It disappeared beyond the waterfall's crest. She remembered having seen similar birds in the skies over the plantations of El Zacate in which she had laboured in another life. Out of place, she thought. Out of time. Like me. Like Adrian. Like us all. 'What are we doing here?' she whispered to herself. We are not fighters. We are peasants. Her heart sank because it finally dawned on her that the offensive for which they had spent so much time and energy preparing was in fact beyond them. Tears welled in her eyes and threatened to spill over. Suddenly Adrian was beside her.

'The *comandantes* are with you one-hundred per cent,' he said quietly, 'as am I.'

Then Emilio emerged at her other side, and when she looked round she saw that the whole troop had gathered with her at the water's edge. 'We are all with you,' a voice said, possibly Wenceslau's, and his sentiment was taken up by other voices until they were overlapping in declarations of solidarity. After a minute or so the chorus died down. Jasmine swallowed the bile that had been creeping up her throat, before turning to Adrian. She lifted his hand and spent a few moments caressing his scuffed knuckles. She kissed them, a *campesina* gesture of profound gratitude.

'Don't injure yourself, amigo,' she cautioned. 'I think you will need good fists in the days ahead.' Then she cast an appreciative look round at her friends, many of whom were clasping her shoulders and arms as if performing a laying on of hands.

Adrian returned the gesture of gratitude by using his thumb to whisk away a tear that was skating down her cheek. 'Because of you, we can hope that our future tears will be joyous ones.'

Again a chorus of agreement rose.

CHAPTER THIRTY-ONE

November 1989

FROM THE MISSION HOUSE veranda Jasmine gazed east at the dawn mist boiling over a forest-laden cordillera to spill like a vast waterfall into a bottomless valley. Now, flooding across the surface of Lake Ilopango, it headed directly for the Valley of Hammocks.

Jasmine dashed out of the forest and into Panchimalco where she called her lookout teams, and from the lip of the escarpment she sent two flares racing towards the stars.

'It is time,' she declared.

* * *

The telephone in the study of the presidential home was taking a hammering. 'Listen, Jorge, the military spokesman is on holiday in Guatemala.' Sorrentino, his silk pyjamas and matching silk dressing gown immaculate, swung the telephone flex over the table lamp before subsiding into his sumptuously upholstered armchair.

The First Lady, her normally flawless pile of hair now in a tumble, was up too, regarding her husband from the corridor, and where Mrs Sorrentino went there also went the maid who peered over the shoulder of her mistress.

'He isn't, neither is my Chief of Psychological Operations for the Joint Chiefs of Staff, he's in New Orleans, can you believe it?' Pause. 'No, bring my helicopter...but land in the garden. I want my wife, kids and maids out of here on the double. Tell everyone to hot foot it to San Miguel.' Pause. 'What?' he yelled.

'Tell the controller that he *is* the General. They must allow him to land.' He rolled his eyes up at the chandeliers. 'I don't care if they think he's a rebel, I tell you he's not, tell the controller that's direct from me.' He came to his feet and, swinging the flex back over the lamp, made his way round to the front of his desk where he stopped and winced as if spiked in his side by a thorn. 'But…but how can anyone be on sick leave for ten years?' Time for considering such mysteries was short, so he blundered on. 'Well then, just get the next available man down the ranks to give the order, even if it comes from the pilots themselves. Now get going and I'll see you in San Miguel.' He clapped the receiver to the cradle and pushed the telephone away in such disgust that it went plunging off the edge of the desk to clatter and ping on the carpeted floor.

'*Hijos de putas*,' he exclaimed, blinking his incredulity at his wife. 'They said they would do it and they did. No one thought they would, and now none of my staff is at hand, and the only one who is on his way, General…shit, what's his name…?'

'Flores?' Mrs Sorrentino helped out in a muted voice.

'Flores, that's it, has been refused landing at Ilopango because the controller believes that the helicopter requesting permission belongs to the rebels. Since *when* have the rebels had helicopters, for *fuck* sake?' He kicked the waste bin across the room. 'Get me the phone.'

The maid hurried forward, gathered up the receiver and its cradle, offered the telephone to the president and ran back to reclaim her position behind Mrs Sorrentino.

'Yes, broadcast the news to the nation, and tell the whole world to tune into Radio Atlacatle…yes…the Air Force radio station…or Radio Nacional. No other station is permitted to go on air…What? What do you mean I can't order that? I'm the President of the Republic…Shut up…Then tell the nation I say they must not listen to any other radio station, apart from the two I mentioned. Does that satisfy your legal quibbling?' He slammed the receiver down and ordered his wife to get dressed, darling, please, and pack our bags. 'You're getting out of here.'

Litter on the tarmac bunched up to the pavements where rain or wind had left it, and along these pavements were dozens of traders' kiosks all boarded up for the night. The combatants huddled in close, leaning forward to better hear Jasmine, their faces, wan and shrouded, peering over the shoulders of those standing closest to her. She raised her voice against the wailing of an ancient air raid siren and the manic barking of a thousand dogs across the city:

'We're about half way down Colonial Street, fifty metres south of the junction with 27th. The guards at the outer junctions must be taken out simultaneously. Use pistols with silencers.' A glance at her watch told her it was coming up to ten to four. Four a.m. was when soldiers were likely to be least alert. 'We go on four.'

A collective synchronising of watches ate up a couple of minutes.

'Once through the outer junctions, proceed towards the inner ones and initiate phase two.' On that reminder she entreated them to remember that the objective is merely to contain the president for a brief period, sufficient to cause him to fret for his safety and that of his family. Nothing more elaborate than that.

'What if we hit him by mistake?' Adrian said flippantly.

'Then he will be dead,' she returned his flippancy before making to address José, but he, hugging himself snugly, forestalled her:

'I'll…w…wait for you b…beside the diner we p…passed at th…the top of the street,' he stammered. 'It's the cold,' he added, by way of explanation, pointing to his chattering teeth.

Jasmine nodded. 'This shouldn't take long. You'll be all right, yeah?'

'I…I can wait. I'll be fine.' He smiled unconvincingly before loping away, back up Colonial Street, his red mop of hair dulling into the night mist, and Jasmine listened to his footfalls until they subsided before she turned to the others.

'Any questions?'

No questions, *comandante*. We are ready, they insisted in a low hum of responses. Having rehearsed for this moment a hundred-plus times and been cooped up in one camp for over a month they were now like horses eager to bolt from their paddocks.

'*Hasta la Victoria!*' she declared.

'*Hasta la Victoria!*' they agreed.

'Then go! *Andando!*' she gave the order.

On a muffled scuffling of many boots, the PCS contingent slipped away to take up positions as rehearsed.

With a hand on the butt of her AK to prevent it from swinging, Jasmine led Adrian, advancing along a pavement that ran between a high graffiti-scribbled wall crowned with rolls of concertina wire, and a chain of boarded-up kiosks. They had not gone far when she hoisted her right fist.

'There they are,' she whispered, crouching low behind a display shelf annexed to one of the kiosks, and peering between its legs. 'Fifteen metres.'

Two military figures stood darkly, seemingly fused to a temporary timber barrier along the foot of which six cones smudged the ground with yellow.

Jasmine motioned for Adrian to take the man on the right while she would take the other. He agreed with a nod, fished out his pistol and fitted it with a silencer.

Jasmine studied her mark. Armed, average height and build, stationary target facing up Colonial Street. She selected the point of impact.

On either side of the kiosk Jasmine and Adrian took up positions and consulted their watches as the seconds ticked away. In unison they raised their pistols and fired. With audible gasps, both soldiers stumbled backwards and twisted over the barricade. Laboured movements were suggestive of attempts to push themselves back up.

'Again,' Jasmine said, and fired a second shot, one that was instantly followed up by Adrian. Her target's head, which had been straining to lift itself, flopped behind the hunch of his shoulders. She held her breath and cringed as their rifles clattered on the tarmac. Adrian's man slid off the barricade and sagged to the ground.

On their way past the fallen men, Jasmine took a moment to ensure that they were dead, and when she was satisfied they posed no threat, she and Adrian recovered the rifles and ammunition and stashed these in a bottle-strewn alleyway that joined Colonial to Metzi. Then they stole forward until they could see a similarly guarded barricade spanning 27th Street, almost adjacent to the factory entrance. Again they settled themselves behind a handy stall. Unlike Colonial, 27th Street was lit by hanging bulbs with halos wilting at the edges.

Peering round the kiosk Jasmine could see that her mark was staring up 27th, presenting her with an angled shot to the flat of his back; while Adrian's was doing miniature patrols on lethargic feet and was now shuffling about to start down the street towards where the guarded gates of the presidential house stood at one side. Single shots fired simultaneously. She saw her man plummet beyond the barrier. Adrian's target reeled backwards, wheeling his arms before keeling back and smacking his head on the road, and again Jasmine winced at the rattle of landing rifles. She tucked her pistol into her boiler suit pockets.

'The south-eastern corner is now secure. Let's hope Emilio and Anabela have taken their junctions.' Adrian squeezed out the first of four fragmentation grenades he was stowing in his array of belt pouches.

'Two minutes and twenty seconds to go,' Jasmine murmured.

They pushed right up to the junction. Across the way, a high perimeter wall seeped into view from the right where it defended the factory, ran unbroken past the presidential residence directly ahead and paled into the light cast by the street lamps. Jasmine couldn't actually make out the entrance she knew stood an equal distance from either end of the perimeter wall. She could, however, see a faceless human hunched atop the wall at the corner closest to the factory, and a similar character two arms' length away at his right side. She could even hear mumbled exchanges, and when one of them turned his head, the helmet's shape became visible. Profiled against the wall below them, two greens stood side by side, rifles hitched inwards so that together they looked like a capital-H. Somewhere distant, the tapping of gunfire mingled with the yapping of dogs, and car alarms cadenced with the air raid siren that still wailed. These sounds were punctuated by the detonations of mortar shells.

Jasmine composed herself. Now she felt a sense of exhilaration, and she listened intently. Again she registered the thump of a mortar; it was a long way off and dulled by the fog that flooded the city. She blotted out all distractions until she could hear those soldiers who stood along the perimeter wall beyond the reach of her eyes. Low mumblings. The scrape of a rubber heel on the pavement.

'Twenty seconds to go,' she said.

They laid their rifles on the pavement, stepped back from the junction and crammed their backs to the wall. Adrian snuck out the pin and held the grenade in a ready-to-throw attitude. Likewise, Jasmine primed one of hers.

'Now,' she told him.

Adrian stepped out and lobbed the small bomb over the corner of the wire above. Silently it dissolved into the mist; but Jasmine saw that his aim was true, that the grenade was on a trajectory that would carry it over 27th Street and into the presidential garden. She stood back and pitched her grenade after Adrian's.

'Nice throw,' Adrian acknowledged generously. He readied his second device and as Jasmine stood aside and unplugged another of her own, he launched his and stepped back in the sequence to allow her to move up and follow through. Adrian threw four to Jasmine's three. Now there was a commotion within the garden as grenades pelted in from three different directions, evidence that Emilio and Anabela had indeed taken their junctions. Some grenades clanged on the tiled roof before rattling down and thudding to the ground, while others landed inaudibly. But once they began exploding it sounded like a motorway pileup was taking place behind those walls; and the tall glass windows of the house were blown inwards, adding further explosive resonance to a growing uproar.

While Adrian stood behind her, his rifle poised, Jasmine crouched, gathered up her rifle, and surveyed the scene. A green on the pavement reacting to the pandemonium behind him, bent over backwards to peer upwards. Above him one of his colleagues, trying to escape from the lethal twists of metal flying within the garden, was wrestling his way through the roll of wire, but he was trapped like a fly in a spider web. Jasmine tossed her last grenade across the street towards the front of the house. She clocked the instant one of the guards spotted her, and in that same split second Adrian shot him square in the chest, angled his rifle mere degrees higher and shot two more who had become embroiled in the coiled trap, leaving these two hanging on the sharp wire spurs with their arms dangling loosely against the wall. Two other soldiers, having had the sense to distance themselves from the mansion, belted along 27th Street and arrived at the factory wall from where they could look down Colonial Street.

Adrian spotted them first, made the instant adjustment to his right and, while they were hefting their rifles into an underarm position, sprayed them with automatic fire. However, neither man went down, but his change of aim had alerted Jasmine. She threw her left shoulder against the wall and, in an awkward seated position, cuddled the rifle butt to her waist. She was about to fire when the grenade she had rolled towards the mansion detonated. She saw the blast wash over both men like a torrent that sent them spinning and stumbling to the ground. She looked up. Adrian was standing a stride into the junction in order to achieve the angle he sought to fire a diagonal left across the road. Jasmine scrambled on to one knee, put her shoulder back on the wall and stared round the corner. A storm of gunfire had broken out to the left, and the belly of the mist was alive with flickering white lights.

The remainder of the column, led by Anabela and Emilio, had secured their junctions and were taking the fight to the soldiers along Metzi. A dead soldier lay in the classical spread-eagled pose in the middle of the road, and another was on his side against the rise of the pavement, his head resting on his up-flung arm. Behind the garden wall the pounding of grenades persisted, and Jasmine could hear the frantic yelling of many men, and in the midst of the tumult the splashing of water. In their haste to dodge the grenade shrapnel, some of the guards were no doubt diving into the swimming pool. The column had advanced along the continuation of Metzi that ran against the eastern side of the target premises, and was engaging the guards at the junction with 27th. That was as far as Jasmine had instructed Emilio and Anabela to proceed. She would not expose combatants to friendly fire by occupying 27th.

She shouldered her AK47, selected automatic fire and spread a fan of fusillade at waist height along the fortified wall, stopping short of where the junction opened. A guard, caught up in her fire, twisted and then collapsed to his knees and thus he remained, sitting on his haunches, arms by his sides, head hanging low. It wasn't until Jasmine retraced her fire and caught him again that he went over with a final twist.

Amid the intermittent clang of explosives, whoosh of shrapnel and clatter of upset turf raining upon the roof, the presidential guards' M16s replied to three dozen guerrilla rifles, all guns gushing automatic rounds. Stray bullets hummed up and down 27th Street, smacking into walls and smashing glass. Street lights shattered, and with each one blown a darker mantle was thrown over the street. Jasmine doubted the soldiers would scramble after the grenades in a hasty attempt to lob them back into the street before they went bang. Caught between the mansion's walls and the garden's perimeter defences with over forty detonating fragmentation grenades for company, it was no wonder they were hurling themselves into the swimming pool or braving the protective wire.

Now she saw that two of the guards had made it through the wire and were clinging by fingertips to the top of those fortifications and about to drop the five metres to the pavement. She fired and held down the trigger, seeing the blurred chain of bullets go forth beyond her jutting muzzle flashes. The deserters relinquished their precarious grip in a hurry. The first man to fall landed on his toes and inadvertently fell forward to smack helmet-first into the wall. The other, with outspread arms, dived backwards in a freefall. Both remained inert once they hit the tarmac.

Jasmine replaced the empty 7.62 ammunition magazine with a fresh one and searched the mist for her next target.

* * *

Under the watchful eyes of his wife and maid who still hadn't packed as he had ordered but remained huddled in the corridor, Sorrentino was placing yet another phone call when, with a crash, the tall window that overlooked his normally green and pleasant garden ruptured inwards. Ten thousand glittering shards gushed across the room and down the opposite wall.

'Down,' he shouted to his wife, dropping the telephone and diving to the carpet in a single movement. Squinting up, he saw the two women flat on their stomachs in the unlit corridor some eight or nine metres away. He sucked in a quick breath which he held in his lungs, and began to crawl towards them with as much coordination as he could rally. He flinched at a piercing crack very close by but continued to paddle forward on hands and knees because paddling is what he was actually doing. The window above him had shattered. It sagged forward and sprinkled his head, back and legs with razor-sharp fragments. He jumped as the stabs told, arching his back and screwing up his eyes.

'*Puta!*' he cried out. What pain!

From far away he heard his wife calling to him. Come on, dear. Keep moving. Don't stop, just keep moving.

He roused himself from the pain, his face streaming with sweat. He resumed his forward motion now wondering why his limbs were pushing in an utterly new way, a clomping lizard-like movement, but it kept him moving in the right direction which was all that really mattered. His wife, who had raised her head, was beckoning with a cupped hand, and in a thin voice screamed encouragement to him from the corridor, but her words were mostly lost in the metallic pounding from outside. He felt blood trickling down the side of his waist, pooling at the base of his spine, seeping between his buttocks, sucking wetly at his pyjamas. Now blood was in his eyes, mingling with the sweat, stinging, and he blinked repeatedly before taking a moment to wipe his eyes with his pyjama sleeve.

He motioned for the women to retreat further into the corridor. They obeyed, backing up deeper into the shadow. He positioned himself like a sprinter at a starting block, ventured one hesitant step and then launched himself into the corridor, belly-flopping on the spot where his wife had lain moments earlier. He spun over just in time to witness the window at the far end of the study rush towards him. Disintegrating into an ocean wave it washed across the length of his private work place, tripping over his desk, toppling the lamp, and petering out as it pitter-pattered up the walls on either side of the corridor, sending a scattering of shards to his feet. Kicking his heels down, he reversed into the waiting arms of his wife who was now kneeling behind him. Wheezing, and starting at each fresh explosion, he glared at the bits of glass that continued to spit into the study where the swinging chandelier was hauling shadows up and down and around the walls.

* * *

Swivelling round Jasmine hunted for the source of a low-pitched clattering that might have belonged to a tractor engine. But this was no tractor.

'Panhard AMLs. Withdraw, now!' she snapped into her radio before tucking it into a webbing pouch at her waist. How many did Adrian think he could hear?

'Not sure. Where do you think they're coming from?'

The tapping of the engines was gathering volume.

'Along 27th, from the east. Probably via Colonia Esperanza.'

She was right; they came down 27th Street. Through the drifting clouds she saw their hulking tank-shapes pointing elongated guns that swivelled with robotic spasms.

'One, two, three, four,' Adrian totted from behind a kiosk while the machines negotiated the barrier and rumbled past the mouth of the junction. '*Hijo de puta!* How many are there?'

'Five,' Jasmine contributed to the count. 'And more coming.'

One of the machines rocked to a halt this side of the check point and swung its 99mm cannon across the road as if to sniff out Colonial Street. Jasmine saw the paleness of skin beneath helmeted heads.

'Two men in the raised turret, one behind at the M60,' she informed Adrian, and smiled inwardly at the folly of the image-conscious greens who, incredibly, were wearing sunglasses. 'They're deploying around the premises,' she added.

'We number over forty. We could take them.' Adrian was fired up.

'No,' Jasmine snapped. 'We pull out now.'

* * *

Yes, he could hear the helicopter, of course, but he couldn't see it for this blasted mist. President Sorrentino had migrated to the cordless telephone in a hallway upon whose slatted walls portraits by a local artist traced his ancestry back a couple of generations. 'There was gunfire and bombs, but they've stopped now. Just tell him to land within the grounds, surely he can do that.' He paused, listened and then rolled his eyes. 'Nothing. All I can do is make stupid phone calls and listen to you giving me excuses while me and my family are trapped in our own home by a bunch of terrorists bent on kidnapping us.'

A boom outside rattled him as much as it did the window frame in the front door.

'You heard that, didn't you? *Mierda!* Tell the pilot to keep hovering until the mist clears…What? …As long as he can, then.' With care he replaced the receiver.

* * *

The first flushes of sunlight began sifting through the thinning mist to gild the rooftops and glow on the streets of the capital. Streets void of civilians save for the vagabonds carrying their pathetic bundles of rags on folded backs. Jasmine, Adrian and José Sabanetas advanced on the high-rise offices from where Radio Nacional was dutifully alarming listeners with news that FMLN terrorists and riffraff had attempted to assassinate *el Presidente de la República*, but were swiftly repelled by the superior capability, bravery and patriotism of our sons in *El Ejército Nacional.* The criminals, frustrated by this embarrassing defeat, had gone berserk, embarking on a vengeful killing spree throughout the capital.

'Max's spies were right; the main entrance is lightly guarded.' Jasmine observed the two sentries poised on the top of three steps, rifles at the ready, capped heads swivelling in slow motion. Behind them double doors marked the main access. Starting at the first rung she scanned the steel scaffold of zigzagging emergency steps that clung to each storey until she reached the roof, then the roof edge for sinister protuberances before checking out the flush-set windows in the two observable walls.

'These aren't private security types,' Adrian made an analysis of the sentries. 'National Police uniforms. Professionals.' As a precaution he left to check on the rear entrance. Max's spies had reported the rear to be locked and unguarded; however, you just had to check again, lest today things were different.

'Well, the mist has all but lifted,' Jasmine said, more to herself than to José. She settled behind a parked car to take the shot. The first policeman died quietly. The second cried out so she plugged him with a follow-up bullet that silenced him but smashed the glass window behind. She waited until Adrian had returned before downing her Beretta.

'The rear door is locked and unguarded,' he confirmed.

367

'We'll go in through the main entrance.' One hand gripping the Beretta, Jasmine used her spare hand and a shoulder to thrust open the double-doors. Once satisfied the short lobby was clear, she began taking the stairs two at a time, closely followed by Adrian and then José, their footfalls padding softly while a diesel generator rumbled somewhere.

They'd already gained the fourth floor when a youth in a green and white polo and white chinos and wearing a harassed expression came scampering down towards them. He froze on the half-landing at the turn of the stairwell, a hand on the wall, another on the banister, and stared wild-eyed at the approaching trio.

'The lifts are out of order,' he blurted.

'The generator doesn't power the lifts,' Jasmine informed him helpfully, which was when his eyes clocked the Beretta. He spun and belted back up the stairs, Jasmine following.

The trio came to a carpeted landing, and Jasmine caught sight of the youth dodging behind a door that had a frosted screen for a window and a laminated plaque with the name of the radio station in black capitals. Through the hazy glass she saw his profile moving to lock the door, and she heard the key engage with a sharp click. The shadow withdrew and faded.

Jasmine booted open the door. The lock spun out of its socket and the glass pane shattered. The offender disappeared behind a door by an unmanned reception desk curved against the far corner. She crunched over the shards into a reception area that was cool from air-conditioning. She pummelled the door twice with her boot before it flung open. Her man, together with a shorter but older gentleman in a grey suit, and a dolly-bird with lots of pink lipstick and jeans so snug they must have been painted on – all hopping nervously, alarm-stricken – had backed up against a long table of polished mahogany on which a host of bowing metal stands pointed microphones towards the empty chairs that surrounded it.

'On the floor and you won't get hurt,' Jasmine demanded.

No fuss. The three Radio Nacional staff dived to the floor

and Adrian began to body search them. Meanwhile, Jasmine pocketed her handgun, unslung the rifle from her shoulder and pinned the stairwell man's head to the floor with the muzzle.

'Get on with it.' She turned and nodded to José.

With forefingers pointing like pistols, José punched two buttons on a standing console and their respective flaps snapped opened simultaneously, and from each housing he plucked a cassette tape which, on an *oh dear, what a pity* and an air of nonchalant impudence, he tossed over his shoulders and then fished two cassettes of his own from his inner jacket pocket, and on a *let's listen to a different tune, shall we?* slotted one into each player.

'They're clean,' Adrian said, and stood up.

'Ready?' Jasmine glanced back at José, who nodded, snapped shut the console flaps, and prodded another button.

'When one tape ends the other will begin automatically,' he told her. 'For the next hour and a half the nation's official radio station will broadcast an informative interview with Xochitletoto on the matter of El Zacate, going out to a larger than usual audience thanks to a presidential decree.'

'What do we do with these?' Adrian asked, pouting towards the floor.

'You can go home,' Jasmine directed her reply at the prisoners, and lifted the rifle muzzle away.

'Big mistake,' Adrian objected. 'They'll return and switch off the tapes.'

'You wouldn't do that, would you?' Jasmine asked sweetly.

The prisoners shook their heads with earnest vigour, and to his credit the stair-man added that he was embarrassed by his earlier outburst of bad language.

'Of course,' Jasmine said, with a tilt of her head. 'Now go, before I change my mind.'

* * *

The roof above the spectators' gallery of the Flor Blanca football stadium must be the platform from where to judge whether their guess was right. And it was right.

369

With one foot forward for enhanced balance on the slant, Jasmine shaded her eyes and gazed across the city towards Radio Nacional.

'Told you they'd return,' Adrian said, taking a step beyond her, binoculars to his eyes.

Three Iroquois gunships buzzing about the building. One helicopter for each miniature figure that waved from a third-floor window. If there were shouts, they were in vain, with the whirr and clatter of the single-engine copters to compete with.

'They haven't even reached their floor,' said José, having plugged his ear with a minute earphone wired to a yellow handheld radio. 'The interview is still in progress. I like this part where you say you saw helicopters. Quite fitting, really.'

Jasmine put her own binoculars on just in time to see one of the airborne gunners level his mounted M60 at the window-revellers who in a blink had dropped their arms and dived from view. The gun rattled. Glass shattered. The gunship pulled out and another drifted in to take its place. Jasmine shifted the lens. More windows shattered on the third and also fourth floors. Glass spilled down the wall, white in the morning sun, like a light sprinkling of salt.

'When they've shot the place to bits, they'll send in the paratroopers,' Adrian predicted. 'The traps upon traps you could set for them!'

'Today they may find themselves overstretched all the same...' Jasmine was replying when a roof of light spread across the sky before vanishing into nothingness. She swung her goggles north, and the hot dry air resonated with a powerful clap and its echo.

'One of Carlos's Strela's has taken out a helicopter,' she announced, feeling a disruption of warm air brush loose spirals of hair across her cheeks. She handed the binoculars to José and offered to hold his portable radio while he checked out the gunship which, with rotors still spinning, drifted, port-side leading, for what seemed like a very long time. With minimal fuss, if you didn't count the smoke pouring from its roof-mounted power plant, it slid into a massive shadow and then onto the lower slopes of the volcano. The tail split away and the flames that engulfed the main fuselage sailed higher than the nearby treetops.

'Look! It fell smack on top of a load of greens climbing to engage Carlos's men. Do you see?' José added a gleeful whoop. No sign of his stammer now. He seemed to be enjoying himself immensely. He handed back the binoculars.

'I had a radio like this,' Jasmine remarked, weighing it in an out held hand.

'Don Serafin gave it to me,' José said defensively, losing his glee, which Jasmine thought was a pity, so she sought to reassure him:

'I didn't mean it like that.'

'No worries,' he acknowledged, and the smile returned to his freckled face.

She surveyed the crash site. Now a dark smear on the sloping scrubland dotted with fires from where sooty smoke wafted up the volcano's side to smudge the sky. Around the burning wreckage were glimpses of green uniforms sheltering in the thickets. She moved the binoculars over the area and then stopped. Sparks flickering in the farmland higher up.

'Good work again from Carlos,' she said. Sending squads down to engage the soldiers.

A tap of distraction on her shoulder.

'*Comandante.*' Adrian pointing up the valley.

She lowered the binoculars. The multi-storey car park was close enough to observe with the naked eye. It was taking fire from a hovering Hughes while behind it, offset a fraction to the right, a similar machine had its bulbous nose sniffing out a complete circumnavigation of a bleak multileveled shopping complex while its gun thudded in short regular sequences.

'Both buildings are crawling with *militares*,' unprompted, Adrian provided commentary. 'I watched them slink in all silent and careful-like through the main entrance.'

'Then Carlos's telephonists are doing their job,' Jasmine

371

said. From a valley echoing with the intermittent mortar thumps and the tapping of small arms fire, more than a dozen sooty plumes were now trickling up to blacken the sky. 'So many people,' she stammered, gulping back a sudden rush of regret.

'Fuck 'em,' grunted Adrian.

* * *

Today the sky above San Salvador turned a patchy grey to sully the spontaneous rosiness of dusk, and by nightfall pockets of fiery orange could be seen from Panchimalco, budding brightest within those asymmetrical sectors of the city whose electricity supply had yet to be restored. A lone grey DC6 droned in endless circles high above the valley. The impatient sirens of fire engines and ambulances percolated to where a full column of PCS combatants were waiting to take to their hammocks. But not before they had tuned into the latest from Serafin, who, in his emotionless reading voice informed his listeners that Adonai and his combatants had, under the dawn mists, penetrated Ilopango Airport and obliterated three stationary UH-1M helicopters and an A-37B bomber. Carlos had hit ANDA – the water company's head offices. Max had given the First Infantry Brigade's barracks a couple of mortars to chew on. Ivan Saavedra had taken on the guards at the power plant and by fluke or flair had killed the electricity supply to a dozen sectors.

After Serafin's good news José switched off the radio and a tangible sense of awe descended over the camp, settling the combatants into a mood of quiet refection. Awe at the scale of the offensive upon which they had embarked; reflection on how much they had achieved in just one day.

But the *comandante* broke the mood by telling everyone that she knew they were tired but we must rehearse tomorrow's objectives before we go to bed.

* * *

She awoke with a jolt, reached for her Beretta, dropped and

crouched beneath the hammock. 'An explosion,' she whispered when she saw the whites of Adrian's eyes in the darkness. '*Vamonos!*'

They scaled the sheer cliff and when they were all above treetop level they gazed back towards the west.

Cuscatlán Tower – the city's only true skyscraper – stood tall and lonesome-looking against the backdrop of the moon-splashed cordillera, but amber flames crinkling within a jagged gash in its floor to ceiling windows three storeys from the top gave the impression of an open wound. As they watched, three A-37B bombers shrieked away along the valley before swinging round over Santa Tecla and galloping back. Two of the bombers disengaged from the formation and dived over the cordillera, but the third one came on apace. The missile was released and abruptly the aircraft lifted and Jasmine could see its gun-metal grey underbelly as it ripped against the stars and disappeared over the cliff's crest. She looked back just in time to see the direct impact precisely half way up the tower. A white glow wrapped in blue folding vapour curtains ballooned and a great chunk from one corner of the tower disintegrated. The resulting cave belched forth a rolling smoke ring beneath which a cascade of rubble and sundry debris plummeted towards the empty car park where it spread with such liquidity that to Jasmine's eye it could have been water from a hosepipe shooting against a hard surface.

It was an impressive display of firepower. But the enemy, overreacting to a false call from one of Carlos's telephonists had predictably shot itself in the foot.

* * *

Good luck favours the prepared mind! Rain (or in this case mist) falls on the good and the wicked! These were a couple of the slogans being bantered by both sides a week into the Offensive. In a news interview General Levi said he couldn't believe the guerrillas' good fortune, even though mist, as the NTV's popular weatherman pointed out afterwards, was as common a feature of the Salvadoran highlands as sun. *La*

Prensa ran a story about the same weatherman's claim to have received death threats from an unknown but enraged source. That the source had demanded he desist from prognosticating any more mist, or else!

For their part the guerrillas didn't question Mother Nature's benevolence. After over a decade of acclimatising in her cloud forests, they had learned to run with her pulse. Dividing into squads and subdividing into squadlets they kept the prodigious military detachments on their metal toes with relentless flash attacks: bolting out of innocuous shadows, getting off no more than a couple of fleeting but succinct rounds before vanishing into the mist. Indirect combatants persisted in clogging up the telephone lines with hysterical reports of guerrilla sightings which invariably prompted a robust response from ground mobiles and air support.

Electricity cables were tampered with in the dead of night, but those clever electricity men in their blue boiler suits and blue vans were impressively swift to return power to the effective sectors. So Adonai struck the power station itself, which left the entire city without ironed shirts or functioning cistern pumps for the better part of three days.

In that desperate time when a battle can go either way, the adversary turned up in endless droves with endless firepower and dextroamphetamine, the guerrilla columns worked with an indomitable resolution that at times spilled into panicked over-enthusiasm, and Jasmine had to rein her column in lest they suffer severe losses. Or worse. Because on day five Segundo was killed together with twenty-seven combatants whose assault on the Hospital Militar had gone horribly wrong. The President promised his startled fans that the insurgents' back had been broken. Jasmine rang Marta Lilian in Santa Rosa de Lima to give her the bad news and to offer condolences.

Day and night Carlos's telephonists set up ambushes and his direct combatants waited for the fall. When a small enough military detachment was directed to look into claims of an insurgent presence in a market square, shuttered shop premises or private house, it was set upon by a larger-than-reported number of sour-eyed guerrillas who, after relieving the soldiers of their M16s and M3A1 grease guns, mercilessly executed them.

From each of the guerrilla columns, accomplished snipers were dispatched into half-finished apartment blocks, into dilapidated townhouses and courtyards, and into long abandoned overgrown gardens. Such deserted vantage points yielded excellent concealment and escape routes, and from them the militants picked off no more than one or two foot or mobile patrols at a time, before abandoning the site never to return.

Under Jasmine's orders and with her by now tattered maps for reference, a systematic destruction of the city's bridges began, until only five remained passable. To get from A to B by army truck you now had to go via Z. To tally with each bridge downed another frantic telephone call to the emergency services prompted mobile military units to go haring to the rescue. At a spot where the vehicles were hindered from making a U-turn due to space restrictions, the guerrillas set upon them. Gun battles developed, most of which were brief. The soldiers fled or risked being routinely slaughtered, and the combatants then stuffed their magazines and belts with ammunition before making off with whatever they could scavenge.

But several of these tricky to coordinate ambushes swelled into running street battles. To Jasmine's horror, more comrades fell. She wept over Wenceslau's blood-soaked body. Adrian sawed off Clementina's mangled right arm but a day later she died in a safe house that was bombed. The same anxious words were spoken every time they gathered round one of their downed colleagues, while Adrian or anyone who took it upon himself to do so, adeptly checked for vital signs: 'He's dead.' 'Is she dead?' Only for the blood-drenched body to stir or groan, which was followed by a flurry of activity to remove the victim further away from the conflict zone in order to receive emergency treatment.

With astonishing speed and at huge personal risk, Red Cross volunteers started appearing and, waving large Red-Cross flags, dodged and ducked and weaved about in the combat zones. With the rattle of fusillade from hidden places hardly abating in consideration of their brave efforts, they set about recovering the wounded guerrillas from the streets and pavements, and ferried them away in the back of vans. When these combat exchanges became prolonged it was the guerrillas who, after losing the element of surprise, were forced by overwhelming numbers and firepower and SAF's imminent arrival to turn tail and beat a hasty retreat.

With mounds of broken masonry, upturned cars and burning tyres, the rabble rousers barricaded boulevards and dual carriageways. When these vital thoroughfares became snarled up, the same combatants picked off the enemy with small arms fire and rotating Gatlings.

In the early mornings, barricades were also set up across pedestrian routes leading to major businesses, banks, factories and foreign embassies. Business stalled, as did industry. According to one angry pharmacist who suddenly had no staff to cater for his abrupt upturn in trade, a lot of people just don't give a shit. They take the week off work. Pull down the shutters and head for the coast, leaving the capital to shut down without them.

Due to multiple bomb scares that mysteriously spread through shopping centres and the capital's various open air markets, workers and customers alike turned away, some to return home, others to join the slow exodus from the city.

The guerrillas' entire stock of explosive devices was discovered and confiscated. An event that was jubilantly paraded for the TV cameras, and the cleavage boasting commentator with her dyed blonde hair and an eye-watering nose job earnestly explained how this was most definitely the breaking of the guerrillas' back and that the citizenry had nothing further to fear. But Jasmine and her avengers were old hands at sourcing weaponry from the enemy. They knocked together home-made replacements with sand from the waysides, petrol siphoned from cars, circuit boards of which Carlos had countless supplies and would be happy to oblige, wood chippings and shards of scrap metal purloined from building sites. With these highly volatile devices they managed to sabotage the city's vital blood lines – its communication systems, its water and drainage systems, and its power supply – again. And all the while they improved on the relentless flash-attacks. Some of these left their hateful foe merely impaired; however, the speed with which they were carried out was eating away at the soldiers' nerves, particularly so with the younger conscript types. Before long the military slipped into its old haphazard methods of guerrilla profiling. On the flimsiest of intelligence they rampaged into the homes of ordinary civilians, rounded up entire families – grandma included – in the living room or rear courtyard and opened fire on them before leaving with grim faces and blood-splattered uniforms to pile into their jeeps or trucks and screech away to the next so-called safe house on their lists.

With five-hundred-pounders, SAF bombers struck suspected FMLN positions within selected neighbourhoods, sending the residents, kids in arms and bundles on backs, scurrying from homes that erupted and disintegrated behind them. Helicopters backed up these initial strikes, sweeping the streets with airborne artillery before the infantry moved in to tidy up.

The fire brigade was run off its feet. So was the ambulance service. The hospitals filled to overflowing. The less seriously wounded were turned away.

As one nurse put in during a shouting match with a frenetic cab driver, 'I may find space in the Hospital de Sonsonate, but I can't reserve it for your passenger. By the time you get there it may be taken. It will be just as quick for you to drive there, and let me get on with looking after my patients instead of making phone calls.'

CHAPTER THIRTY-TWO

DAY EIGHT OF THE OFFENSIVE. DAWN. The PCS was in the city and by good fortune so was the mist. With a rearguard following a short distance behind and named flankers and scouts detaching themselves to hurriedly scrutinise and secure a junction or other potential hazard, Jasmine led the column through the quiet lanes, avoiding the main thoroughfares. The occasional flush of a porch lamp or the glimmer of a cat's eyes were the only lights that penetrated the cloud. Not even the sound of mortar shells to disturb such stillness. Jasmine had ordered the bombing be withheld until five a.m. by which time the PCS aimed to be in position to take out a good number of military vehicles as they sped towards Ilopango. Adonai and his column waited in readiness for their second offensive on the airfield – installations to be targeted principally. Anything else was a bonus. Nevertheless, after last week's siege, security at Ilopango had no doubt increased, and would be operating with greater alertness. Today Adonai and his columns would have their work cut out.

Struggling to keep pace, Adrian was a one-man band, with a lot of paraphernalia: one blowtorch from a leather strap around his neck, one ten-litre explosion-resistant petrol tank, ten-metres of armoured petrol hose slung round his shoulder, and one hand pump gripped in his left hand. The combatants crept down a sloping concrete bank and gathered beneath a steel truss bridge that spanned a stream on the outskirts of Colonia Ivu. Several of the combatants squeezed their hands over their noses and mouths against the stench of raw sewage that rose in steam from frothy, petrol-coloured waters.

'Three birds with one stone,' Jasmine reminded her night brigade while Adrian set to work assembling his gear. 'Divert military mobile units by sabotage, take out units, and replenish ammunition.'

'We're ready,' said Adrian, rubbing the blowtorch.

'*Andando, pues,*' Jasmine urged him.

Adrian set the blowtorch hissing a long white flame with just a soupçon of blue.

'Everyone else, take up defensive positions and warn us of foot or vehicle approaches,' Jasmine ordered.

'You too, *comandante*, I can do this by myself,' said Adrian. But she insisted on staying to help lug his accessories after him. He donned a pair of protective goggles. 'I'll leave the floor beams and end posts intact,' he announced, pointing into the mist. 'The trick is to get the midsection that runs between the end verticals to fall out.'

'Save the explanations, Ade. We're somewhat pressed for time.'

Standing on the concrete bank beneath the bridge, Adrian employed the tool against the expansion end of the construction, and fired the main beam amid showers of amber sparks at a point a metre from where it met the bank. Every now and then he stood back to examine his workmanship. It was a delicate operation, for he had to take care to sever the beams to within a few inches of their ability to sustain the weight of the bridge.

When he was satisfied with his first incision, he moved beneath the bridge and set the flame to the parallel main beam and repeated the process. He drank some water from his bottle and then climbed up the bank and began to work the upper beam at a point precisely above the damage he had made below, pausing only to inspect the channel he was driving through the metal.

'Now to repeat the process at the fixed end,' he grunted,

dipping his head in a vain attempt to wipe his sweaty brow on a raised shoulder.

They trotted a little way down river and found a wide pebbled shallow. Careful to get as little of the foul waters on her clothing as possible Jasmine picked her way across, while Adrian sloshed a pace ahead. Once on dry land they jogged back to the bridge where, pitching the blowtorch aloft, Adrian went to work. When he had seen to all the joists, he told Jasmine that the whole lot could tumble with the slightest application of weight. He would go on to the bridge alone to sever the upper spars.

So, drumming her fingers on the polished wood of her AK, Jasmine watched as Adrian attacked the first of two upper beams. Despite her anxiety, Jasmine knew there would be no hurrying him. He flamed the second of the upper beams with the same care and attention he had shown the others.

'That should do it,' he said at long, long last.

From a public telephone Jasmine called 911 and hysterically reported *muchachos* marauding in Colonia Ivu and neighbouring Vista Hermosa. When she returned to the column she called Isabela and Emilio forward for instructions.

'Our destruction of the flyovers listed makes this the most direct route from the military compound to the southern sector, and that implies crossing this bridge. I'm leaving two squads with you. Stay close to the bridge and wait for the arrival of the army. Due to the curfew no civilian traffic should be on the roads, but if ambulances or the fire service try to cross in the meantime, you must turn them away.'

Without further ado Jasmine selected eight volunteers and assigned four each to the command of Emilio and Anabela. 'Once the bridge is down, military traffic will take the Santa Tecla road on its way to back up SAF at Ilopango. We will be waiting for them in the dip that runs between the filter road and the flyover to Merliot. You know the place. Meet us there if you have time, if not, I'll see you back at the waterfall.'

Anabela replied by whipping back and releasing the rifle

380

charger.

Jasmine led the remainder of the column through the built up areas along the lower flanks of the cordillera towards the Pan American Highway.

* * *

Emilio and Anabela divided their two squads into four. After sending these to conceal themselves along the banks but within earshot, the two lieutenants took up positions on opposite approaches to the bridge, and with rifles at the ready they waited to turn away any civilian traffic that might seek to cross. Emilio could make out Anabela's slight figure only because he knew she was there. With her rifle angled across her midriff, she was a small-t, or perhaps the number 4.

The all-night curfew afforded the armed forces free range of the city's roads, so it wasn't long before Emilio heard the rattling diesel engine of a personnel carrier labouring towards Colonia Ivu. Anabela must have heard it too because she was doing a very convincing *zenzontle*, and Emilio selected his owl effort for the acknowledgement, at which the number 4 promptly vanished. Emilio slid behind a carpenter's workshop from where his flair for shapes took the bridge, seen now from the side, to be the bottom half of a triangle.

The engine staggered down the gears. The headlights poked into view, dimly at first but quickly intensifying as they drew near. Snub-nosed, with a long rectangular carrier, the truck's profile was otherwise rinsed of colour and feature as it crawled on to the bridge. Emilio flattened his back to the wall and cupped a hand at either side of his mouth. This time he opted for his *manakin* call: three successive "doo" notes, subtly falling in pitch. Thus cued his assigned team rose from the riverbank, and were still pushing up beside him when a grinding noise made him look back towards the truck that was now at least half way across the river and for a worrying moment it appeared would make it all the way. But how could he have ever doubted Adrian's skills? True to form, they were spot on. The steel truss bridge gave out a bell-like clang. It jolted.

The central span dropped a metre only to come up sharply with an excruciating crunch. Amid a lot more grinding, many men hollered while suspended in mid-fall. With bewildering speed the entire steel structure plunged twenty feet, sucking the truck after it. Spitting sparks it ploughed deep crevices into the sloping cement walls, and then thundered into the shallow waters where with an eternity of shrieking metal it eventually settled. The support beams ended up crippled into a V-shape trapping the truck in its jaws.

Emilio, Anabela and their merry men descended on the wreckage from all sides, and finished off the stunned and wounded soldiers in a merciless act of slaughter. Within minutes the butchery was over and the guerrillas confiscated weapons, ammunition, cash, food and anything else that might come in handy, before slipping through the network of lanes to make their escape.

* * *

Over the past eight days Captain Escobar had worked very diligently indeed. He had gathered scraps of intelligence on the guerrillas' advance and dotted them on his wall-map with red-headed pins; he'd numbered the pins and scribbled annotations in a variety of inks. Now the numbered dots looked like a road to nowhere, but there were a lot of them and so many dots must lead somewhere, and because three heads are better than one he had called Anastasio and his pilot-of-few-words to the assembly hall in SAF's splinter-operations base at Comalapa, in the humid coastal plains. Anastasio arrived in full uniform and cap and loads of firepower racked on his belt. An equally eager Flight Lieutenant Cabrera was already flight-suited and now stood clutching his helmet in a gloved hand while peering closely at Escobar's unfinished painting by numbers.

'Adonai is driving in from the east.' By ploughing his thumbnail across the wall-map Escobar showed his onlookers what he meant.

'Heading back to Ilopango Airport,' Anastasio surmised.

'Carlos was launching attacks from the volcano.' Escobar

pointed out the volcano as if that colossal hump needed any more limelight. 'Maximiliano started off on the cordillera. Then he divided his column, so they're been coming down through La Cima in dribs and… '

'What about Saavedra and the bitch?' Anastasio interrupted, allowing his impatience to get the better of him.

'I'm not sure,' Escobar admitted. 'The high number of false leads they're putting out makes it tricky to plot or establish patterns from the guerrilla advance once they've penetrated the city. The only way really is to link up confirmed assaults.'

'Show me the confirmed assaults,' Anastasio demanded.

'Well, day one, after a strike on the Casa Presidencial, from which we dislodged them, they hit Radio Nacional.'

'I heard about that,' Anastasio said, with a spiteful smirk for Cabrera. 'Apparently your boys shot the place to bits. When our boys went in, all they found were three radio staff – very dead.'

'That remains to be established, doesn't it?' Cabrera cautioned in his standard stress-free approach to everything.

'Whatever!' said Anastasio, chasing the last word.

'Then they took out a helicopter by firing from positions along the cordillera,' Escobar recovered collective attention. 'Later on they withdrew and split into small squads, doing their sporadic hit and run thing throughout the afternoon. Because they came to us wherever we moved, rather than following a circuit of their own, well, you see what I mean by *difficult*. How do you draw clear conclusions as to a target order? Aside from static targets such as installations and features of the city's infrastructure, the militants' hit and runs are seemingly random. Their next targets could be any of the units our combined forces have deployed throughout the city, and with the fog coming in so thickly, the militants have moved about for the most part unseen.'

Escobar is building himself up for a grand entrance, Anastasio decided. 'So go on, you haven't called us here just to say we're no further forward. Stop parading your feathers.

What have you discovered?'

Escobar tried in vain to conceal his smugness, but his dimples puckered into a poorly stifled smirk that said it all. 'Twenty minutes ago we lost a personnel carrier on the bridge at Colonia Ivu.' He broke off to allow the penny to drop. 'Got it?'

After a moment's consideration old-hat Anastasio had. 'A diversion.' He put his face close to the map, picked out Escobar's pinhead where the map had neglected to depict the bridge in question, and underscored it with a groove from his thumbnail. His thumb struck out in several directions, as if sketching in the spokes of a cartwheel, but only one spoke led unhindered back to the city's most transited artery – The Pan American Highway. Now, with the destruction of that un-depicted bridge, even that route was cut. He dug his thumbnail in deep, almost tearing the paper, as if to squash the guerrillas for making his life difficult. 'It's a small bridge to destroy, but when related to our compound at La Ceiba behind the Basílica de Guadalupe, the cordillera, and Ilopango, access to these districts is cut off, and traffic – ours in this case because of the curfew – is forced to divert up the Pan Americana.'

'That's my conclusion also,' Escobar got in before Anastasio could hog all the glory. 'And unless I'm missing something, at some point along that route they'll be waiting to ambush our mobiles.'

'But where, exactly?' Cabrera enquired, bringing his compatriots back to earth. Being a man of the skies, he was not expected to know the miniature detail of the terrain. Cabrera looked at Escobar. Escobar at Anastasio.

Anastasio invited guesswork because he too subscribed to the three heads notion, especially when the stakes were volcanically high, as they were now.

Cabrera plucked at his earlobe a couple of times, and then prodded the map with his little finger. 'Behind the basilica,' he offered. 'It's just across from the army compound, which must be on their target list.'

Air force fairies don't know jackshit about real combat. Have to be spoon-fed. But Anastasio didn't say that, instead he encouraged participation from Escobar.

'I disagree,' Escobar said, to Anastasio's relief. 'The risk-effort-gain equation makes the compound unviable. If you're a guerrilla – right? – you've got no difficulty taking on roaming ground units. So why go for a heavily guarded compound?'

'So what *do* you suggest?' Anastasio demanded. Escobar was quick to rubbish Cabrera's suggestion; but where's his pearl of wisdom?

'I suggest we look for the most direct alternative route between the southern sector and Ilopango.'

'Quit fucking around,' said Anastasio, losing his rag a little. 'That's what we *are* doing. But check out the map, will you; we're talking at least ten kilometres of road. We can't cover every inch of it, can we? Narrow it down for me.'

They continued to conjecture, picking out the most likely positions and debating their worth from the point of uncivilised guerrillas hell-bent on returning the country to prehistoric epochs.

* * *

Pan American Highway on San Salvador's south-western outskirts.

Jasmine could make out tin sheets and timber that served as roofs and walls. In places they glistened, in others they faded.

'Believe the forecast and we have an hour tops before the mist begins to lift,' she said, breaking out of her jog several paces ahead of Adrian. As she waited for the column to assemble, she could hear shells slamming in the east. 'Sounds like Adonai's lot are throwing everything they have at the airbase.'

'The old rover was never one for half measures,' Adrian said with unbridled fondness. 'Won't be long before a bunch of greens go rushing to thwart his mischief.'

It was easier to do a roll call than to count the combatants and when all sixty-four had admitted to being present and correct, Jasmine referred them to their maps. But Adrian the spokesman reminded her that it wouldn't be an exaggeration to say we've been through this a hundred times already with each member. They know where to go when, and what to do when.

'Very well. But remember…'

'To halt our fire at the first sound of a helicopter,' Adrian interrupted.

'And move into the second phase.'

'That too.'

'*Ándale, pues.*'

With the grass hissing at their ankles the combatants skirted the tin *champas* to where a long gravel-sided gully separated the Pan American from a used-car dealer's place. Within the high-fenced forecourt, up to seventy cars for sale lurked in the power cut. Although she knew from her observations during the planning stages that only two security guards were ever on site at any one time, she decided a cursory search would be appropriate.

'I'm going to secure the forecourt and check on the *sentinelas,*' she told Adrian.

'I'll meet you in the gully, village-side,' he answered.

Reluctant to run risks she considered unnecessary, Jasmine disposed of both security men by way of her Beretta. Then she worked her way through the entire car park, casting the narrow beam of her pencil torch beneath the cars and in through side windows. There were a hundred treacherous possibilities, hiding places from where a rear attack could be mounted with devastating consequences for the PCS.

Meanwhile a dozen snipers took up positions on the smart new flyover that bridged the Pan American three hundred metres beyond the *champas* settlement.

When Jasmine was satisfied that the car dealer's place posed no direct threat, she jogged up to beyond the forecourt to check on the three combatants she had posted as lookouts. Their instructions were to warn the column of every advance on their position that came from beyond the high perimeter fence. To her relief she found them exactly where she had expected. Squatting between the upper end of the forecourt and a recently trimmed hedgerow, they had a potential sniper's view through the bushes on to a half-finished housing estate, and good escape routes at either side. When they gave her the thumbs-up, she jogged back down the grassy gradient beside the forecourt and found Adrian lying belly-down on the gully's sloping bank, peering directly on to the tarmac. By now the other combatants would be in position. Beyond Adrian, along the gully at the side of the highway, and wherever the land was uneven, dipped or rutted, they lay in ambush with rifles and shotguns at the ready. She looked back towards the village even though it was hidden in the cloud. Are we far enough from the settlement not to prompt reprisals from the armed forces? She wondered, as she had when first she'd surveyed the area for its potential, and had measured two hundred paces from the nearest shack to where they now lay in waiting. There was no definitive answer.

She settled down beside Adrian, lying flat on the gravel, feeling it scratch her stomach and thighs through her boiler suit. Cradling her rifle barrel in her left hand, she laid her cheek on the butt's wooden side panel and began tapping the trigger guard with her forefinger.

'By now the route through Colonia Ivu should be non-viable,' she went over the theory yet again.

'With restricted access to the southern sector and air field, and none via the bridge, military back-up will turn back and detour through Merliot, bringing them up towards us and the flyover,' Adrian added in the monotone of a man who's recited this story a hundred times already.

The crickets were silent tonight. But dogs howled at every dull boom of mortars that rose in the east.

'I hope Adonai achieves his objective,' Jasmine said, noticing the odours of charcoal and engine oil on the muggy air.

* * *

387

'What about here?' Escobar jabbed yet another potential site with his thumbnail. 'I did a good few foot patrols along this stretch. If I remember right, there's a gully runs along the side of the highway, someone's idea of a drainage ditch. Gets waterlogged in June, bone dry for the rest of the year. Get yourself hunkered down in there…'

'A gully…hmm,' Anastasio interrupted, and commenced examination of Escobar's discovery. 'And a flyover – what? – perhaps fifty metres further up the road.' He straightened up and clapped Escobar on the back. 'Nice one, Nathan. No better place along the entire route from where to launch a pretty little surprise assault.' He turned to Flt Lt Cabrera. 'Fly us in that general direction so as to be at hand when things kick off. While Cazador keeps the insurgents busy with sky-fire, Matador will fly on…let's say…just short of a kilometre towards the west, and set its paratroopers down on the highway. They'll wheel round and fan out through La Cima and mount a rear assault from the south.'

'We have a bad weather warning for the capital,' Cabrera advised dutifully. 'Visibility is down due to thick fog.'

'Listen now and listen well,' Anastasio said with studied restraint. He cupped a palm on Cabrera's shoulder and grabbed a handful of flight suit. 'Has it not occurred to you that Jasmine Gavidia purposely delayed the offensive until the weather was against us? Has it not occurred to you, *either*, that if we do nothing tonight, severer consequences will befall us tomorrow? Now,' be broke off to pat down Cabrera's ruffled shoulder, 'your equipment includes NVGs?'

'For sure.'

'Tracer, only the dim variety, yeah?' Bright tracer would betray the copter gunners' position and overwhelm the NVGs. The subdued type he always found tricky to follow. Dim tracer would be clearly visible with NVGs but not so to the naked eyes of the bastards on the ground, and he didn't reckon on their funds running to a full complement of night-vision equipment.

'For sure,' Cabrera agreed again.

'Good, now let's use them, shall we?'

Twenty minutes later Anastasio and twelve paratroopers were belted into canvass seats in Cazador's twilit rear cabin. The UH-1M Hughes helicopter bristled with weaponry: a pintle mounted six-barrelled Gatling; twin M60s; and one M79 grenade launcher. To each a gunner was assigned, and for Anastasio a huge mounted searchlight angled downwards. The Gatling gunner, a bull-terrier-cum-ruffian with a skinhead sunken between hunched shoulders, slid the door shut. Cabrera was on the radio to the tower.

Here in the lowland coastal plains the airport lay beneath the dense cloud bank. Through the wide rectangular window Anastasio could see Matador, in which Captain Escobar was rucked up together with a further dozen veteran troopers. A similarly armed gunship swathed in camouflage, Matador was preparing for takeoff. Mounted aft of the transmission on top of the fuselage and enclosed in cowlings, the single turboshaft power plant was humming, its spinning rotors picking up pace.

Peering beyond Cabrera, Anastasio could see through the curved cockpit windshield and across the landing zone towards SAF's annex – a single storey box separated from the passenger terminal by a fenced car park and twin landing circles. Now the whine of Cazador's power plant was quickening against Cabrera's terse verbal exchanges with the control tower. The ship lifted, nose down and tail up. The tarmac slid beneath and then fell away as they gained altitude.

With navigation lights bright and rotating beacons flashing the two helicopters raced skywards in a staggered right formation. Anastasio gazed across the unlit farmland plain as far as the coast, where crested waves curled upon a long silvery beach, and huts and lanterns dotted the silhouetted fringe of coconut palms.

Cazador leading, they soared into the cloud bank and at once the panorama vanished and the cabin dimmed to almost pitch black. In the thick cloud that was cuffing the window

389

Anastasio could see the reflection of the navigation lights. He swivelled his head to study the instrument panel – circular dials glowing a soft red. He noted the gyromatic compass system and direction-finder, and although these were signalled in English he had flown enough to recognise their functions.

With wisps of white clinging to the landing gear they burst out of the cloud and climbed into a canopy of stars. Anastasio leaned forward to get a better view. Below him a moonlit cloudscape ranged across the earth to a faded indigo belt that saddled the eastern horizon. Through it rose the flanks of the San Salvador volcano to preside above it all with its crown of red antennae. The gunship levelled off and banked fractionally to the left before surging towards the looming summit. Scanning across the great valley, Anastasio could see the cordillera's long, toothed heights and trickles of moonlight running like streams down its creviced mountainside.

In a flight of fancy he debated whether this panoramic grandeur was the most beautiful thing his eyes had ever beheld. But reluctantly he conceded that ever since he'd first set eyes on Jasmine laying the table in Pa's house, he'd been drowning miserably in her thrall. Why should that be when she'd caused him so much grief? The silent indignity he'd taken on the chin at rumours that she'd left him for the sloppy alcoholic brother of one of the country's most notorious insurgents. Not satisfied with assassinating his colonel and in so doing depriving Anastasio of a promotion, she goes on to smash his cocaine operation and expose him to ONUSAL, and all the while she's wresting key departments from army command. Fuck sake! She was a menace to him personally and to the army as a whole. He shook his head in dismay because he had hated her and desired her with equal ferocity these past seven years. Shapeless dungarees and complete absence of makeup, yet she maddened his wits until he could as easily daydream of tender lovemaking as slit her slender throat. If anyone should discover he'd actually taken to washing himself daily with the very same brand of soap that she used, well, there'd be a few raised eyebrows. But the soap kept the scent of her skin fresh in his memory, and added another dimension to the images of her that strolled in and out of his mind whenever they felt the urge. He'd taken a hundred mind journeys back to key crossroads in his thirty-four years on this planet and opted for different turns. Had he applied his charm, he might have groomed Jasmine for the future, because, unlike the tarts he'd used and discarded in his wake, Jasmine was marriage material. Now she'd be his faithful wife looking after their five kids and he wouldn't be sitting here in Cazador taking on an offensive mounted – if Escobar was right – by *her*! But he hadn't taken those turns, had he? And here he was on his way to face her head on. Or was it Saavedra? he thought, fretting for a moment that he was chucking the best counterinsurgency resources in the land after a fat bastard who couldn't mount a mule, let alone an ambush.

It was the girl!

Through a bullshit-baffles-brains effort he'd managed to hold off the down payment to the assassin who Gabriel in his eagerness to please had sounded out. He didn't know the guy, but there again that was the nature of the game. There'd be no need of him after today's mission. Tonight he would greet Jasmine with twenty-four elite SAF troopers. Tonight there were no young conscripts or bungling army types amongst them. These were skilled professionals at the top of their game on whom he could rely to perform as such. Tonight, Jasmine, my love, I will kill you.

Anastasio's stomach churned as the ship commenced its descent, and he surfaced from his moody reflections. They had crossed the volcano's summit and were now pitching towards the mist that floated like a great steaming river up the Valley of Hammocks. They plunged into it, and the ship rattled as it drove earthwards. Anastasio swallowed to unblock his ears. The gunners slid the door aft and took hold of their weapons. Mist flooded the cabin, cold and damp on Anastasio's face. The darkness might have been absolute were it not for the red

391

glow from the instrument panel and the intermittent flash of the navigation lights reflecting off the mist. The gunners pulled their NVGs down over their eyes. Anastasio did likewise, staining the clouds with shades of green and better defining their shapes and allowed him to penetrate their depths with greater scrutiny than with the naked eye but not as well as he would have wished.

'Our flight plan takes us across the highway and over the flyover. We will then bank round to approach the guerrillas from the south,' Cabrera's composed voice informed through the intercom.

Anastasio answered with a raised thumb. The wipers were pelting across the windshield. Mist must be very wet.

'ETA two minutes,' said Cabrera.

* * *

With the first stirrings of a breeze came the howl of a diesel engine labouring.

'Here they come.' Adrian had heard it too. 'Two.'

Conversation was switched off. Jasmine wriggled to achieve greater comfort. She nudged her left elbow into the gravel and steadied her grip on the rifle barrel before moving her finger on to the trigger. She turned her eyes towards the approaching motors and remained absolutely still. Then she felt the earth shudder beneath her.

With single headlights blazing on full beam the massive M900 burst out of the mist. Even at this distance, Jasmine could smell the acridness of brake friction. Painted a dull military olive the mammoth rumbled past above her, the carrier's canvas canopy rippling like bed sheets hung out to dry, huge tyres spinning beneath the angular mudguard.

She allowed the monster to continue. It is imperative, she reasoned, that however many vehicles compose the convoy, they carry on deep into the area commanded by the PCS before she triggered her comrades' fire by getting off the first shot.

The second truck emerged. An M813, its carrier also roofed with soft fabric, bellowed past. No other engines in earshot.

Two it was!

She fired the first shot at the M813's front nearside tyre and watched it deflate. An instant later she had punctured all three nearside tyres, the truck was lurching to its left, shotguns were blasting the tarpaulin, and Jasmine added automatic fire to the assault, shredding the tyres before sending streams of bullets towards the carrier's rear-end. The truck accelerated, attempting to manoeuvre out of danger, except it was inadvertently driving itself deeper into the thick of it. Now Jasmine could angle her shots into the carrier's open end. Soldiers were jostling and scrambling. As they tried to leg it over the tailgate, she aimed for their chests and heads. Judging by the blare of automatic fire and shotgun blasts at her left, the lead truck was coming under similar assault. Some of the soldiers managed to get a few rounds off, but disorientated by surprise, darkness and fog, their bullets skimmed ineffectually over the gully, a handful drummed into the rise behind the prostrated PCS.

Amid the bedlam Jasmine heard a terrific crunch. The M900 had come to a halt, its driver probably picked off by one of the snipers on the flyover. The M813 had slammed into its rear-end.

Remaining at positions low in the gully the combatants pounded merciless rounds into the tattered tarpaulins, exposing the soldiers, and then chopping them down with brutal accuracy, while from the bridge the snipers rained their fire upon the lead truck. Shedding spent magazines and reloading with fresh ones or hurriedly stuffing loose rounds into emptied magazines, the militants paused for mere seconds before taking up the assault once again. Bullets clanged off metal, crashed glass, and tore through the now ragged sails of the soft tops.

Jasmine honed in on the drone of a helicopter approach. 'Helicopter squadron,' she called to Adrian, and the warning was carried verbally down the line and their gunfire came to a staggered halt. From the resulting quiet emerged the pitiful

393

whimpering of their victims.

'My knee! My knee!' one cried in agony, and others even called for mother.

The combatants climbed out of the gully and hastened to the flyover. Gathering beneath its four-lane width they took up infantry positions; some kneeling on the tarmac across the Pan American while others stood, their rifles angled upwards, over the heads of their kneeling comrades. Jasmine tucked herself behind a supporting pilaster, aimed her rifle at the front of the M900 and fired twice, smashing both headlights whose beams had, up until that moment, lit up the short tunnel beneath the flyover. Now, only the somewhat obstructed headlights of the M813 buried in the lead vehicle's tailgate would be visible on close inspection. If close inspection was of any interest to the helicopters, all the better.

'Two threats from above,' she warned.

One engine thudded overhead and receded. The other followed suit.

* * *

'Get us in close,' Anastasio demanded of Cabrera. He wasn't fooled by those images of Jasmine's face peering up at him. She would be a phantom soon enough.

The gunship embarked on a gradual left turn but continued the descent. Now it was Cabrera's terse commentary on air. Now the Operations Base controller's. Now Matador's pilot was chipping in. They were coordinating flight paths on a radio talk-through. Visibility close to zilch. Fifty-nine knots. Stop turn after thirty degrees.

Finally the ship levelled off and decelerated. The torch would provide a bright target at which ground fire could be aimed. Anastasio would not use the torch unless absolutely necessary. So he narrowed his eyes, because even with the benefit of NVGs he had to draw on all his powers of focus. These fucking goggles are not all they're cracked up to be. Perhaps Cabrera, you could drop a couple of flares and light up the area because, frankly, I'm struggling to see a thing.

'Negative. That would light us up too. I'll bank round and come at them from behind, a little lower than we are now.'

Anastasio could only guess at the complexities the pilot faced in these treacherous conditions. He could not have appreciated the skill required to manoeuvre and coordinate with another pilot in an urban area where electricity cables, bridges and ground fire could hook you out of the sky at any turn.

Lightning flickered below, except it couldn't have been lightning because judging by the row of muzzle flashes and intermittent tracers, the gunners were already giving it some. So Anastasio whipped out his pistol and joined in. The lightning disappeared beneath the deck. The no-neck Gatling man bellowed at Cabrera to come round, come round again!

Sitting neck-deep in cloud Anastasio hunted for fresh signs of lightning. He felt the helicopter gain a little altitude, then bank so steeply on a left turn that he reached out and steadied himself on the doorsill for fear of being lobbed overboard. They descended and reduced speed. The fog abated. The ship came to a stable hover inside a bubble created by the rotors' downward current.

'That's as low as I can take her,' Cabrera's voice came from all around.

'Lower,' Anastasio yelled at the helmet. 'Lower.'

In response Cabrera told him to fuck off. Safety first. This is as close as we go. Now do what you came to do.

Anastasio glared. 'Are we directly over where we saw the gunfire?'

They were, said a raised thumb.

Anastasio pushed the NVGs up on to his forehead. 'Bloody useless piece of kit,' he muttered in disgust, and grabbed the searchlight and directed it earthwards. He thumbed the slide switch but the powerful glare reflected off the clouds in a blinding sheen. '*Mierda!*' he yelled in utter exasperation, and he slammed his fist down on top of the torch. 'The light makes it even worse. What is this? Who designed this shit?'

No sooner had lightning flaunted itself a second time than the gunners pounced on it. But there was something disconcerting about seeing hundreds of rounds vanishing almost as soon as they emerged from their muzzle flashes. If the torch wasn't enough to betray the gunners' position, the tracers could do the job almost as well. And to add to Anastasio's sense of disconcertedness, wasn't that Cabrera yelling now?

'We're taking ground fire. I'm pulling pitch.' It was Cabrera, tense but decisive.

While the gunners pummelled, the helicopter climbed sharply. So sharply that Anastasio gulped at the abrupt gravitational press that drove him deep into his seat, forcing him to relinquish his grip on the searchlight. He turned aside, about to make his protestations known to the pilot but when he distinctly heard the metallic clattering of bullets against the fuselage's shell he thought better of it. Cabrera needed no distractions right now. Anastasio was dazzled by the searchlight and for a while the cockpit was an empty black void.

'*Madre mia*,' he exclaimed, reeling at the sensations of vertigo and nausea. 'Are we hit?' But the Gatling gunner, hunched over his weapon, was too absorbed to reply.

Fighting himself out of his seat Anastasio reached out, fumbled for the torch and turned off the powerful beam. He slumped back and again looked towards the cockpit, blinking repeatedly in his effort to recover some vision. Like a theatre curtain going up, the darkness lifted from the pilot's shoulders and helmeted head. The circles on the instrument panel materialised, though they swam from their positions and overlapped. But he reined them back into focus. He spotted the winding vertical speed indicator signalling a rapid climb rate. However, to his relief, the attitude indicator showed the aircraft was level. He laid his head back. They were not hit.

The gunners were still at it, all credit to the fellows, but a blast of atmospherics pierced the racket and a male voice bellowed on the FM radio: 'Look out, Cazador!'

Anastasio blinked at the open door because Matador's navigational lights were inexplicably looming out of the clouds above. His heart slammed into his ribcage as if it had fathomed the phenomenon before his mind had cottoned on. Swirling beacons plunged past the open door on a downward oblique, so close that Anastasio jumped back in his seat, bracing his boots against the searchlight mount. He recovered his wits quickly enough to lean forward and peer after the navigation lights that faded in the same split second he caught sight of them. Perhaps because he refused to believe his eyes, he still hadn't made sense of what they'd seen. Or still seeing: no sooner had a bubbling whiteness infused the clouds than it had filtered away.

'Matador is down,' the Gatling gunner shouted at Cabrera.

'Matador is down?' Anastasio echoed to himself. *Is down*, as in *crashed*! At which the same bubbling light of a moment ago repeated itself in his head. And he lost it. 'Put down. Put down,' he was screaming. 'Put down. We must go after her.' He punched his fist high and swung it down upon the terrier's skinhead. His hand hurt. He shut his eyes, kicked out, felt the lamp's mount under his boot, and tried to dislodge it with more kicking. He opened his eyes but couldn't see a thing. Strong paws – probably the terrier's – were shoving his neck back, making him cough for breath; others were on his chest, pinning him to his seat; and others still were clamped to his ankles.

While Cabrera was directed back to Operations Base on a radar approach, Anastasio slept peacefully under the effects of heavy sedation.

CHAPTER THIRTY-THREE

ARENA's more liberal supporters complained it was a long time. They protested at their Party's "tardy response", urging President Sorrentino, who had eventually managed to get away to his emergency digs in San Miguel, towards dialogue with the FMLN. The more conservative residents reckoned it was too short, that the armed forces still had lots to give, that with a little more time they would defeat the guerrillas. Nevertheless, the San Salvador offensive lasted twelve days and nights before President Sorrentino finally called Iqbal Haq. He had sent out his depleted squadron of A-37 bombers, but despite the assault on Cuscatlán Tower and the reports from the SAF general that five hundred rebels had perished there and thousands more on the slopes of the volcano, the guerrillas had lost none of their ability to mount coordinated flash attacks and disappear into the city. Indeed, the reported attacks being carried out against military targets had increased steadily throughout those twelve days. So had the varying figures published in the press showing the number of downed SAF helicopters. Precise data, however, was characteristically absent. None of those statistics published by his armed forces, or shown or leaked to the press, reported by the American Embassy, or those highly exaggerated numbers claimed by the rebel radio station, agreed. Nevertheless, whichever statistic Sorrentino chose to believe, they all made for grim reading. These incidents and accidents were claiming the lives of military personnel in alarmingly high numbers. Privately he admitted that the constant A-37s and Skymaster forays over the city were now little more than a show of force.

'The guerrillas have no care for human life,' he complained bitterly to Iqbal. 'Hundreds of innocents have died during their illegal incursion, and the rebels continue to shell civilian targets.'

'Would you like me to schedule a meeting with Señor Gadala?' Iqbal asked quietly. 'The United Nations and its staff will do all we can to assist in this difficult but urgent process towards peace.'

'If you think it would help,' said Sorretino.

CHAPTER THIRTY-FOUR

BESIDE A DEEP CONCRETE sump in a walled courtyard an average man stood naked, spun the tap and rinsed both hands. To dry them he used a green flannel. He pulled a white roman cassock over his greying mop of hair. Clutching both lengths of cord he flipped the amice over his head and tied it round his shoulders, concealing the cassock's collar. He reached into the white cloak-like alb and pulled it on. It floated down to his ankles, and he fastened the twisted rope securely around his waist. The chasuble was a poncho-like garment elaborately embroidered with images of birds and flowers, and he secured this over his shoulders and smoothed it down until its hems reached his knees.

He took up the gun. The Accuracy International Arctic Warfare rifle – AW for short – is a British-made bolt-action rifle designed with snipers in mind. Among its notable features, a light aluminum chassis made for easy maneuverability, while a 6x42 telescopic sight with variable magnification was great for close-ups.

By now the agent Gabriel had commissioned on Anastasio's behalf was anything but average.

* * *

A breezy Monday morning and Iqbal Haq had ordered a fleet of UN helicopters to airlift the Five from wherever they wished to the Church of San Marcos in the village of Olocuilta.

A vexed Anastasio loitered by the kerb. How the FMLN had

turned the odds upside down stunned him still. That they'd managed to achieve the prominence the US had financed ARENA to prevent was a question for historians to examine. There may have been no clear winner here, but if the FMLN were granted legal status to compete in the nation's presidential elections they will have achieved what they'd fought for, and in that sense the victory would be theirs. If that happened, would the FMLN agree to a concession hitherto unforthcoming in their negotiations – that of a general amnesty? Because if they didn't there was any amount of bad stuff that could happen.

He drifted amid the milling reporters and cameramen, feeling like one of the foreigners also gathered on the wide frangipani avenue, off which the church was set.

It was a cheerful, sunny day with birdsong in the trees. Yet Anastasio didn't share in its cheer, couldn't share in it, not until he was certain that El Zacate and several other failed Hammer and something endeavours would not return to bite.

Having shot up Radio Nacional, SAF had committed the further gaffe of allowing a full hour to pass before paratroopers gained access to the building and turned off Sochitle-toto's incendiary interview. By then she had named and shamed him no less than five times, linking him to the assault on El Zacate and made assertions that he'd engaged a death squad to murder Chachi Flint, brother to the PCS leader. Subsequently the name of Major Anastasio Menesses, son of the Mayor of Nejapa, had been splashed across the newspapers of North, Central, and South America. Should he be indicted, the flower-bird's eye-witness evidence would, in light of the increasing international sympathy for the campesinos, carry significant weight. Moreover, ONUSAL was already meddling where they had no business meddling. An Argentine forensic anthropology team had begun nosing around the silent remains of El Zacate. They'd discovered human bones, half of them children's. So what? Back in the day he could so easily have buried the meddlers with their precious human bones. But ONUSAL and the Catholics had complicated everything.

401

Even the Americans, who'd previously turned a blind eye to – even secretly encouraged – military methods, had suddenly developed a conscience. Things were changing at a giddy rate. Old powers were suddenly not so powerful. Those who were never expected to rise from beneath the feet of the *terratenientes* were now eyeing government.

Just as well he'd put together a contingency plan.

'Fried plantain,' he said to the street seller. '*Mucha salsa.*'

She was stuffing plantain sticks into a sandwich bag when Anastasio heard the hubbub rising behind him. He looked round. All reporters scuttling towards steps that led to the church's heavy double doors from which suited overfed bureaucrats were filing out in ones and twos on an apparent collision course. Anastasio attempted to read their faces, but they were giving away nothing.

Had peace been agreed? And if so, under what terms?

Aside from Vice President Ernesto González and Abraham Gadala, the politicians, their legal executives and bodyguards pushed through the throng and into waiting SUVs to be whisked away before they said anything that departed from the nascent accord.

So the reporters swarmed round the two authorised spokesmen. A statement would be read aloud. Or perhaps not, because the reporters were already shouting out questions, overlapping each other and thrusting forward microphones. In khaki and trim white beard Abraham held up hands in a call for silence while González clasped his hands over his bollocks like a footballer defending a free kick.

As the shouts died down Anastasio moved closer to the action.

'Have you reached an agreement with ARENA?' A beauty queen in lots of makeup and a bright body-hugging mini-dress caught Abraham's eye.

The "yes" brought a roar of approval and clapping from the gallery, which was replaced by a flood of competing questions; but the beauty queen again won through:

'Has a ceasefire been agreed?'

'I'm very pleased to announce that a ceasefire has been agreed, effective from the 1st of February, 1992. However, we don't anticipate renewed hostilities between now and then.' He looked towards González who nodded his agreement.

'What terms were agreed?'

'As of this day the Frente Farabundo Martí para la Liberación Nacional is a legal political party, at liberty to democratically participate in the decisions all our peoples make on our collective and inclusive future.'

They got what they wanted; now give me what I want. But a backlist of other questions unrelated to what Anastasio wanted had him rolling his eyes and whipping up his hand in frustration. When eventually the question came there was so much noise that Anastasio held his breath, fingers poised midway into the snack bag, and called upon all his powers of focus.

'Will an amnesty be declared for those found to have committed war crimes?'

'For the sake of peace for all Salvadorans, the FMLN has conceded that a national amnesty is desirable,' Abraham declared.

'Yes!' Anastasio breathed again. Hardly able to contain a smile, he shut his eyes and basked in the relief that washed over him.

'However,' Abraham went on ominously, 'this doesn't impede your right to seek justice through the international courts.'

'International courts!' Anastasio repeated, whirling from profound relief to acute alarm. He put away his premature smile. He hadn't considered that matters might be heard by foreigners. 'She could still take me down. Play safe not sorry.'

He didn't have long to wait before Jasmine Gavidia emerged through the church doors. Big hair topped with a Basque beret fronting the FMLN's star insignia. Shapeless boiler suit zipped to the neck.

403

She was alone, he noted with small relief, and steeling himself against his qualms he dialled a number on his mobile phone. 'Proceed. Green boiler suit. Burgundy beret.' He stuffed the phone into a leather pouch, and as Jasmine descended the steps he went forward, reached out and seized her wrist. It felt odd but good to be close to her again. He marvelled at her face framed in spirals of black, auburn and blonde, and the sultry shadow across her eyes, all so familiar, yet so different. So close, yet so unreachable.

'Happy now?' he heard himself say far more softly than he'd planned. 'You've got what you wanted.' He searched for something truly hideous to say, but the best he could muster was *it won't last you know*. An impulse to take her in his arms shook him. But she would never allow that. Then another to kneel before her, humiliate himself in front of everyone here and ask for forgiveness. Suddenly he was capable of any extreme to right the wrongs between them.

But she had a faintly mystified expression, and he panicked that she might actually have forgotten him, and all his loving inclinations turned themselves on their head and became the exact opposite, not because she was a guerrilla but because she was able to chuck his sense of worth into the abyss with a single glance.

He boiled.

Her tiny hand on his cheek, and he jumped back at the shock of it.

'I too did things I regret,' she said, her Cuscatlán accent calling him home. 'Be at peace, friend, I have nothing against you.'

Anastasio thought he would burst with love. What started as a cough turned into a whimper, and his attempt at correction turned to open weeping, and before he could check himself he fell heavily on his knees. He had a thousand confessions to get off his chest. But then he remembered the job. He must cancel it and began a frantic fumbling for phone to do just that.

* * *

404

A battered yellow taxi with blacked-out windows drifted past the Church of San Marcos. A rear-seat passenger in priestly garb removed the backrest and wriggled through. Legs still in the back seat area, torso in the boot, he assumed the shooting position. The driver flicked the boot lever, triggering the boot to open, but the assassin prevented it from fully opening by tugging on a regular cupboard handle that had been welded into the boot ceiling precisely for just such occasions. He adjusted the boot lid, settling it centimetres short of shutting, enough for the sight to view the outside world. No need for the bipod, the end of the stainless steel barrel slots into a precut angular groove in the rear wall of the boot, allowing the barrel to sweep left and right. He knew from having observed his brother take up the same position during practice, that in urban settings this arrangement was scarcely noticeable from the outside. Barely an inch of the AW's barrel protrudes beyond the boot, and once the shot is fired you draw the gun inside, while the car, like every other car in a neighbourhood that's being shot at, screeches away to be lost in the confusion.

On the verge opposite the church the driver parked between two other taxis, their recumbent drivers waiting for clients who, once the show was over, would be clamouring for a ride back into San Salvador.

'Stop, brother,' he said, when the panorama was favourable.

From this distance the target would be identifiable with the naked eye. He checked the position of the security suits and the UN Police. Dark glasses and blank expressions preoccupied with the reporters' proximity to the Vice-President and the FMLN chief, both of whom were parading on the steps like preachers before a congregation.

'Boiler suit...Red beret...Where are you?' Beneath frangipanis a scene dappled with sunlight. 'There you are,' he said, the familiar missed heartbeat at spotting the mark. 'Having a nice chat with that tall guy, are you?'

He put his eye to the telescopic lens and the woman's green-clad shoulder danced up close. He notched the lens up

405

a fraction to study her face. Could she possibly be as deadly as the contractor's envoy insists? Some measure of regret always surfaced when the target was a child or a lovely woman. Who in this business hadn't discussed this pang of conscience with fellow professionals? Best not to question a contractor's motives! So, like the professional he was, he pitted his nerves against distracting sentimentality. At any rate, this would be his final such undertaking, even if the peace talks turned out to be yet another farcical venture and the war were to continue for another twelve years.

'She's saying something to him.' Was he holding off destroying such loveliness, or was there time enough to satisfy his curiosity? The taxi was partially screened behind a parked SUV. The security guards and UN Police still preoccupied with jostling reporters. For a few seconds, at least, he would have a clear shot. He nudged the rifle to the left.

'Tall man,' he sighed, 'vaguely familiar.' He frowned, looked away from the lens and screwed up his eyes, searching his mind for that remote memory. 'Nothing.' He shook his head. 'Back to the woman with the beret.' He fixed his eye to the lens and guided her back into view. Steadying his breathing now, composing for the shot, bringing his heart rate down to that calm and silent place where the perfect shot was possible. Then out of darkness the face sprang at him, and recognition dawned with a jolt, his heart pumping very, very hard. 'I know that man.' He shifted the lens again and rediscovered Anastasio's chiselled profile and flat-top hairdo much lower than expected. The guy must be kneeling!

The assassin drew in a long deep breath and exhaled. 'Six thousand dollars to take her out. More than I've ever earned for a contract anywhere.' His finger on the trigger guard, giving it procrastinating taps. 'A lot of money down the drain.'

He fired. Anastasio vanished from his lens. The girl jumped free as the major slumped forward, arse in the air and head to the ground, eyes already shut, mouth pouting slackly.

'That's for Maria and my unborn son,' he said, and then bellowed at the driver, 'Go Alejandro.'

CHAPTER THIRTY-FIVE

February 1992

BIENVENIDOS A RESTAURANTE CABAÑA DE LEÑA. So read the sign lettered in bamboo segments above the hilltop restaurant's entrance of designer-rustic timber.

Hands in pockets and the light of an enthusiast in his eyes, Leonel was appraising the selection of motor vehicles parked in the car park and secretly deciding which one or one very much like it would be his when he could afford to replace his pickup, which Jasmine had admitted swapping for a nice canoe with some crafty fisherman she'd met on her travels. However, if he was prudent, now that he was gainfully employed by the FMLN, a replacement vehicle might come sooner rather than later. That one over there, he settled for a new-looking SUV, glossy under the security lamps. He turned to observe the stage where members of Los Hermanos Flores and an impressive array of musical instruments were taking up positions.

'*Damas y Caballeros*, this song is for you. *Mi Pais*,' the leggy lead-singer announced to a roar of approval from the packed house. Then the nine-piece ensemble was belting out an emotionally charged cumbia number, and the slatted dance floor flooded with spinning bodies, swirling skirts and clacking heels.

Leonel smiled as he observed a waiter elevate a tray of bottled beer on a brace of fingertips and foxtrot his way round the edge of the dance floor, fraternising at every turn with those he met on his journey. Eventually he sashayed over to where two young couples were seated at a table close to a kitchen that was conjuring up a fiesta of mouth-watering aromas. Adopting a half-bow he lowered the tray and served up the beers with exaggerated flourishes.

A crackling of tyres on gravel prompted Leonel to turn his attention once again to the car park where a taxi was pulling up. A driver in a white guayabera shirt popped out and hurried round to the rear, swinging open the door. A shapely calf emerged below the door, and when Jasmine alighted fully Leonel straightened up and adjusted the knot in his red tie. Reflected light shimmered across her mass of corkscrew curls as she drew them back over her shoulders. She wore a strapless black evening gown to below her knees. Her lipstick was a deep cherry; it was the first time Leonel had seen her wear any makeup. She came forward and he marvelled at how the dress remained suspended.

'No poetry in the world could describe your beauty,' he proclaimed, and would have proclaimed a lot more but mercifully good sense leapt to his rescue. So he leaned in and kissed her cheek and as he lingered in her fragrance he spotted a flower-shaped earring clinging to her earlobe. '*Encanta'o.*'

'You brush up quite nicely yourself, Don Leonel,' she admitted, smiling up at him. 'Combatant fatigues for a pinstripe.'

'I'm a politician now,' he replied, tugging at his lapels with mock smugness. 'Shall we?' Gently he took her elbow and together they strolled like the couple he fancied them to be into the restaurant. Two waiters closed in with wide-smile welcomes and led them on a slalom mission to avoid diners and dancers.

'Your table on the veranda has been reserved, Señor Flint.'

'Oh, it's beautiful!' Jasmine exclaimed, disengaging her arm and gliding over to the bamboo veranda rail. Far below, the lights of San Salvador washed across the Valley of Hammocks to the where the volcano rose darkly into a brush-stroke of white cloud. Above the valley, stars clung to the night like coffee blossoms to a vast plantation.

'Cappuccino, please.' She turned to the hovering waiter, while the other drew back a chair to seat her.

Leonel plumped for a cold beer and the waiters left to make good the order.

'So, Jasmine,' Leonel began, feeling rather awkward, 'where have you been since the Olocuilta talks? In hiding? Keeping a low profile? Whatever you like to call it, you simply disappeared. Adonai suggested contacting you through Padre Melgar. Is he psychic? Or did you tell him and not me where you were?'

'You really want to know?'

'I really want to know.'

Her hands were below the tabletop, probably fidgeting with interlinked fingers. She was again the girl he'd met over seven years ago. 'In church, confessing, renewing my faith.'

'What? For six months?'

'No,' she admitted with a little laugh and a little shrug. 'I've been living on Chachi's farm, actually, reviving the orchard. It's looking quite reasonable now. I've even had to prune back some of the bushes.'

'After all you achieved, Jasmine. Abraham wanted you to witness his signing of the peace treaty.'

'Did he?' she replied, rocking dreamily to the live cumbia.

'Iqbal sent a helicopter to fly you to Chapultepec Castle in Mexico. I was looking forward to doing the tourist thing together. But Adrian said you'd left the PCS. No forwarding address.'

'His loyalty is absolute. That's what I asked him to say.' Folding her arms she settled her elbows on the tabletop and gazed longingly towards the dance floor.

Leonel blinked as if to refocus, to accommodate her abrupt return to farmhand which, going by her look tonight, was hard to picture. 'Abraham's hopeful you'll accept a position at Party Headquarters,' he laboured on, feeling inexplicably defeated. 'He's even holding several open for you – says you can choose.'

A do-we-have-to-talk-about-this look dissolved into a remote sigh on the apparent concession that they should talk about it. 'That's not for me.'

'Well, what is for you?' Leonel retorted, not unkindly. And then he knew the reason behind her reticence: in a job market increasingly calling for university graduates, she was going to struggle when, owing to the outbreak of the conflict, she hadn't even completed her baccalaureate – basic secondary school education. 'I would be happy to see you through the rest of your schooling and university. I'm sure Abraham would enrol you in all courses necessary for your post in the FMLN.'

She beamed at him as if she were going to say yes, thank you; but she said no, it's not that, but thank you, all the same.

'What *will* you do for work?'

'I was wondering…' she paused to lean back and smile her thanks up at the waiter who set a coffee cup and saucer on the table in front of her, 'whether you'd allow me to take up the running of Chachi's farm. I think I could make a real go of it.'

'You want to go back to farming?' Leonel said doubtfully.

'It's what I am. A *campesina.*'

'It's yours,' he declared with an amused shake of his head. 'I'll have the deeds drawn up on Monday.'

'I didn't mean for you to give it…'

'No, no. It's yours,' he chuckled. 'It's what Chachi would have wanted, I'm sure. But if you change your mind…'

'Thanks. I won't.' She sipped frothy cappuccino. 'Did it go well?' – brightening, now that the embarrassing stuff was over. 'The ceremony, I mean.'

A deep intake of breath. 'What can I say? Of course the ceremony itself was a solemn occasion. But, hey, there was loads of good food and we met lots of people we'd only ever heard of – politicians of course, but also writers, poets and artists. You would have loved it. It was good.'

She was glad it was good.

There was a short break between songs. Jasmine turned towards the musicians and soon they struck up another energetic number.

'So, tell me,' said Leonel, and she faced him with her wide eyes. 'What happened to that sweet little girl who adored flowers?'

'Oh, she's still here. If Señor Dexterous cares to look,' she replied, lips pursed to forbid a smile.

'I do care to look.' Leonel held out his hand and tipped his head towards the dance floor. 'I care very much.'

The Civil War in El Salvador

The civil war in El Salvador lasted from 1980 through to 1992. On one side the military, driven by deep-rooted historical motives and often acting independently of the elected governments; on the other the Farabundo Marti National Liberation Front (FMLN), a coalition of five guerrilla groups set up to achieve, among other aims, the armed defence of the peasantry from military operations and the right to participate in the democratic process. 75,000 people lost their lives in the fighting, and eight thousand disappeared. In 1992, Peace Accords were signed at Chapultepec Castle, Mexico. Despite the deep and bitter divisions that existed, the Salvadorans have since built an impressive record of reconciliation that many, including the US State Department and the UN Secretary-General Ban Ki-moon, have praised as a peace model for current conflicts elsewhere in the world.

Further Reading

The Massacre at El Mozote by Mark Danner, Granta Books, 2005.
Salvador by Joan Didion, Granta Books, 2006.
They Won't Take Me Alive: Salvadoran Women in Struggle for National Liberation by Claribel Alegria, The Women's Press, 1987.

and a film: *Innocent Voices.*

Also from The Merlin Press

Broad and Alien is the World
by Ciro Alegria

A classic of its kind: a fictional recreation of life in poor
indigenous agricultural communities in the Peruvian Andes
from the turn of the last century until the 1930s.
A book which captures the beliefs, traditions and customs of
these people just as the base of their social organisation was
facing extinction.

1983, 470 pages, paperback

www.merlinpress.co.uk